DEC 0 8 2018

VAULT COMICS PRESENTS

STALAG X

VAULT

PUBLISHER DAMIAN A. WASSEL

EDITOR-IN-CHIEF ADRIAN F. WASSEL

V.P. VISUAL BRANDING + DESIGN NATHAN C. GOODEN

ART DIRECTOR TIM DANIEL

PRINCIPAL DAMIAN A. WASSEL, SR.

STALAG X, VOLUME ONE, MARCH, 2018. COPYRIGHT © 2018 KEVIN J. ANDERSON AND STEVEN L. SEARS. ALL RIGHTS RESERVED. "STALAG X", THE STALAG X LOGO, AND THE LIKENESSES OF ALL CHARACTERS HEREIN ARE TRADEMARKS OF EVIN J. ANDERSON AND STEVEN L. SEARS, UNLESS OTHERWISE NOTED. "VAULT" AND THE VAULT LOGO ARE TRADEMARKS OF CREATIVE MIND ENERGY, LLC. NO PART OF THIS WORK MAY BE REPRODUCED, TRANSMITTED, STORED OR USED IN ANY FORM OR BY ANY MEANS GRAPHIC, ELECTRONIC, OR MECHANICAL, INCLUDING BUT NOT LIMITED TO PHOTOCOPYING, RECORDING, SCANNING, DIGITIZING, TAPING, WEB DISTRIBUTION, INFORMATION NETWORKS, OR INFORMATION STORAGE AND RETRIEVAL SYSTEMS, EXCEPT AS PERMITTED UNDER SECTION 107 OR 108 OF THE 1976 UNITED STATES COPYRIGHT ACT, WITHOUT THE PRIOR WRITTEN PERMISSION OF THE PUBLISHER. ALL NAMES, CHARACTERS, EVENTS, AND LOCALES IN THIS PUBLICATION ARE ENTIRELY FICTIONAL. ANY RESEMBLANCE TO ACTUAL PERSONS (LIVING OR DEAD, INCLUDING THOSE IMPRISONED AT THE STALAG), EVENTS, INSTITUTIONS, OR PLACES, WITHOUT SATIRIC INTENT, IS COINCIDENTAL. PRINTED IN CANADA. FOR INFORMATION ABOUT FOREIGN OR MULTIMEDIA RIGHTS, CONTACT: RIGHTS@VAULTCOMICS.COM

WRITTEN BY

KEVIN J. ANDERSON STEVEN L. SEARS

ILLUSTRATED BY

MIKE RATERA

COLORED BY

ANGELINA LIM   SKYE OGDEN   GONÇALO LOPES

LETTERED BY

NIC J. SHAW   ADAM WOLLET

DESIGNED BY

TIM DANIEL

PRODUCTION BY

KIM MCLEAN

COVERS BY

DAVE DORMAN
BEN TEMPLESMITH

NOVELLA ILLUSTRATIONS BY

NATHAN GOODEN

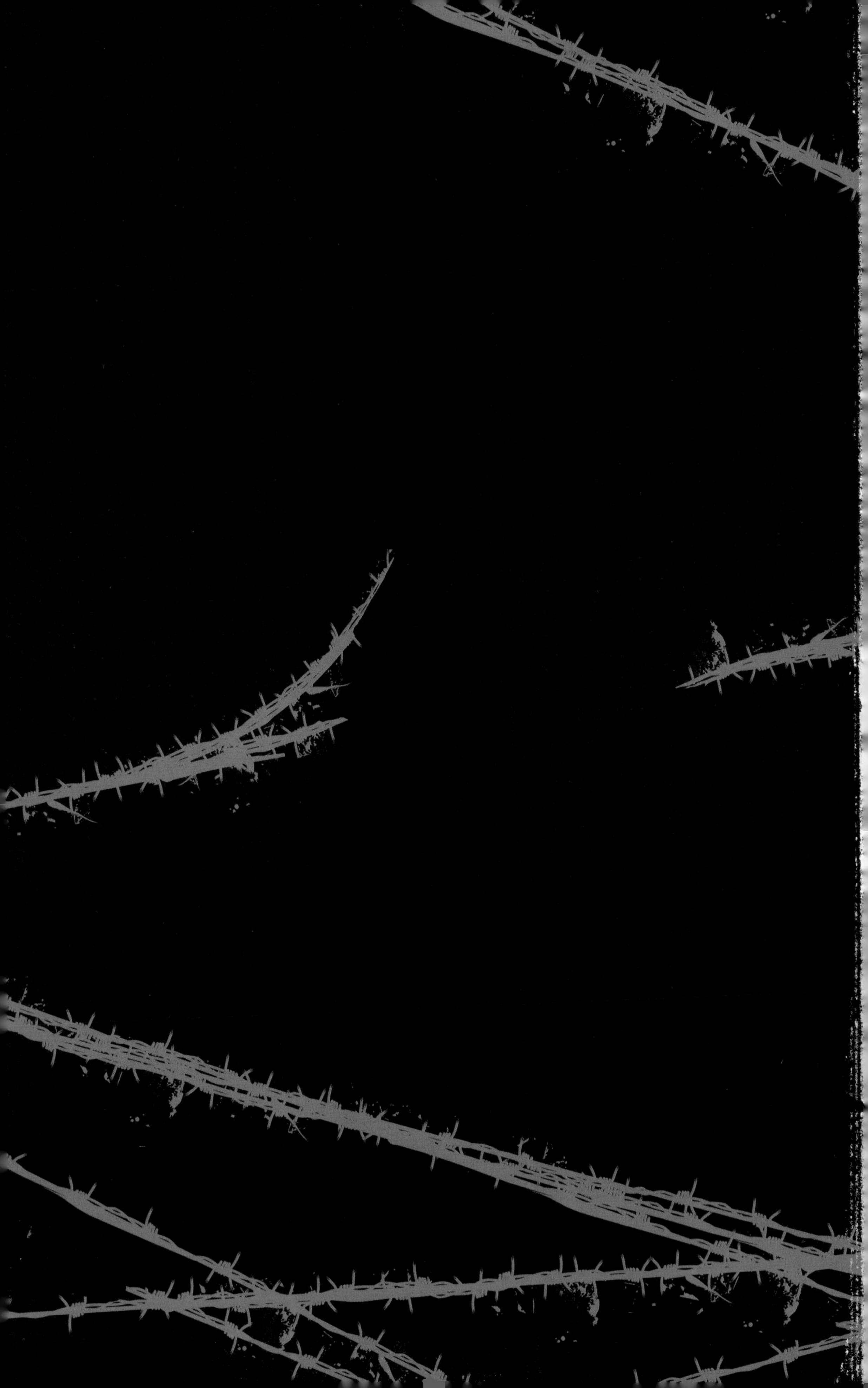

CHAPTER

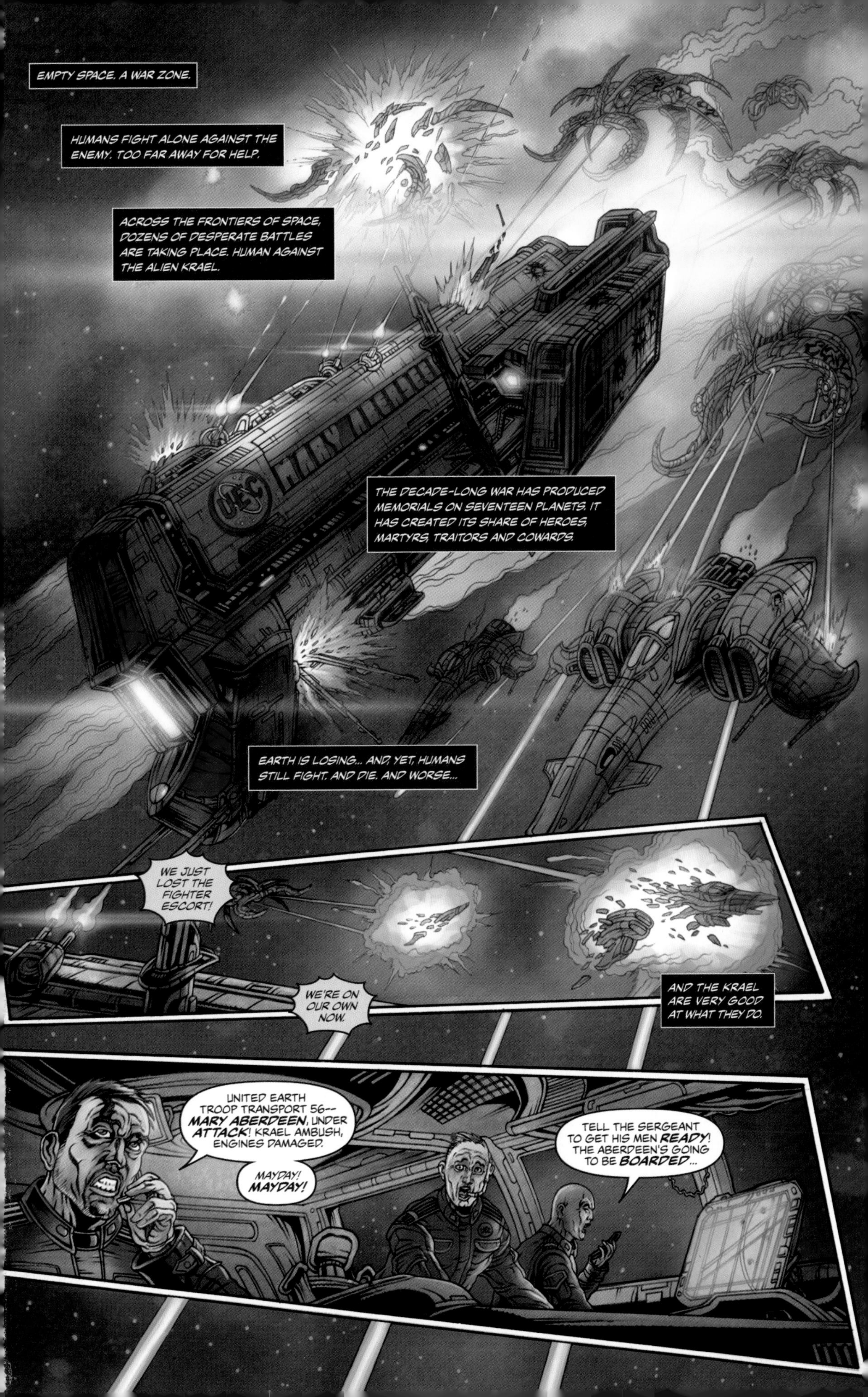
EMPTY SPACE. A WAR ZONE.
HUMANS FIGHT ALONE AGAINST THE ENEMY. TOO FAR AWAY FOR HELP.
ACROSS THE FRONTIERS OF SPACE, DOZENS OF DESPERATE BATTLES ARE TAKING PLACE. HUMAN AGAINST THE ALIEN KRAEL.
UEC
MARY ABERDEEN
THE DECADE-LONG WAR HAS PRODUCED MEMORIALS ON SEVENTEEN PLANETS. IT HAS CREATED ITS SHARE OF HEROES, MARTYRS, TRAITORS AND COWARDS.
EARTH IS LOSING... AND, YET, HUMANS STILL FIGHT. AND DIE. AND WORSE...
WE JUST LOST THE FIGHTER ESCORT!
WE'RE ON OUR OWN NOW.
AND THE KRAEL ARE VERY GOOD AT WHAT THEY DO.
UNITED EARTH TROOP TRANSPORT 56-- MARY ABERDEEN, UNDER ATTACK! KRAEL AMBUSH, ENGINES DAMAGED.
MAYDAY! MAYDAY!
TELL THE SERGEANT TO GET HIS MEN READY! THE ABERDEEN'S GOING TO BE BOARDED...

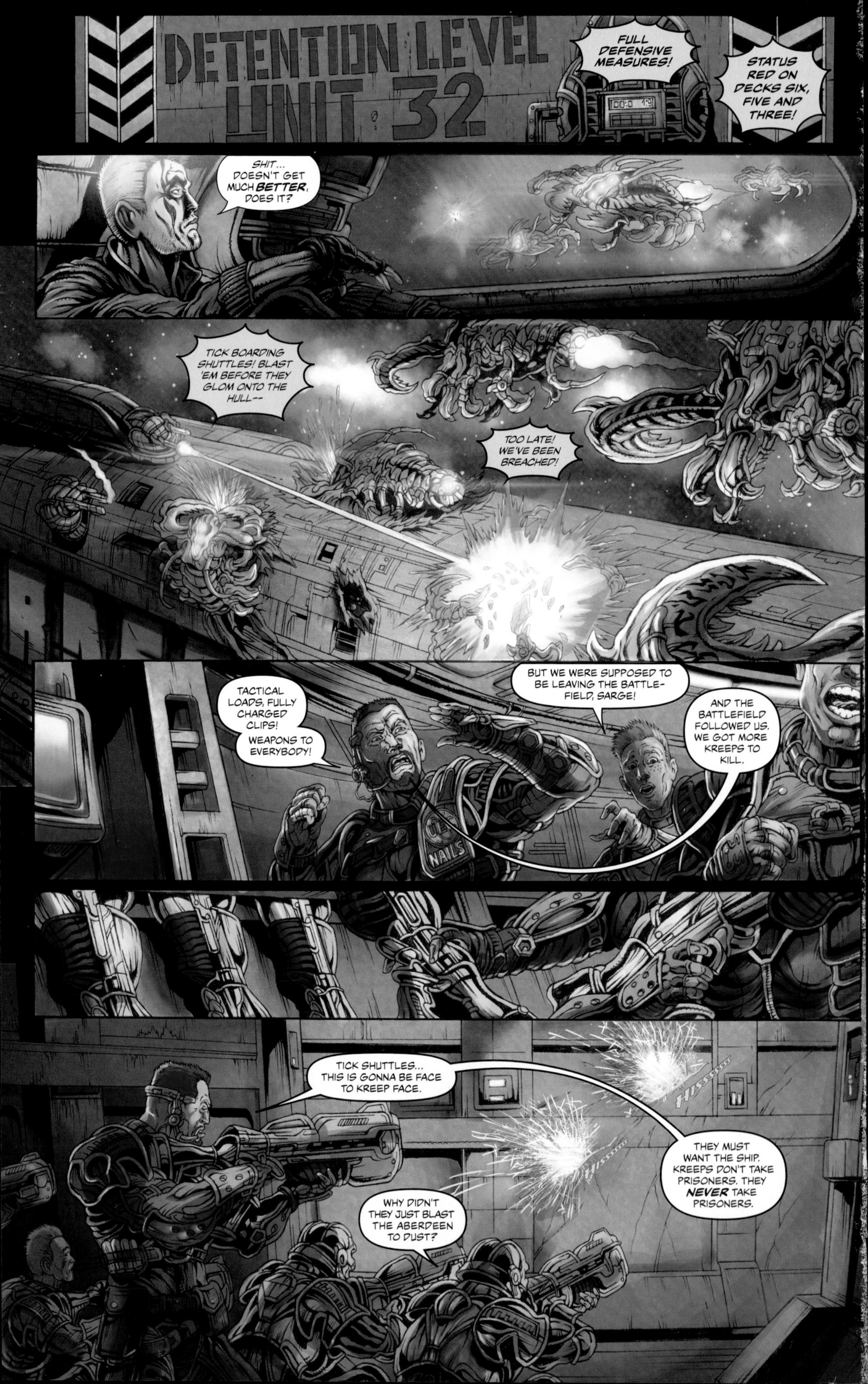
DETENTION LEVEL UNIT 32
FULL DEFENSIVE MEASURES!
STATUS RED ON DECKS SIX, FIVE AND THREE!
SHIT... DOESN'T GET MUCH BETTER, DOES IT?
TICK BOARDING SHUTTLES! BLAST 'EM BEFORE THEY GLOM ONTO THE HULL--
TOO LATE! WE'VE BEEN BREACHED!
TACTICAL LOADS, FULLY CHARGED CLIPS!
WEAPONS TO EVERYBODY!
BUT WE WERE SUPPOSED TO BE LEAVING THE BATTLE-FIELD, SARGE!
AND THE BATTLEFIELD FOLLOWED US. WE GOT MORE KREEPS TO KILL.
NAILS
TICK SHUTTLES... THIS IS GONNA BE FACE TO KREEP FACE.
THEY MUST WANT THE SHIP. KREEPS DON'T TAKE PRISONERS. THEY NEVER TAKE PRISONERS.
WHY DIDN'T THEY JUST BLAST THE ABERDEEN TO DUST?

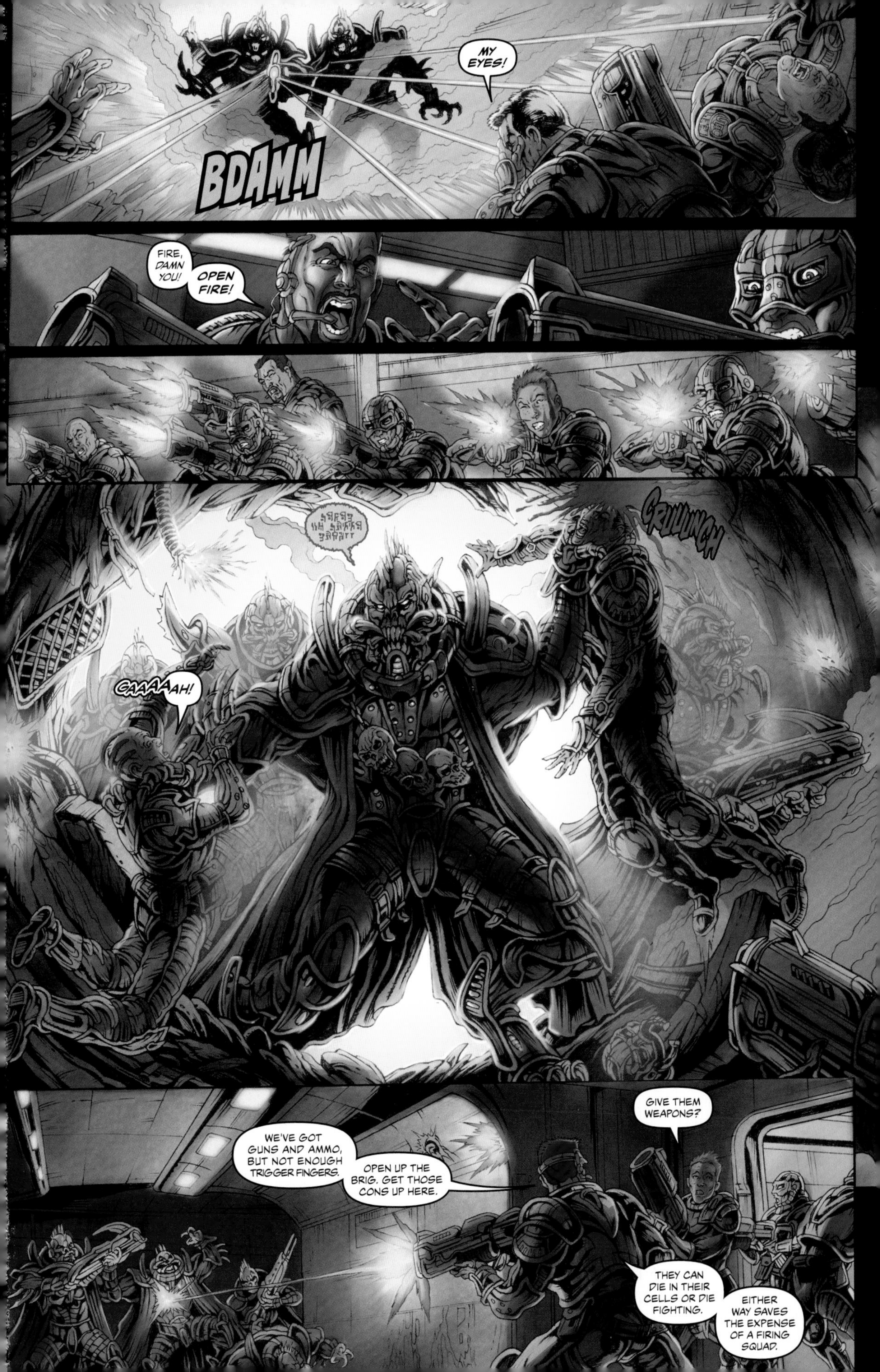

MY EYES!
BDAMM
FIRE, DAMN YOU!
OPEN FIRE!
CRUUNCH
CAAAAAH!
WE'VE GOT GUNS AND AMMO, BUT NOT ENOUGH TRIGGER FINGERS.
OPEN UP THE BRIG. GET THOSE CONS UP HERE.
GIVE THEM WEAPONS?
THEY CAN DIE IN THEIR CELLS OR DIE FIGHTING.
EITHER WAY SAVES THE EXPENSE OF A FIRING SQUAD.

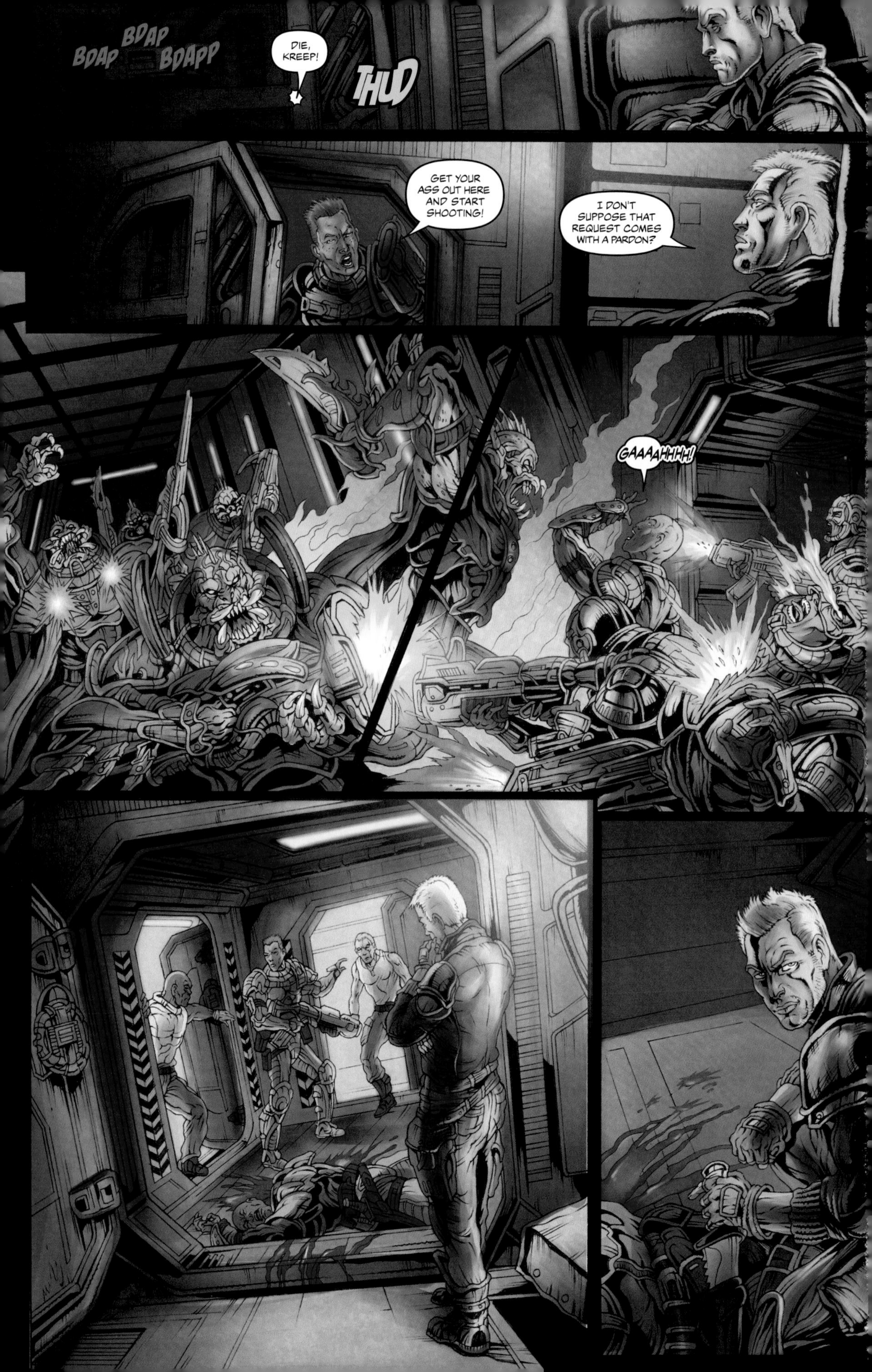
BDAP BDAP BDAPP
DIE, KREEP!
THUD
GET YOUR ASS OUT HERE AND START SHOOTING!
I DON'T SUPPOSE THAT REQUEST COMES WITH A PARDON?
GAAAAHHHH!

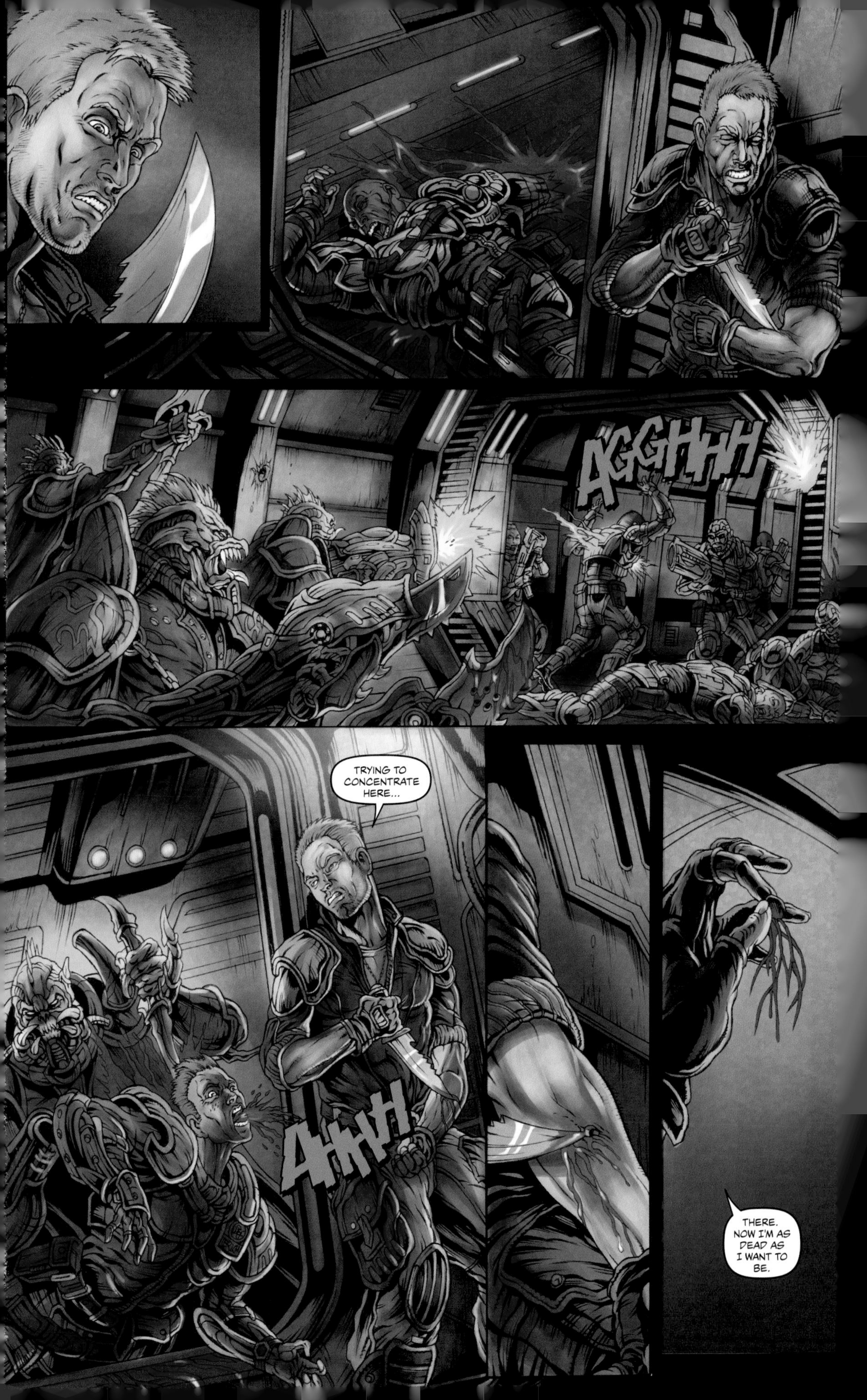
AGGHHH
TRYING TO CONCENTRATE HERE...
AHHH
THERE. NOW I'M AS DEAD AS I WANT TO BE.

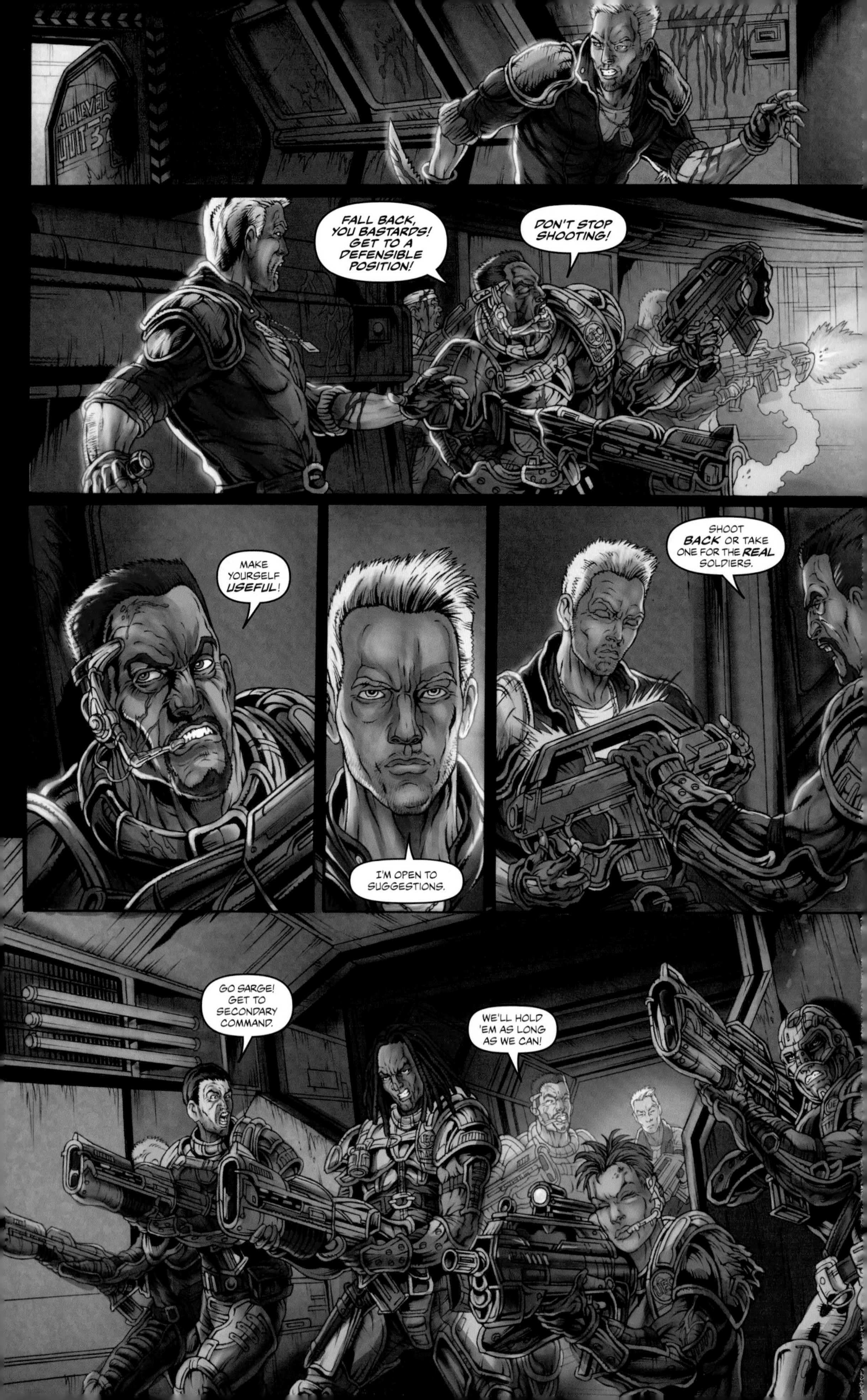
FALL BACK, YOU BASTARDS! GET TO A DEFENSIBLE POSITION!
DON'T STOP SHOOTING!
MAKE YOURSELF USEFUL!
I'M OPEN TO SUGGESTIONS.
SHOOT BACK OR TAKE ONE FOR THE REAL SOLDIERS.
GO SARGE! GET TO SECONDARY COMMAND.
WE'LL HOLD 'EM AS LONG AS WE CAN!

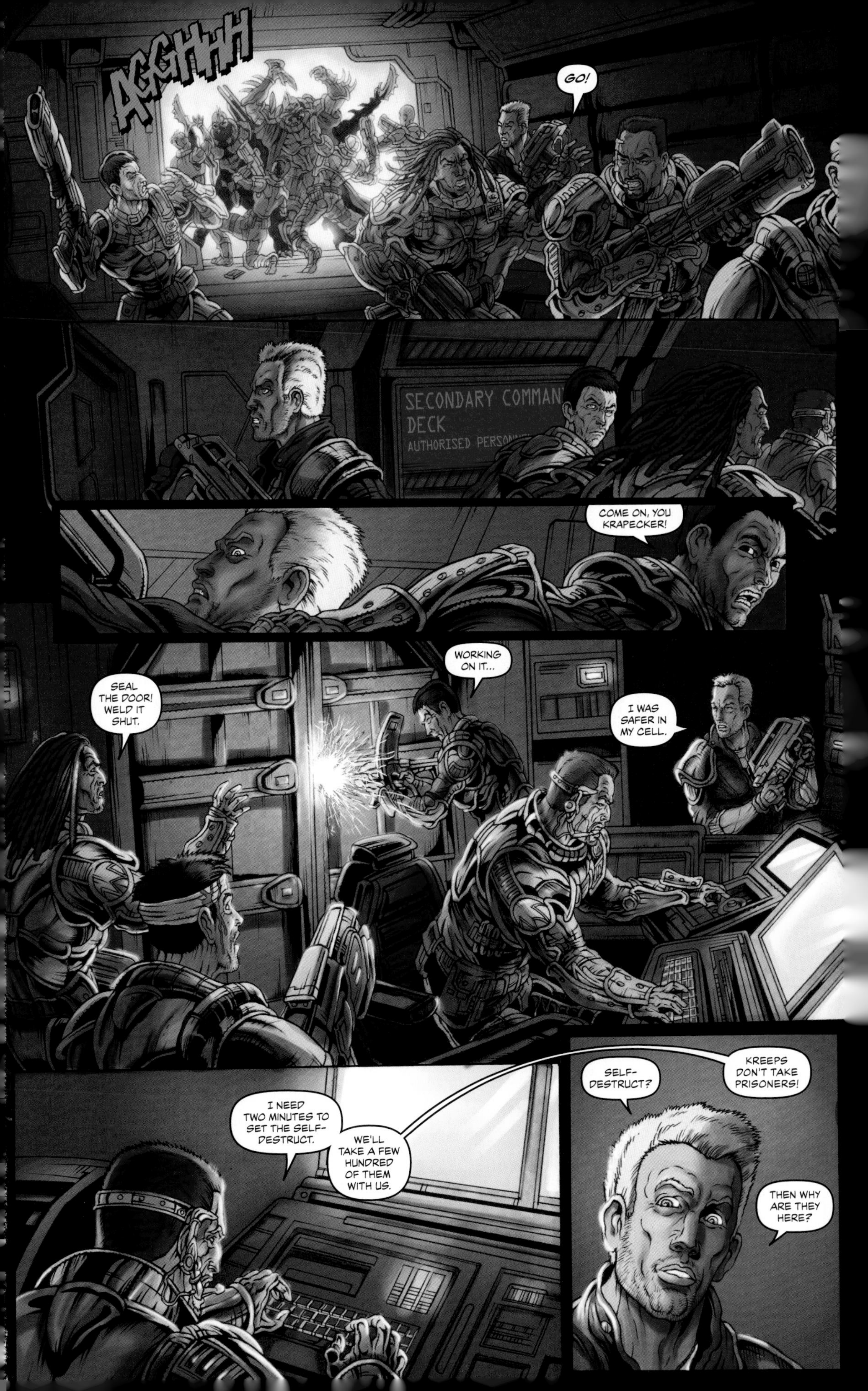
AGGHHH
GO!
SECONDARY COMMAN
DECK
AUTHORISED PERSON
COME ON, YOU KRAPECKER!
SEAL THE DOOR! WELD IT SHUT.
WORKING ON IT...
I WAS SAFER IN MY CELL.
I NEED TWO MINUTES TO SET THE SELF-DESTRUCT.
WE'LL TAKE A FEW HUNDRED OF THEM WITH US.
SELF-DESTRUCT?
KREEPS DON'T TAKE PRISONERS!
THEN WHY ARE THEY HERE?

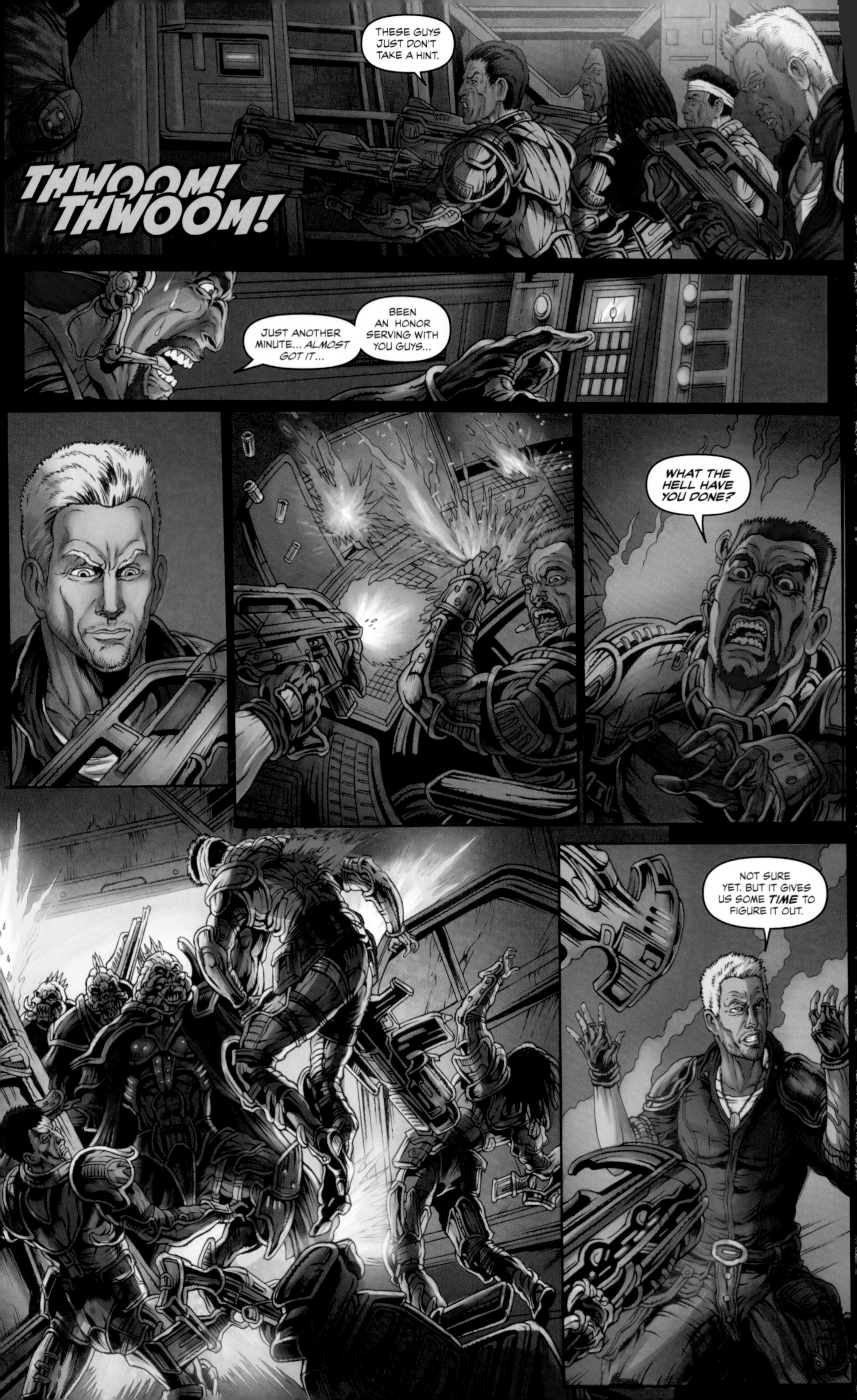
THESE GUYS JUST DON'T TAKE A HINT.
THWOOM! THWOOM!
JUST ANOTHER MINUTE... ALMOST GOT IT...
BEEN AN HONOR SERVING WITH YOU GUYS...
WHAT THE HELL HAVE YOU DONE?
NOT SURE YET. BUT IT GIVES US SOME TIME TO FIGURE IT OUT.

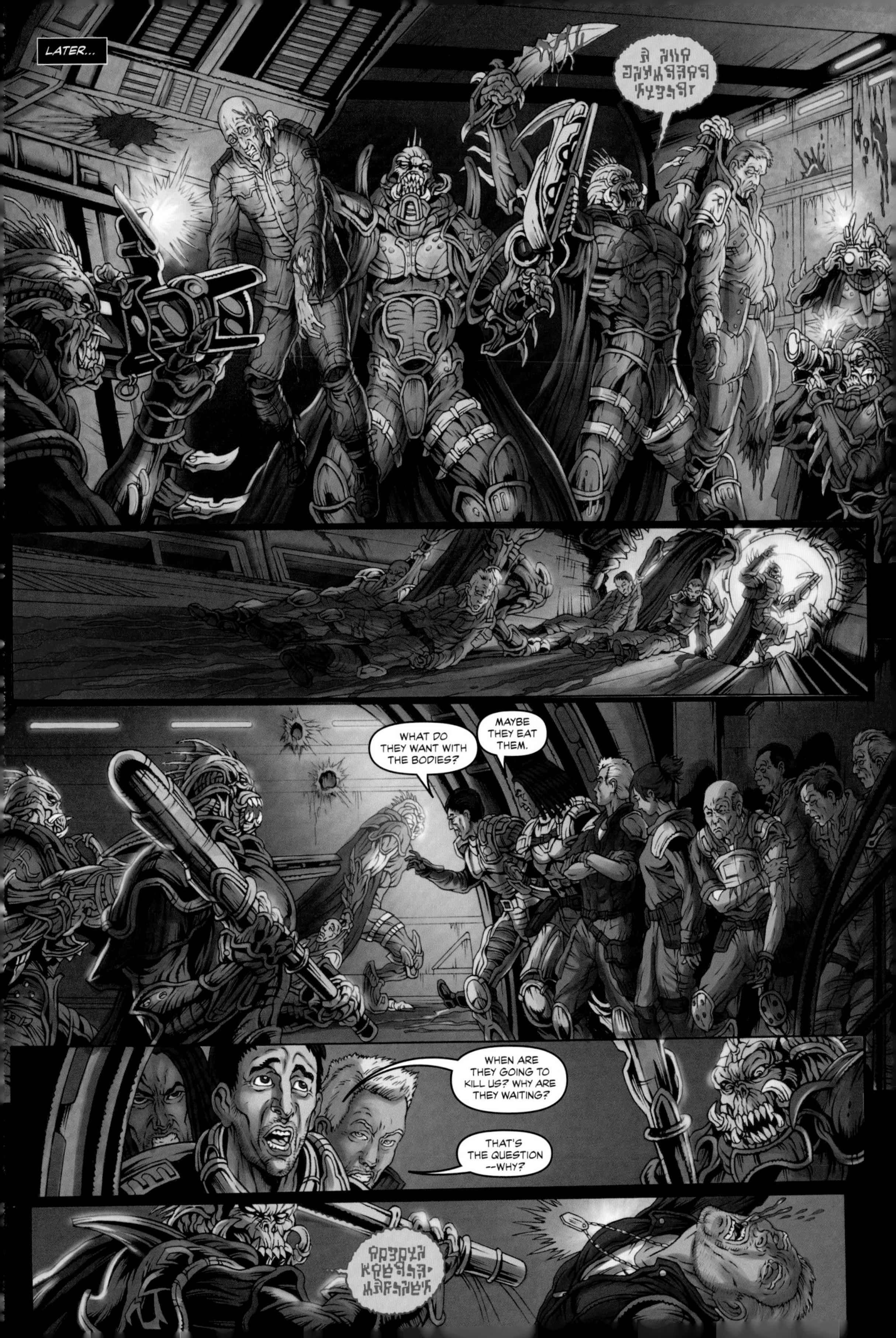
LATER...
WHAT DO THEY WANT WITH THE BODIES?
MAYBE THEY EAT THEM.
WHEN ARE THEY GOING TO KILL US? WHY ARE THEY WAITING?
THAT'S THE QUESTION --WHY?

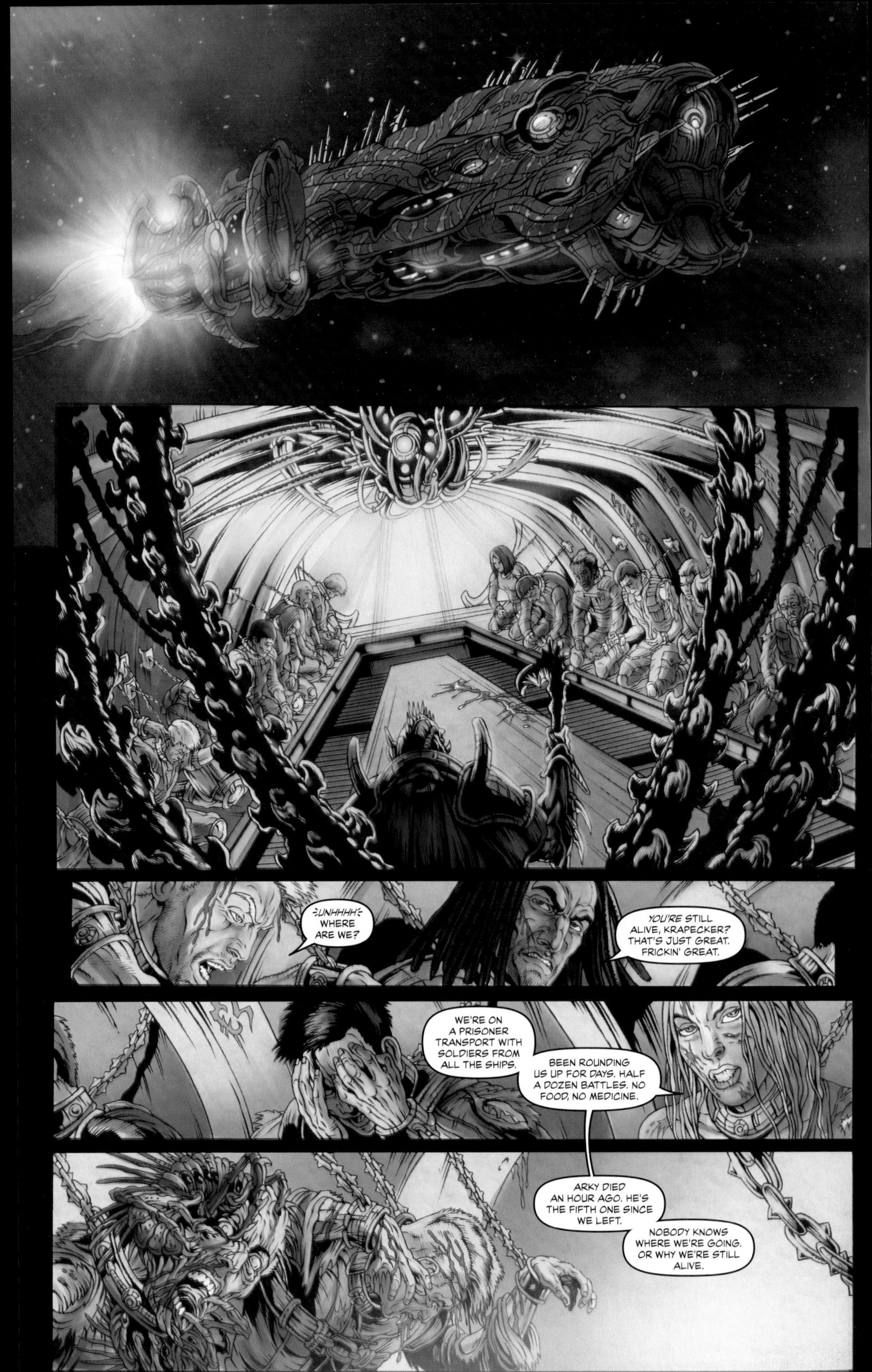
UNHHHH WHERE ARE WE?
YOU'RE STILL ALIVE, KRAPECKER? THAT'S JUST GREAT. FRICKIN' GREAT.
WE'RE ON A PRISONER TRANSPORT WITH SOLDIERS FROM ALL THE SHIPS.
BEEN ROUNDING US UP FOR DAYS. HALF A DOZEN BATTLES. NO FOOD, NO MEDICINE.
ARKY DIED AN HOUR AGO. HE'S THE FIFTH ONE SINCE WE LEFT.
NOBODY KNOWS WHERE WE'RE GOING. OR WHY WE'RE STILL ALIVE.

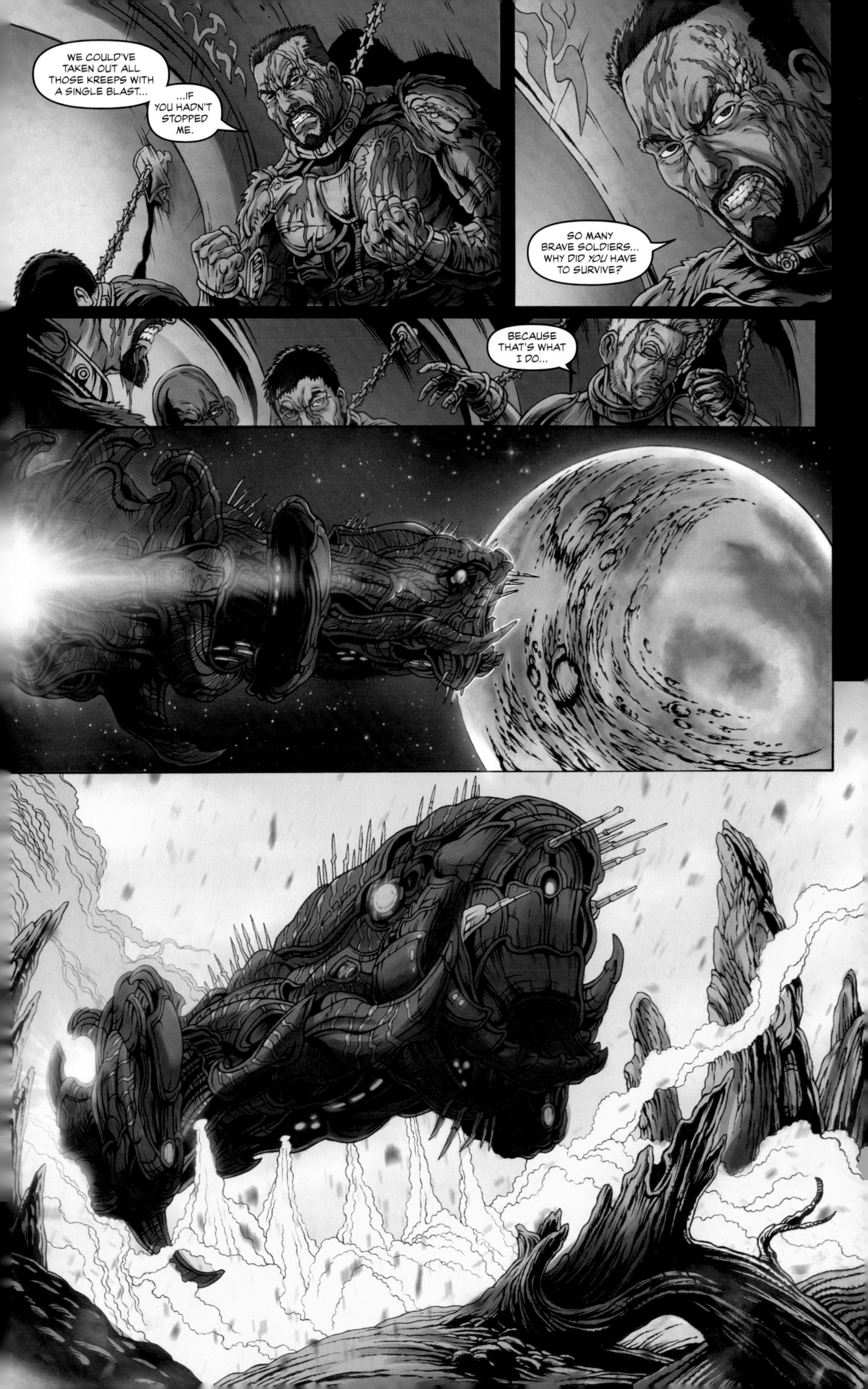
WE COULD'VE TAKEN OUT ALL THOSE KREEPS WITH A SINGLE BLAST...
...IF YOU HADN'T STOPPED ME.
SO MANY BRAVE SOLDIERS... WHY DID *YOU* HAVE TO SURVIVE?
BECAUSE THAT'S WHAT I DO...

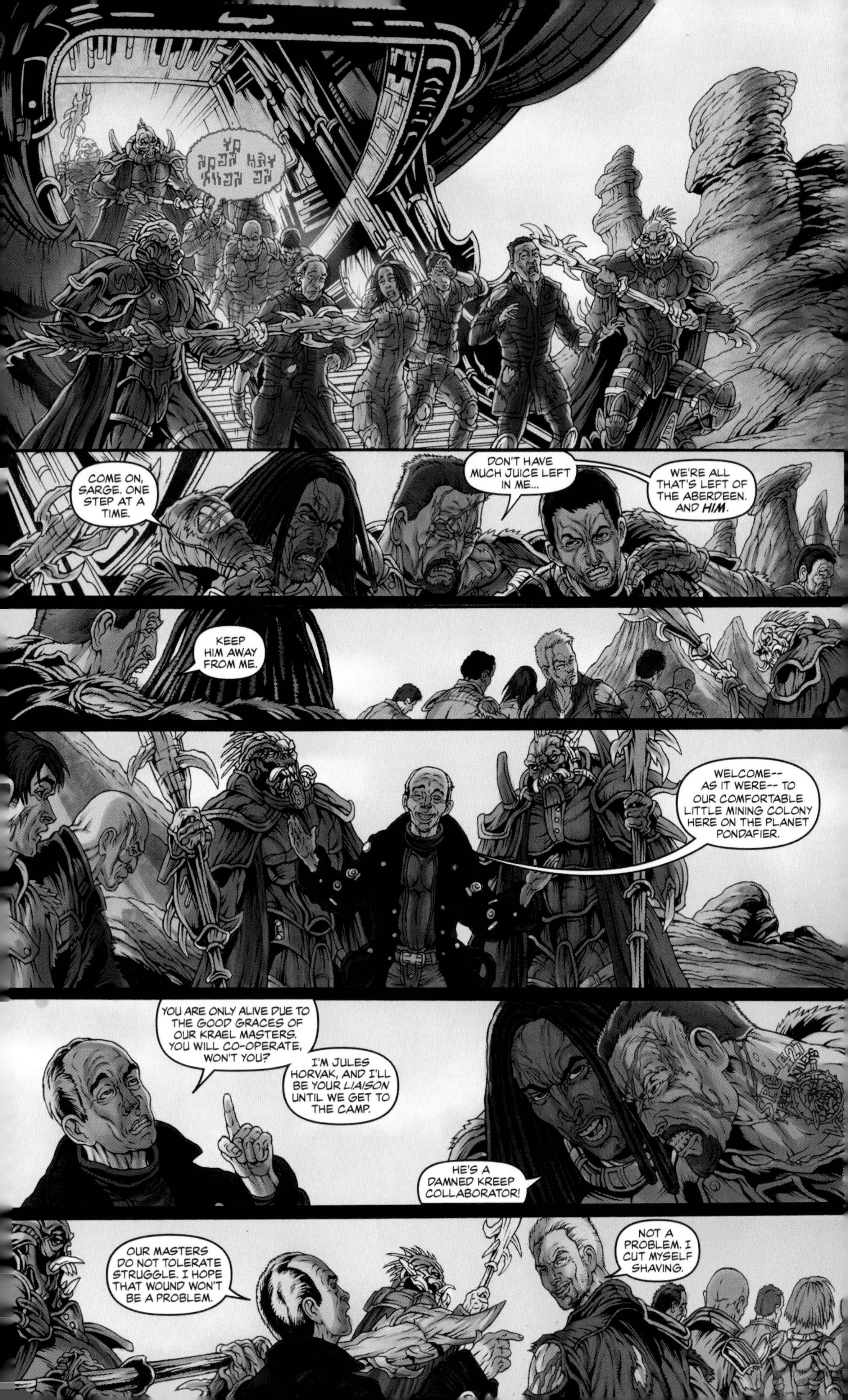
COME ON, SARGE. ONE STEP AT A TIME.
DON'T HAVE MUCH JUICE LEFT IN ME...
WE'RE ALL THAT'S LEFT OF THE ABERDEEN. AND ***HIM***.
KEEP HIM AWAY FROM ME.
WELCOME-- AS IT WERE-- TO OUR COMFORTABLE LITTLE MINING COLONY HERE ON THE PLANET PONDAFIER.
YOU ARE ONLY ALIVE DUE TO THE GOOD GRACES OF OUR KRAEL MASTERS. YOU WILL CO-OPERATE, WON'T YOU?
I'M JULES HORVAK, AND I'LL BE YOUR *LIAISON* UNTIL WE GET TO THE CAMP.
HE'S A DAMNED KREEP COLLABORATOR!
OUR MASTERS DO NOT TOLERATE STRUGGLE. I HOPE THAT WOUND WON'T BE A PROBLEM.
NOT A PROBLEM. I CUT MYSELF SHAVING.

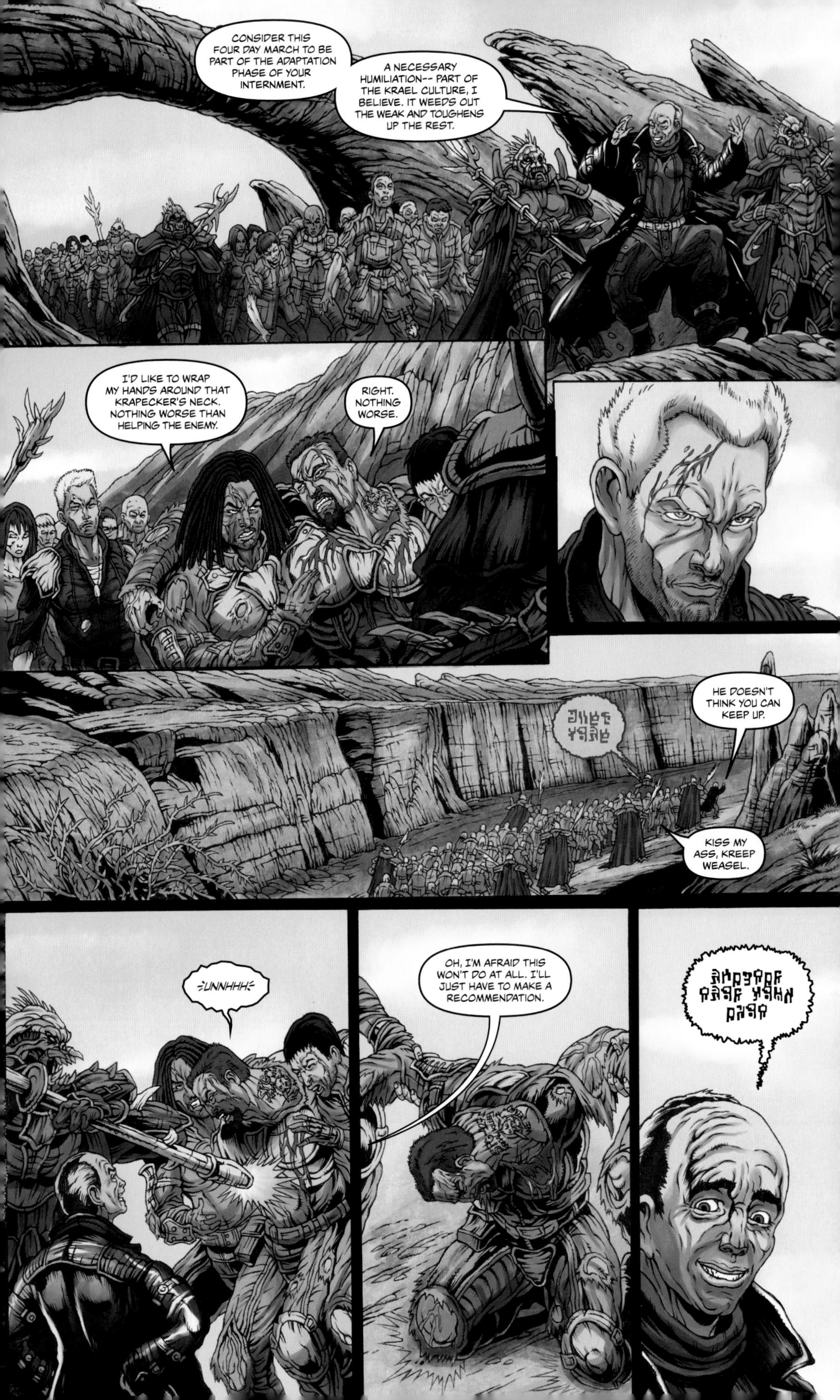
CONSIDER THIS FOUR DAY MARCH TO BE PART OF THE ADAPTATION PHASE OF YOUR INTERNMENT.
A NECESSARY HUMILIATION-- PART OF THE KRAEL CULTURE, I BELIEVE. IT WEEDS OUT THE WEAK AND TOUGHENS UP THE REST.
I'D LIKE TO WRAP MY HANDS AROUND THAT KRAPECKER'S NECK. NOTHING WORSE THAN HELPING THE ENEMY.
RIGHT. NOTHING WORSE.
HE DOESN'T THINK YOU CAN KEEP UP.
KISS MY ASS, KREEP WEASEL.
UNNHHH
OH, I'M AFRAID THIS WON'T DO AT ALL. I'LL JUST HAVE TO MAKE A RECOMMENDATION.

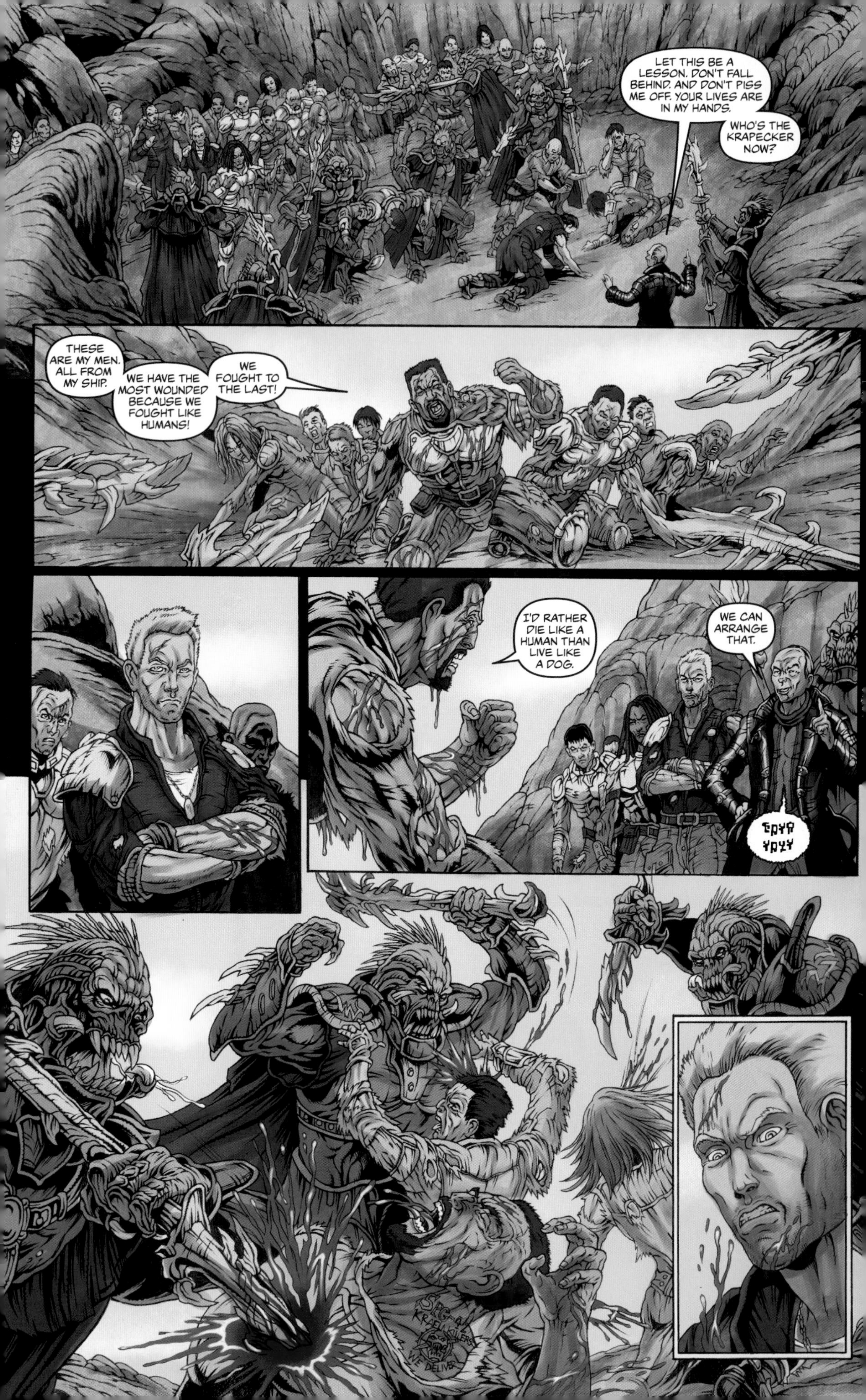
LET THIS BE A LESSON. DON'T FALL BEHIND. AND DON'T PISS ME OFF. YOUR LIVES ARE IN MY HANDS.
WHO'S THE KRAPECKER NOW?
THESE ARE MY MEN. ALL FROM MY SHIP.
WE HAVE THE MOST WOUNDED BECAUSE WE FOUGHT LIKE HUMANS!
WE FOUGHT TO THE LAST!
I'D RATHER DIE LIKE A HUMAN THAN LIVE LIKE A DOG.
WE CAN ARRANGE THAT.

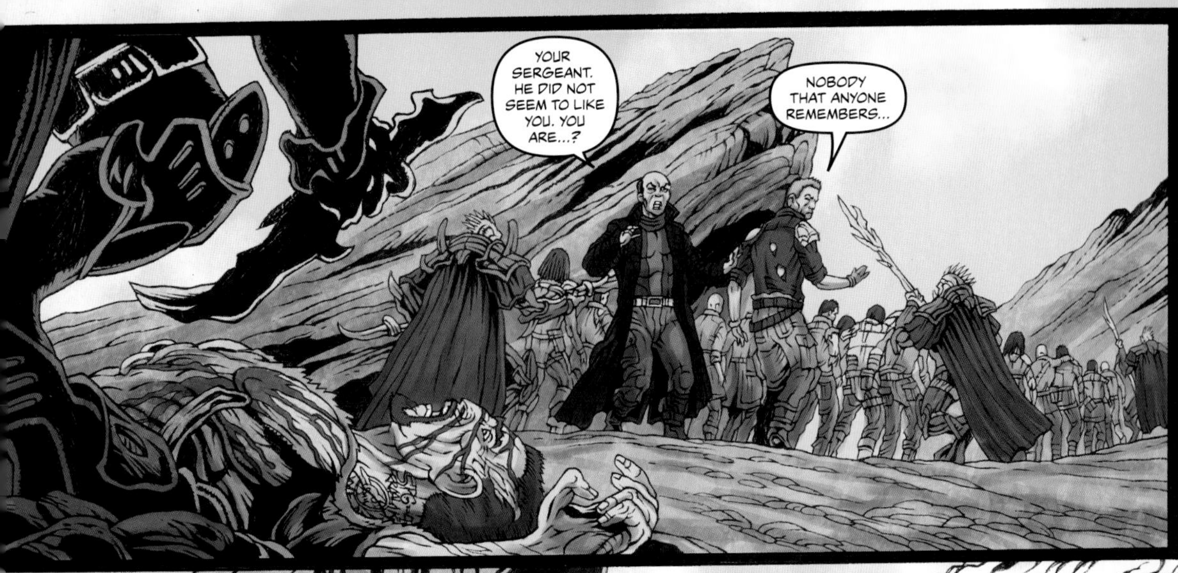
YOUR SERGEANT. HE DID NOT SEEM TO LIKE YOU. YOU ARE...?
NOBODY THAT ANYONE REMEMBERS...
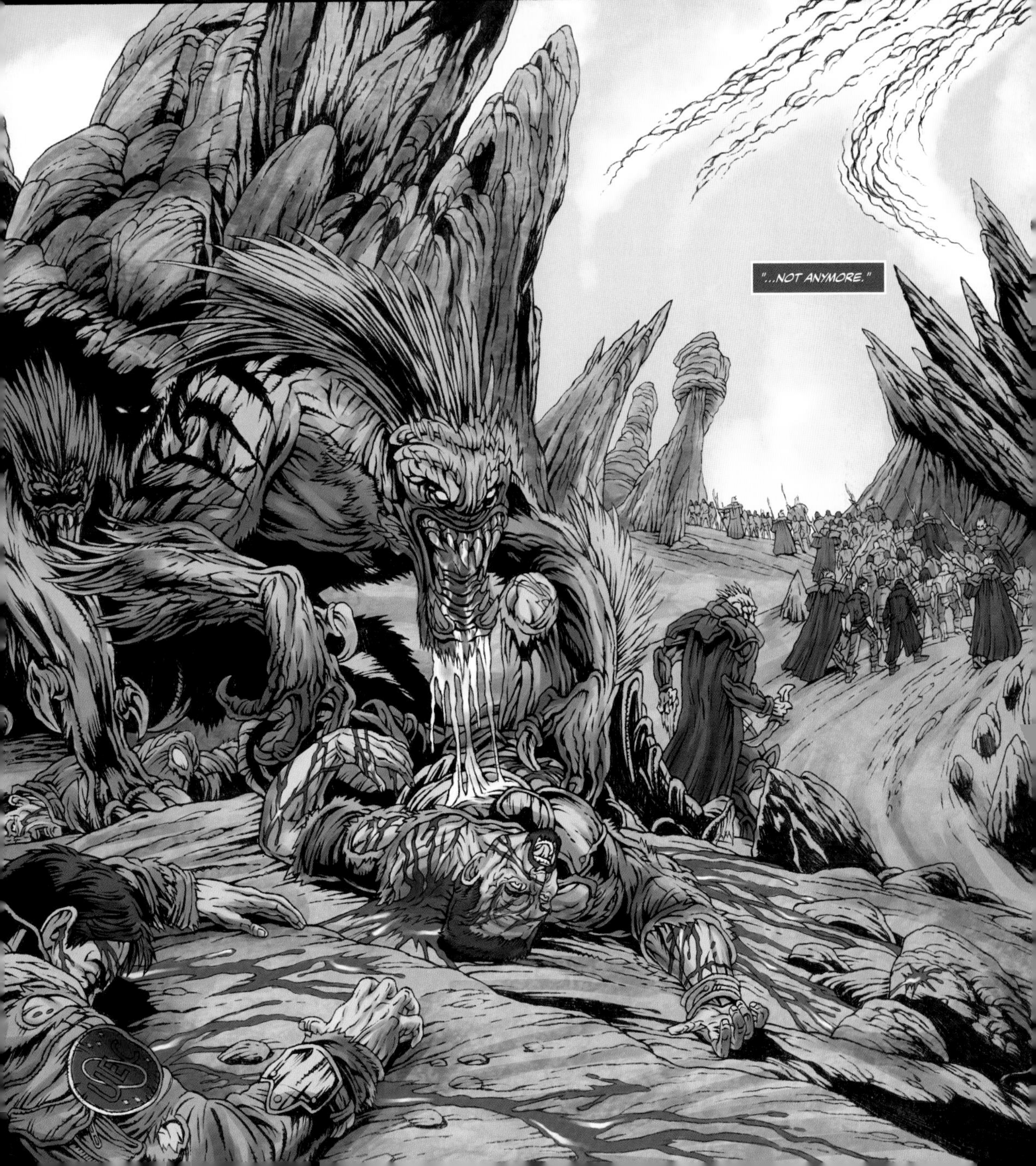
"...NOT ANYMORE."

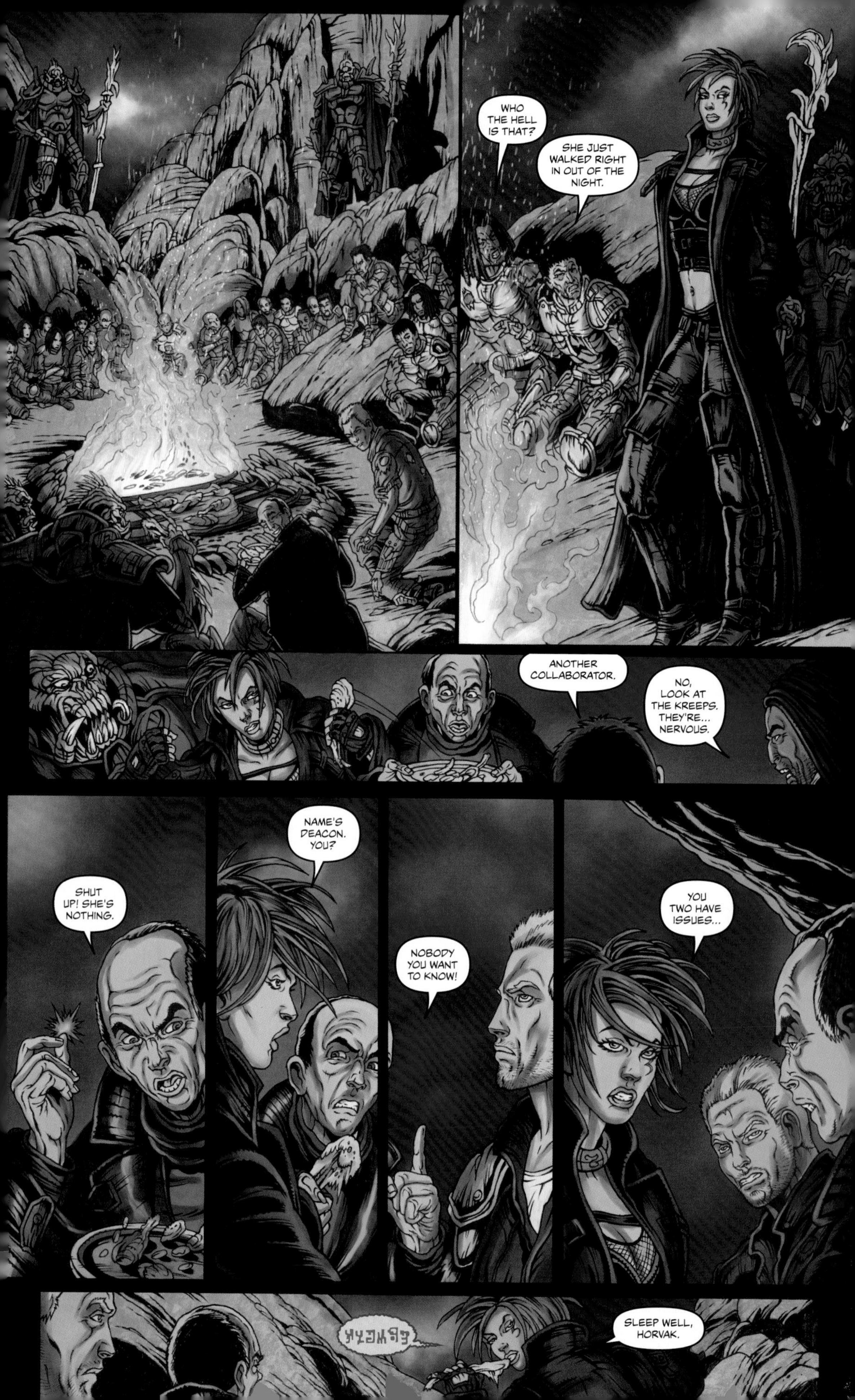
WHO THE HELL IS THAT?
SHE JUST WALKED RIGHT IN OUT OF THE NIGHT.
ANOTHER COLLABORATOR.
NO, LOOK AT THE KREEPS. THEY'RE... NERVOUS.
SHUT UP! SHE'S NOTHING.
NAME'S DEACON. YOU?
NOBODY YOU WANT TO KNOW!
YOU TWO HAVE ISSUES...
SLEEP WELL, HORVAK.

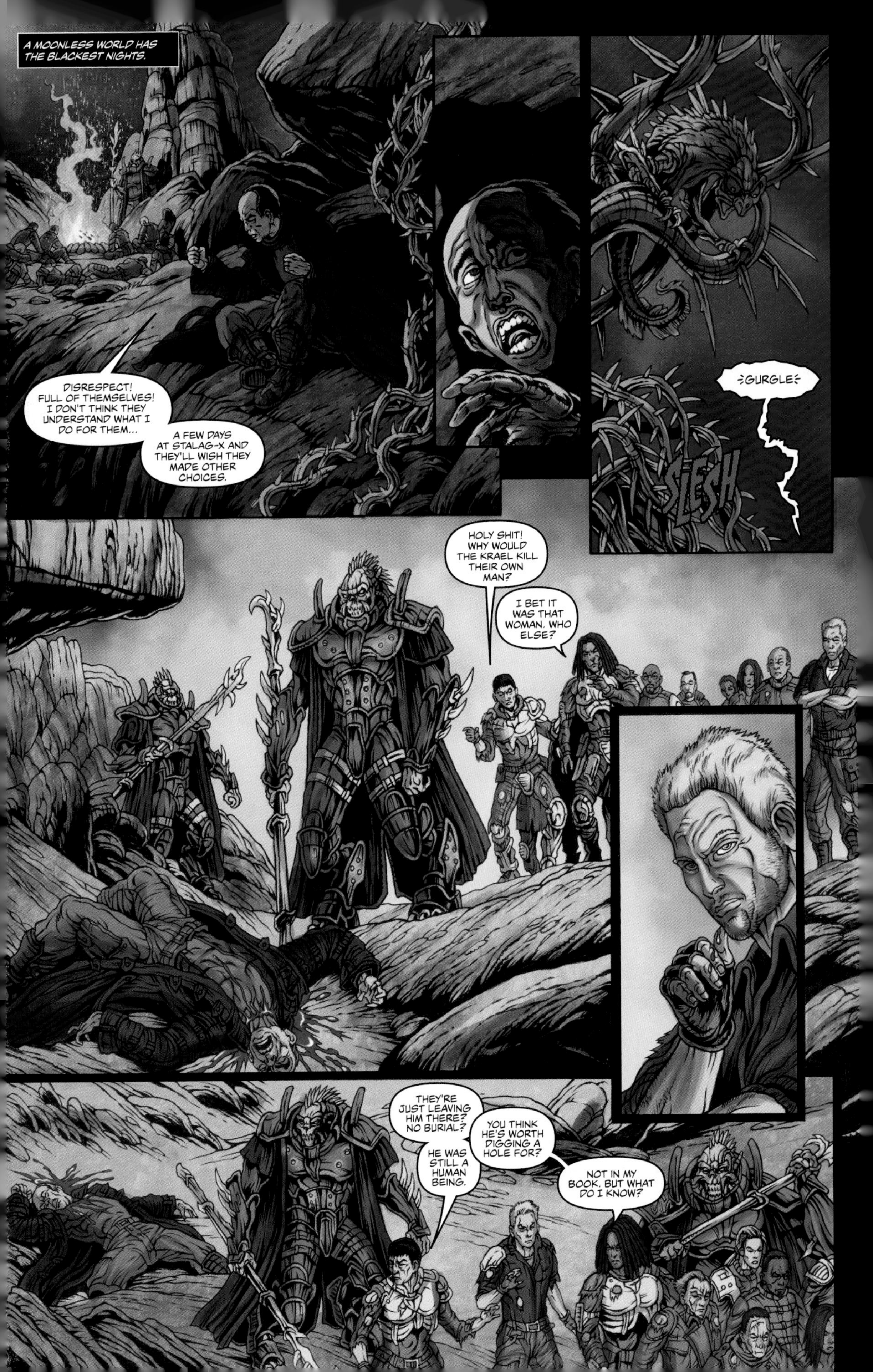
A MOONLESS WORLD HAS THE BLACKEST NIGHTS.
DISRESPECT! FULL OF THEMSELVES! I DON'T THINK THEY UNDERSTAND WHAT I DO FOR THEM...
A FEW DAYS AT STALAG-X AND THEY'LL WISH THEY MADE OTHER CHOICES.
GURGLE
SLESH
HOLY SHIT! WHY WOULD THE KRAEL KILL THEIR OWN MAN?
I BET IT WAS THAT WOMAN. WHO ELSE?
THEY'RE JUST LEAVING HIM THERE? NO BURIAL?
HE WAS STILL A HUMAN BEING.
YOU THINK HE'S WORTH DIGGING A HOLE FOR?
NOT IN MY BOOK. BUT WHAT DO I KNOW?

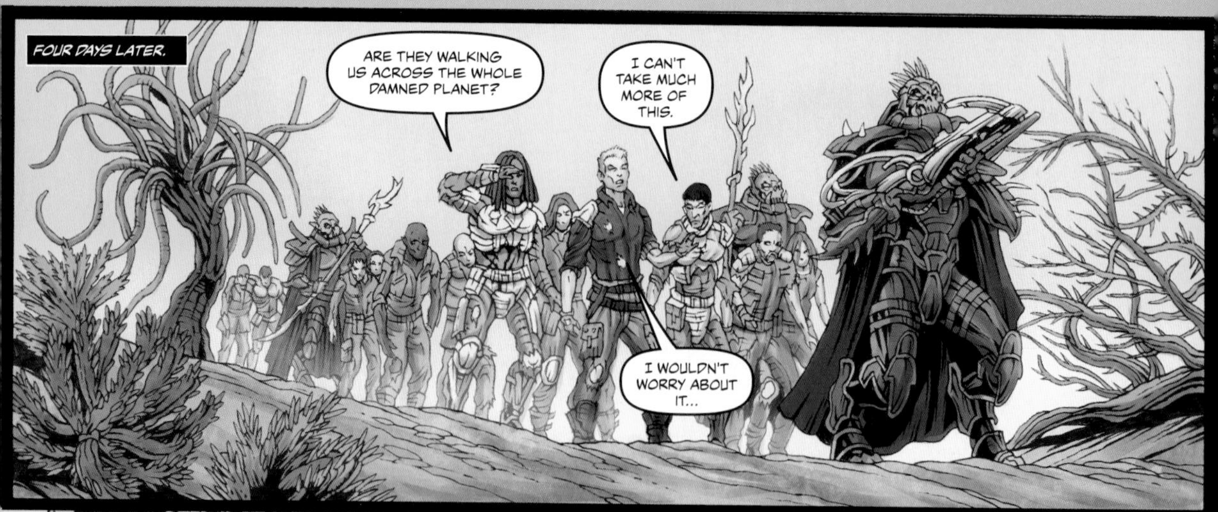
FOUR DAYS LATER.
ARE THEY WALKING US ACROSS THE WHOLE DAMNED PLANET?
I CAN'T TAKE MUCH MORE OF THIS.
I WOULDN'T WORRY ABOUT IT...

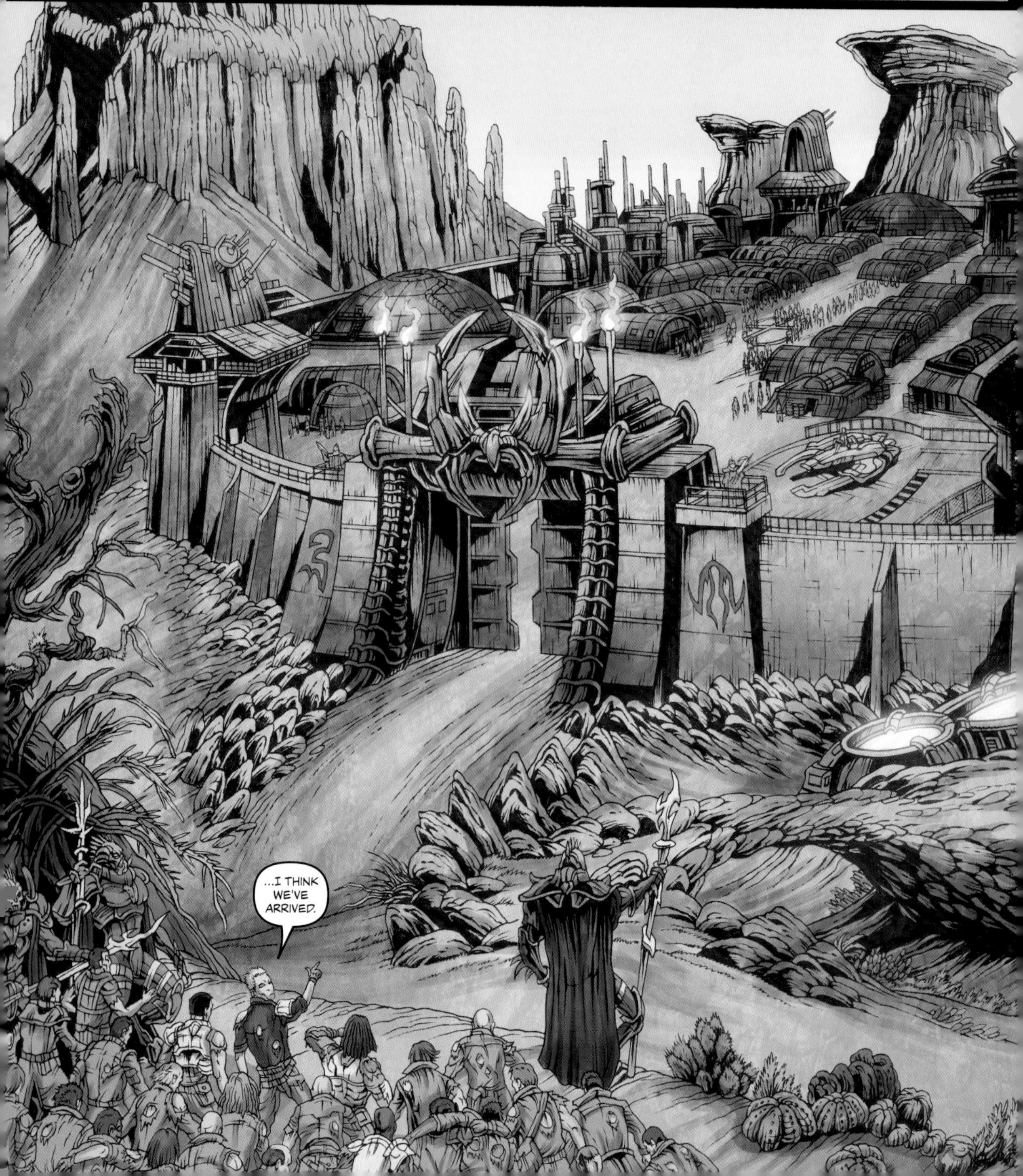
...I THINK WE'VE ARRIVED.

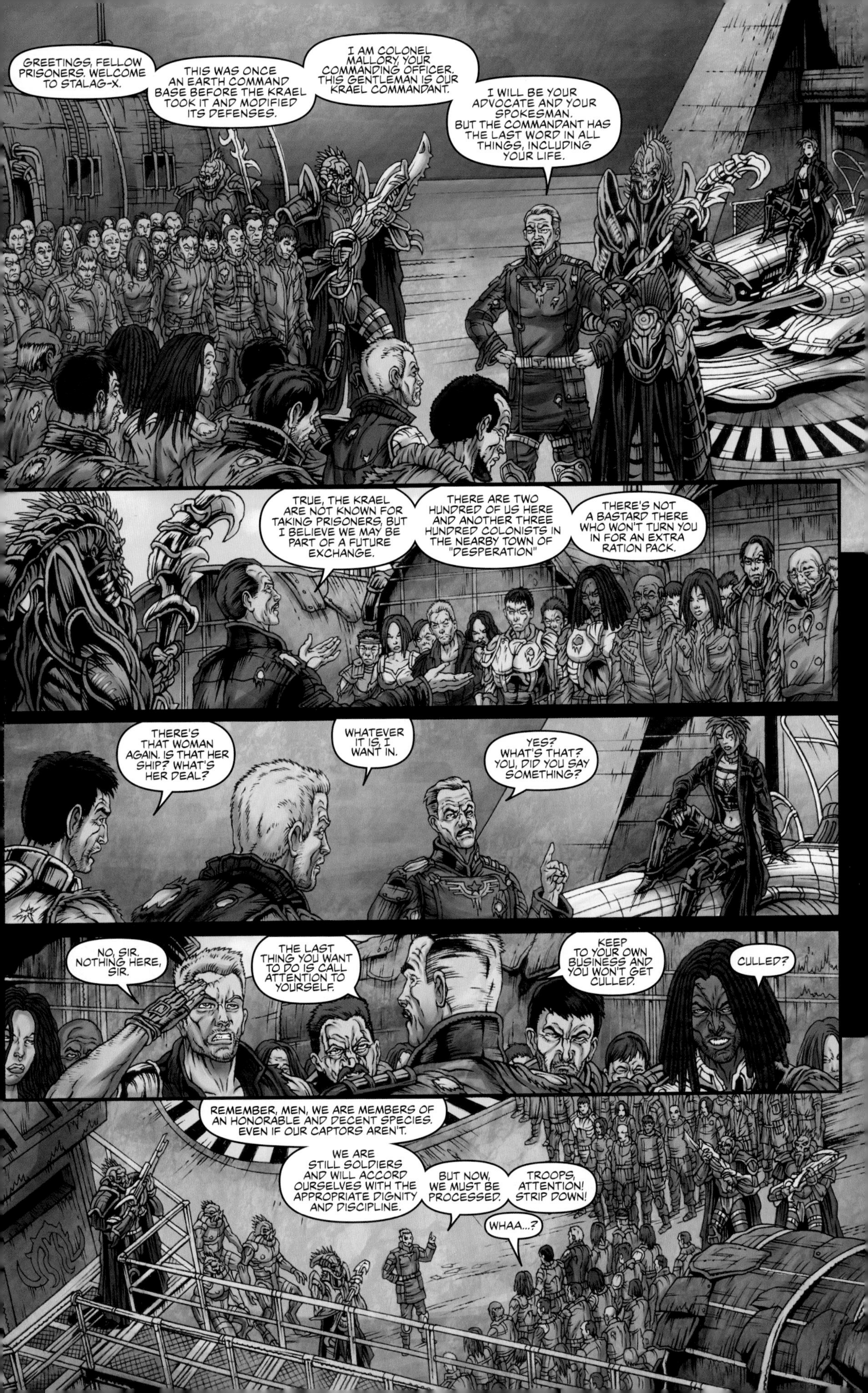
GREETINGS, FELLOW PRISONERS. WELCOME TO STALAG-X.
THIS WAS ONCE AN EARTH COMMAND BASE BEFORE THE KRAEL TOOK IT AND MODIFIED ITS DEFENSES.
I AM COLONEL MALLORY, YOUR COMMANDING OFFICER. THIS GENTLEMAN IS OUR KRAEL COMMANDANT.
I WILL BE YOUR ADVOCATE AND YOUR SPOKESMAN. BUT THE COMMANDANT HAS THE LAST WORD IN ALL THINGS, INCLUDING YOUR LIFE.
TRUE, THE KRAEL ARE NOT KNOWN FOR TAKING PRISONERS, BUT I BELIEVE WE MAY BE PART OF A FUTURE EXCHANGE.
THERE ARE TWO HUNDRED OF US HERE AND ANOTHER THREE HUNDRED COLONISTS IN THE NEARBY TOWN OF "DESPERATION"
THERE'S NOT A BASTARD THERE WHO WON'T TURN YOU IN FOR AN EXTRA RATION PACK.
THERE'S THAT WOMAN AGAIN. IS THAT HER SHIP? WHAT'S HER DEAL?
WHATEVER IT IS, I WANT IN.
YES? WHAT'S THAT? YOU, DID YOU SAY SOMETHING?
NO, SIR. NOTHING HERE, SIR.
THE LAST THING YOU WANT TO DO IS CALL ATTENTION TO YOURSELF.
KEEP TO YOUR OWN BUSINESS AND YOU WON'T GET CULLED.
CULLED?
REMEMBER, MEN, WE ARE MEMBERS OF AN HONORABLE AND DECENT SPECIES. EVEN IF OUR CAPTORS AREN'T.
WE ARE STILL SOLDIERS AND WILL ACCORD OURSELVES WITH THE APPROPRIATE DIGNITY AND DISCIPLINE.
BUT NOW, WE MUST BE PROCESSED.
TROOPS, ATTENTION! STRIP DOWN!
WHAA...?

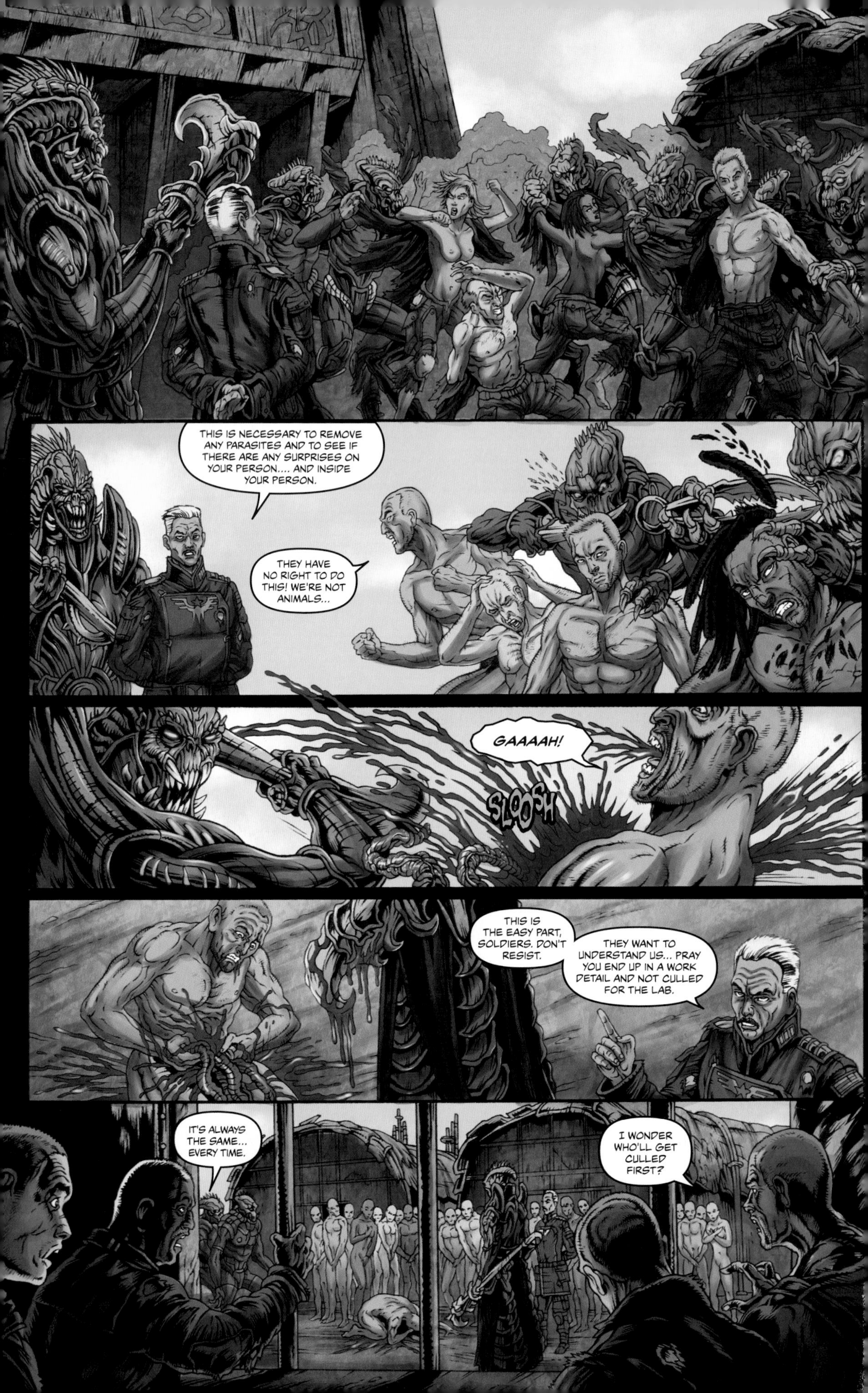
THIS IS NECESSARY TO REMOVE ANY PARASITES AND TO SEE IF THERE ARE ANY SURPRISES ON YOUR PERSON.... AND INSIDE YOUR PERSON.
THEY HAVE NO RIGHT TO DO THIS! WE'RE NOT ANIMALS...
GAAAAH!
SLOOSH
THIS IS THE EASY PART, SOLDIERS. DON'T RESIST.
THEY WANT TO UNDERSTAND US... PRAY YOU END UP IN A WORK DETAIL AND NOT CULLED FOR THE LAB.
IT'S ALWAYS THE SAME... EVERY TIME.
I WONDER WHO'LL GET CULLED FIRST?

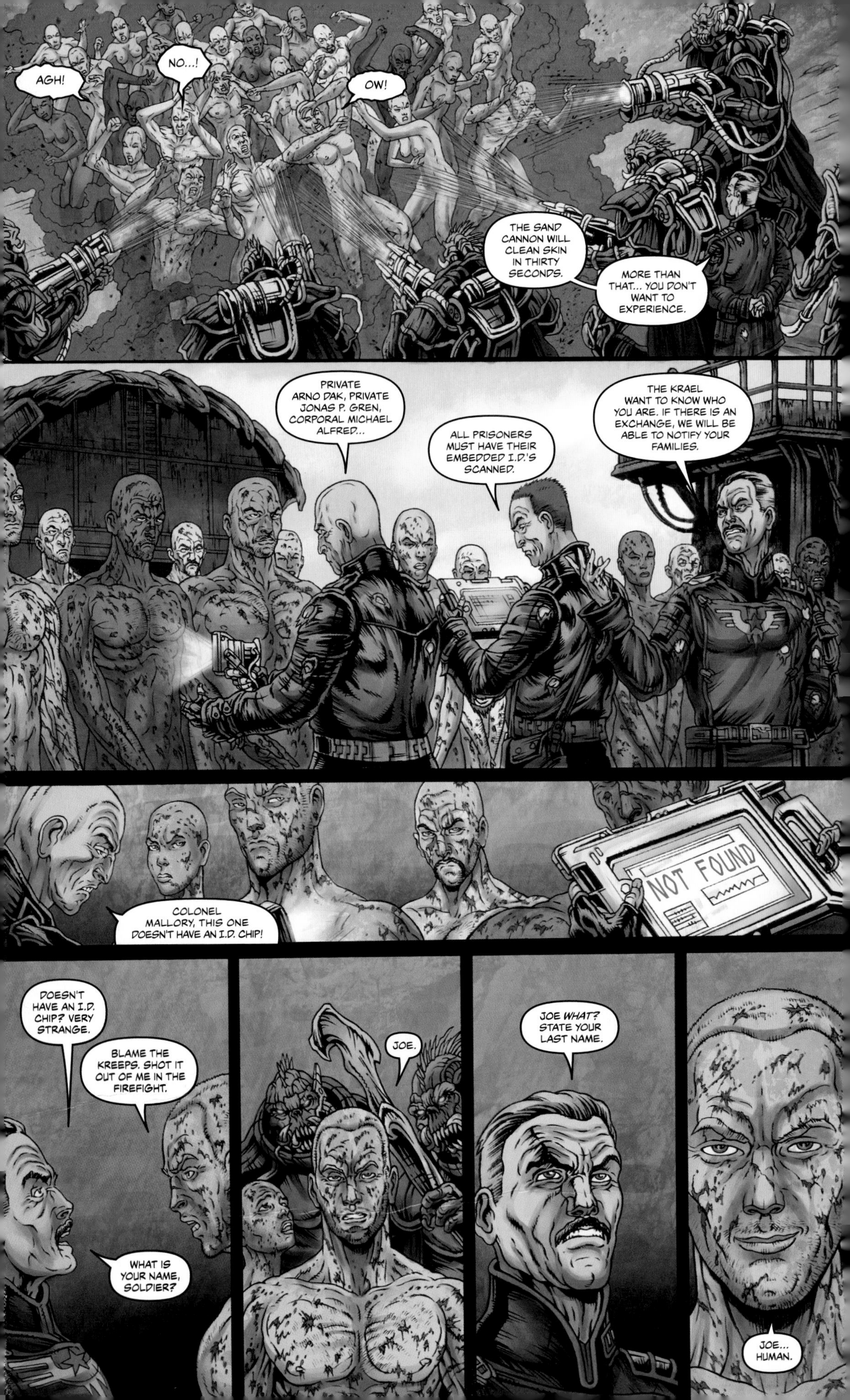
AGH!
NO...!
OW!
THE SAND CANNON WILL CLEAN SKIN IN THIRTY SECONDS.
MORE THAN THAT... YOU DON'T WANT TO EXPERIENCE.
PRIVATE ARNO DAK, PRIVATE JONAS P. GREN, CORPORAL MICHAEL ALFRED...
ALL PRISONERS MUST HAVE THEIR EMBEDDED I.D.'S SCANNED.
THE KRAEL WANT TO KNOW WHO YOU ARE. IF THERE IS AN EXCHANGE, WE WILL BE ABLE TO NOTIFY YOUR FAMILIES.
NOT FOUND
COLONEL MALLORY, THIS ONE DOESN'T HAVE AN I.D. CHIP!
DOESN'T HAVE AN I.D. CHIP? VERY STRANGE.
BLAME THE KREEPS. SHOT IT OUT OF ME IN THE FIREFIGHT.
WHAT IS YOUR NAME, SOLDIER?
JOE.
JOE WHAT? STATE YOUR LAST NAME.
JOE... HUMAN.

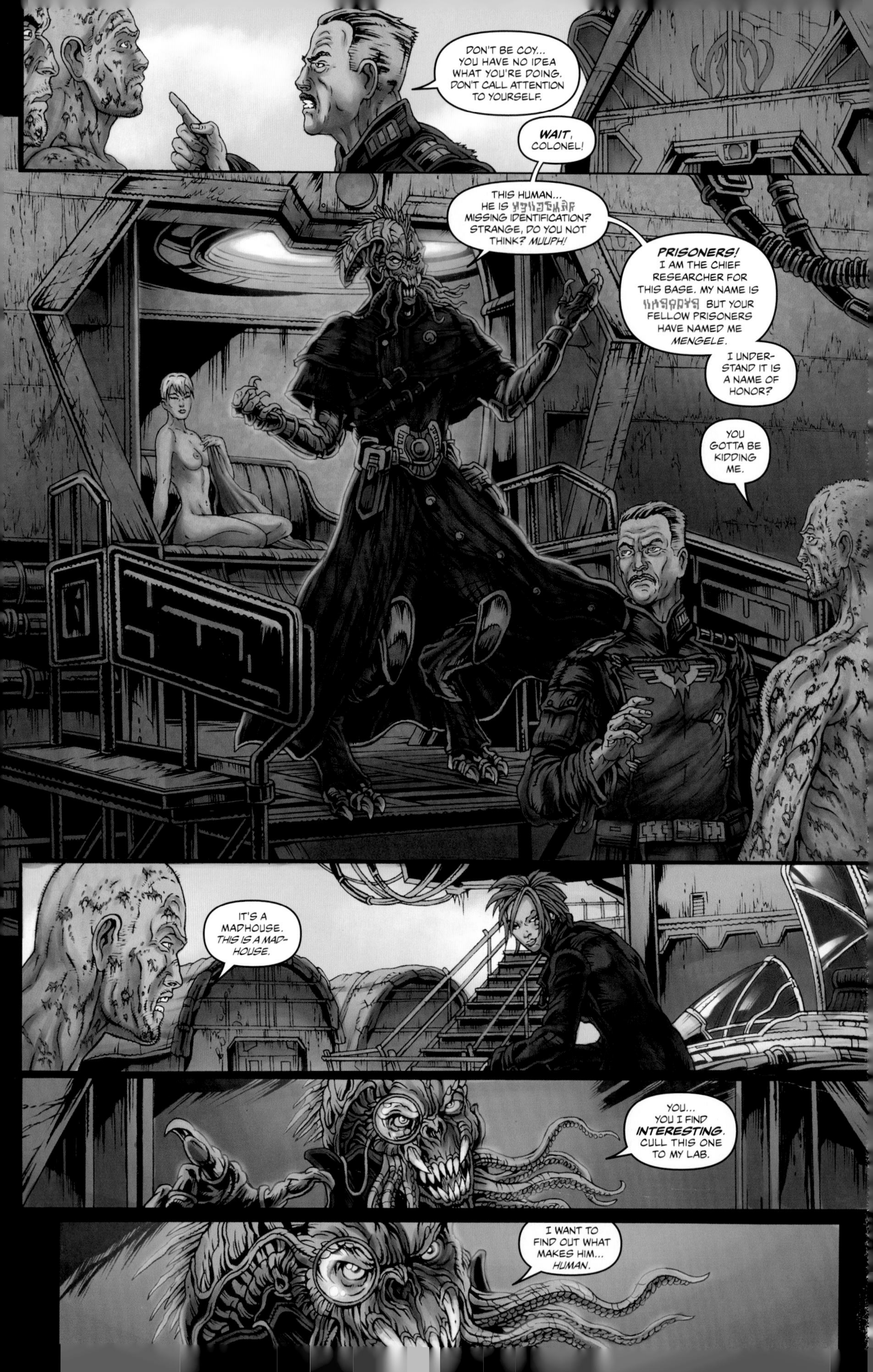
DON'T BE COY... YOU HAVE NO IDEA WHAT YOU'RE DOING. DON'T CALL ATTENTION TO YOURSELF.
WAIT, COLONEL!
THIS HUMAN... HE IS MISSING IDENTIFICATION? STRANGE, DO YOU NOT THINK? MUUPH!
PRISONERS! I AM THE CHIEF RESEARCHER FOR THIS BASE. MY NAME IS BUT YOUR FELLOW PRISONERS HAVE NAMED ME MENGELE.
I UNDERSTAND IT IS A NAME OF HONOR?
YOU GOTTA BE KIDDING ME.
IT'S A MADHOUSE. THIS IS A MADHOUSE.
YOU... YOU I FIND INTERESTING. CULL THIS ONE TO MY LAB.
I WANT TO FIND OUT WHAT MAKES HIM... HUMAN.

CHAPTER II

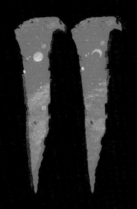

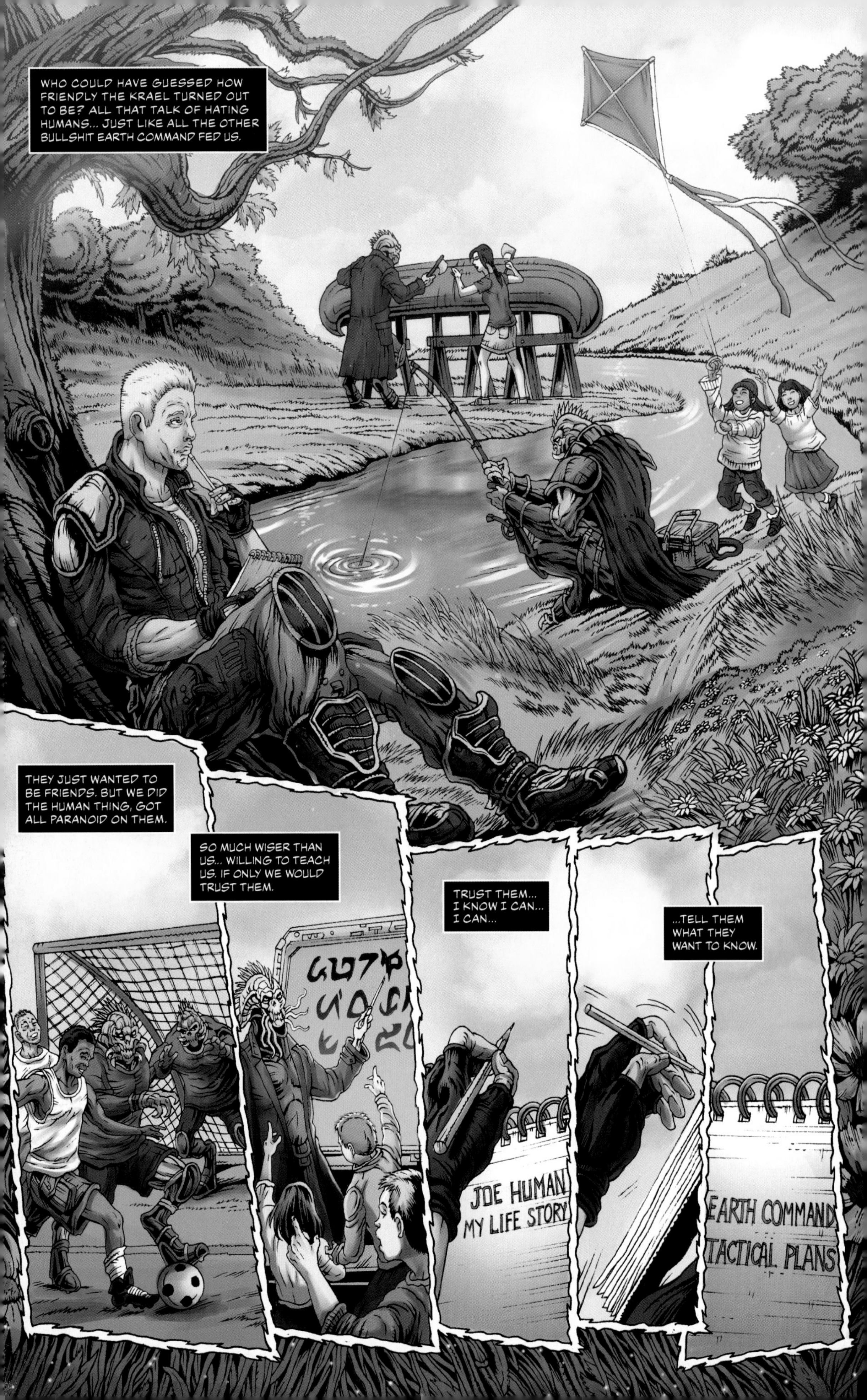
WHO COULD HAVE GUESSED HOW FRIENDLY THE KRAEL TURNED OUT TO BE? ALL THAT TALK OF HATING HUMANS... JUST LIKE ALL THE OTHER BULLSHIT EARTH COMMAND FED US.
THEY JUST WANTED TO BE FRIENDS. BUT WE DID THE HUMAN THING, GOT ALL PARANOID ON THEM.
SO MUCH WISER THAN US... WILLING TO TEACH US. IF ONLY WE WOULD TRUST THEM.
TRUST THEM... I KNOW I CAN... I CAN...
JOE HUMAN
MY LIFE STORY
...TELL THEM WHAT THEY WANT TO KNOW.
EARTH COMMAND
TACTICAL PLANS

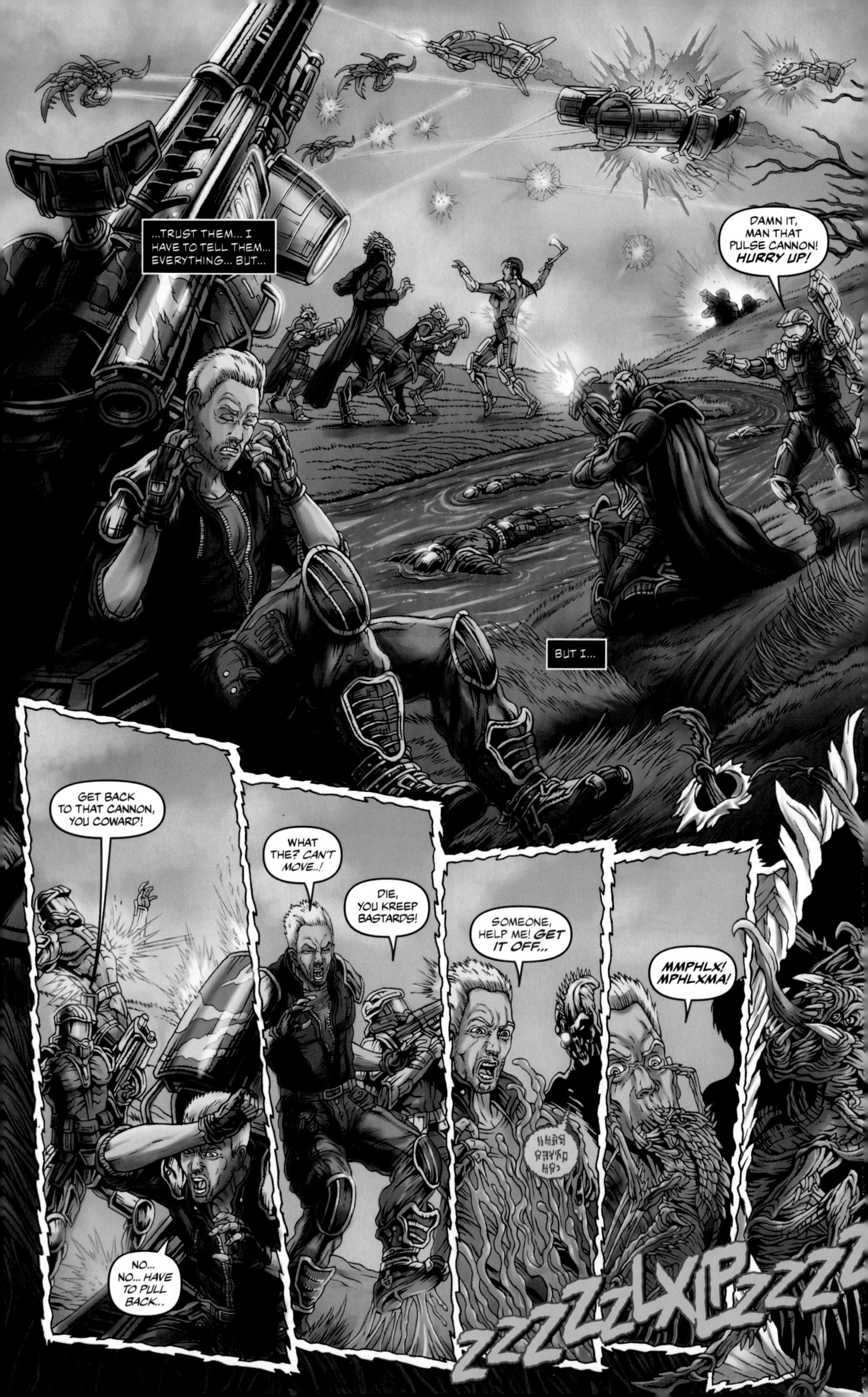
...TRUST THEM... I HAVE TO TELL THEM... EVERYTHING... BUT...
DAMN IT, MAN THAT PULSE CANNON! *HURRY UP!*
BUT I...
GET BACK TO THAT CANNON, YOU COWARD!
NO... NO... HAVE TO PULL BACK...
WHAT THE? *CAN'T MOVE..!*
DIE, YOU KREEP BASTARDS!
SOMEONE, HELP ME! *GET IT OFF...*
MMPHLX! MPHLXMA!
ZZZZZZLXLPZZZZ

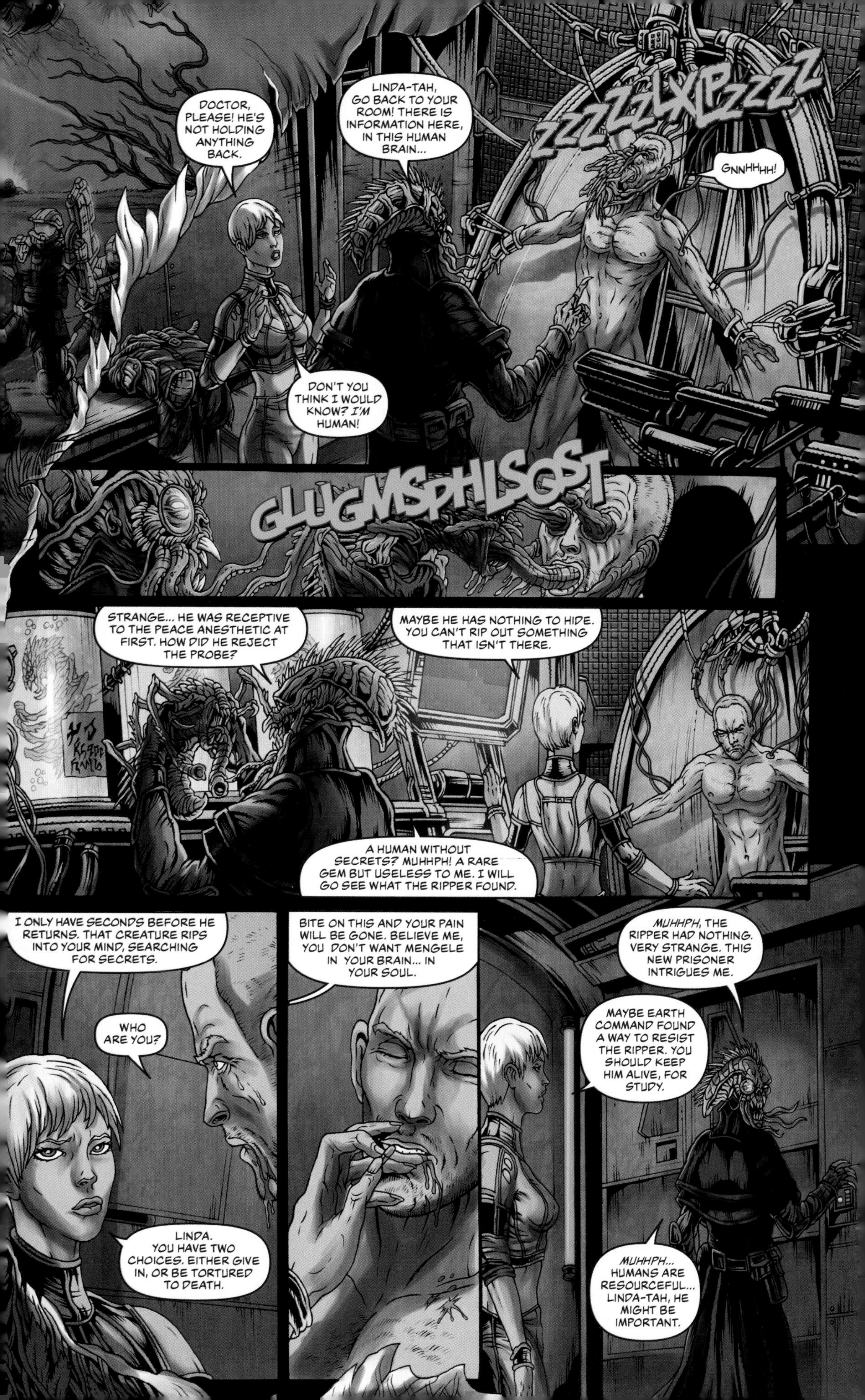

DOCTOR, PLEASE! HE'S NOT HOLDING ANYTHING BACK.
LINDA-TAH, GO BACK TO YOUR ROOM! THERE IS INFORMATION HERE, IN THIS HUMAN BRAIN...
ZZZZZZLXLPZZZZ
GNNHHHH!
DON'T YOU THINK I WOULD KNOW? I'M HUMAN!
GLUGMSPHLSGST
STRANGE... HE WAS RECEPTIVE TO THE PEACE ANESTHETIC AT FIRST. HOW DID HE REJECT THE PROBE?
MAYBE HE HAS NOTHING TO HIDE. YOU CAN'T RIP OUT SOMETHING THAT ISN'T THERE.
A HUMAN WITHOUT SECRETS? MUHHPH! A RARE GEM BUT USELESS TO ME. I WILL GO SEE WHAT THE RIPPER FOUND.
I ONLY HAVE SECONDS BEFORE HE RETURNS. THAT CREATURE RIPS INTO YOUR MIND, SEARCHING FOR SECRETS.
WHO ARE YOU?
LINDA. YOU HAVE TWO CHOICES. EITHER GIVE IN, OR BE TORTURED TO DEATH.
BITE ON THIS AND YOUR PAIN WILL BE GONE. BELIEVE ME, YOU DON'T WANT MENGELE IN YOUR BRAIN... IN YOUR SOUL.
MUHHPH, THE RIPPER HAD NOTHING. VERY STRANGE. THIS NEW PRISONER INTRIGUES ME.
MAYBE EARTH COMMAND FOUND A WAY TO RESIST THE RIPPER. YOU SHOULD KEEP HIM ALIVE, FOR STUDY.
MUHHPH... HUMANS ARE RESOURCEFUL... LINDA-TAH, HE MIGHT BE IMPORTANT.

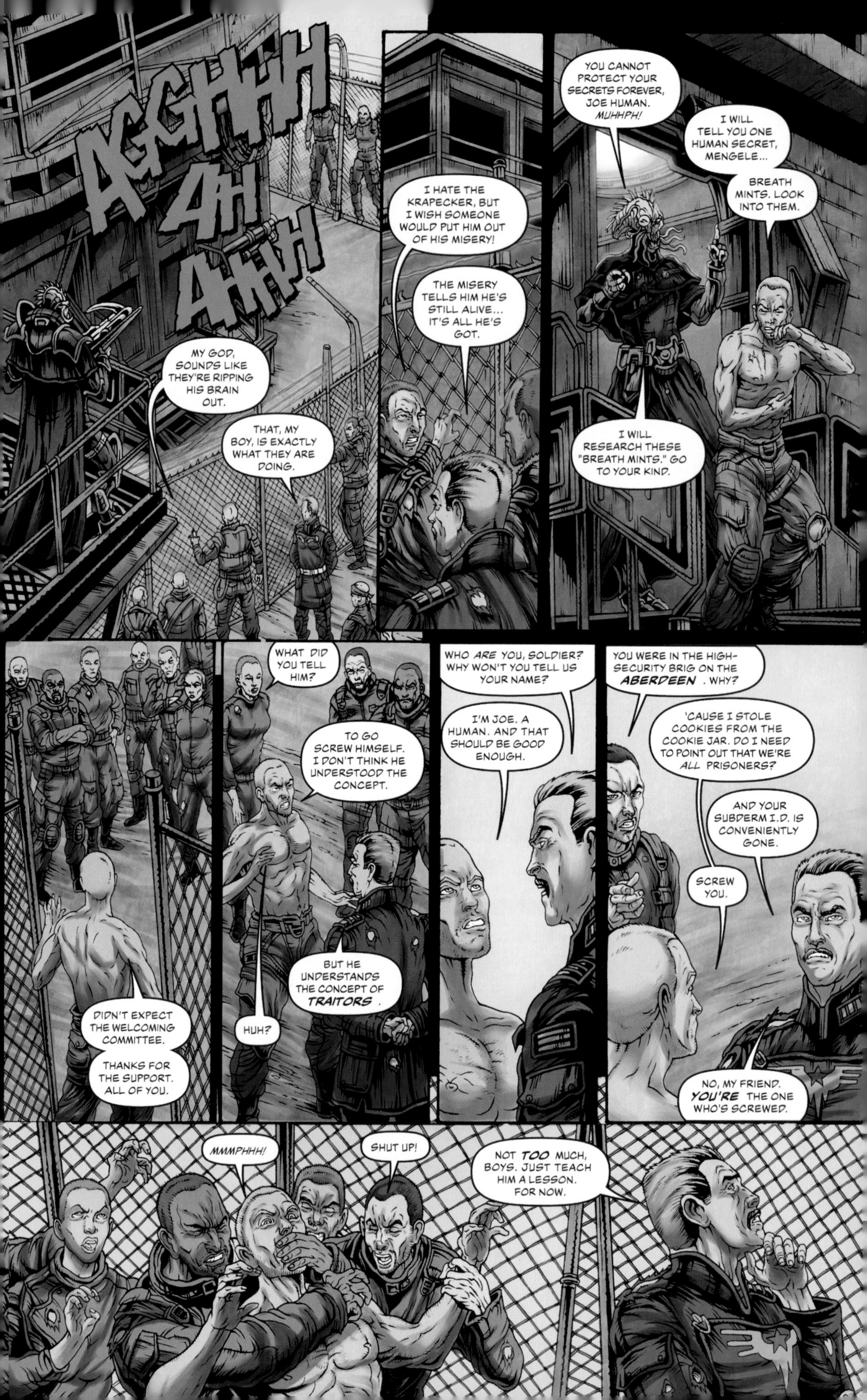
AGGHHH AHH AHHH
MY GOD, SOUNDS LIKE THEY'RE RIPPING HIS BRAIN OUT.
THAT, MY BOY, IS EXACTLY WHAT THEY ARE DOING.
I HATE THE KRAPECKER, BUT I WISH SOMEONE WOULD PUT HIM OUT OF HIS MISERY!
THE MISERY TELLS HIM HE'S STILL ALIVE... IT'S ALL HE'S GOT.
YOU CANNOT PROTECT YOUR SECRETS FOREVER, JOE HUMAN. *MUHHPH!*
I WILL TELL YOU ONE HUMAN SECRET, MENGELE...
BREATH MINTS. LOOK INTO THEM.
I WILL RESEARCH THESE "BREATH MINTS." GO TO YOUR KIND.
DIDN'T EXPECT THE WELCOMING COMMITTEE.
THANKS FOR THE SUPPORT. ALL OF YOU.
WHAT DID YOU TELL HIM?
TO GO SCREW HIMSELF. I DON'T THINK HE UNDERSTOOD THE CONCEPT.
BUT HE UNDERSTANDS THE CONCEPT OF ***TRAITORS***.
HUH?
WHO *ARE* YOU, SOLDIER? WHY WON'T YOU TELL US YOUR NAME?
I'M JOE. A HUMAN. AND THAT SHOULD BE GOOD ENOUGH.
YOU WERE IN THE HIGH-SECURITY BRIG ON THE ***ABERDEEN***. WHY?
'CAUSE I STOLE COOKIES FROM THE COOKIE JAR. DO I NEED TO POINT OUT THAT WE'RE *ALL* PRISONERS?
AND YOUR SUBDERM I.D. IS CONVENIENTLY GONE.
SCREW YOU.
NO, MY FRIEND. ***YOU'RE*** THE ONE WHO'S SCREWED.
MMMPHHH!
SHUT UP!
NOT ***TOO*** MUCH, BOYS. JUST TEACH HIM A LESSON. FOR NOW.

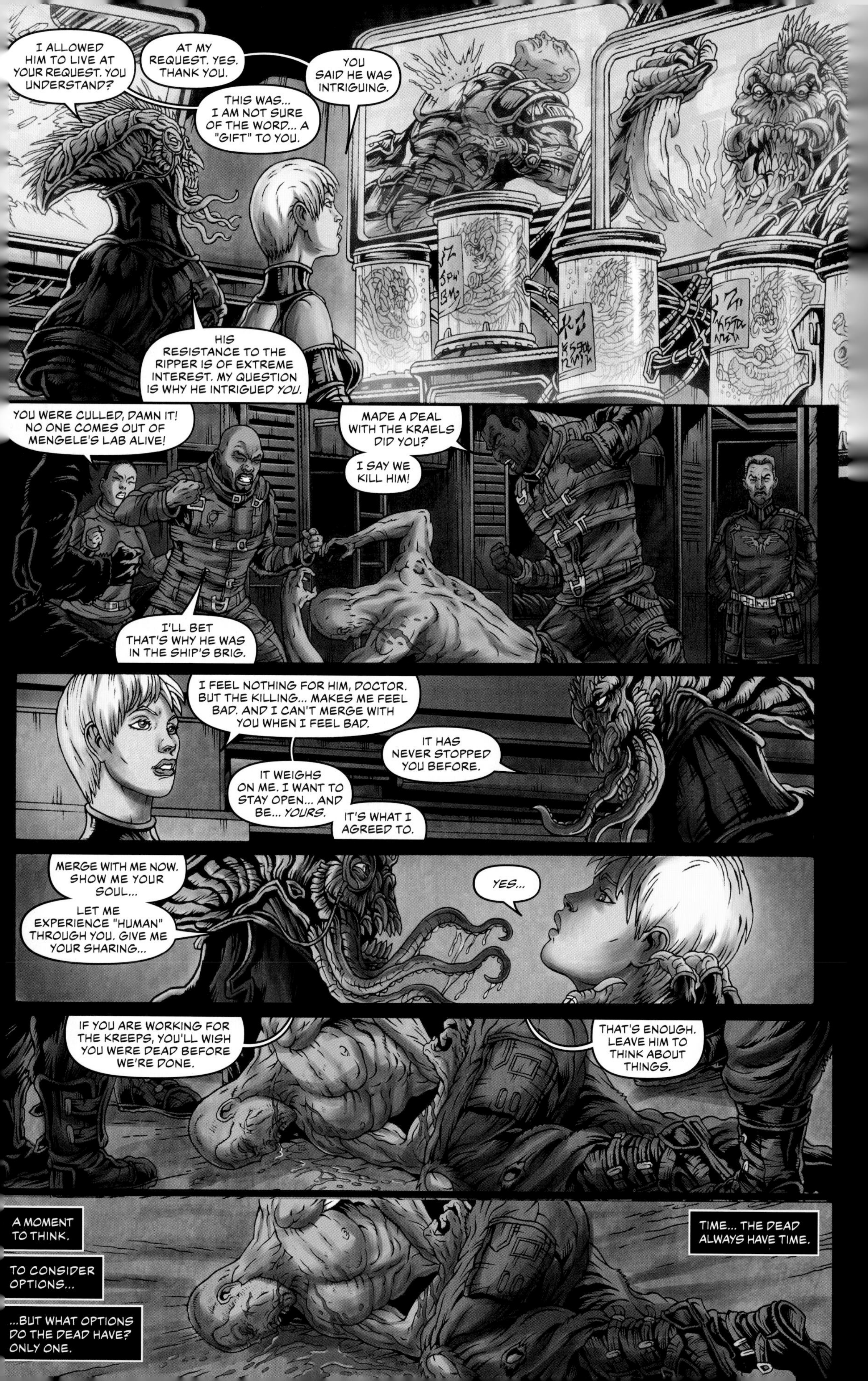
I ALLOWED HIM TO LIVE AT YOUR REQUEST. YOU UNDERSTAND?
AT MY REQUEST. YES. THANK YOU.
YOU SAID HE WAS INTRIGUING.
THIS WAS... I AM NOT SURE OF THE WORD... A "GIFT" TO YOU.
HIS RESISTANCE TO THE RIPPER IS OF EXTREME INTEREST. MY QUESTION IS WHY HE INTRIGUED *YOU*.
YOU WERE CULLED, DAMN IT! NO ONE COMES OUT OF MENGELE'S LAB ALIVE!
MADE A DEAL WITH THE KRAELS DID YOU?
I SAY WE KILL HIM!
I'LL BET THAT'S WHY HE WAS IN THE SHIP'S BRIG.
I FEEL NOTHING FOR HIM, DOCTOR. BUT THE KILLING... MAKES ME FEEL BAD. AND I CAN'T MERGE WITH YOU WHEN I FEEL BAD.
IT HAS NEVER STOPPED YOU BEFORE.
IT WEIGHS ON ME. I WANT TO STAY OPEN... AND BE... *YOURS*.
IT'S WHAT I AGREED TO.
MERGE WITH ME NOW. SHOW ME YOUR SOUL...
LET ME EXPERIENCE "HUMAN" THROUGH YOU. GIVE ME YOUR SHARING...
YES...
IF YOU ARE WORKING FOR THE KREEPS, YOU'LL WISH YOU WERE DEAD BEFORE WE'RE DONE.
THAT'S ENOUGH. LEAVE HIM TO THINK ABOUT THINGS.
A MOMENT TO THINK.
TO CONSIDER OPTIONS...
...BUT WHAT OPTIONS DO THE DEAD HAVE? ONLY ONE.
TIME... THE DEAD ALWAYS HAVE TIME.

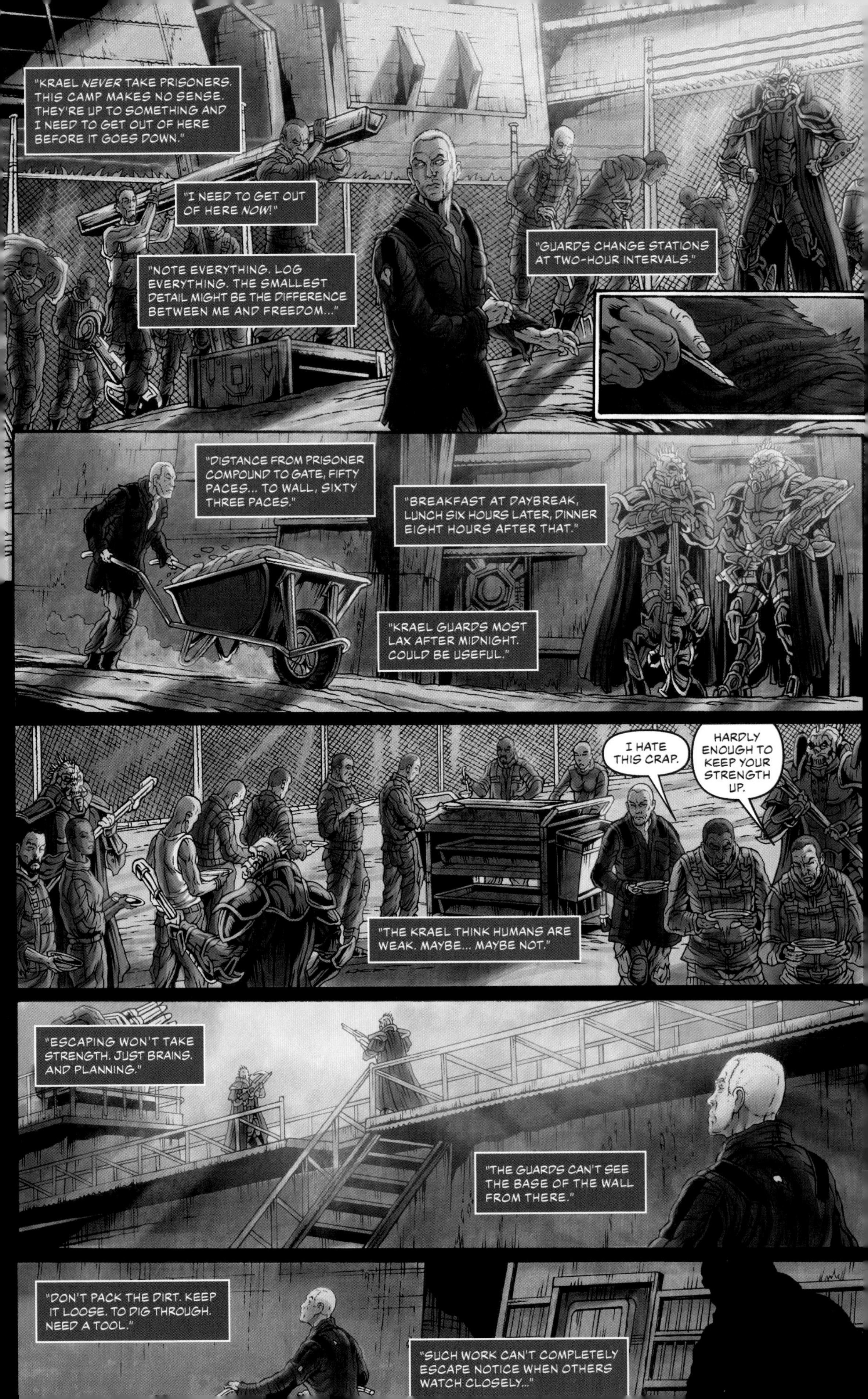
"KRAEL NEVER TAKE PRISONERS. THIS CAMP MAKES NO SENSE. THEY'RE UP TO SOMETHING AND I NEED TO GET OUT OF HERE BEFORE IT GOES DOWN."
"I NEED TO GET OUT OF HERE NOW!"
"NOTE EVERYTHING. LOG EVERYTHING. THE SMALLEST DETAIL MIGHT BE THE DIFFERENCE BETWEEN ME AND FREEDOM..."
"GUARDS CHANGE STATIONS AT TWO-HOUR INTERVALS."
"DISTANCE FROM PRISONER COMPOUND TO GATE, FIFTY PACES... TO WALL, SIXTY THREE PACES."
"BREAKFAST AT DAYBREAK, LUNCH SIX HOURS LATER, DINNER EIGHT HOURS AFTER THAT."
"KRAEL GUARDS MOST LAX AFTER MIDNIGHT. COULD BE USEFUL."
I HATE THIS CRAP.
HARDLY ENOUGH TO KEEP YOUR STRENGTH UP.
"THE KRAEL THINK HUMANS ARE WEAK. MAYBE... MAYBE NOT."
"ESCAPING WON'T TAKE STRENGTH. JUST BRAINS. AND PLANNING."
"THE GUARDS CAN'T SEE THE BASE OF THE WALL FROM THERE."
"DON'T PACK THE DIRT. KEEP IT LOOSE. TO DIG THROUGH. NEED A TOOL."
"SUCH WORK CAN'T COMPLETELY ESCAPE NOTICE WHEN OTHERS WATCH CLOSELY..."

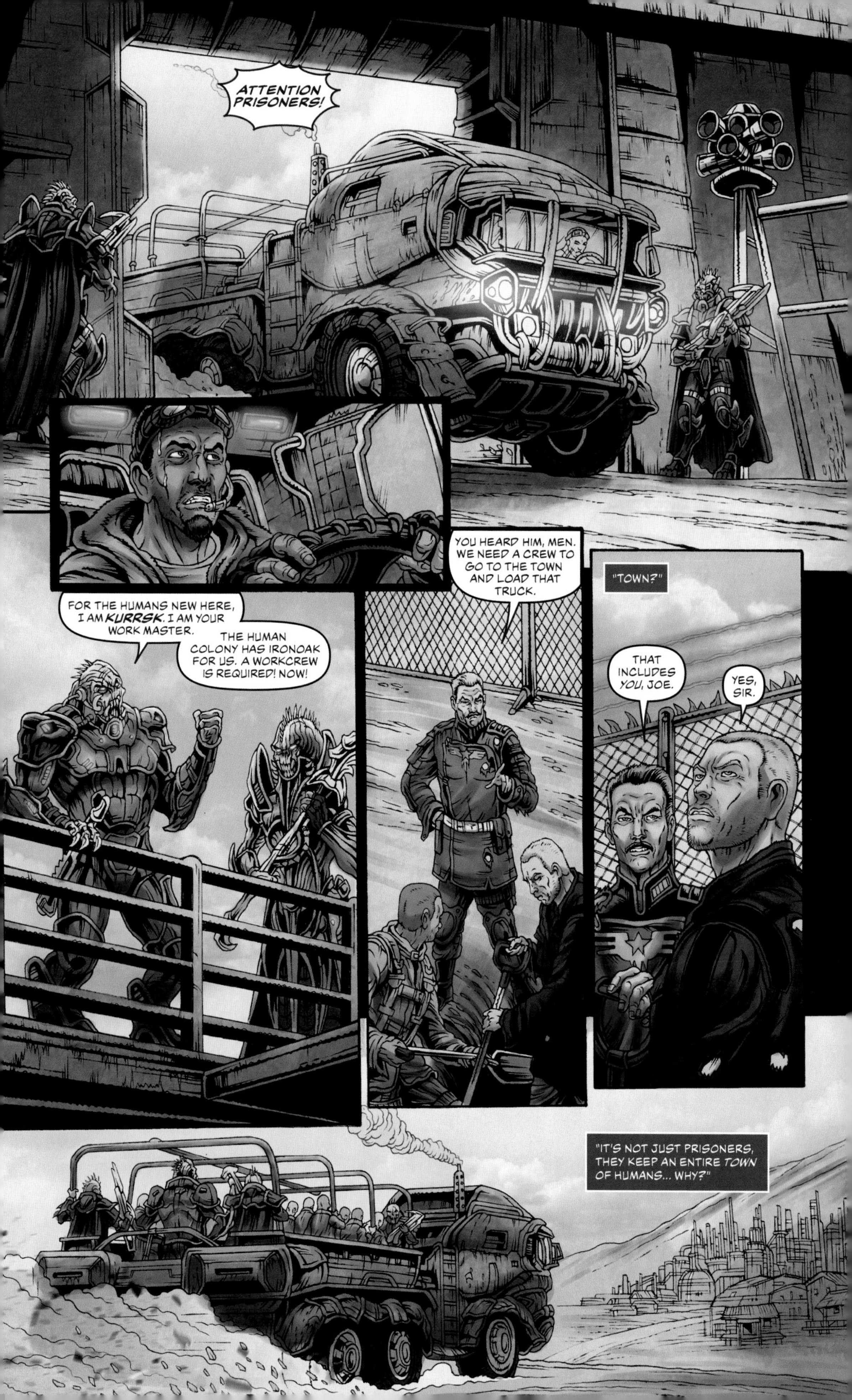
ATTENTION PRISONERS!
FOR THE HUMANS NEW HERE, I AM KURRSK. I AM YOUR WORK MASTER.
THE HUMAN COLONY HAS IRONOAK FOR US. A WORKCREW IS REQUIRED! NOW!
YOU HEARD HIM, MEN. WE NEED A CREW TO GO TO THE TOWN AND LOAD THAT TRUCK.
"TOWN?"
THAT INCLUDES YOU, JOE.
YES, SIR.
"IT'S NOT JUST PRISONERS, THEY KEEP AN ENTIRE TOWN OF HUMANS... WHY?"

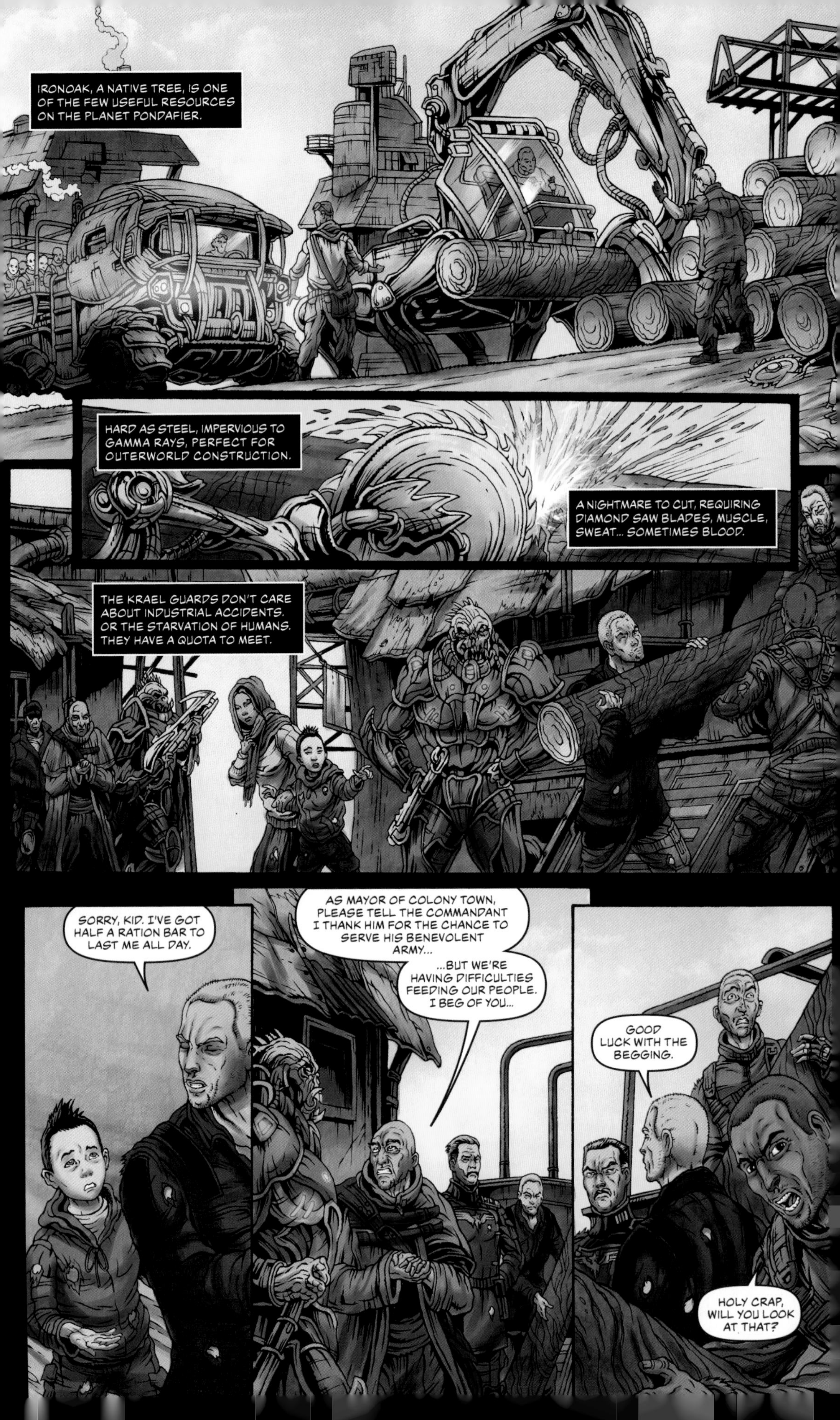
IRONOAK, A NATIVE TREE, IS ONE OF THE FEW USEFUL RESOURCES ON THE PLANET PONDAFIER.
HARD AS STEEL, IMPERVIOUS TO GAMMA RAYS, PERFECT FOR OUTERWORLD CONSTRUCTION.
A NIGHTMARE TO CUT, REQUIRING DIAMOND SAW BLADES, MUSCLE, SWEAT... SOMETIMES BLOOD.
THE KRAEL GUARDS DON'T CARE ABOUT INDUSTRIAL ACCIDENTS. OR THE STARVATION OF HUMANS. THEY HAVE A QUOTA TO MEET.
SORRY, KID. I'VE GOT HALF A RATION BAR TO LAST ME ALL DAY.
AS MAYOR OF COLONY TOWN, PLEASE TELL THE COMMANDANT I THANK HIM FOR THE CHANCE TO SERVE HIS BENEVOLENT ARMY...
...BUT WE'RE HAVING DIFFICULTIES FEEDING OUR PEOPLE. I BEG OF YOU...
GOOD LUCK WITH THE BEGGING.
HOLY CRAP, WILL YOU LOOK AT THAT?

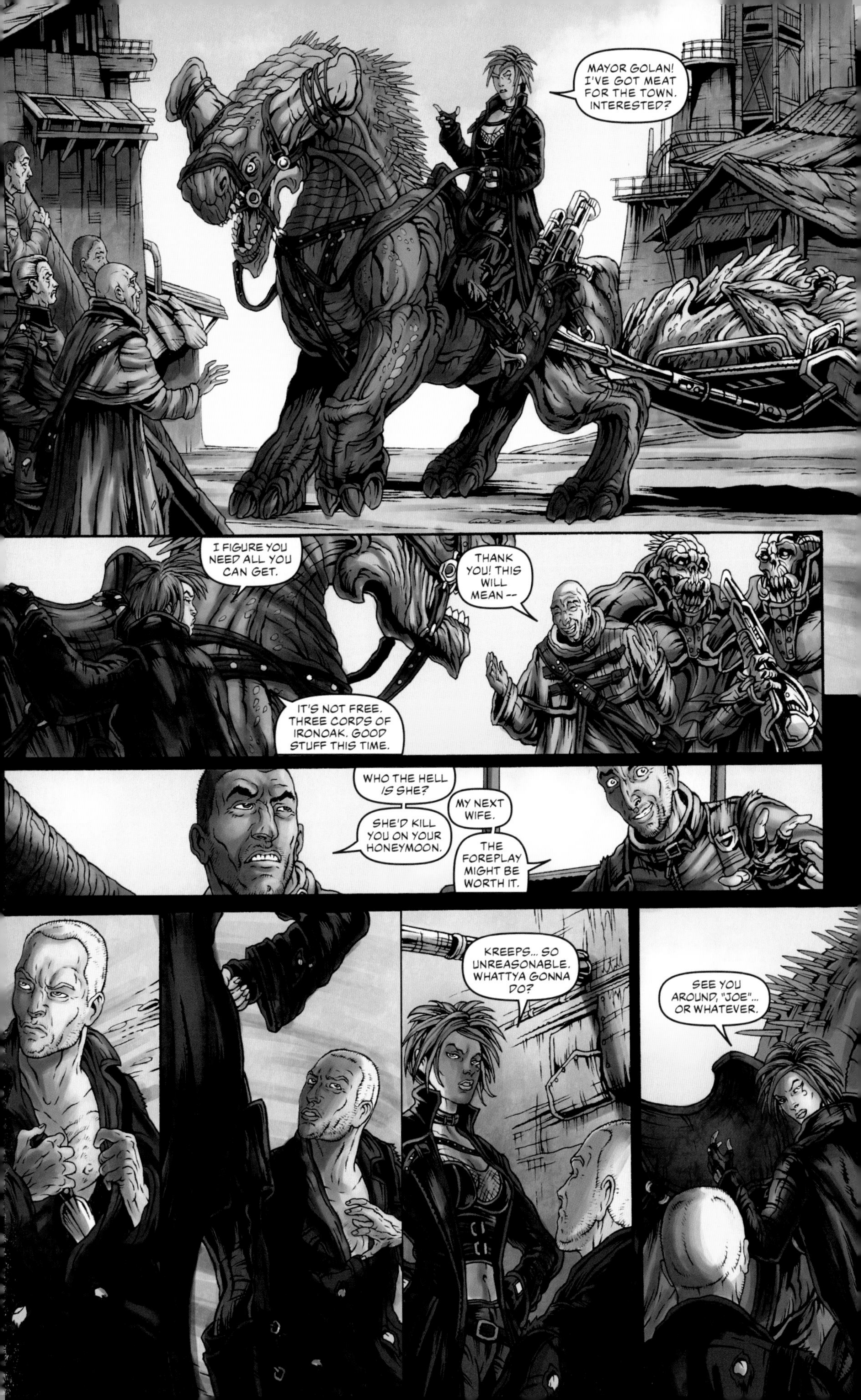
MAYOR GOLAN! I'VE GOT MEAT FOR THE TOWN. INTERESTED?
I FIGURE YOU NEED ALL YOU CAN GET.
THANK YOU! THIS WILL MEAN --
IT'S NOT FREE. THREE CORDS OF IRONOAK. GOOD STUFF THIS TIME.
WHO THE HELL *IS* SHE?
SHE'D KILL YOU ON YOUR HONEYMOON.
MY NEXT WIFE.
THE FOREPLAY MIGHT BE WORTH IT.
KREEPS... SO UNREASONABLE. WHATTYA GONNA DO?
SEE YOU AROUND, "JOE"... OR WHATEVER.

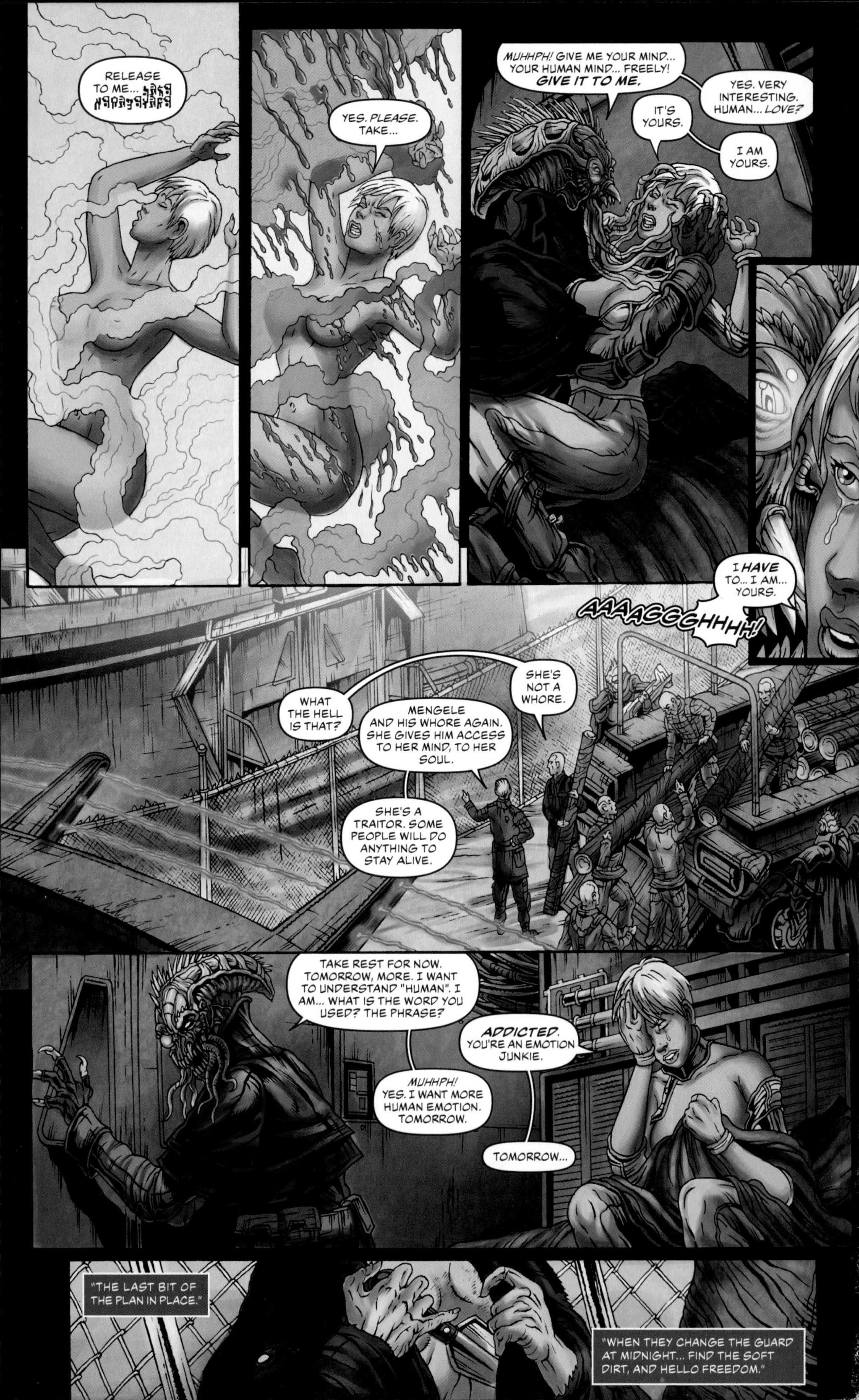
RELEASE TO ME...
YES. *PLEASE.* TAKE...
MUHHPH! GIVE ME YOUR MIND... YOUR HUMAN MIND... FREELY! ***GIVE IT TO ME.***
IT'S YOURS.
YES. VERY INTERESTING. HUMAN... *LOVE?*
I AM YOURS.
I ***HAVE*** TO... I AM... YOURS.
AAAAGGGHHHH!
WHAT THE HELL IS THAT?
MENGELE AND HIS WHORE AGAIN. SHE GIVES HIM ACCESS TO HER MIND, TO HER SOUL.
SHE'S NOT A WHORE.
SHE'S A TRAITOR. SOME PEOPLE WILL DO ANYTHING TO STAY ALIVE.
TAKE REST FOR NOW. TOMORROW, MORE. I WANT TO UNDERSTAND "HUMAN". I AM... WHAT IS THE WORD YOU USED? THE PHRASE?
ADDICTED. YOU'RE AN EMOTION JUNKIE.
MUHHPH! YES. I WANT MORE HUMAN EMOTION. TOMORROW.
TOMORROW...
"THE LAST BIT OF THE PLAN IN PLACE."
"WHEN THEY CHANGE THE GUARD AT MIDNIGHT... FIND THE SOFT DIRT, AND HELLO FREEDOM."

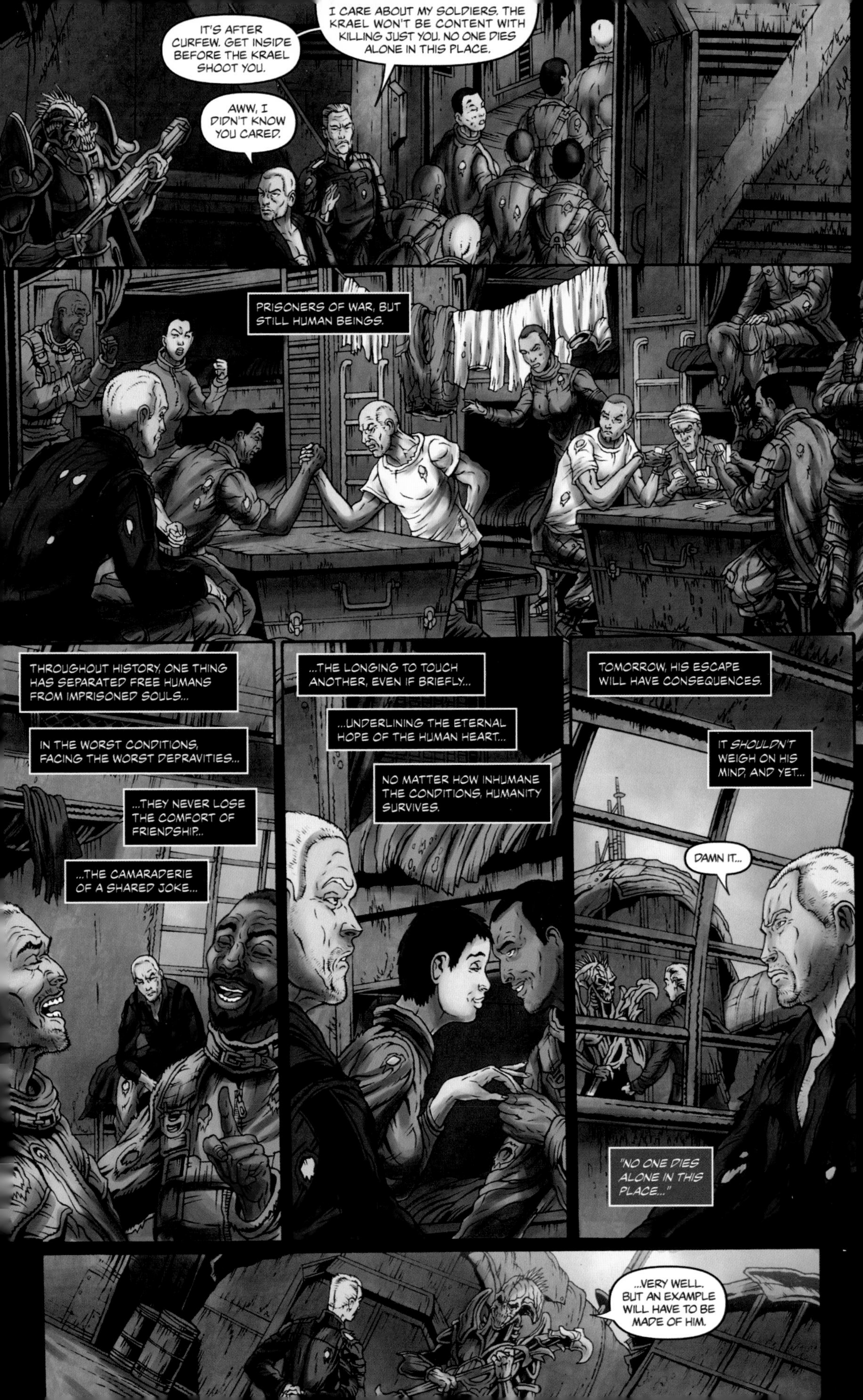

IT'S AFTER CURFEW. GET INSIDE BEFORE THE KRAEL SHOOT YOU.
I CARE ABOUT MY SOLDIERS. THE KRAEL WON'T BE CONTENT WITH KILLING JUST YOU. NO ONE DIES ALONE IN THIS PLACE.
AWW, I DIDN'T KNOW YOU CARED.
PRISONERS OF WAR, BUT STILL HUMAN BEINGS.
THROUGHOUT HISTORY, ONE THING HAS SEPARATED FREE HUMANS FROM IMPRISONED SOULS...
IN THE WORST CONDITIONS, FACING THE WORST DEPRAVITIES...
...THEY NEVER LOSE THE COMFORT OF FRIENDSHIP...
...THE CAMARADERIE OF A SHARED JOKE...
...THE LONGING TO TOUCH ANOTHER, EVEN IF BRIEFLY...
...UNDERLINING THE ETERNAL HOPE OF THE HUMAN HEART...
NO MATTER HOW INHUMANE THE CONDITIONS, HUMANITY SURVIVES.
TOMORROW, HIS ESCAPE WILL HAVE CONSEQUENCES.
IT *SHOULDN'T* WEIGH ON HIS MIND, AND YET...
DAMN IT...
"NO ONE DIES ALONE IN THIS PLACE..."
...VERY WELL. BUT AN EXAMPLE WILL HAVE TO BE MADE OF HIM.

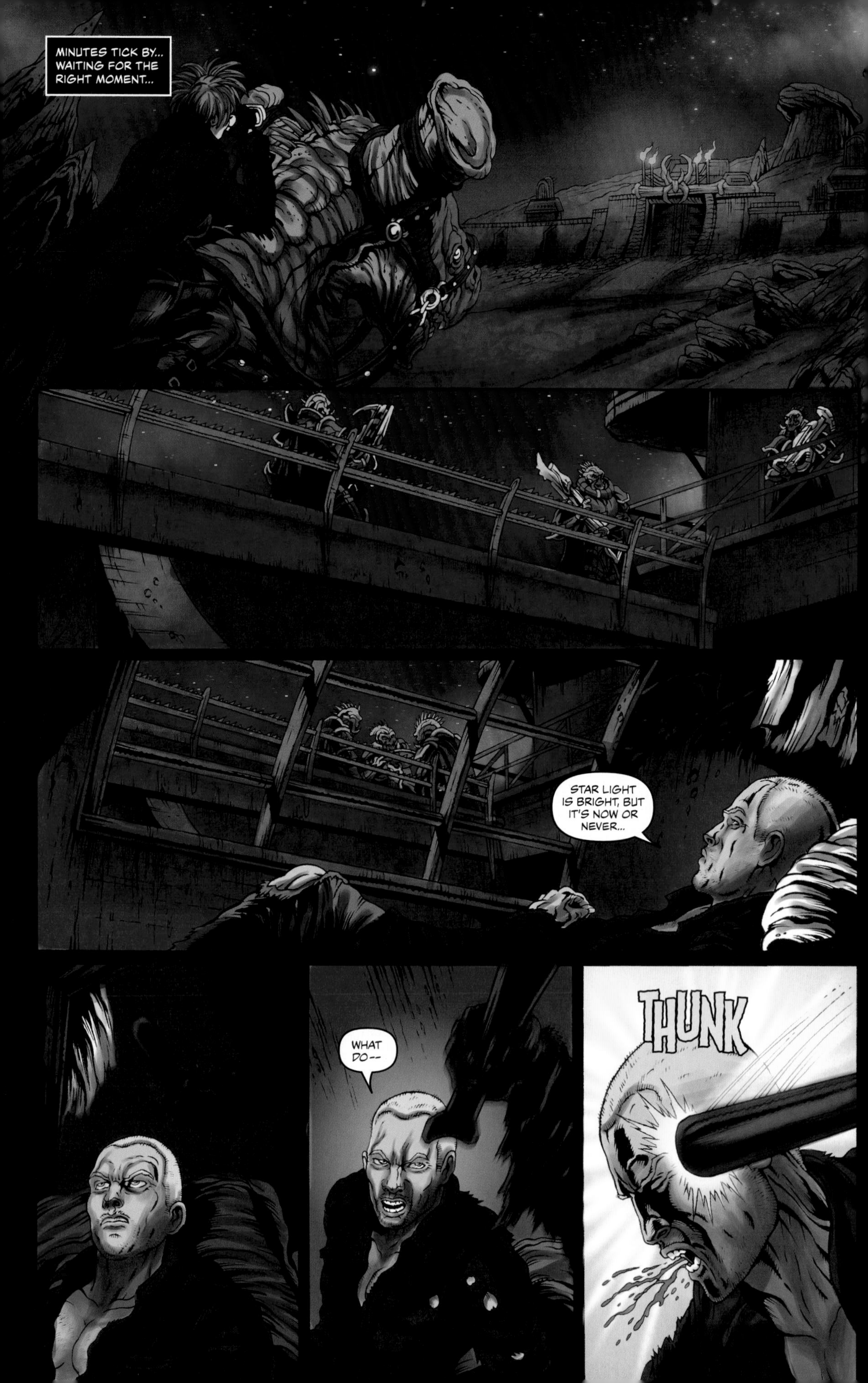
MINUTES TICK BY... WAITING FOR THE RIGHT MOMENT...
STAR LIGHT IS BRIGHT, BUT IT'S NOW OR NEVER...
WHAT DO--
THUNK

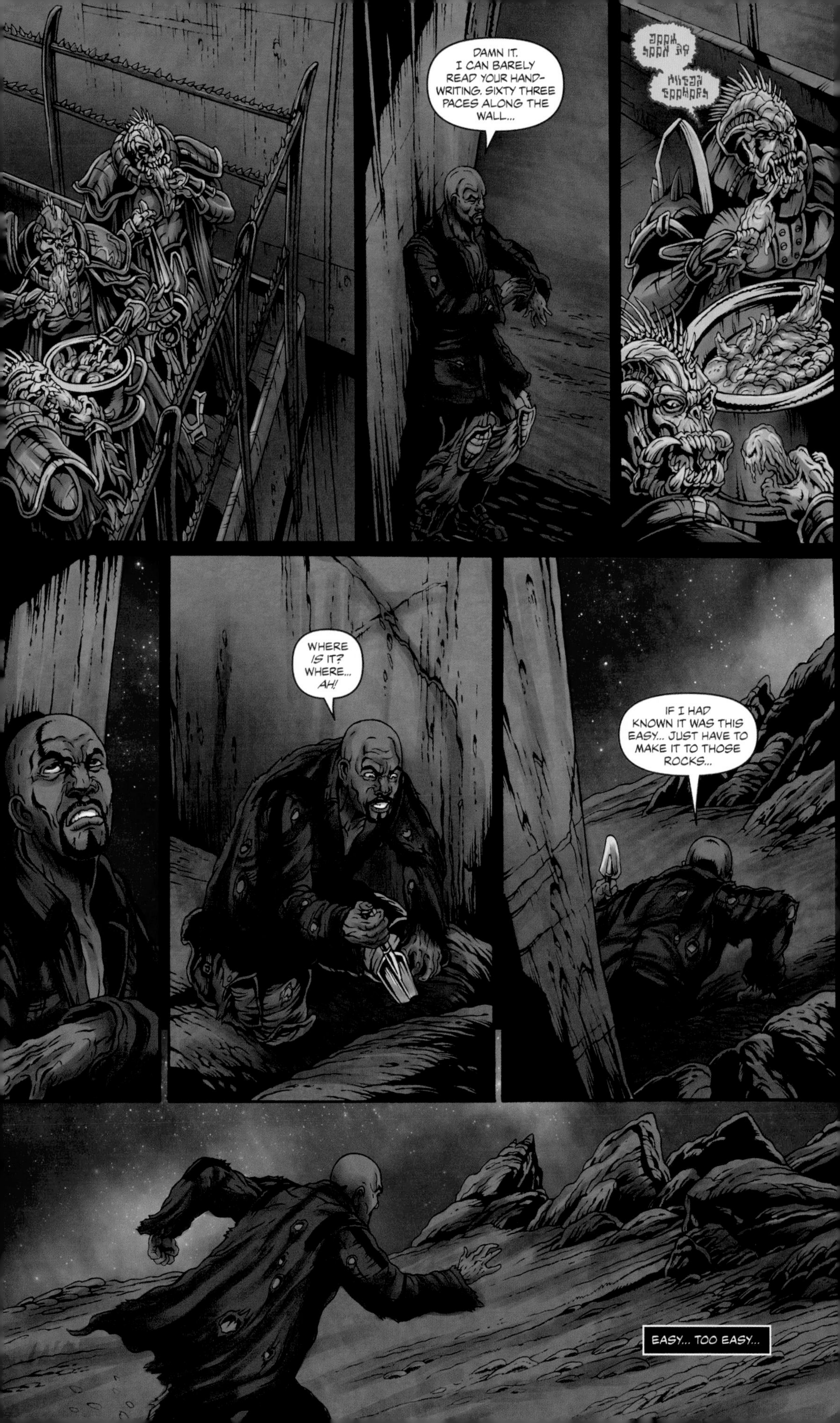
DAMN IT. I CAN BARELY READ YOUR HAND-WRITING. SIXTY THREE PACES ALONG THE WALL...
WHERE *IS* IT? WHERE... *AH!*
IF I HAD KNOWN IT WAS THIS EASY... JUST HAVE TO MAKE IT TO THOSE ROCKS...
EASY... TOO EASY...

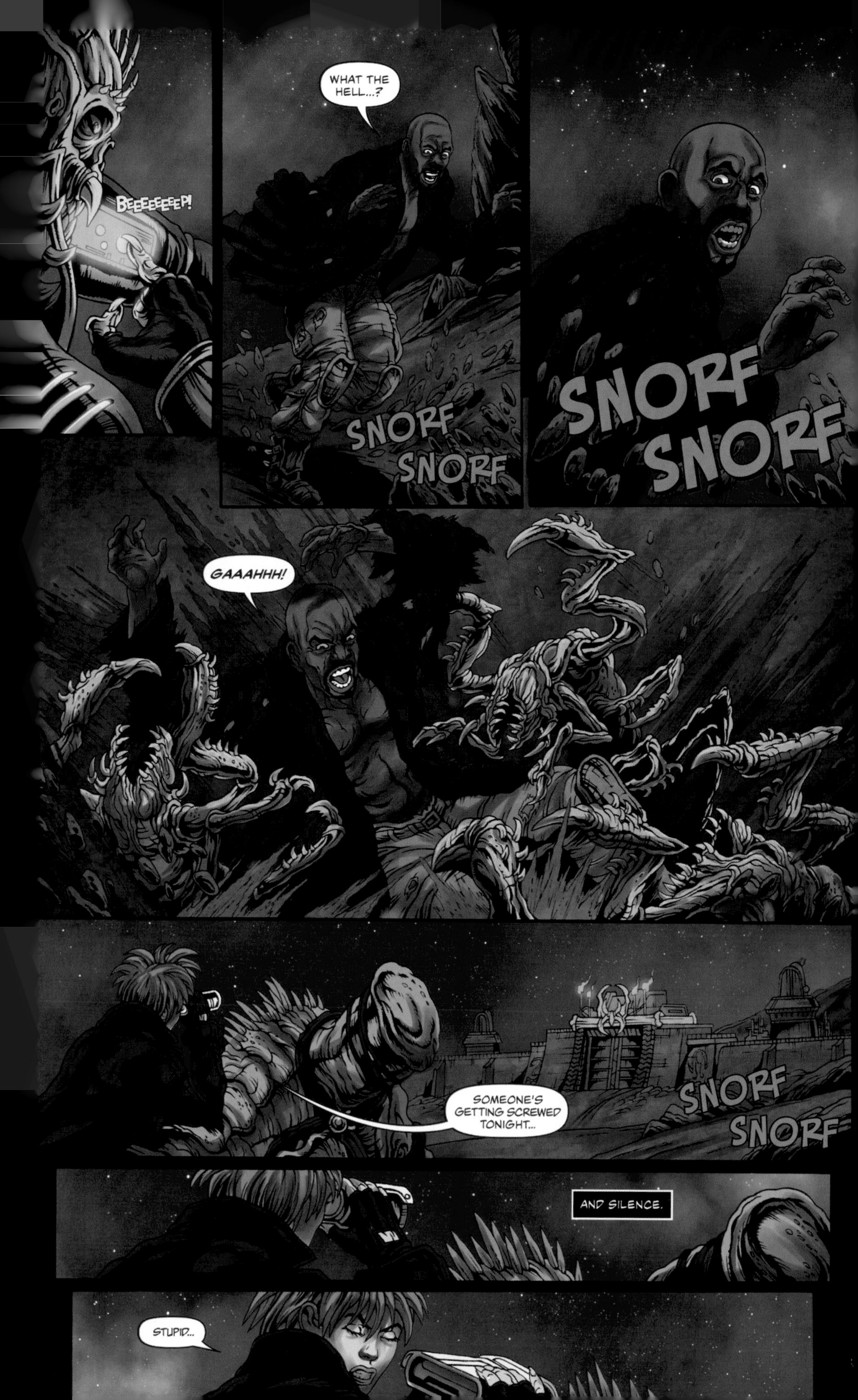

BEEEEEEEEP!
WHAT THE HELL...?
SNORF
SNORF
SNORF
SNORF
GAAAHHH!
SOMEONE'S GETTING SCREWED TONIGHT...
SNORF
SNORF
AND SILENCE.
STUPID...

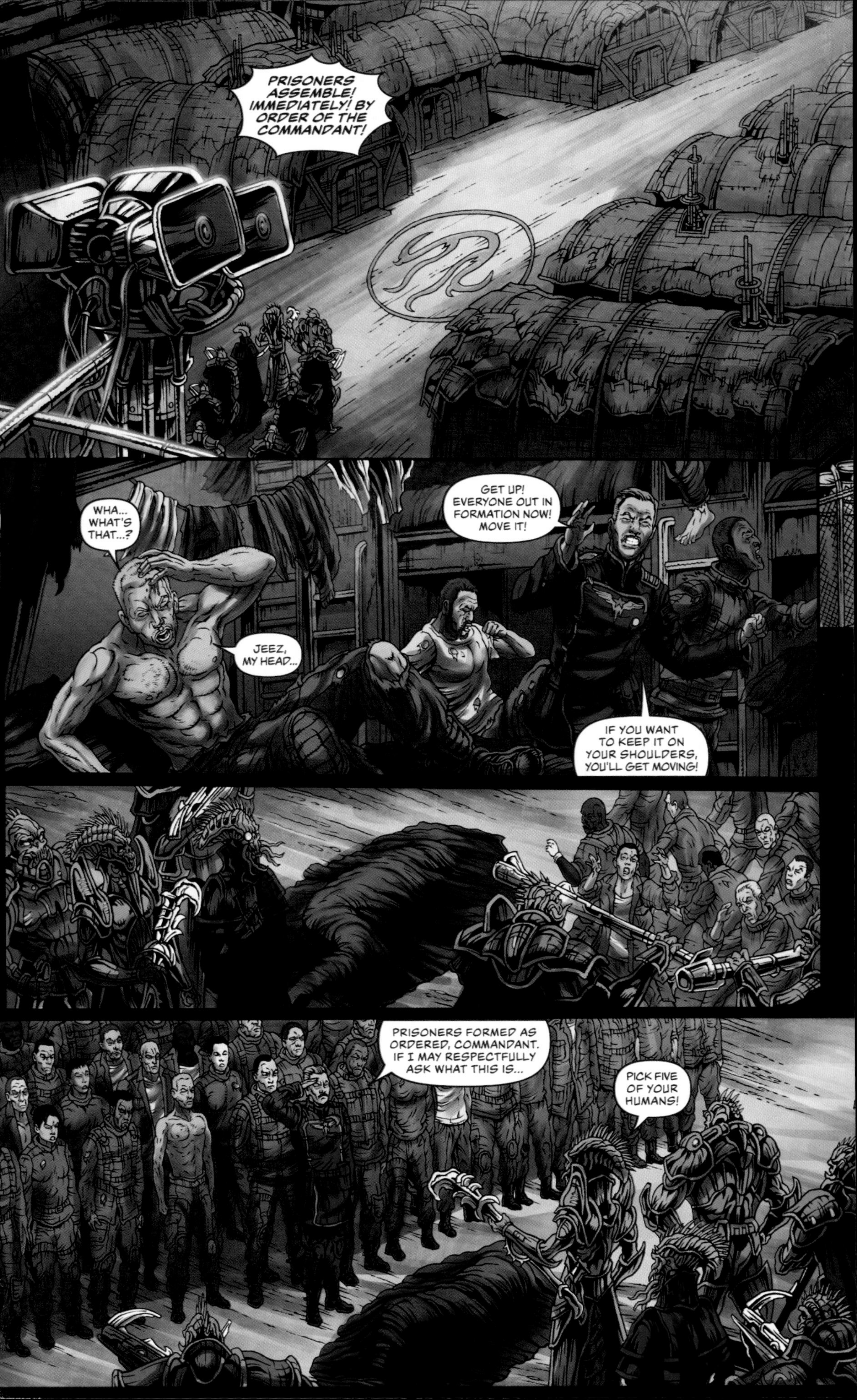
PRISONERS ASSEMBLE! IMMEDIATELY! BY ORDER OF THE COMMANDANT!
WHA... WHAT'S THAT...?
GET UP! EVERYONE OUT IN FORMATION NOW! MOVE IT!
JEEZ, MY HEAD...
IF YOU WANT TO KEEP IT ON YOUR SHOULDERS, YOU'LL GET MOVING!
PRISONERS FORMED AS ORDERED, COMMANDANT. IF I MAY RESPECTFULLY ASK WHAT THIS IS...
PICK FIVE OF YOUR HUMANS!

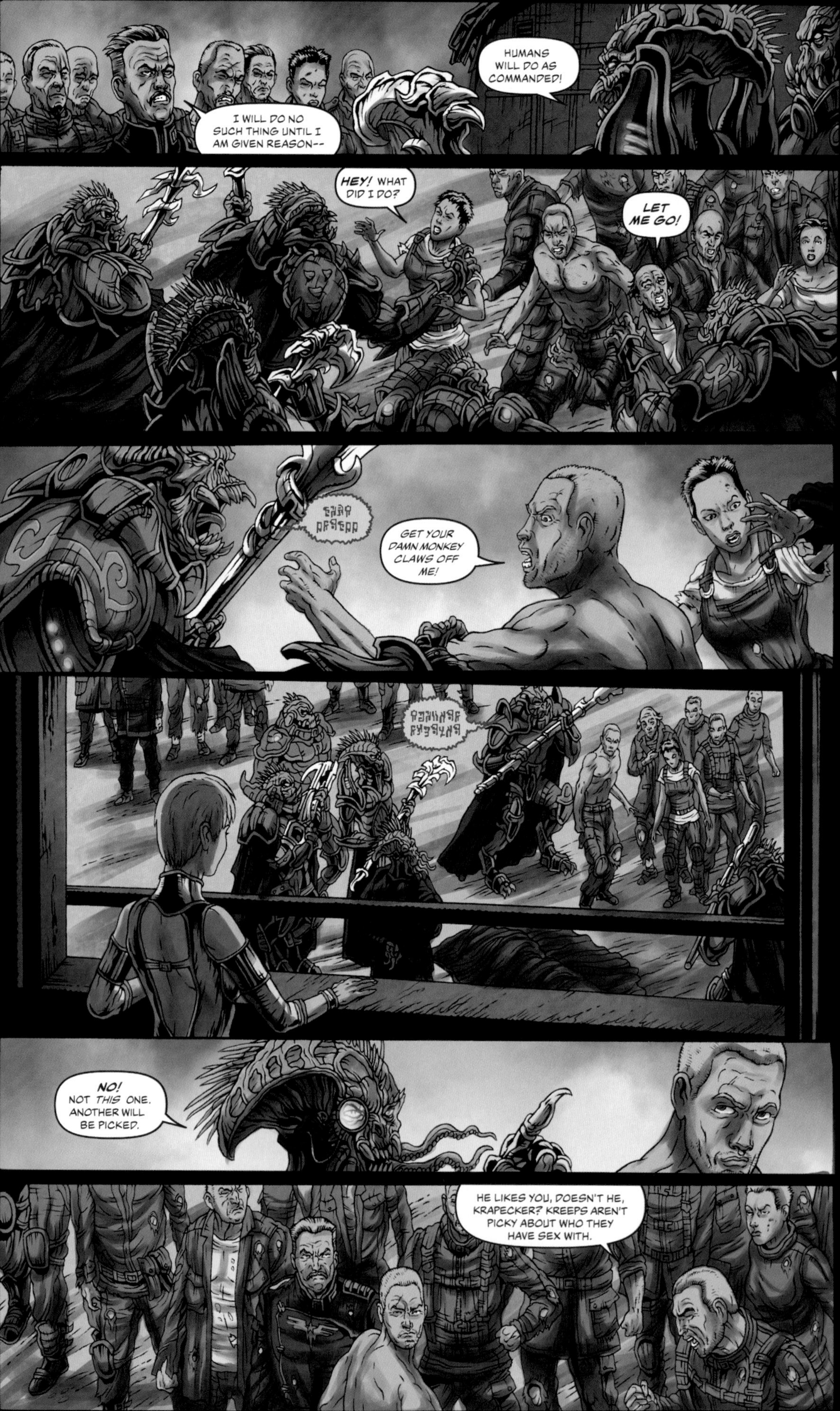
I WILL DO NO SUCH THING UNTIL I AM GIVEN REASON--
HUMANS WILL DO AS COMMANDED!
HEY! WHAT DID I DO?
LET ME GO!
GET YOUR DAMN MONKEY CLAWS OFF ME!
NO! NOT THIS ONE. ANOTHER WILL BE PICKED.
HE LIKES YOU, DOESN'T HE, KRAPECKER? KREEPS AREN'T PICKY ABOUT WHO THEY HAVE SEX WITH.

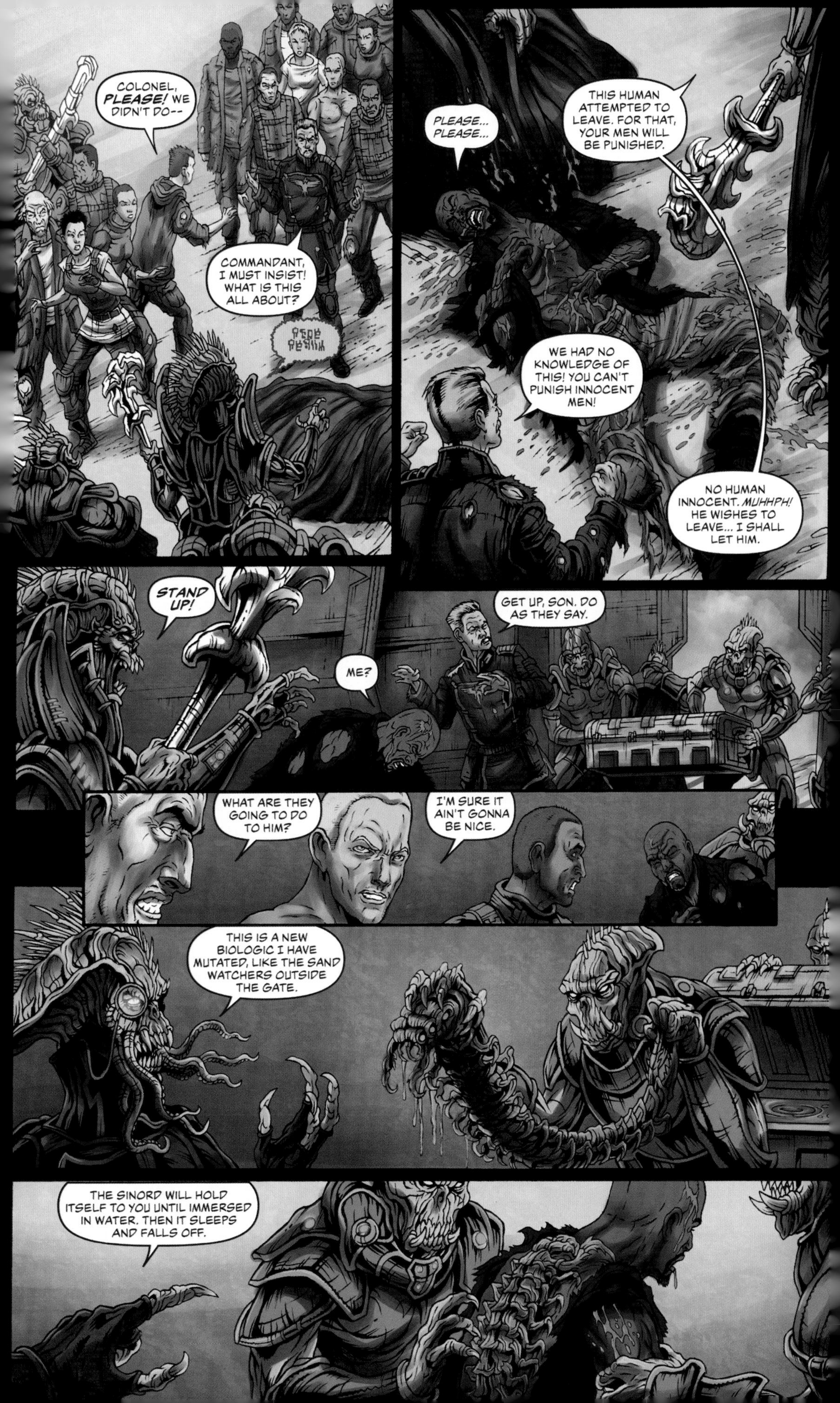
COLONEL, PLEASE! WE DIDN'T DO--
COMMANDANT, I MUST INSIST! WHAT IS THIS ALL ABOUT?
PLEASE... PLEASE...
THIS HUMAN ATTEMPTED TO LEAVE. FOR THAT, YOUR MEN WILL BE PUNISHED.
WE HAD NO KNOWLEDGE OF THIS! YOU CAN'T PUNISH INNOCENT MEN!
NO HUMAN INNOCENT. MUHHPH! HE WISHES TO LEAVE... I SHALL LET HIM.
STAND UP!
ME?
GET UP, SON. DO AS THEY SAY.
WHAT ARE THEY GOING TO DO TO HIM?
I'M SURE IT AIN'T GONNA BE NICE.
THIS IS A NEW BIOLOGIC I HAVE MUTATED, LIKE THE SAND WATCHERS OUTSIDE THE GATE.
THE SINORD WILL HOLD ITSELF TO YOU UNTIL IMMERSED IN WATER. THEN IT SLEEPS AND FALLS OFF.

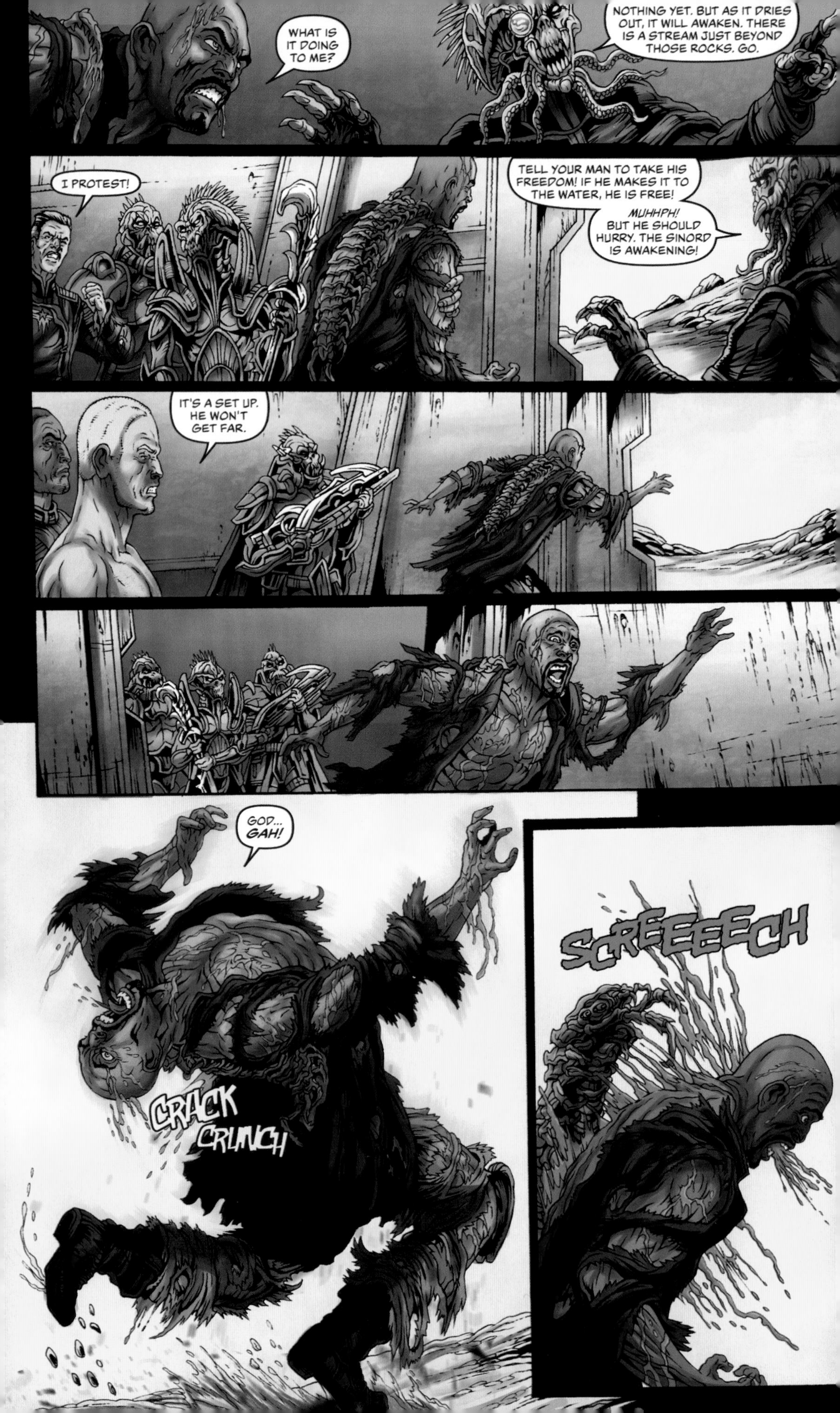

WHAT IS IT DOING TO ME?
NOTHING YET. BUT AS IT DRIES OUT, IT WILL AWAKEN. THERE IS A STREAM JUST BEYOND THOSE ROCKS. GO.
I PROTEST!
TELL YOUR MAN TO TAKE HIS FREEDOM! IF HE MAKES IT TO THE WATER, HE IS FREE!
MUHHPH! BUT HE SHOULD HURRY. THE SINORD IS AWAKENING!
IT'S A SET UP. HE WON'T GET FAR.
GOD... **GAH!**
CRACK
CRUNCH
SCREEEECH

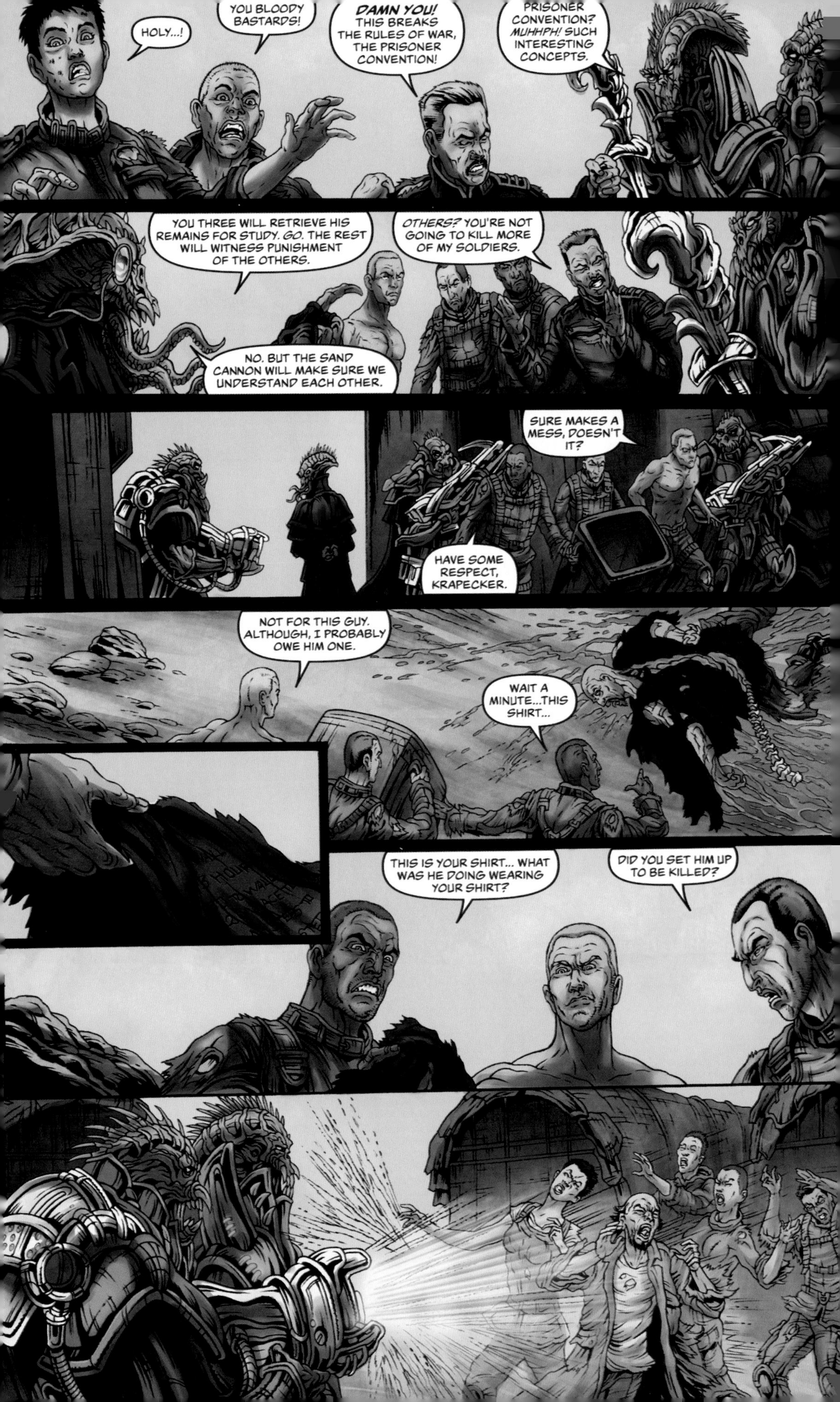
HOLY...!
YOU BLOODY BASTARDS!
DAMN YOU! THIS BREAKS THE RULES OF WAR, THE PRISONER CONVENTION!
PRISONER CONVENTION? MUHHPH! SUCH INTERESTING CONCEPTS.
YOU THREE WILL RETRIEVE HIS REMAINS FOR STUDY. GO. THE REST WILL WITNESS PUNISHMENT OF THE OTHERS.
OTHERS? YOU'RE NOT GOING TO KILL MORE OF MY SOLDIERS.
NO. BUT THE SAND CANNON WILL MAKE SURE WE UNDERSTAND EACH OTHER.
SURE MAKES A MESS, DOESN'T IT?
HAVE SOME RESPECT, KRAPECKER.
NOT FOR THIS GUY. ALTHOUGH, I PROBABLY OWE HIM ONE.
WAIT A MINUTE...THIS SHIRT...
THIS IS YOUR SHIRT... WHAT WAS HE DOING WEARING YOUR SHIRT?
DID YOU SET HIM UP TO BE KILLED?

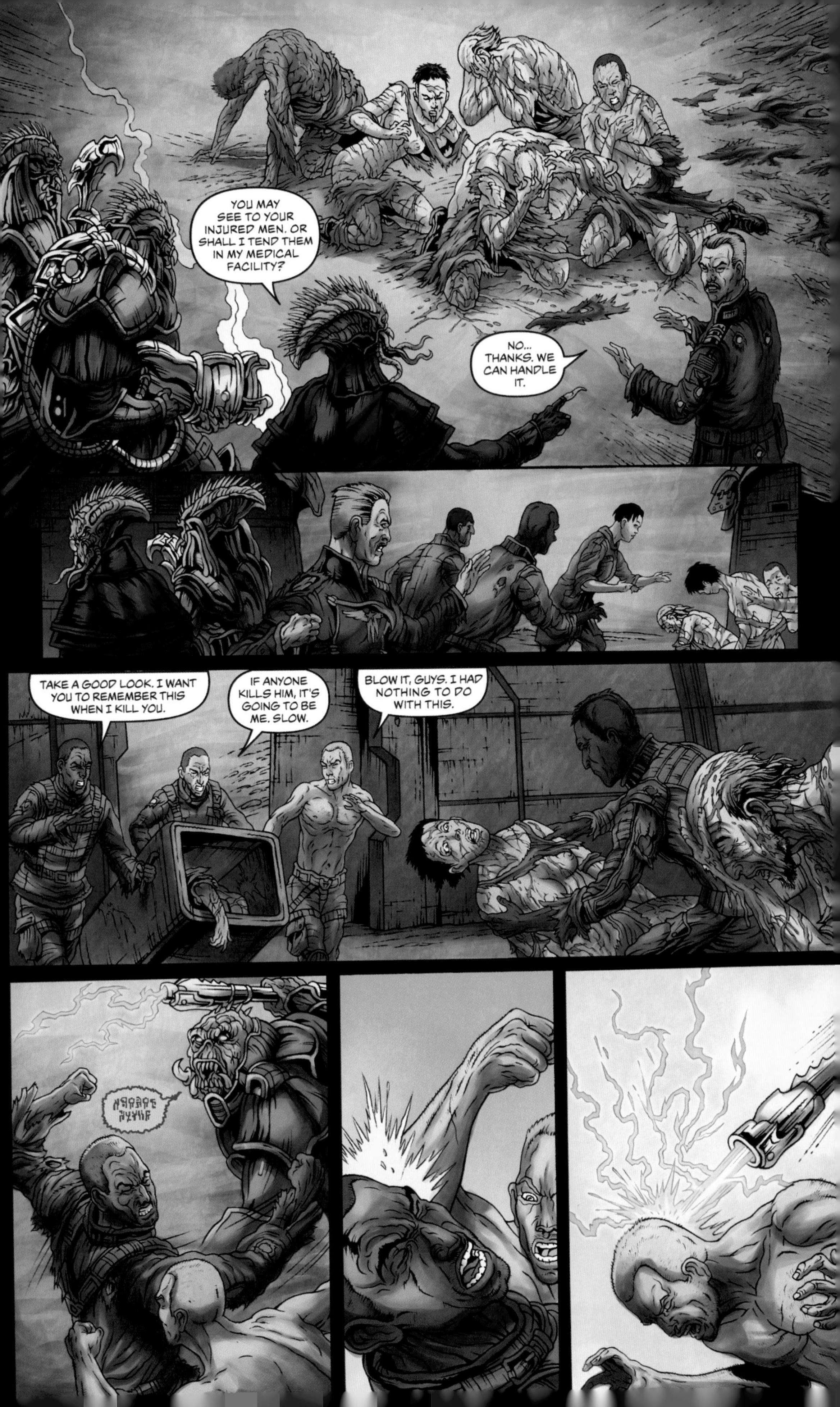
YOU MAY SEE TO YOUR INJURED MEN. OR SHALL I TEND THEM IN MY MEDICAL FACILITY?
NO... THANKS. WE CAN HANDLE IT.
TAKE A GOOD LOOK. I WANT YOU TO REMEMBER THIS WHEN I KILL YOU.
IF ANYONE KILLS HIM, IT'S GOING TO BE ME. SLOW.
BLOW IT, GUYS. I HAD NOTHING TO DO WITH THIS.

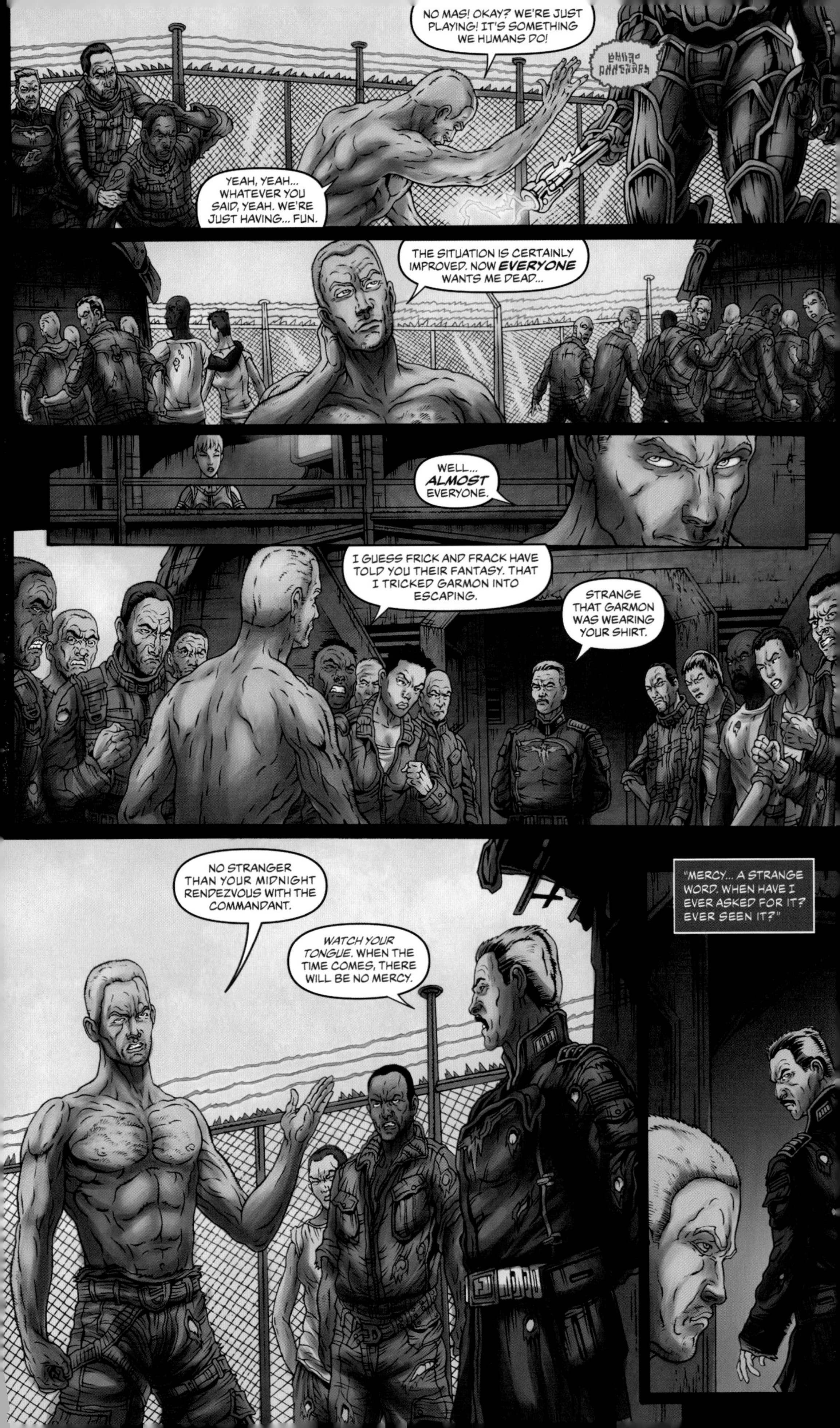
NO MAS! OKAY? WE'RE JUST PLAYING! IT'S SOMETHING WE HUMANS DO!
YEAH, YEAH... WHATEVER YOU SAID, YEAH. WE'RE JUST HAVING... FUN.
THE SITUATION IS CERTAINLY IMPROVED. NOW EVERYONE WANTS ME DEAD...
WELL... ALMOST EVERYONE.
I GUESS FRICK AND FRACK HAVE TOLD YOU THEIR FANTASY. THAT I TRICKED GARMON INTO ESCAPING.
STRANGE THAT GARMON WAS WEARING YOUR SHIRT.
NO STRANGER THAN YOUR MIDNIGHT RENDEZVOUS WITH THE COMMANDANT.
WATCH YOUR TONGUE. WHEN THE TIME COMES, THERE WILL BE NO MERCY.
"MERCY... A STRANGE WORD. WHEN HAVE I EVER ASKED FOR IT? EVER SEEN IT?"

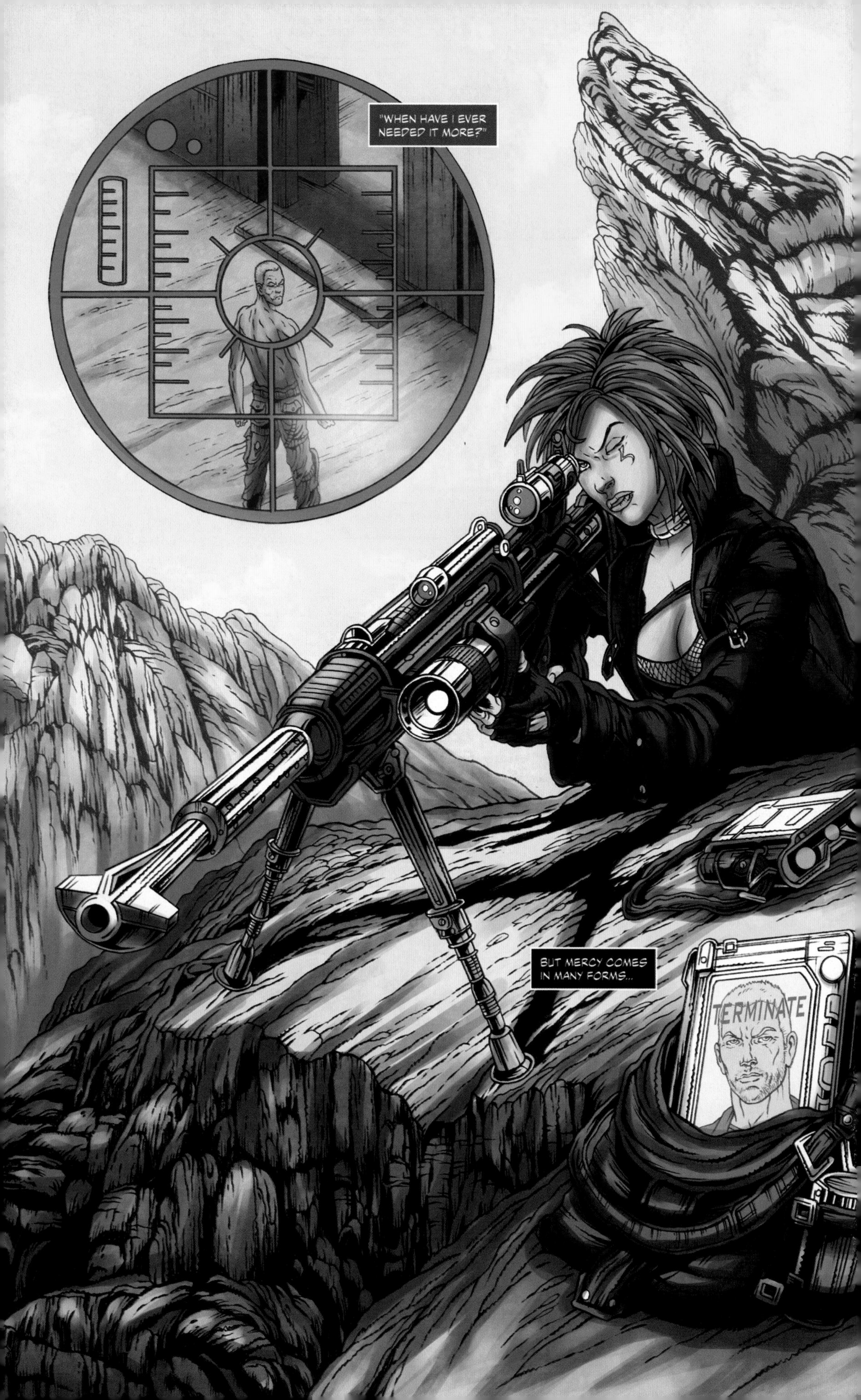
"WHEN HAVE I EVER NEEDED IT MORE?"
BUT MERCY COMES IN MANY FORMS...
TERMINATE

CHAPTER III

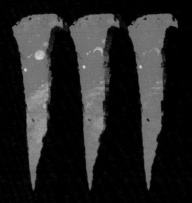

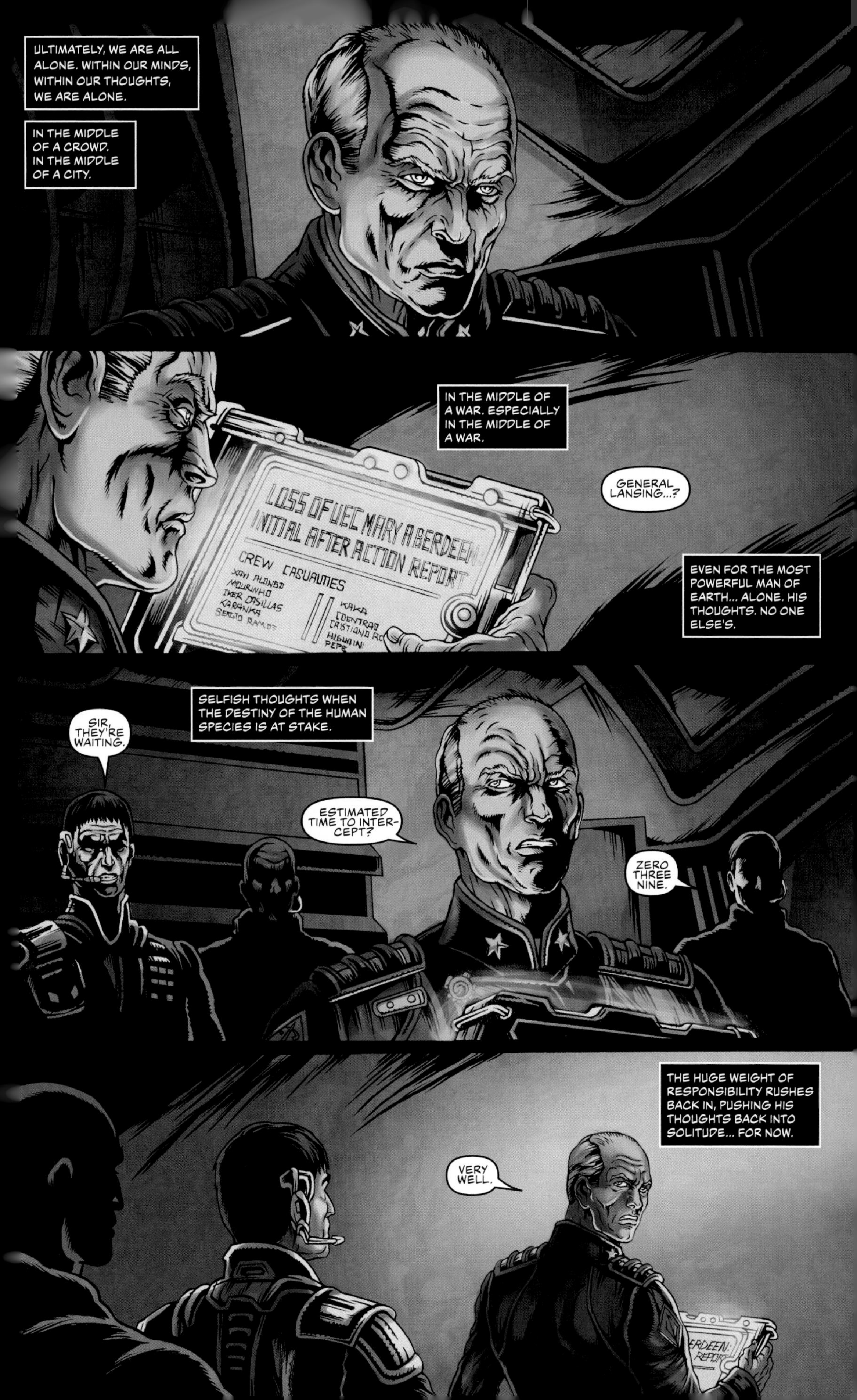
ULTIMATELY, WE ARE ALL ALONE. WITHIN OUR MINDS, WITHIN OUR THOUGHTS, WE ARE ALONE.
IN THE MIDDLE OF A CROWD. IN THE MIDDLE OF A CITY.
IN THE MIDDLE OF A WAR. ESPECIALLY IN THE MIDDLE OF A WAR.
LOSS OF UEC MARY ABERDEEN: INITIAL AFTER ACTION REPORT
GENERAL LANSING...?
EVEN FOR THE MOST POWERFUL MAN OF EARTH... ALONE. HIS THOUGHTS. NO ONE ELSE'S.
SELFISH THOUGHTS WHEN THE DESTINY OF THE HUMAN SPECIES IS AT STAKE.
SIR, THEY'RE WAITING.
ESTIMATED TIME TO INTER-CEPT?
ZERO THREE NINE.
THE HUGE WEIGHT OF RESPONSIBILITY RUSHES BACK IN, PUSHING HIS THOUGHTS BACK INTO SOLITUDE... FOR NOW.
VERY WELL.

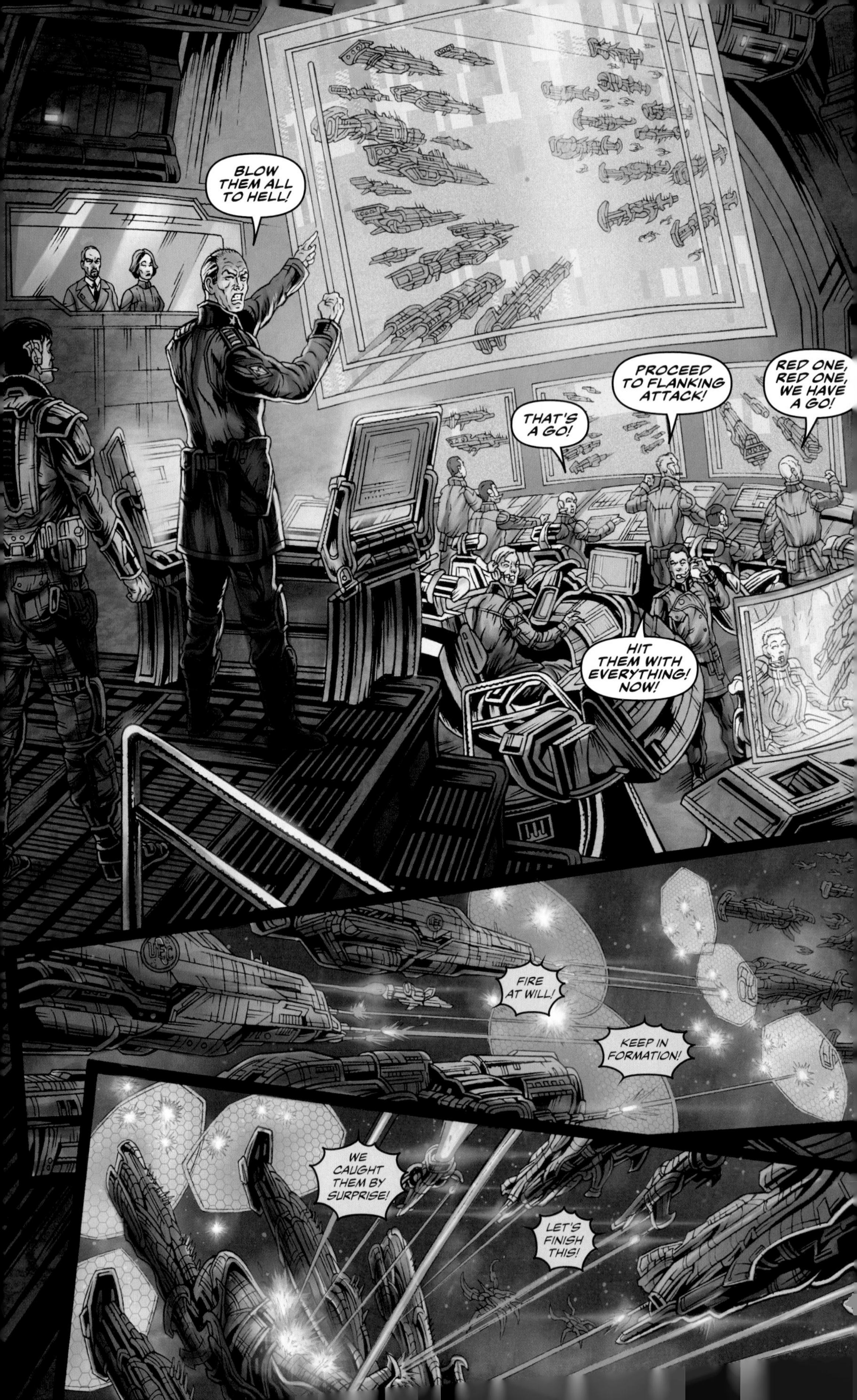
BLOW THEM ALL TO HELL!
THAT'S A GO!
PROCEED TO FLANKING ATTACK!
RED ONE, RED ONE, WE HAVE A GO!
HIT THEM WITH EVERYTHING! NOW!
FIRE AT WILL!
KEEP IN FORMATION!
WE CAUGHT THEM BY SURPRISE!
LET'S FINISH THIS!

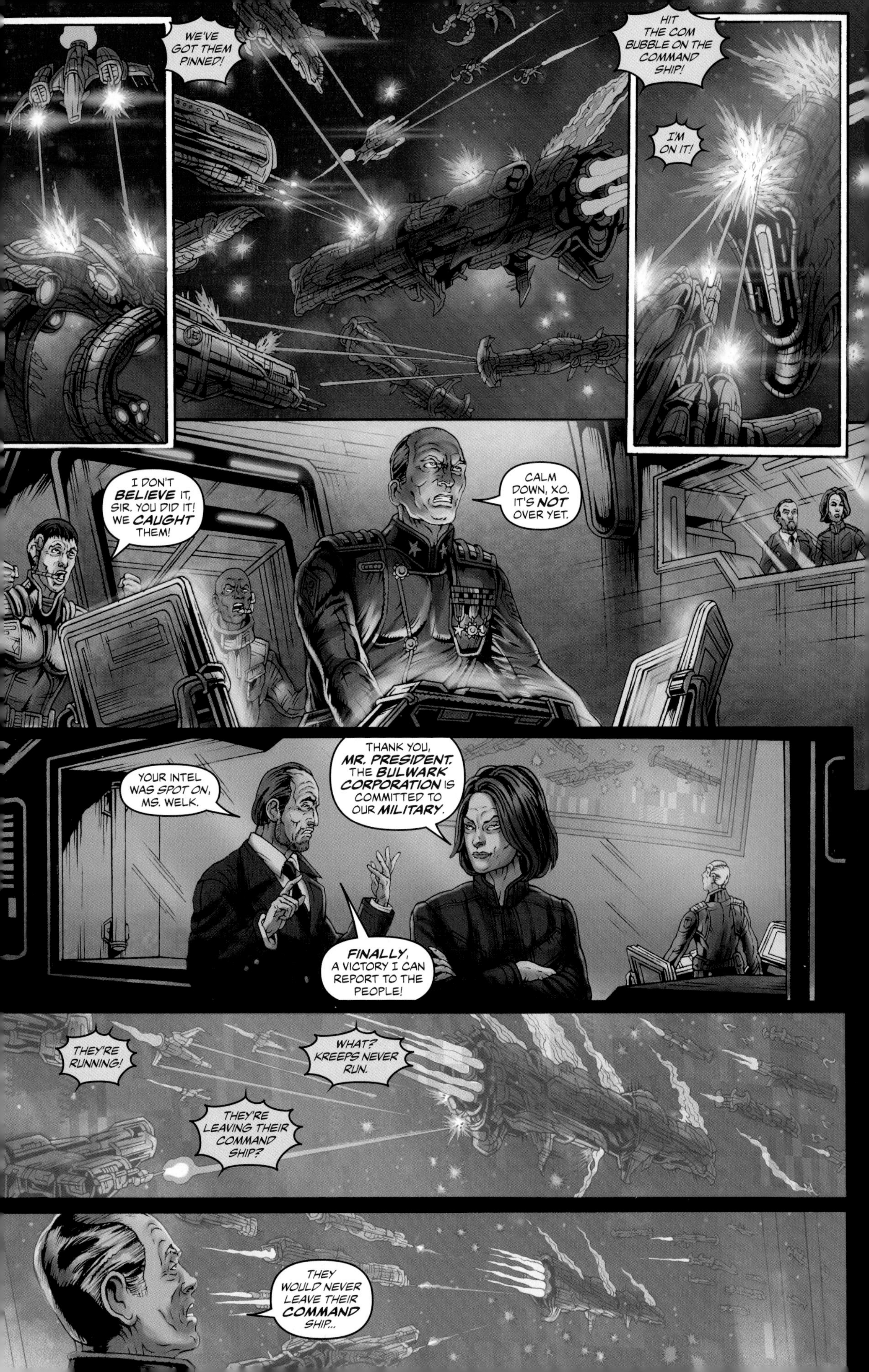
WE'VE GOT THEM PINNED!
HIT THE COM BUBBLE ON THE COMMAND SHIP!
I'M ON IT!
I DON'T BELIEVE IT, SIR. YOU DID IT! WE CAUGHT THEM!
CALM DOWN, XO. IT'S NOT OVER YET.
YOUR INTEL WAS SPOT ON, MS. WELK.
THANK YOU, MR. PRESIDENT. THE BULWARK CORPORATION IS COMMITTED TO OUR MILITARY.
FINALLY, A VICTORY I CAN REPORT TO THE PEOPLE!
THEY'RE RUNNING!
WHAT? KREEPS NEVER RUN.
THEY'RE LEAVING THEIR COMMAND SHIP?
THEY WOULD NEVER LEAVE THEIR COMMAND SHIP...

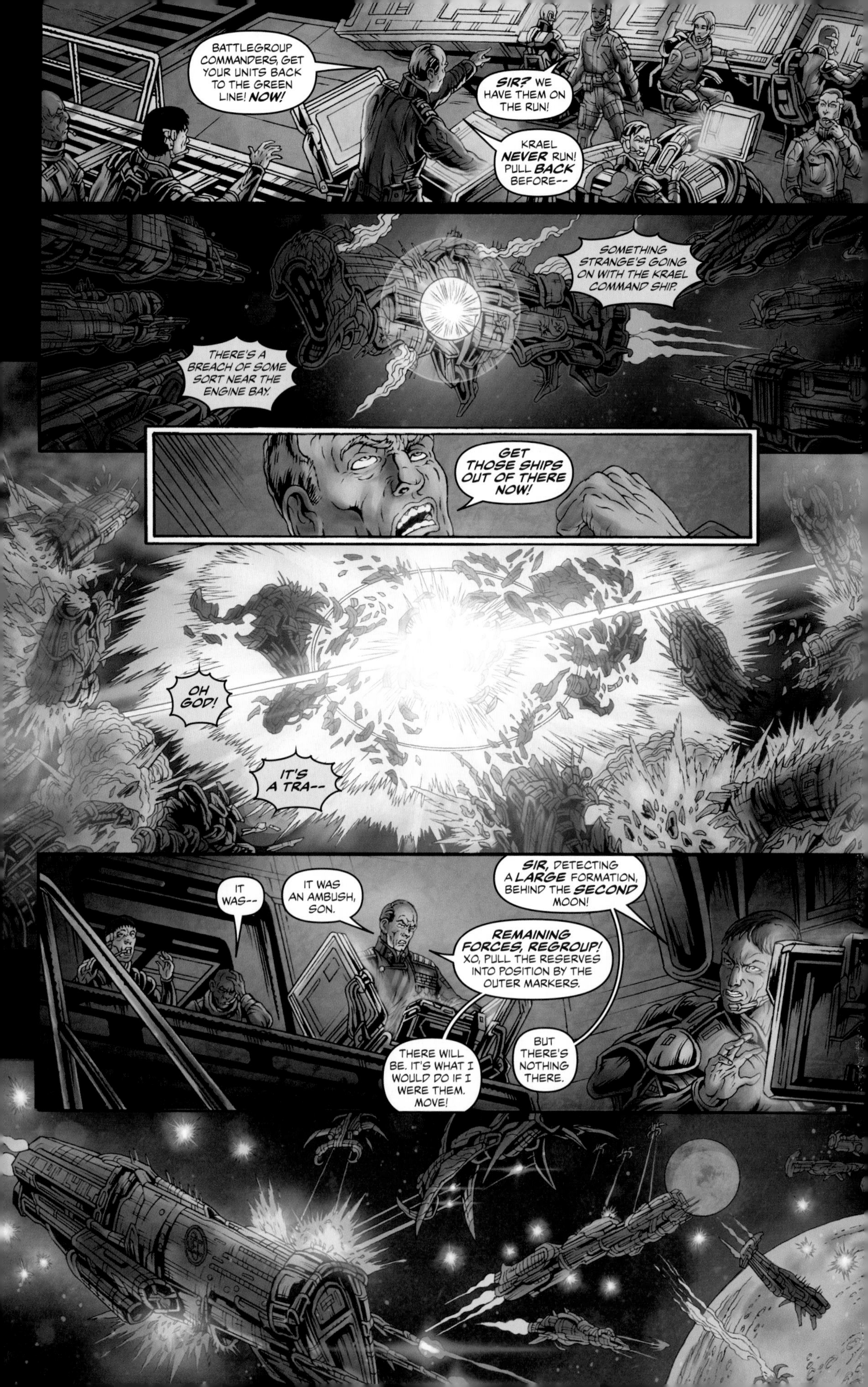
BATTLEGROUP COMMANDERS, GET YOUR UNITS BACK TO THE GREEN LINE! NOW!
SIR? WE HAVE THEM ON THE RUN!
KRAEL NEVER RUN! PULL BACK BEFORE--
SOMETHING STRANGE'S GOING ON WITH THE KRAEL COMMAND SHIP.
THERE'S A BREACH OF SOME SORT NEAR THE ENGINE BAY.
GET THOSE SHIPS OUT OF THERE NOW!
OH GOD!
IT'S A TRA--
IT WAS--
IT WAS AN AMBUSH, SON.
SIR, DETECTING A LARGE FORMATION, BEHIND THE SECOND MOON!
REMAINING FORCES, REGROUP! XO, PULL THE RESERVES INTO POSITION BY THE OUTER MARKERS.
BUT THERE'S NOTHING THERE.
THERE WILL BE. IT'S WHAT I WOULD DO IF I WERE THEM. MOVE!

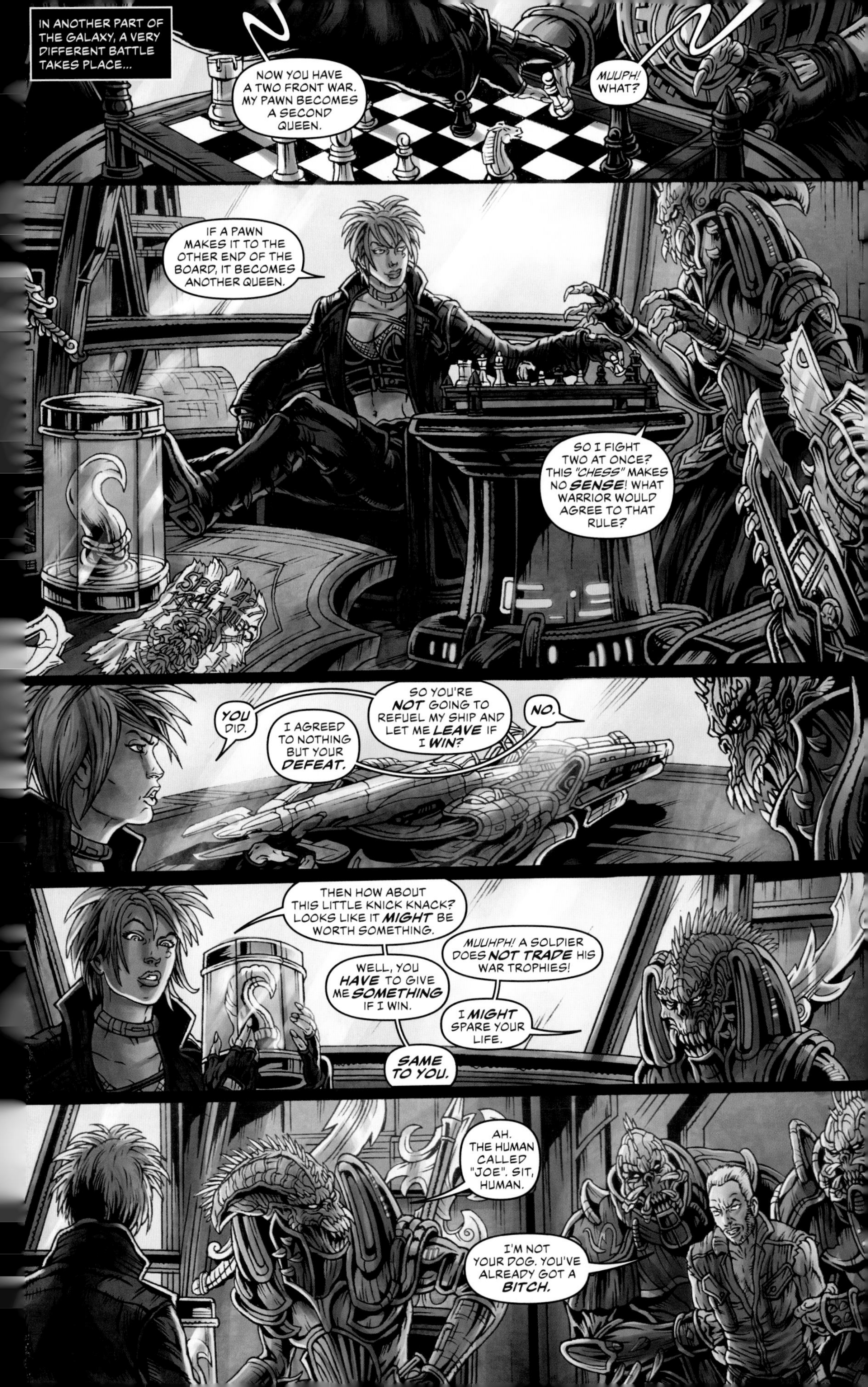
IN ANOTHER PART OF THE GALAXY, A VERY DIFFERENT BATTLE TAKES PLACE...
NOW YOU HAVE A TWO FRONT WAR. MY PAWN BECOMES A SECOND QUEEN.
MUUPH! WHAT?
IF A PAWN MAKES IT TO THE OTHER END OF THE BOARD, IT BECOMES ANOTHER QUEEN.
SO I FIGHT TWO AT ONCE? THIS "CHESS" MAKES NO SENSE! WHAT WARRIOR WOULD AGREE TO THAT RULE?
YOU DID.
I AGREED TO NOTHING BUT YOUR DEFEAT.
SO YOU'RE NOT GOING TO REFUEL MY SHIP AND LET ME LEAVE IF I WIN?
NO.
THEN HOW ABOUT THIS LITTLE KNICK KNACK? LOOKS LIKE IT MIGHT BE WORTH SOMETHING.
MUUHPH! A SOLDIER DOES NOT TRADE HIS WAR TROPHIES!
WELL, YOU HAVE TO GIVE ME SOMETHING IF I WIN.
I MIGHT SPARE YOUR LIFE.
SAME TO YOU.
AH. THE HUMAN CALLED "JOE". SIT, HUMAN.
I'M NOT YOUR DOG. YOU'VE ALREADY GOT A BITCH.

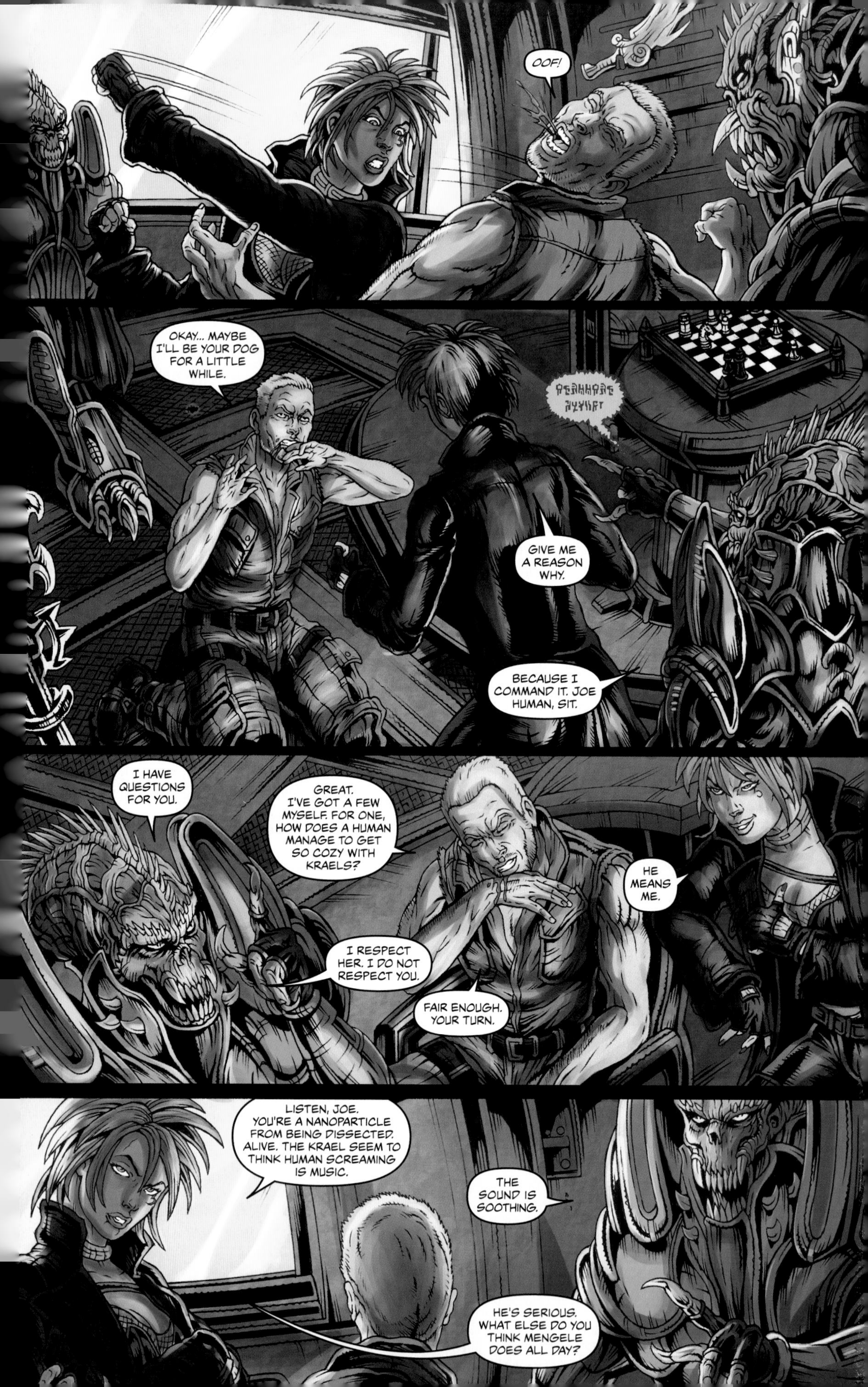
OOF!
OKAY... MAYBE I'LL BE YOUR DOG FOR A LITTLE WHILE.
GIVE ME A REASON WHY.
BECAUSE I COMMAND IT. JOE HUMAN, SIT.
I HAVE QUESTIONS FOR YOU.
GREAT. I'VE GOT A FEW MYSELF. FOR ONE, HOW DOES A HUMAN MANAGE TO GET SO COZY WITH KRAELS?
HE MEANS ME.
I RESPECT HER. I DO NOT RESPECT YOU.
FAIR ENOUGH. YOUR TURN.
LISTEN, JOE. YOU'RE A NANOPARTICLE FROM BEING DISSECTED. ALIVE. THE KRAEL SEEM TO THINK HUMAN SCREAMING IS MUSIC.
THE SOUND IS SOOTHING.
HE'S SERIOUS. WHAT ELSE DO YOU THINK MENGELE DOES ALL DAY?

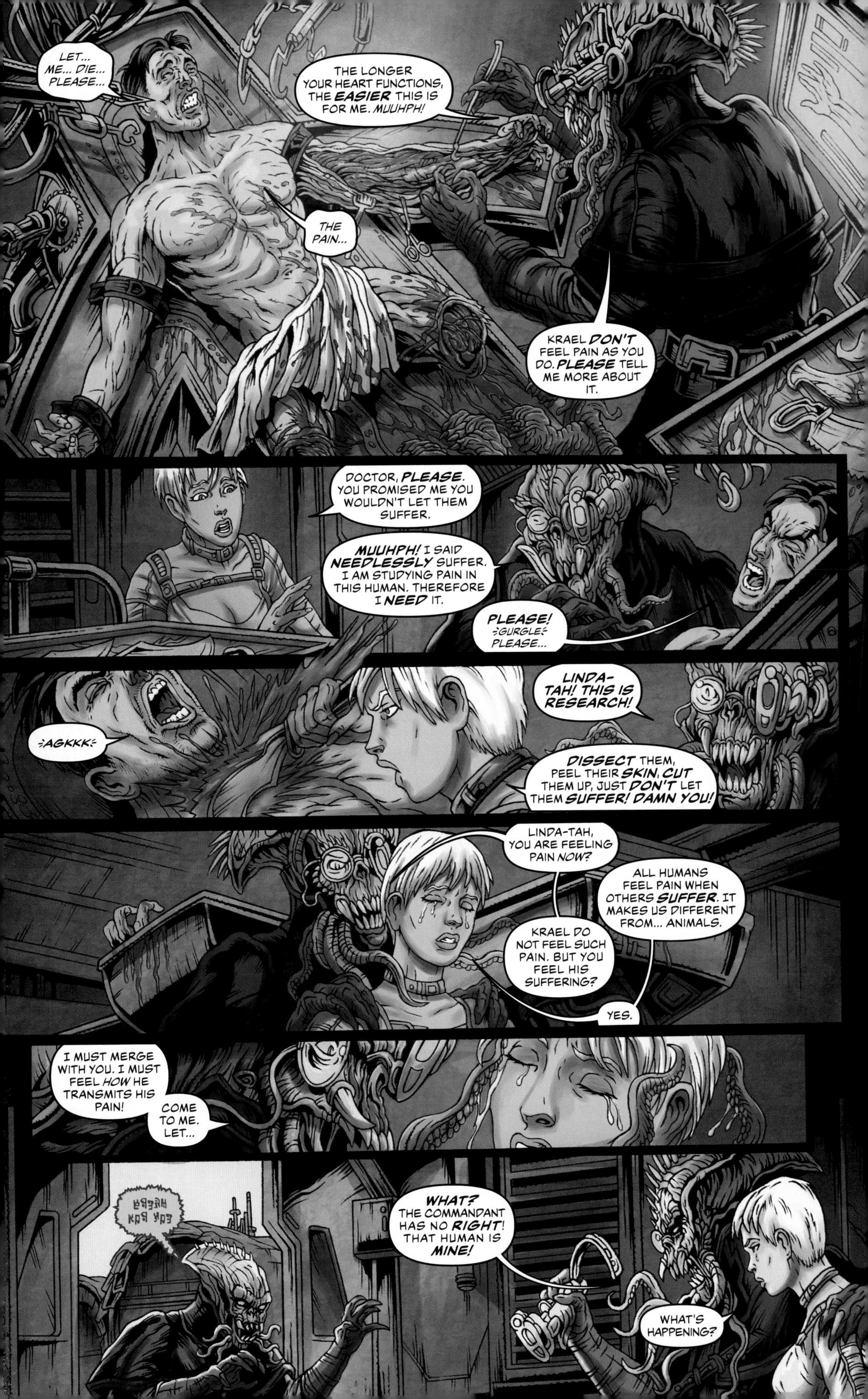
LET... ME... DIE... PLEASE...
THE LONGER YOUR HEART FUNCTIONS, THE EASIER THIS IS FOR ME. MUUHPH!
THE PAIN...
KRAEL DON'T FEEL PAIN AS YOU DO. PLEASE TELL ME MORE ABOUT IT.
DOCTOR, PLEASE. YOU PROMISED ME YOU WOULDN'T LET THEM SUFFER.
MUUHPH! I SAID NEEDLESSLY SUFFER. I AM STUDYING PAIN IN THIS HUMAN. THEREFORE I NEED IT.
PLEASE! GURGLE PLEASE...
AGKKK
LINDA-TAH! THIS IS RESEARCH!
DISSECT THEM, PEEL THEIR SKIN, CUT THEM UP, JUST DON'T LET THEM SUFFER! DAMN YOU!
LINDA-TAH, YOU ARE FEELING PAIN NOW?
ALL HUMANS FEEL PAIN WHEN OTHERS SUFFER. IT MAKES US DIFFERENT FROM... ANIMALS.
KRAEL DO NOT FEEL SUCH PAIN. BUT YOU FEEL HIS SUFFERING?
YES.
I MUST MERGE WITH YOU. I MUST FEEL HOW HE TRANSMITS HIS PAIN!
COME TO ME. LET...
WHAT? THE COMMANDANT HAS NO RIGHT! THAT HUMAN IS MINE!
WHAT'S HAPPENING?

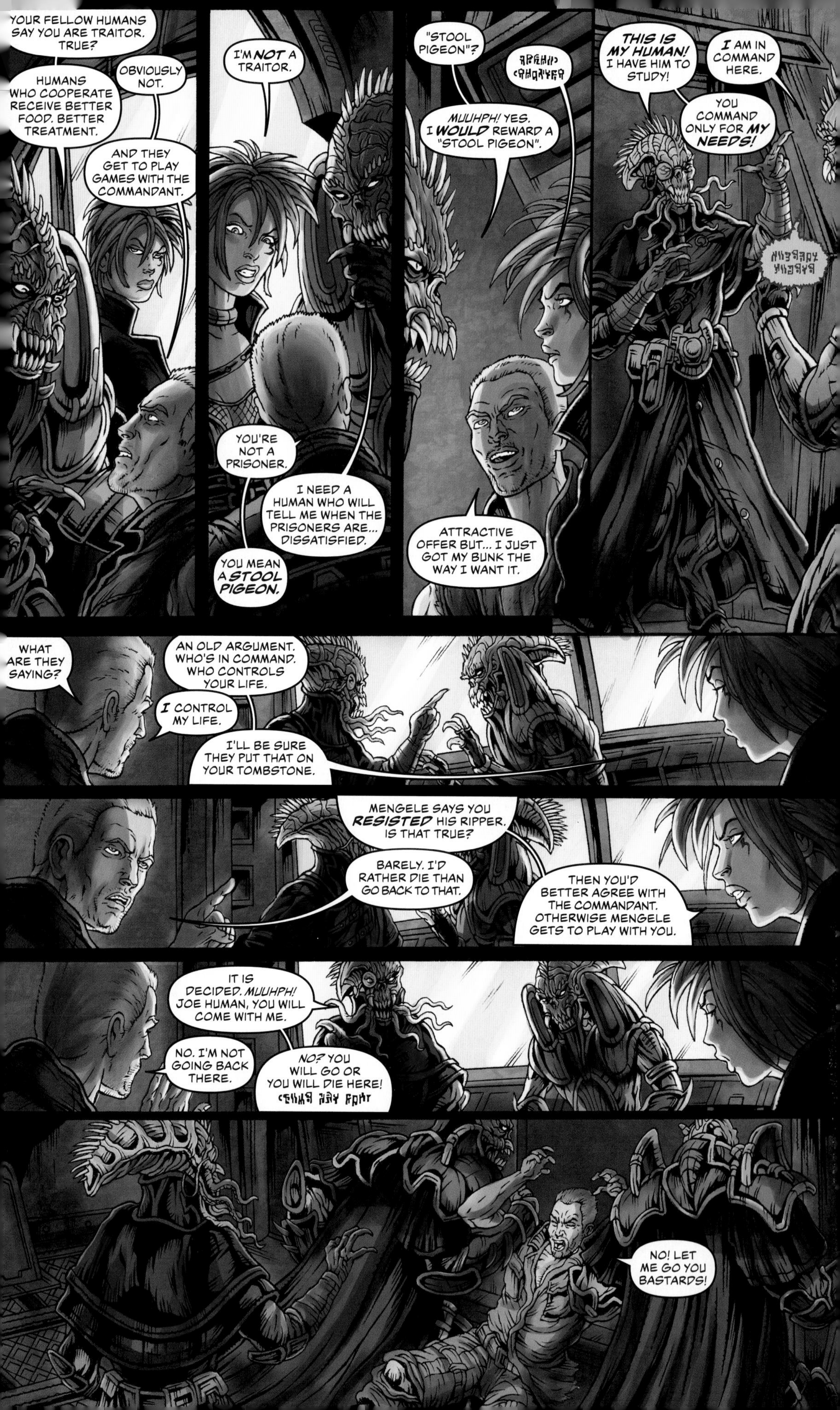

YOUR FELLOW HUMANS SAY YOU ARE TRAITOR. TRUE?
HUMANS WHO COOPERATE RECEIVE BETTER FOOD. BETTER TREATMENT.
OBVIOUSLY NOT.
AND THEY GET TO PLAY GAMES WITH THE COMMANDANT.
I'M NOT A TRAITOR.
YOU'RE NOT A PRISONER.
I NEED A HUMAN WHO WILL TELL ME WHEN THE PRISONERS ARE... DISSATISFIED.
YOU MEAN A STOOL PIGEON.
"STOOL PIGEON"?
MUUHPH! YES. I WOULD REWARD A "STOOL PIGEON".
ATTRACTIVE OFFER BUT... I JUST GOT MY BUNK THE WAY I WANT IT.
THIS IS MY HUMAN! I HAVE HIM TO STUDY!
I AM IN COMMAND HERE.
YOU COMMAND ONLY FOR MY NEEDS!
WHAT ARE THEY SAYING?
AN OLD ARGUMENT. WHO'S IN COMMAND. WHO CONTROLS YOUR LIFE.
I CONTROL MY LIFE.
I'LL BE SURE THEY PUT THAT ON YOUR TOMBSTONE.
MENGELE SAYS YOU RESISTED HIS RIPPER. IS THAT TRUE?
BARELY. I'D RATHER DIE THAN GO BACK TO THAT.
THEN YOU'D BETTER AGREE WITH THE COMMANDANT. OTHERWISE MENGELE GETS TO PLAY WITH YOU.
IT IS DECIDED. MUUHPH! JOE HUMAN, YOU WILL COME WITH ME.
NO. I'M NOT GOING BACK THERE.
NO? YOU WILL GO OR YOU WILL DIE HERE!
NO! LET ME GO YOU BASTARDS!

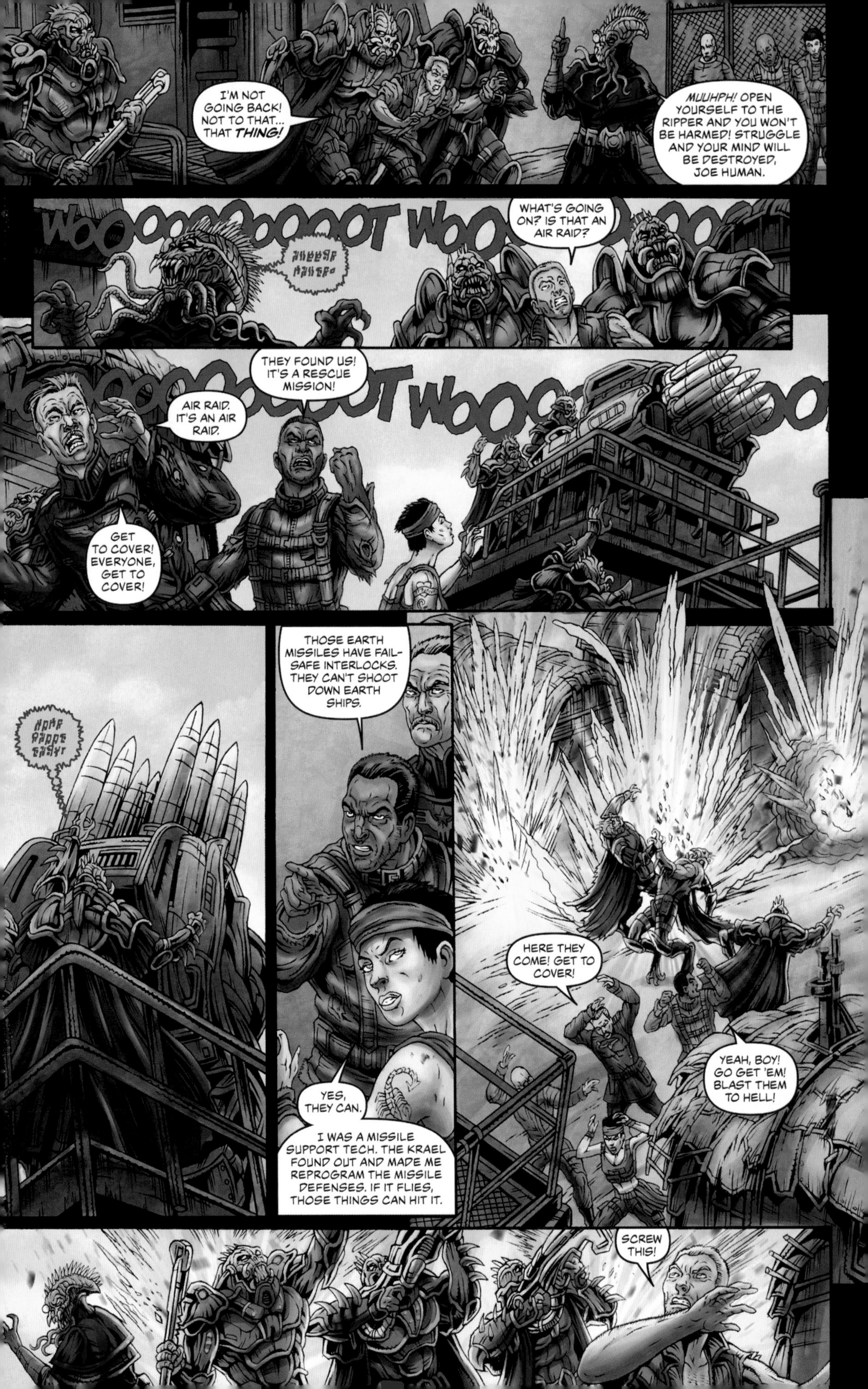
I'M NOT GOING BACK! NOT TO THAT... THAT *THING!*
MUUHPH! OPEN YOURSELF TO THE RIPPER AND YOU WON'T BE HARMED! STRUGGLE AND YOUR MIND WILL BE DESTROYED, JOE HUMAN.
WOOOOOOOOOOT WOOOOOOOOO
WHAT'S GOING ON? IS THAT AN AIR RAID?
WOOOOOOOOOOT WOOOOOOOO
THEY FOUND US! IT'S A RESCUE MISSION!
AIR RAID. IT'S AN AIR RAID.
GET TO COVER! EVERYONE, GET TO COVER!
THOSE EARTH MISSILES HAVE FAIL-SAFE INTERLOCKS. THEY CAN'T SHOOT DOWN EARTH SHIPS.
YES, THEY CAN.
I WAS A MISSILE SUPPORT TECH. THE KRAEL FOUND OUT AND MADE ME REPROGRAM THE MISSILE DEFENSES. IF IT FLIES, THOSE THINGS CAN HIT IT.
HERE THEY COME! GET TO COVER!
YEAH, BOY! GO GET 'EM! BLAST THEM TO HELL!
SCREW THIS!

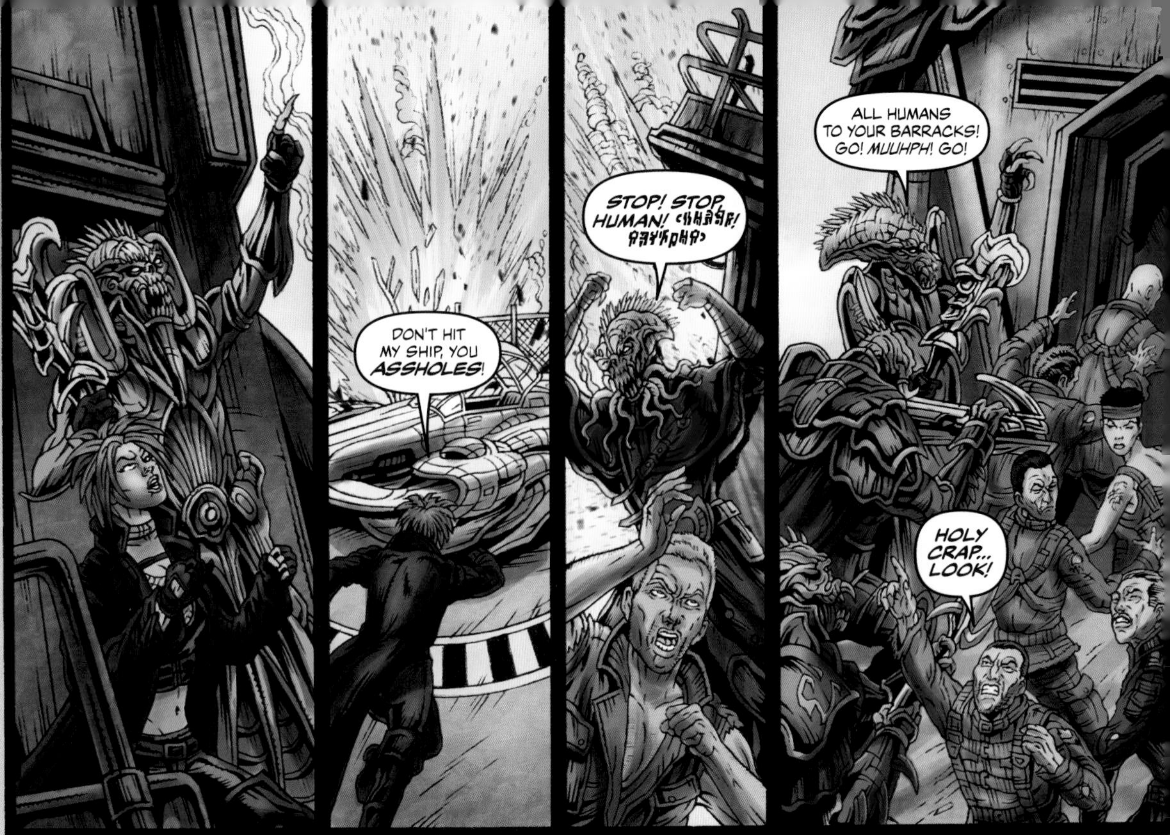
DON'T HIT MY SHIP, YOU ASSHOLES!
STOP! STOP, HUMAN!
ALL HUMANS TO YOUR BARRACKS! GO! MUUHPH! GO!
HOLY CRAP... LOOK!

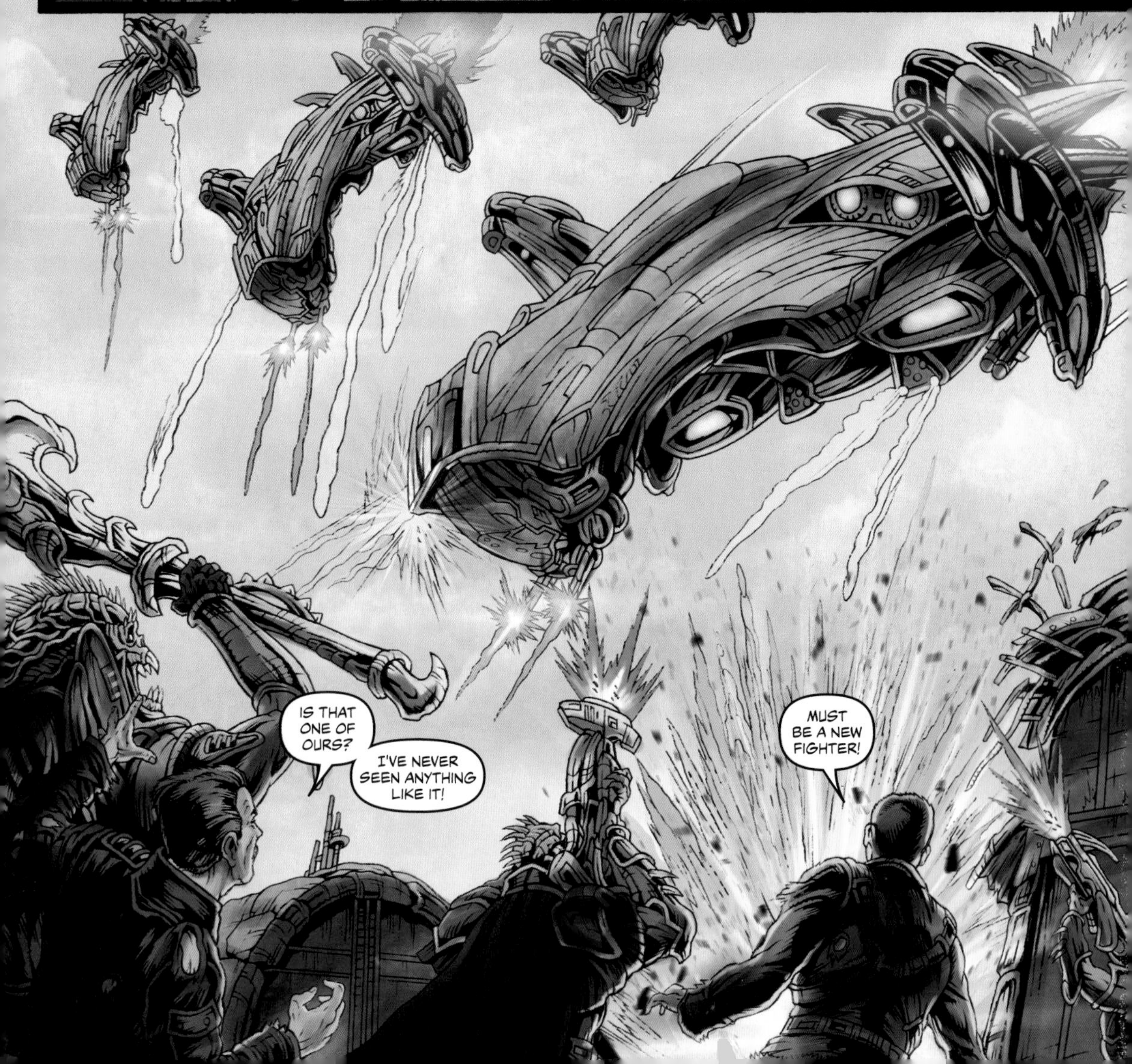
IS THAT ONE OF OURS?
I'VE NEVER SEEN ANYTHING LIKE IT!
MUST BE A NEW FIGHTER!

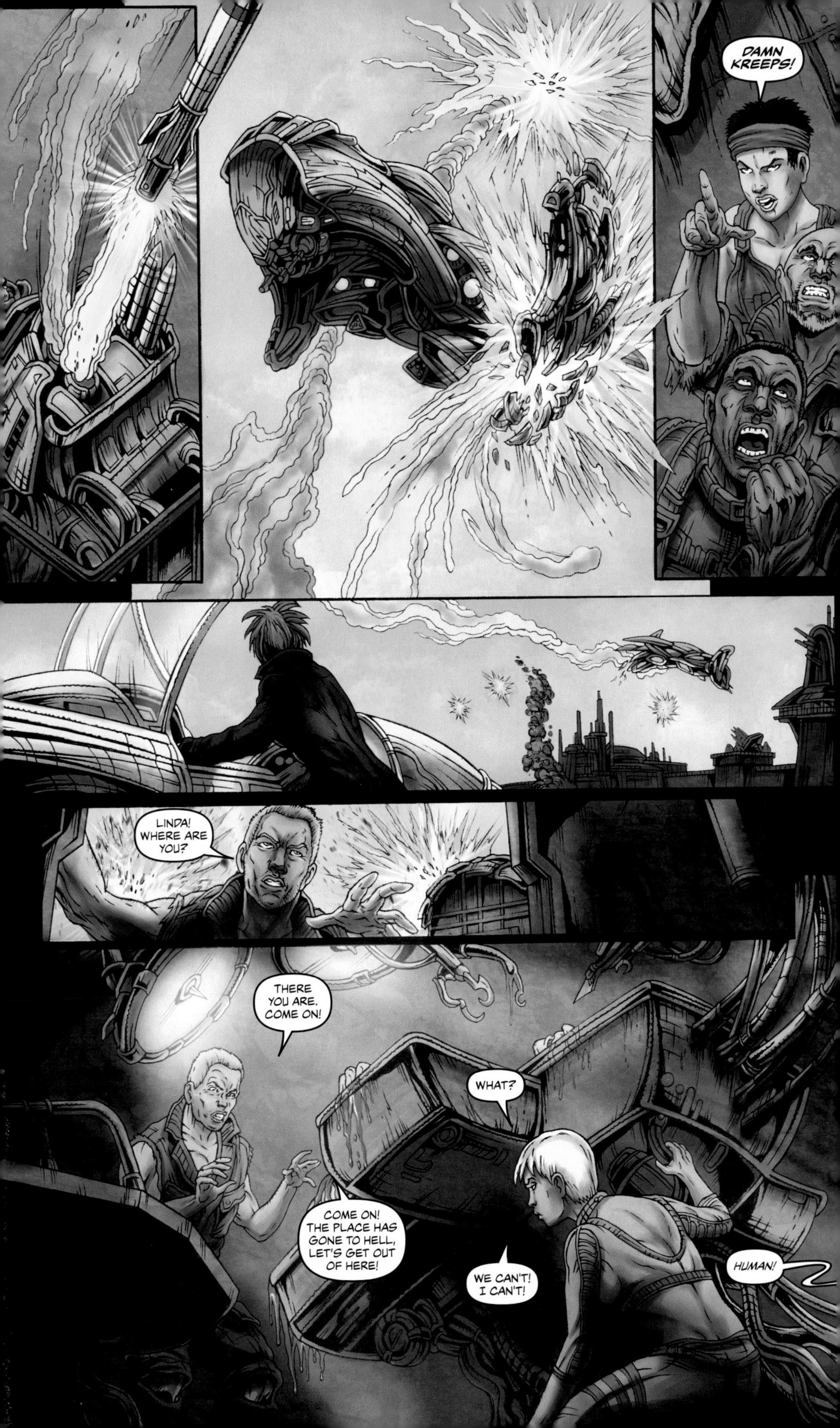
DAMN KREEPS!
LINDA! WHERE ARE YOU?
THERE YOU ARE. COME ON!
WHAT?
COME ON! THE PLACE HAS GONE TO HELL, LET'S GET OUT OF HERE!
WE CAN'T! I CAN'T!
HUMAN!

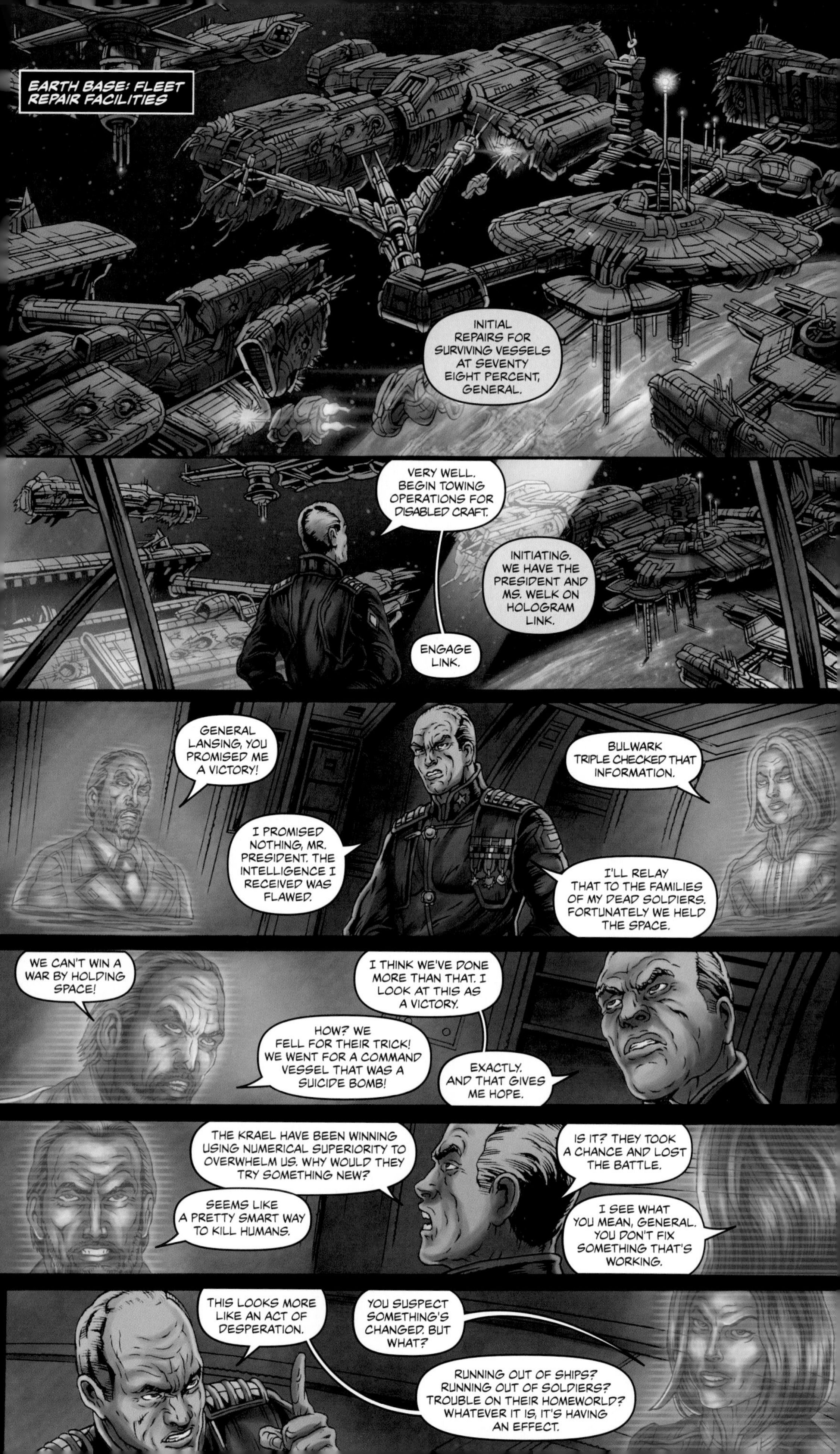
EARTH BASE: FLEET REPAIR FACILITIES
INITIAL REPAIRS FOR SURVIVING VESSELS AT SEVENTY EIGHT PERCENT, GENERAL.
VERY WELL. BEGIN TOWING OPERATIONS FOR DISABLED CRAFT.
INITIATING. WE HAVE THE PRESIDENT AND MS. WELK ON HOLOGRAM LINK.
ENGAGE LINK.
GENERAL LANSING, YOU PROMISED ME A VICTORY!
I PROMISED NOTHING, MR. PRESIDENT. THE INTELLIGENCE I RECEIVED WAS FLAWED.
BULWARK TRIPLE CHECKED THAT INFORMATION.
I'LL RELAY THAT TO THE FAMILIES OF MY DEAD SOLDIERS. FORTUNATELY WE HELD THE SPACE.
WE CAN'T WIN A WAR BY HOLDING SPACE!
I THINK WE'VE DONE MORE THAN THAT. I LOOK AT THIS AS A VICTORY.
HOW? WE FELL FOR THEIR TRICK! WE WENT FOR A COMMAND VESSEL THAT WAS A SUICIDE BOMB!
EXACTLY. AND THAT GIVES ME HOPE.
THE KRAEL HAVE BEEN WINNING USING NUMERICAL SUPERIORITY TO OVERWHELM US. WHY WOULD THEY TRY SOMETHING NEW?
SEEMS LIKE A PRETTY SMART WAY TO KILL HUMANS.
IS IT? THEY TOOK A CHANCE AND LOST THE BATTLE.
I SEE WHAT YOU MEAN, GENERAL. YOU DON'T FIX SOMETHING THAT'S WORKING.
THIS LOOKS MORE LIKE AN ACT OF DESPERATION.
YOU SUSPECT SOMETHING'S CHANGED. BUT WHAT?
RUNNING OUT OF SHIPS? RUNNING OUT OF SOLDIERS? TROUBLE ON THEIR HOMEWORLD? WHATEVER IT IS, IT'S HAVING AN EFFECT.

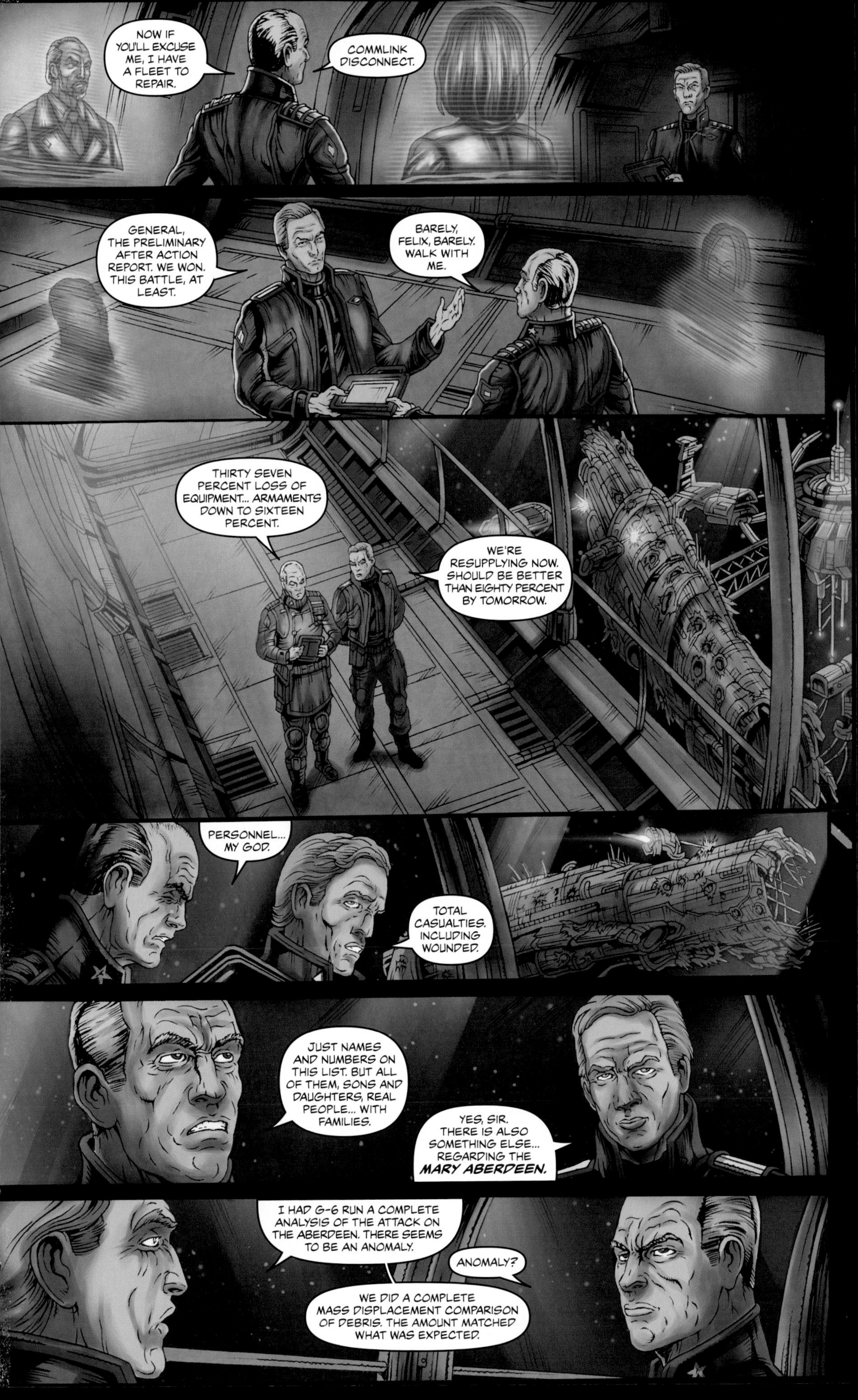

NOW IF YOU'LL EXCUSE ME, I HAVE A FLEET TO REPAIR.
COMMLINK DISCONNECT.
GENERAL, THE PRELIMINARY AFTER ACTION REPORT. WE WON. THIS BATTLE, AT LEAST.
BARELY, FELIX, BARELY. WALK WITH ME.
THIRTY SEVEN PERCENT LOSS OF EQUIPMENT... ARMAMENTS DOWN TO SIXTEEN PERCENT.
WE'RE RESUPPLYING NOW. SHOULD BE BETTER THAN EIGHTY PERCENT BY TOMORROW.
PERSONNEL... MY GOD.
TOTAL CASUALTIES. INCLUDING WOUNDED.
JUST NAMES AND NUMBERS ON THIS LIST. BUT ALL OF THEM, SONS AND DAUGHTERS, REAL PEOPLE... WITH FAMILIES.
YES, SIR. THERE IS ALSO SOMETHING ELSE... REGARDING THE ***MARY ABERDEEN.***
I HAD G-6 RUN A COMPLETE ANALYSIS OF THE ATTACK ON THE ABERDEEN. THERE SEEMS TO BE AN ANOMALY.
ANOMALY?
WE DID A COMPLETE MASS DISPLACEMENT COMPARISON OF DEBRIS. THE AMOUNT MATCHED WHAT WAS EXPECTED.

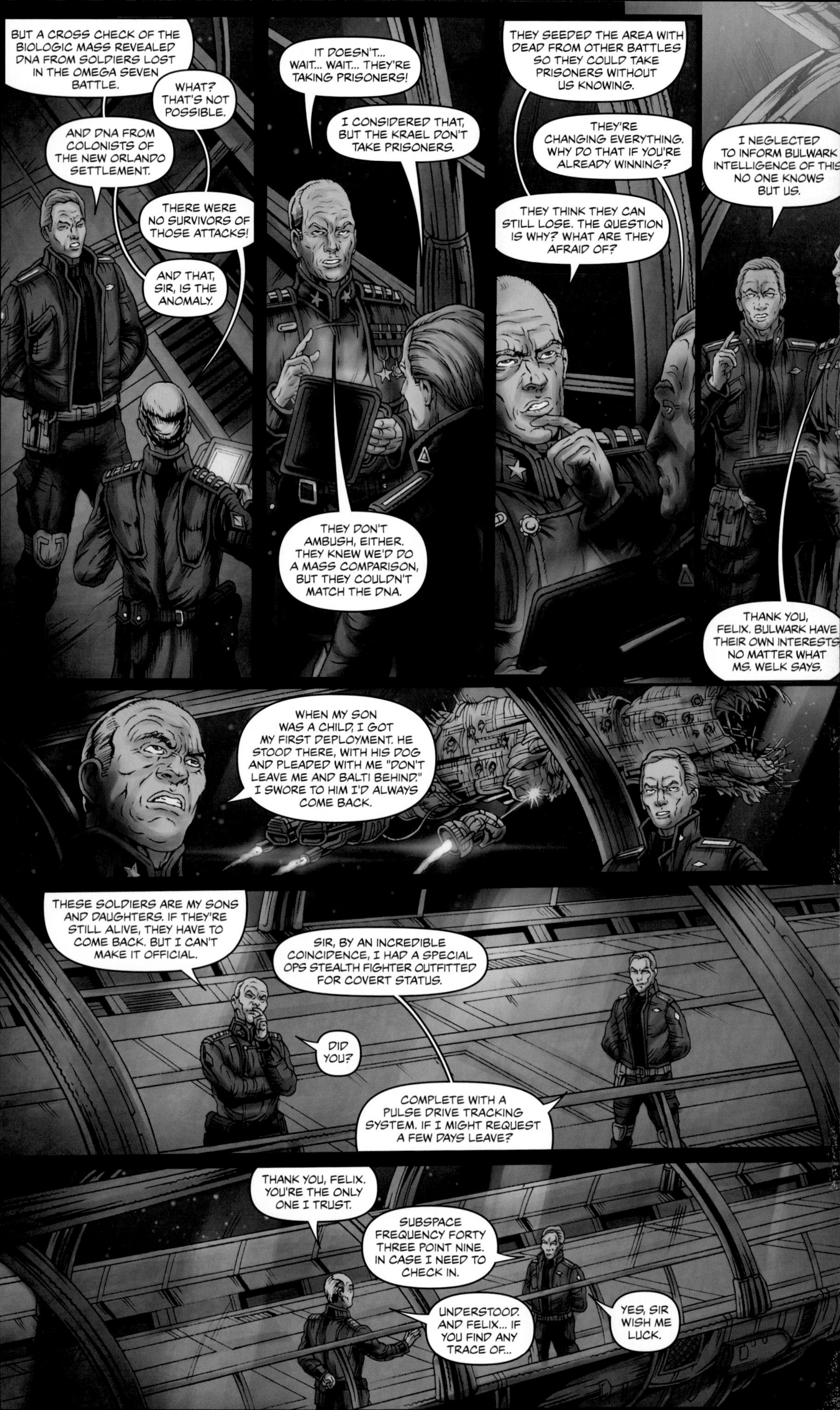

BUT A CROSS CHECK OF THE BIOLOGIC MASS REVEALED DNA FROM SOLDIERS LOST IN THE OMEGA SEVEN BATTLE.
WHAT? THAT'S NOT POSSIBLE.
AND DNA FROM COLONISTS OF THE NEW ORLANDO SETTLEMENT.
THERE WERE NO SURVIVORS OF THOSE ATTACKS!
AND THAT, SIR, IS THE ANOMALY.
IT DOESN'T... WAIT... WAIT... THEY'RE TAKING PRISONERS!
I CONSIDERED THAT, BUT THE KRAEL DON'T TAKE PRISONERS.
THEY DON'T AMBUSH, EITHER. THEY KNEW WE'D DO A MASS COMPARISON, BUT THEY COULDN'T MATCH THE DNA.
THEY SEEDED THE AREA WITH DEAD FROM OTHER BATTLES SO THEY COULD TAKE PRISONERS WITHOUT US KNOWING.
THEY'RE CHANGING EVERYTHING. WHY DO THAT IF YOU'RE ALREADY WINNING?
THEY THINK THEY CAN STILL LOSE. THE QUESTION IS WHY? WHAT ARE THEY AFRAID OF?
I NEGLECTED TO INFORM BULWARK INTELLIGENCE OF THIS NO ONE KNOWS BUT US.
THANK YOU, FELIX. BULWARK HAVE THEIR OWN INTERESTS NO MATTER WHAT MS. WELK SAYS.
WHEN MY SON WAS A CHILD, I GOT MY FIRST DEPLOYMENT. HE STOOD THERE, WITH HIS DOG AND PLEADED WITH ME "DON'T LEAVE ME AND BALTI BEHIND." I SWORE TO HIM I'D ALWAYS COME BACK.
THESE SOLDIERS ARE MY SONS AND DAUGHTERS. IF THEY'RE STILL ALIVE, THEY HAVE TO COME BACK. BUT I CAN'T MAKE IT OFFICIAL.
SIR, BY AN INCREDIBLE COINCIDENCE, I HAD A SPECIAL OPS STEALTH FIGHTER OUTFITTED FOR COVERT STATUS.
DID YOU?
COMPLETE WITH A PULSE DRIVE TRACKING SYSTEM. IF I MIGHT REQUEST A FEW DAYS LEAVE?
THANK YOU, FELIX. YOU'RE THE ONLY ONE I TRUST.
SUBSPACE FREQUENCY FORTY THREE POINT NINE. IN CASE I NEED TO CHECK IN.
UNDERSTOOD. AND FELIX... IF YOU FIND ANY TRACE OF...
YES, SIR WISH ME LUCK.

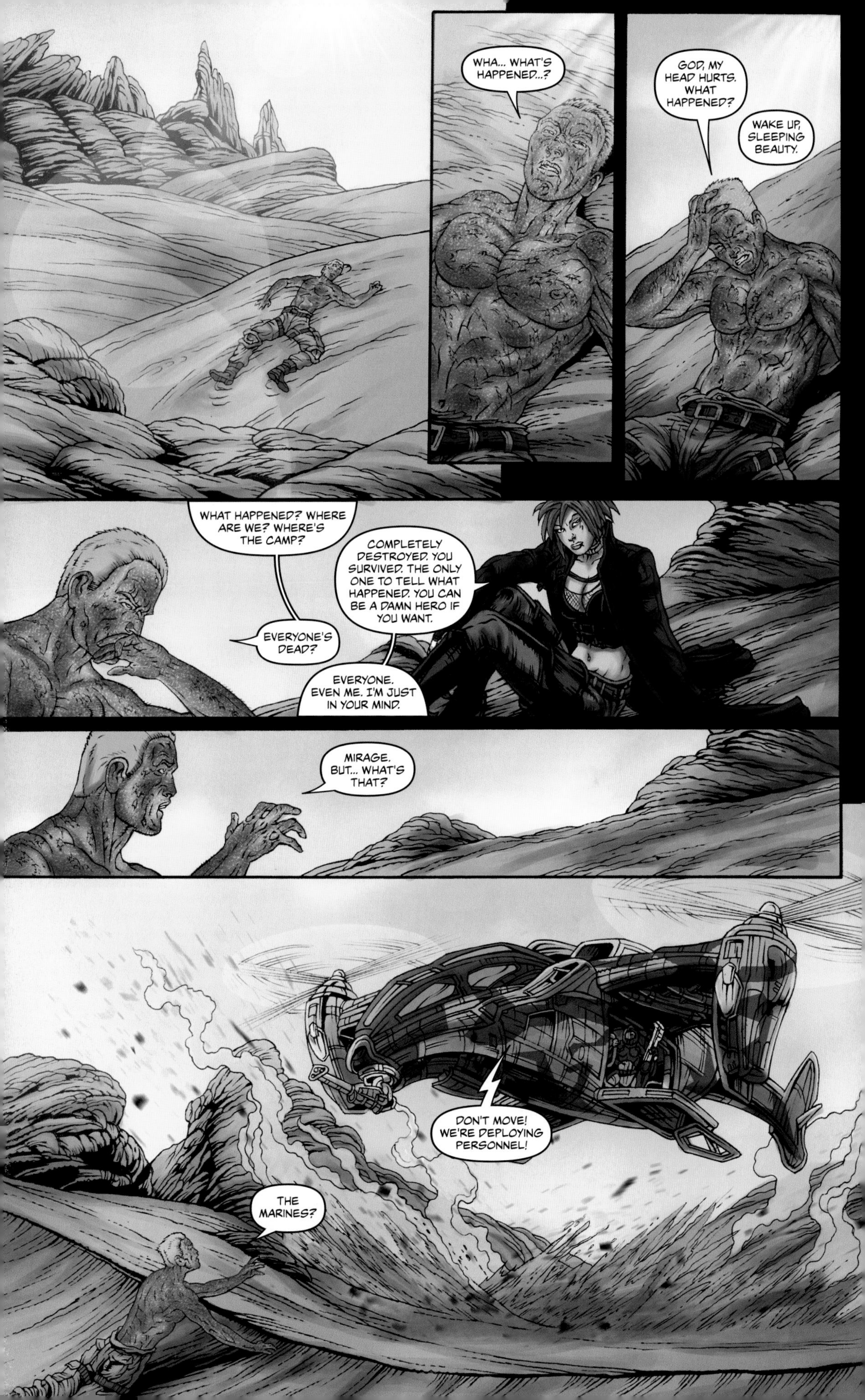
WHA... WHAT'S HAPPENED...?
GOD, MY HEAD HURTS. WHAT HAPPENED?
WAKE UP, SLEEPING BEAUTY.
WHAT HAPPENED? WHERE ARE WE? WHERE'S THE CAMP?
COMPLETELY DESTROYED. YOU SURVIVED. THE ONLY ONE TO TELL WHAT HAPPENED. YOU CAN BE A DAMN HERO IF YOU WANT.
EVERYONE'S DEAD?
EVERYONE. EVEN ME. I'M JUST IN YOUR MIND.
MIRAGE. BUT... WHAT'S THAT?
DON'T MOVE! WE'RE DEPLOYING PERSONNEL!
THE MARINES?

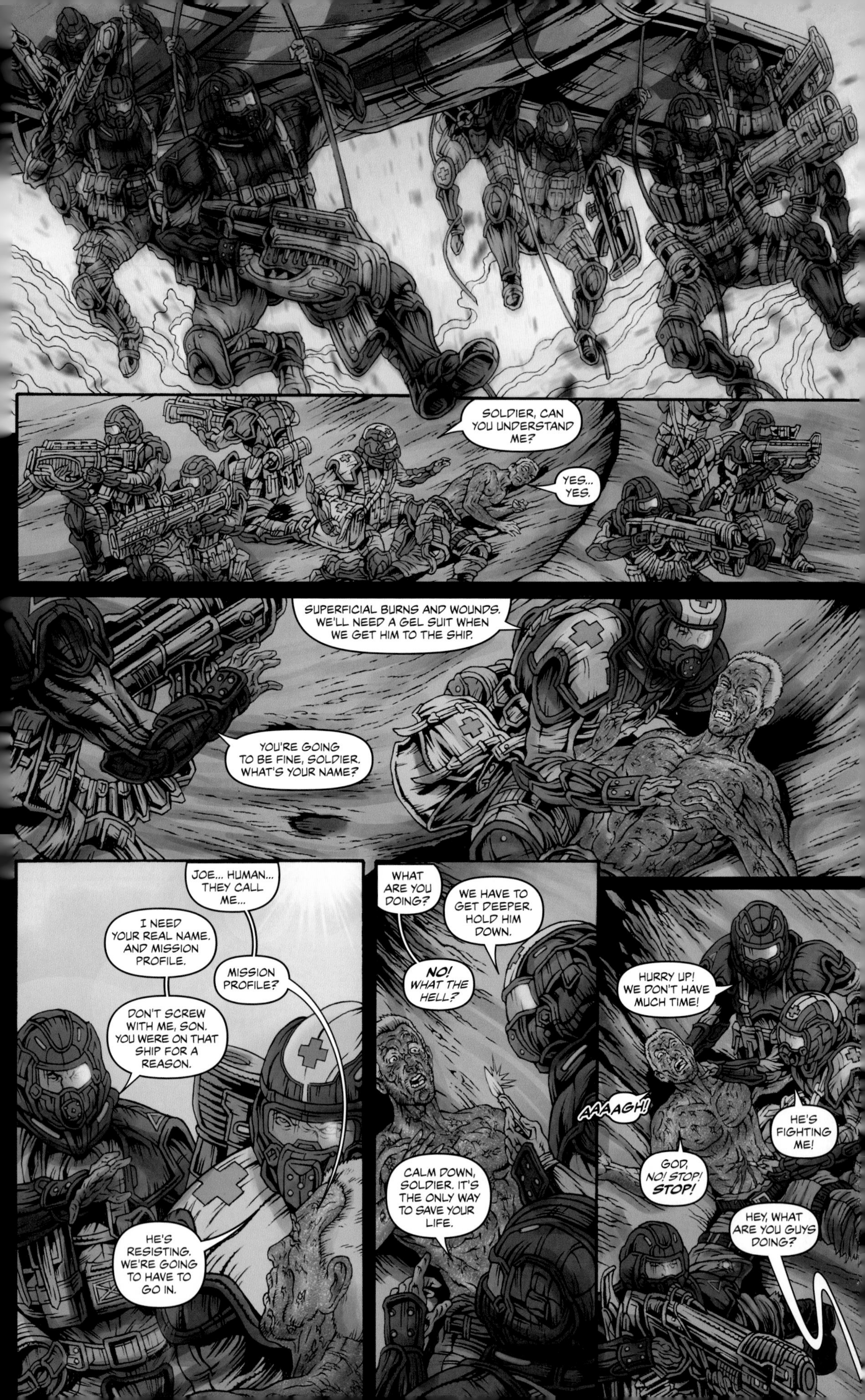
SOLDIER, CAN YOU UNDERSTAND ME?
YES... YES.
SUPERFICIAL BURNS AND WOUNDS. WE'LL NEED A GEL SUIT WHEN WE GET HIM TO THE SHIP.
YOU'RE GOING TO BE FINE, SOLDIER. WHAT'S YOUR NAME?
JOE... HUMAN... THEY CALL ME...
I NEED YOUR REAL NAME. AND MISSION PROFILE.
MISSION PROFILE?
DON'T SCREW WITH ME, SON. YOU WERE ON THAT SHIP FOR A REASON.
HE'S RESISTING. WE'RE GOING TO HAVE TO GO IN.
WHAT ARE YOU DOING?
WE HAVE TO GET DEEPER. HOLD HIM DOWN.
NO! WHAT THE HELL?
CALM DOWN, SOLDIER. IT'S THE ONLY WAY TO SAVE YOUR LIFE.
HURRY UP! WE DON'T HAVE MUCH TIME!
AAAAGH!
HE'S FIGHTING ME!
GOD, NO! STOP! STOP!
HEY, WHAT ARE YOU GUYS DOING?

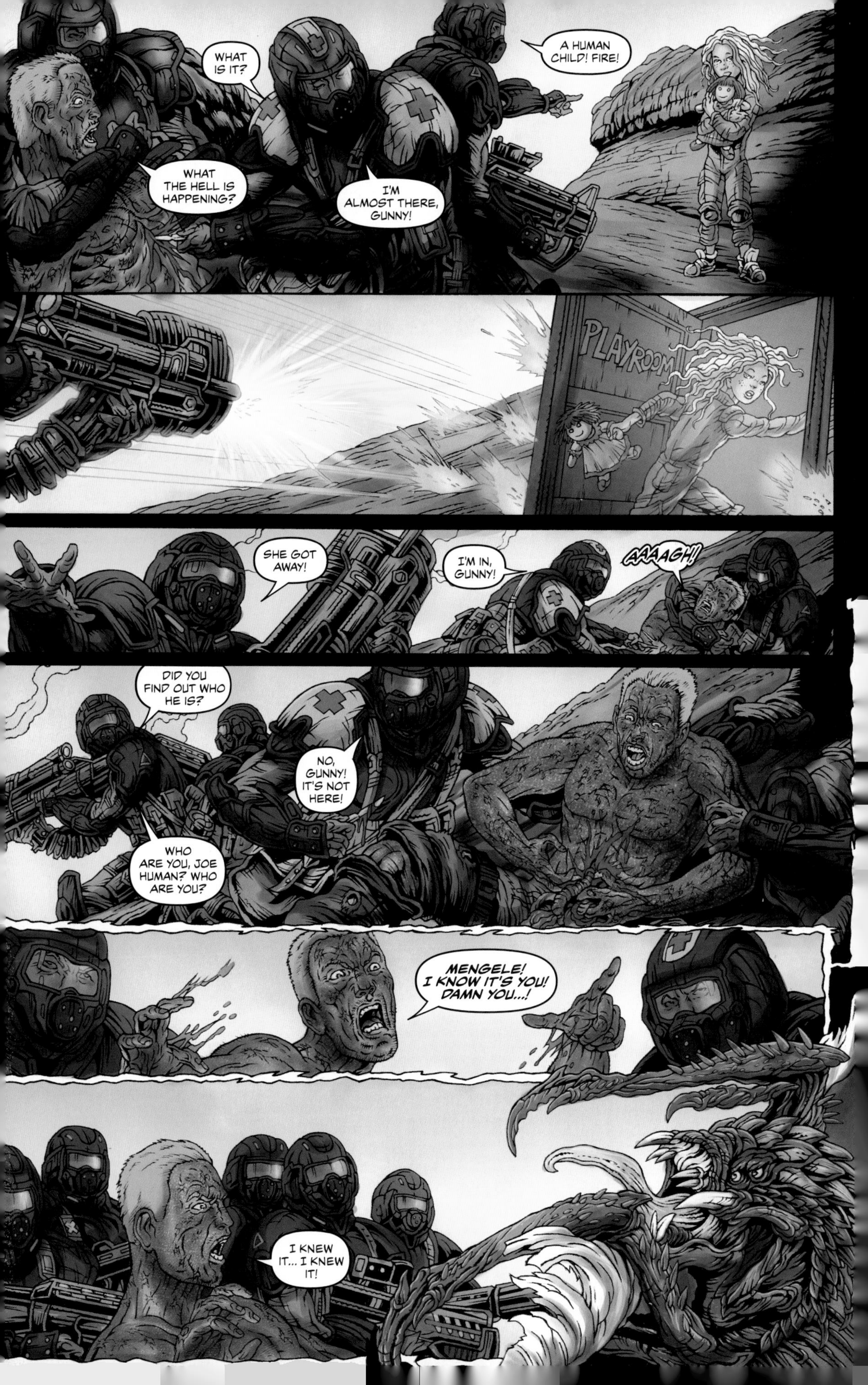
WHAT IS IT?
A HUMAN CHILD! FIRE!
WHAT THE HELL IS HAPPENING?
I'M ALMOST THERE, GUNNY!
PLAYROOM
SHE GOT AWAY!
I'M IN, GUNNY!
AAAAGH!
DID YOU FIND OUT WHO HE IS?
NO, GUNNY! IT'S NOT HERE!
WHO ARE YOU, JOE HUMAN? WHO ARE YOU?
MENGELE! I KNOW IT'S YOU! DAMN YOU...!
I KNEW IT... I KNEW IT!

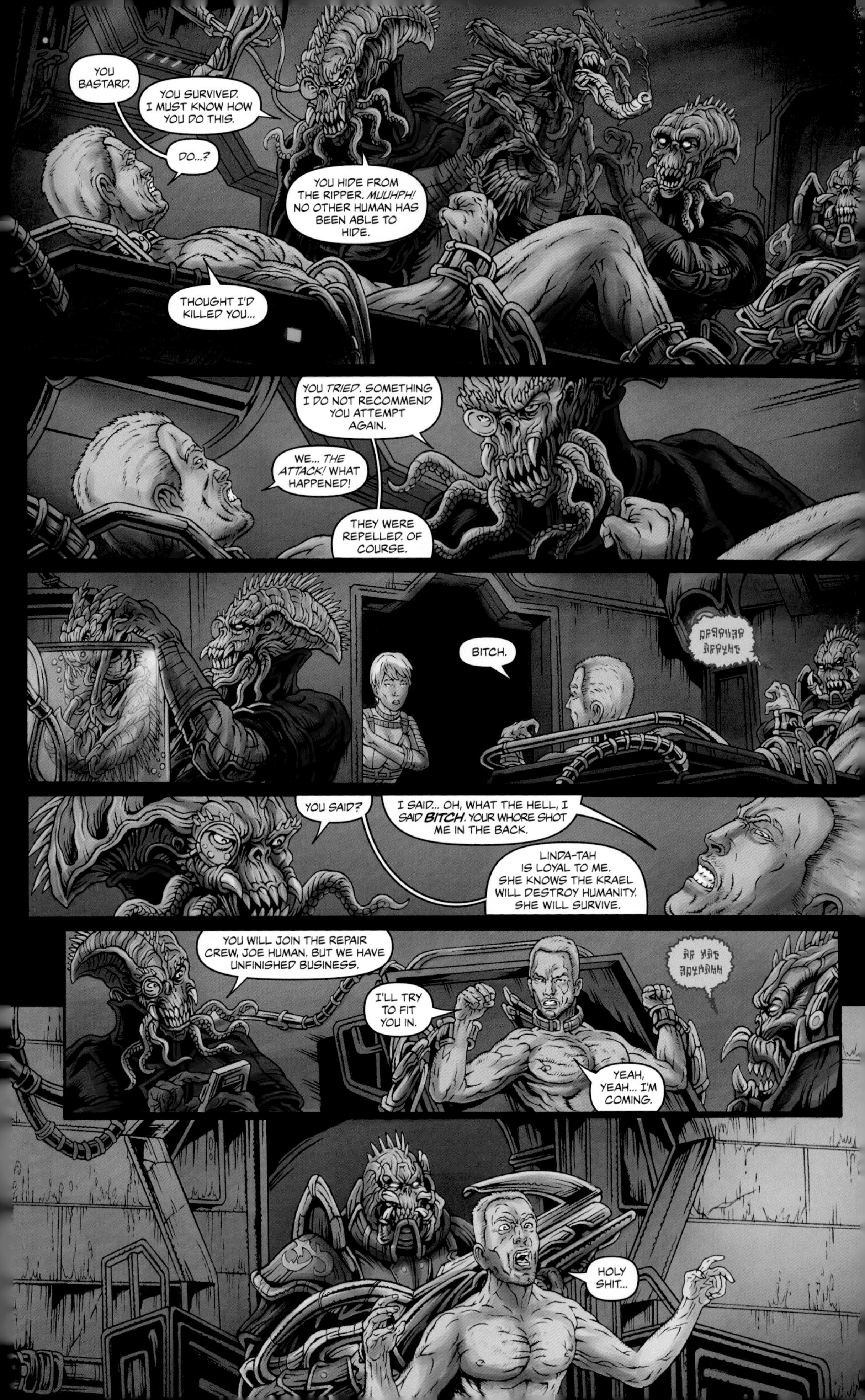
YOU BASTARD.
YOU SURVIVED. I MUST KNOW HOW YOU DO THIS.
DO...?
YOU HIDE FROM THE RIPPER. *MUUHPH!* NO OTHER HUMAN HAS BEEN ABLE TO HIDE.
THOUGHT I'D KILLED YOU...
YOU *TRIED*. SOMETHING I DO NOT RECOMMEND YOU ATTEMPT AGAIN.
WE... *THE ATTACK!* WHAT HAPPENED!
THEY WERE REPELLED. OF COURSE.
BITCH.
YOU SAID?
I SAID... OH, WHAT THE HELL, I SAID ***BITCH***. YOUR WHORE SHOT ME IN THE BACK.
LINDA-TAH IS LOYAL TO ME. SHE KNOWS THE KRAEL WILL DESTROY HUMANITY. SHE WILL SURVIVE.
YOU WILL JOIN THE REPAIR CREW, JOE HUMAN. BUT WE HAVE UNFINISHED BUSINESS.
I'LL TRY TO FIT YOU IN.
YEAH, YEAH... I'M COMING.
HOLY SHIT...

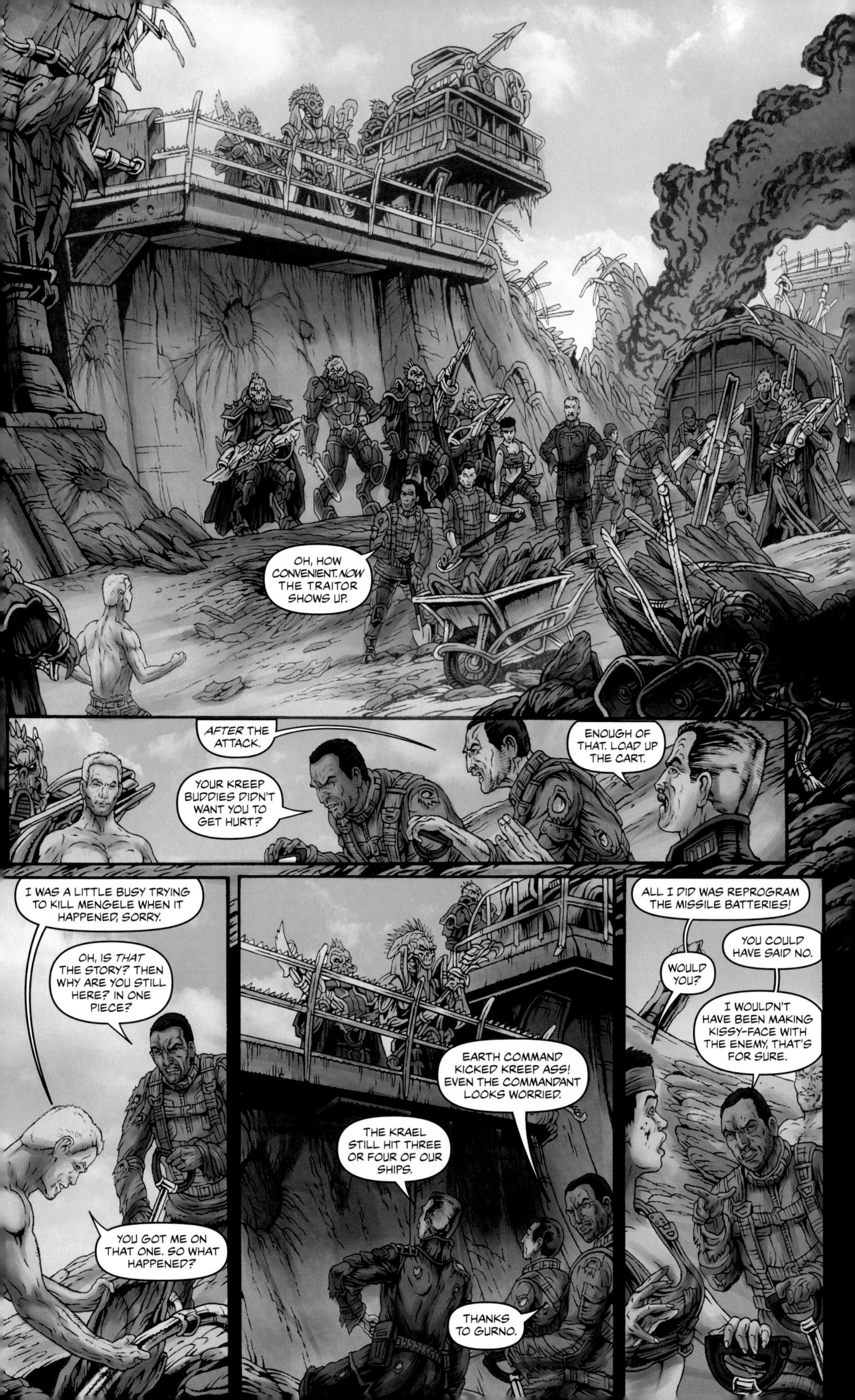
OH, HOW CONVENIENT. *NOW* THE TRAITOR SHOWS UP.
AFTER THE ATTACK.
YOUR KREEP BUDDIES DIDN'T WANT YOU TO GET HURT?
ENOUGH OF THAT. LOAD UP THE CART.
I WAS A LITTLE BUSY TRYING TO KILL MENGELE WHEN IT HAPPENED, SORRY.
OH, IS *THAT* THE STORY? THEN WHY ARE YOU STILL HERE? IN ONE PIECE?
YOU GOT ME ON THAT ONE. SO WHAT HAPPENED?
EARTH COMMAND KICKED KREEP ASS! EVEN THE COMMANDANT LOOKS WORRIED.
THE KRAEL STILL HIT THREE OR FOUR OF OUR SHIPS.
THANKS TO GURNO.
ALL I DID WAS REPROGRAM THE MISSILE BATTERIES!
WOULD YOU?
YOU COULD HAVE SAID NO.
I WOULDN'T HAVE BEEN MAKING KISSY-FACE WITH THE ENEMY, THAT'S FOR SURE.

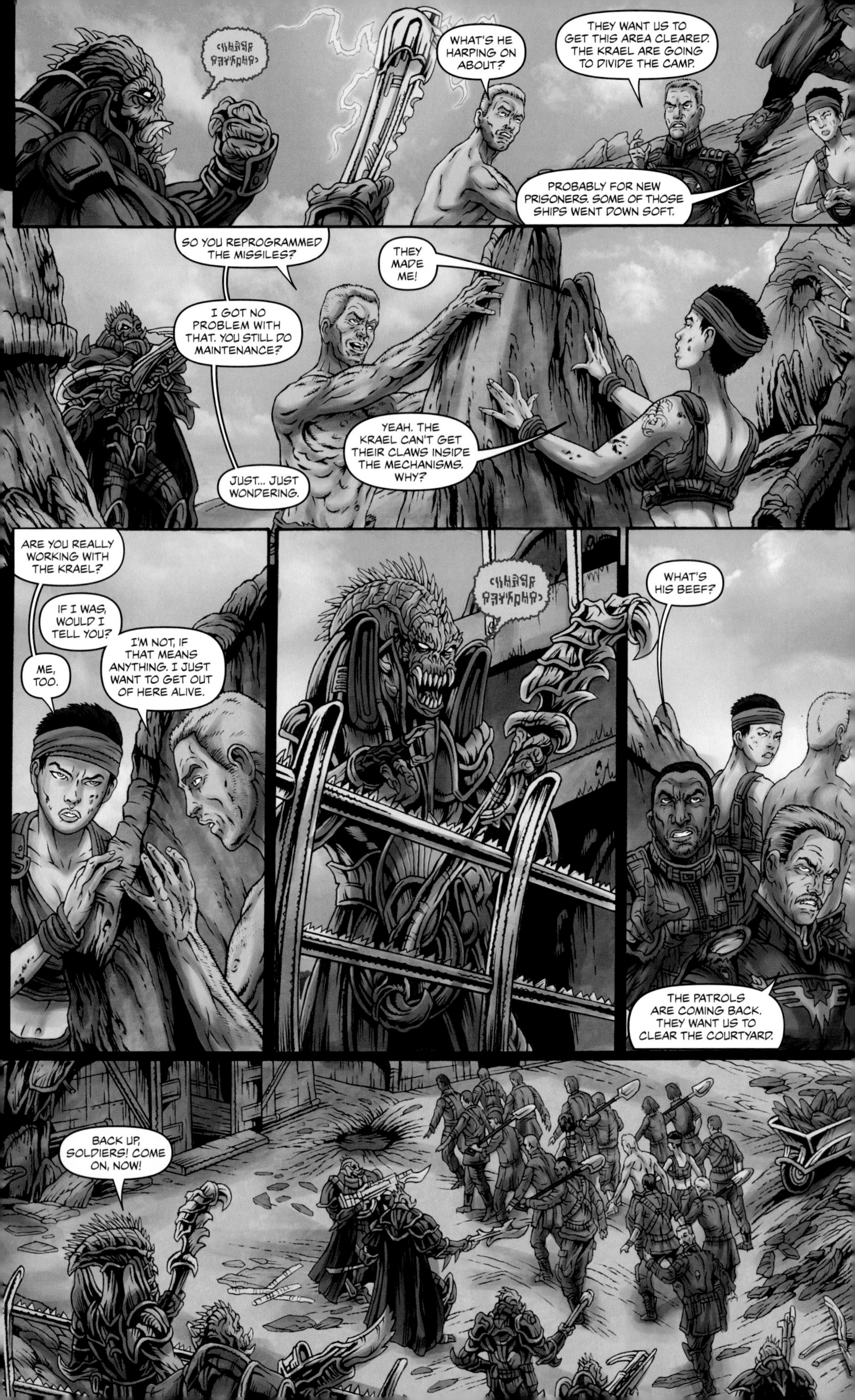
WHAT'S HE HARPING ON ABOUT?
THEY WANT US TO GET THIS AREA CLEARED. THE KRAEL ARE GOING TO DIVIDE THE CAMP.
PROBABLY FOR NEW PRISONERS. SOME OF THOSE SHIPS WENT DOWN SOFT.
SO YOU REPROGRAMMED THE MISSILES?
THEY MADE ME!
I GOT NO PROBLEM WITH THAT. YOU STILL DO MAINTENANCE?
YEAH. THE KRAEL CAN'T GET THEIR CLAWS INSIDE THE MECHANISMS. WHY?
JUST... JUST WONDERING.
ARE YOU REALLY WORKING WITH THE KRAEL?
IF I WAS, WOULD I TELL YOU?
I'M NOT, IF THAT MEANS ANYTHING. I JUST WANT TO GET OUT OF HERE ALIVE.
ME, TOO.
WHAT'S HIS BEEF?
THE PATROLS ARE COMING BACK. THEY WANT US TO CLEAR THE COURTYARD.
BACK UP, SOLDIERS! COME ON, NOW!

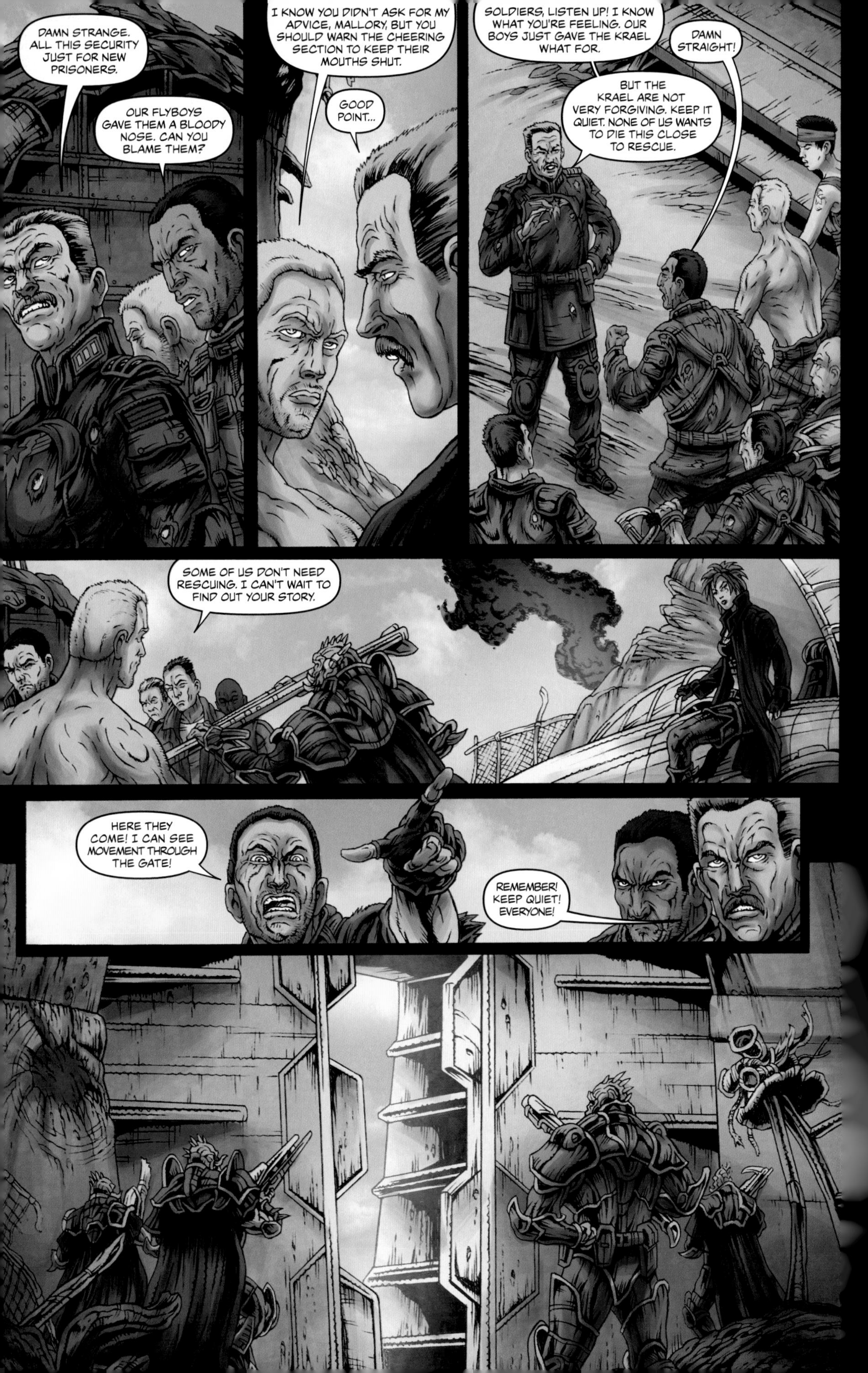
DAMN STRANGE. ALL THIS SECURITY JUST FOR NEW PRISONERS.
OUR FLYBOYS GAVE THEM A BLOODY NOSE. CAN YOU BLAME THEM?
I KNOW YOU DIDN'T ASK FOR MY ADVICE, MALLORY, BUT YOU SHOULD WARN THE CHEERING SECTION TO KEEP THEIR MOUTHS SHUT.
GOOD POINT...
SOLDIERS, LISTEN UP! I KNOW WHAT YOU'RE FEELING. OUR BOYS JUST GAVE THE KRAEL WHAT FOR.
DAMN STRAIGHT!
BUT THE KRAEL ARE NOT VERY FORGIVING. KEEP IT QUIET. NONE OF US WANTS TO DIE THIS CLOSE TO RESCUE.
SOME OF US DON'T NEED RESCUING. I CAN'T WAIT TO FIND OUT YOUR STORY.
HERE THEY COME! I CAN SEE MOVEMENT THROUGH THE GATE!
REMEMBER! KEEP QUIET! EVERYONE!

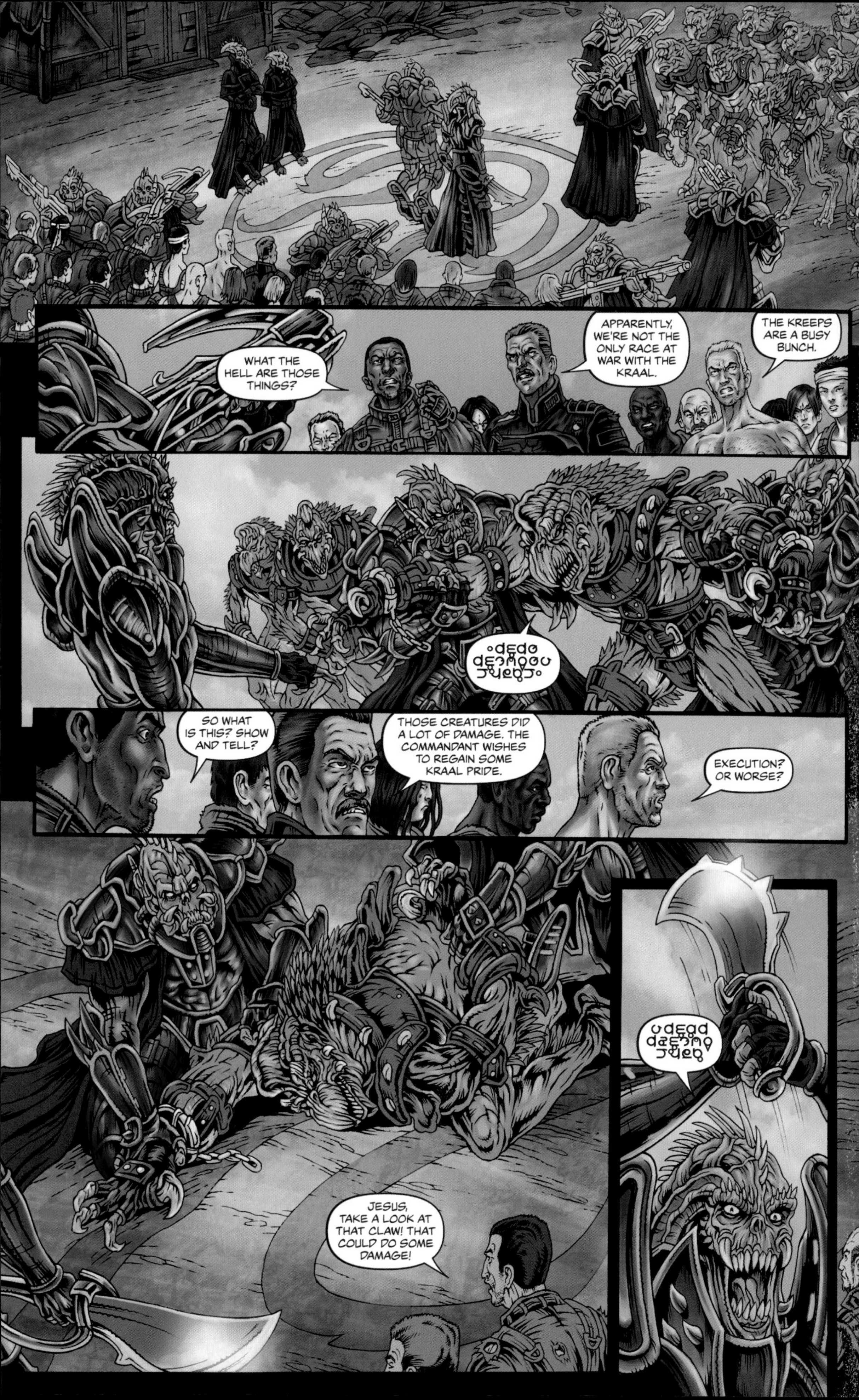
WHAT THE HELL ARE THOSE THINGS?
APPARENTLY, WE'RE NOT THE ONLY RACE AT WAR WITH THE KRAAL.
THE KREEPS ARE A BUSY BUNCH.
SO WHAT IS THIS? SHOW AND TELL?
THOSE CREATURES DID A LOT OF DAMAGE. THE COMMANDANT WISHES TO REGAIN SOME KRAAL PRIDE.
EXECUTION? OR WORSE?
JESUS, TAKE A LOOK AT THAT CLAW! THAT COULD DO SOME DAMAGE!

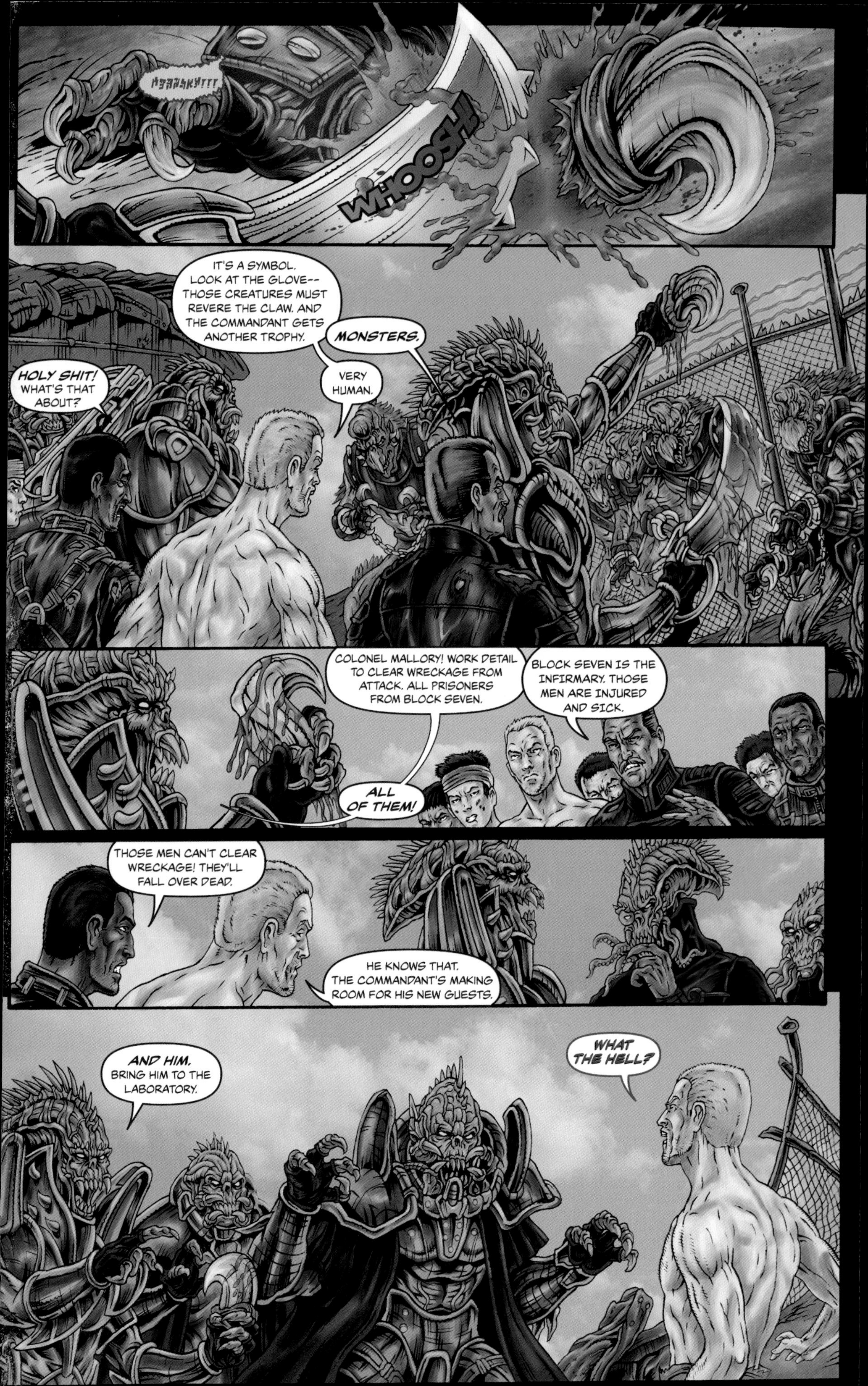
WHOOSH!
IT'S A SYMBOL. LOOK AT THE GLOVE-- THOSE CREATURES MUST REVERE THE CLAW. AND THE COMMANDANT GETS ANOTHER TROPHY.
HOLY SHIT! WHAT'S THAT ABOUT?
MONSTERS.
VERY HUMAN.
COLONEL MALLORY! WORK DETAIL TO CLEAR WRECKAGE FROM ATTACK. ALL PRISONERS FROM BLOCK SEVEN.
ALL OF THEM!
BLOCK SEVEN IS THE INFIRMARY. THOSE MEN ARE INJURED AND SICK.
THOSE MEN CAN'T CLEAR WRECKAGE! THEY'LL FALL OVER DEAD.
HE KNOWS THAT. THE COMMANDANT'S MAKING ROOM FOR HIS NEW GUESTS.
AND HIM. BRING HIM TO THE LABORATORY.
WHAT THE HELL?

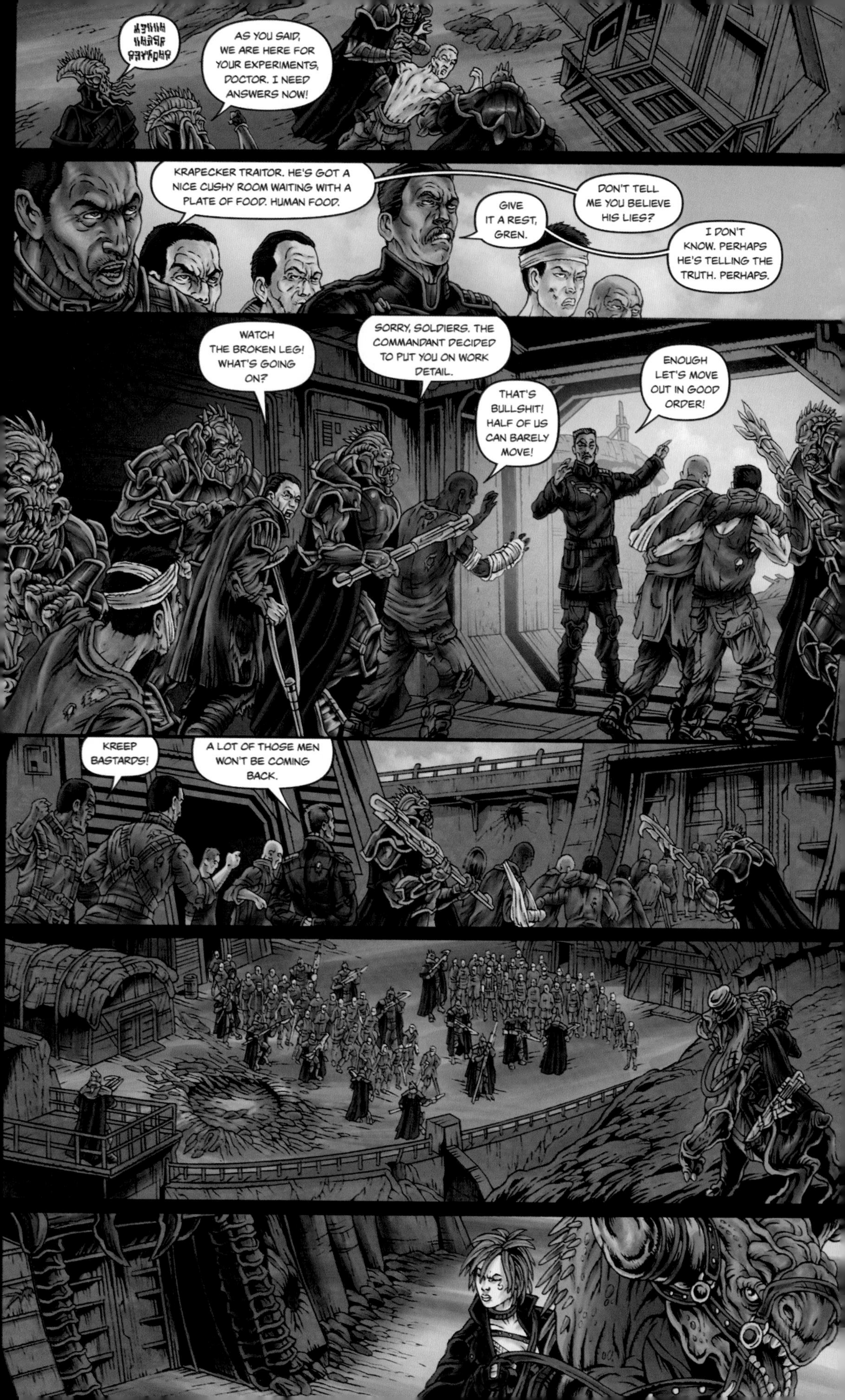
AS YOU SAID, WE ARE HERE FOR YOUR EXPERIMENTS, DOCTOR. I NEED ANSWERS NOW!
KRAPECKER TRAITOR. HE'S GOT A NICE CUSHY ROOM WAITING WITH A PLATE OF FOOD. HUMAN FOOD.
DON'T TELL ME YOU BELIEVE HIS LIES?
GIVE IT A REST, GREN.
I DON'T KNOW. PERHAPS HE'S TELLING THE TRUTH. PERHAPS.
WATCH THE BROKEN LEG! WHAT'S GOING ON?
SORRY, SOLDIERS. THE COMMANDANT DECIDED TO PUT YOU ON WORK DETAIL.
THAT'S BULLSHIT! HALF OF US CAN BARELY MOVE!
ENOUGH LET'S MOVE OUT IN GOOD ORDER!
KREEP BASTARDS!
A LOT OF THOSE MEN WON'T BE COMING BACK.

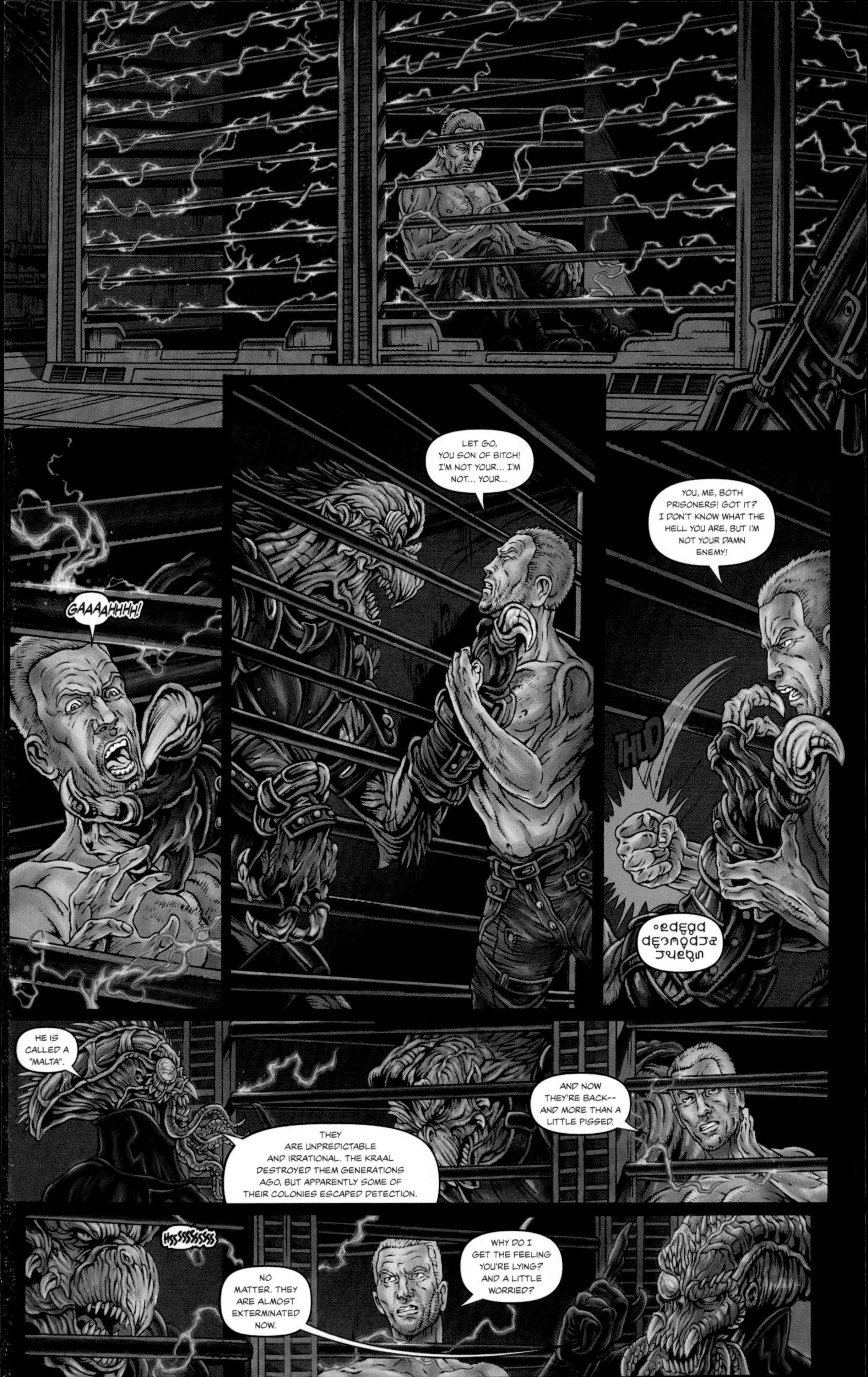
GAAAAHHHH!
LET GO, YOU SON OF BITCH! I'M NOT YOUR... I'M NOT... YOUR...
YOU, ME, BOTH PRISONERS! GOT IT? I DON'T KNOW WHAT THE HELL YOU ARE, BUT I'M NOT YOUR DAMN ENEMY!
THUD
HE IS CALLED A "MALTA".
THEY ARE UNPREDICTABLE AND IRRATIONAL. THE KRAAL DESTROYED THEM GENERATIONS AGO, BUT APPARENTLY SOME OF THEIR COLONIES ESCAPED DETECTION.
AND NOW THEY'RE BACK-- AND MORE THAN A LITTLE PISSED.
HSSSSSSSSSS
NO MATTER. THEY ARE ALMOST EXTERMINATED NOW.
WHY DO I GET THE FEELING YOU'RE LYING? AND A LITTLE WORRIED?

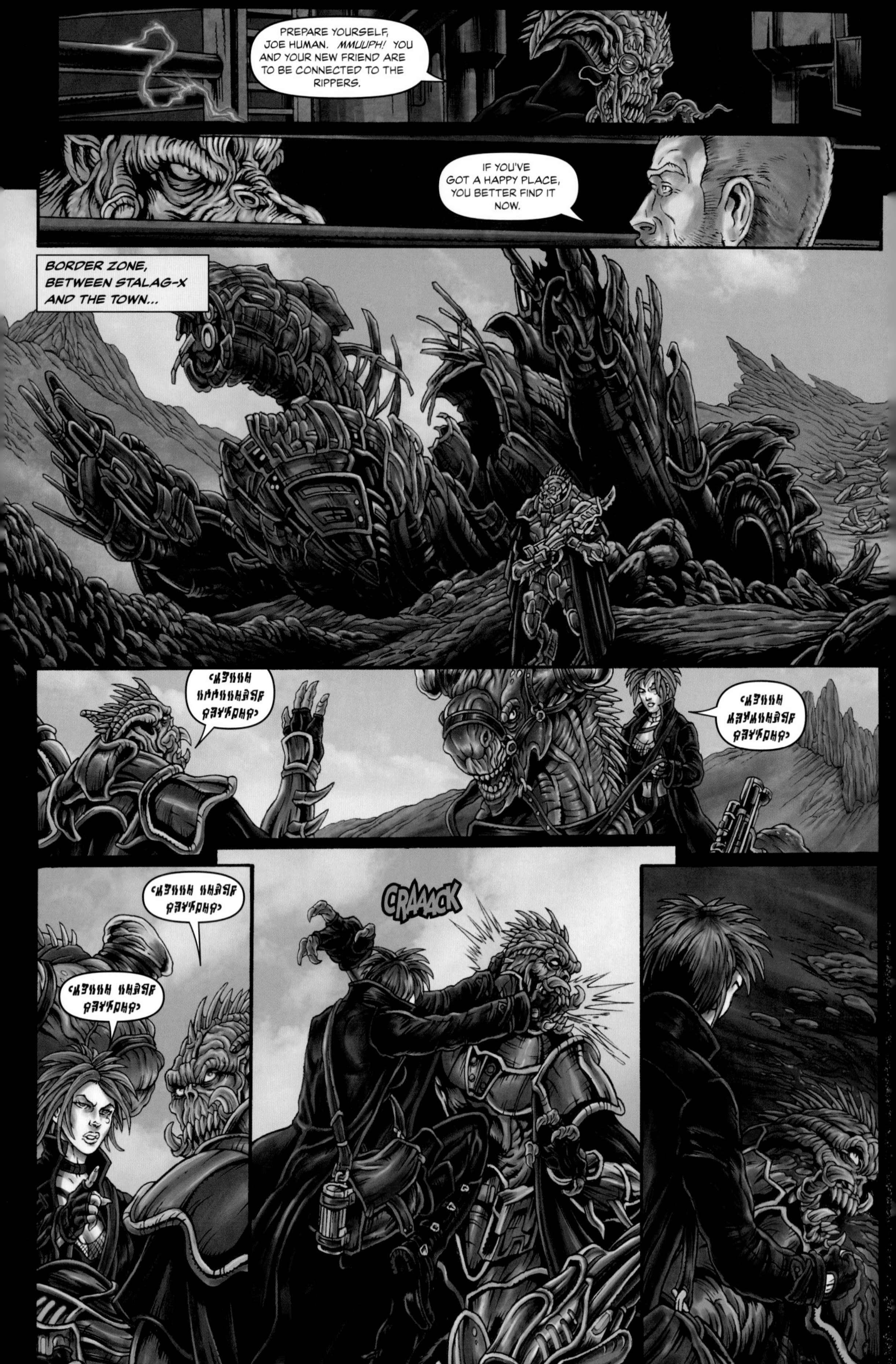
PREPARE YOURSELF, JOE HUMAN. MMUUPH! YOU AND YOUR NEW FRIEND ARE TO BE CONNECTED TO THE RIPPERS.
IF YOU'VE GOT A HAPPY PLACE, YOU BETTER FIND IT NOW.
BORDER ZONE, BETWEEN STALAG-X AND THE TOWN...
CRAAACK

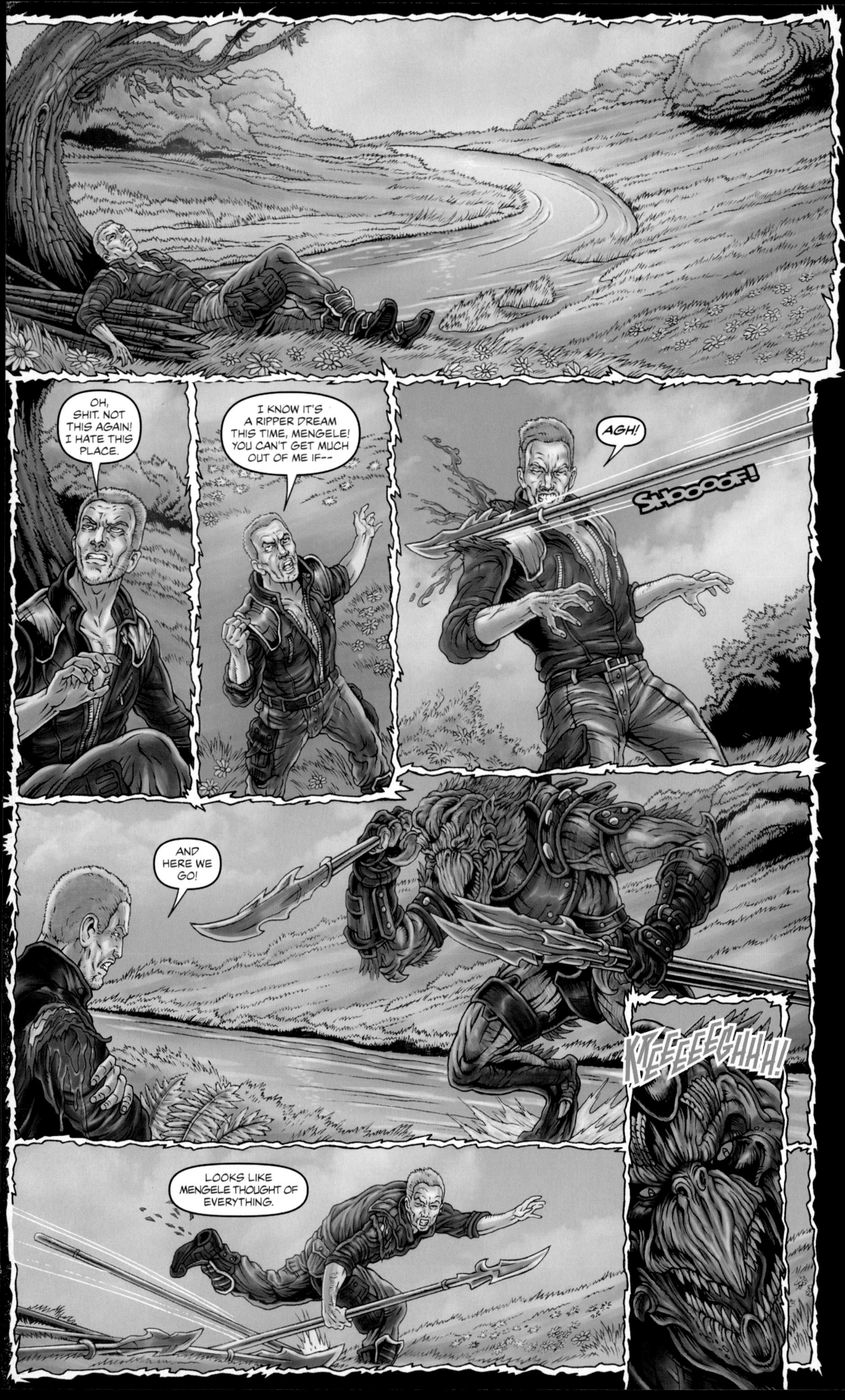
OH, SHIT. NOT THIS AGAIN! I HATE THIS PLACE.
I KNOW IT'S A RIPPER DREAM THIS TIME, MENGELE! YOU CAN'T GET MUCH OUT OF ME IF--
AGH!
SHOOOOF!
AND HERE WE GO!
KREEEEEGHHH!
LOOKS LIKE MENGELE THOUGHT OF EVERYTHING.

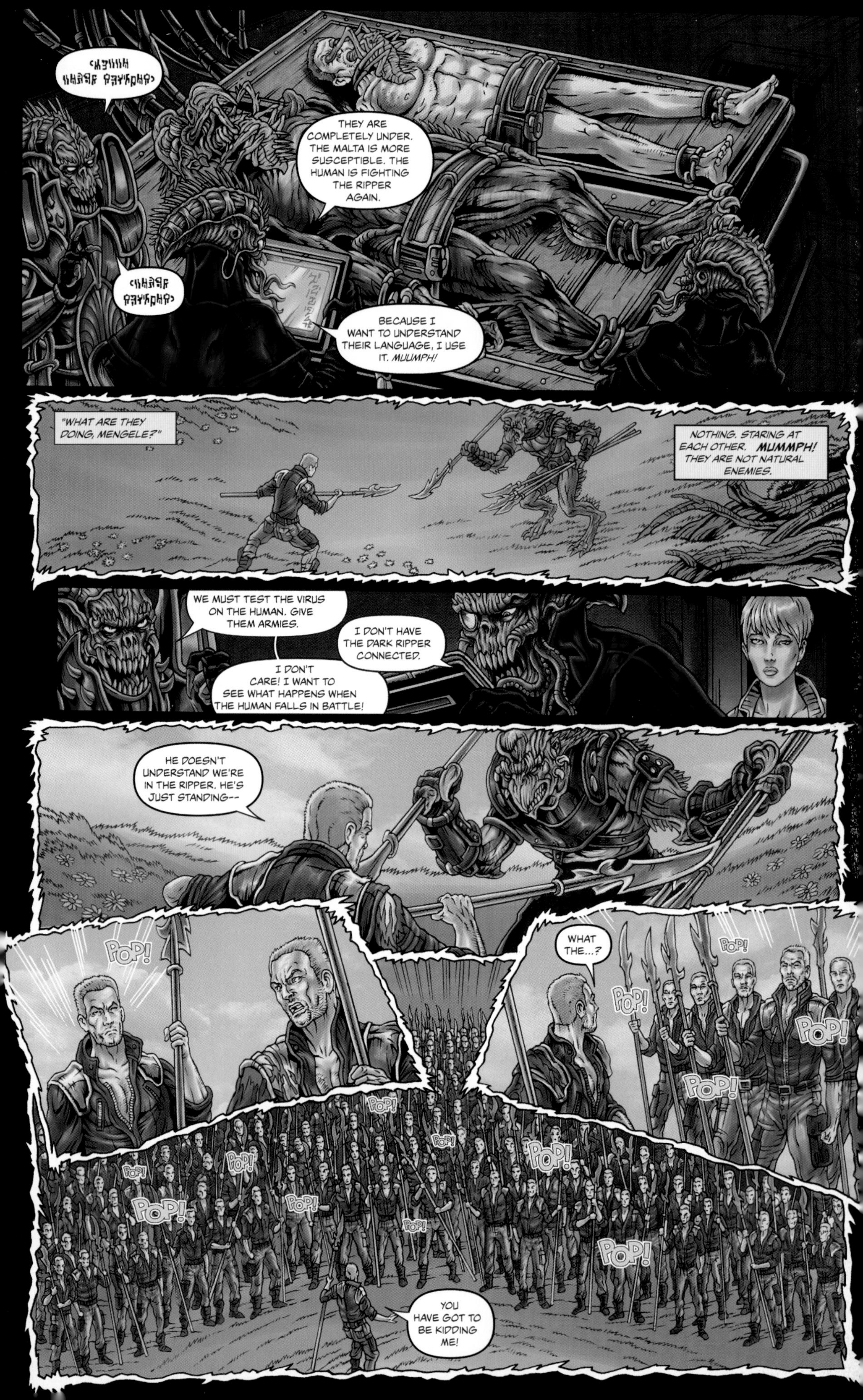
THEY ARE COMPLETELY UNDER. THE MALTA IS MORE SUSCEPTIBLE. THE HUMAN IS FIGHTING THE RIPPER AGAIN.
BECAUSE I WANT TO UNDERSTAND THEIR LANGUAGE, I USE IT. MUUMPH!
"WHAT ARE THEY DOING, MENGELE?"
NOTHING. STARING AT EACH OTHER. MUMMPH! THEY ARE NOT NATURAL ENEMIES.
WE MUST TEST THE VIRUS ON THE HUMAN. GIVE THEM ARMIES.
I DON'T HAVE THE DARK RIPPER CONNECTED.
I DON'T CARE! I WANT TO SEE WHAT HAPPENS WHEN THE HUMAN FALLS IN BATTLE!
HE DOESN'T UNDERSTAND WE'RE IN THE RIPPER. HE'S JUST STANDING--
POP!
WHAT THE...?
POP!
POP!
POP!
POP!
POP!
POP!
POP!
POP!
POP!
POP!
POP!
POP!
YOU HAVE GOT TO BE KIDDING ME!

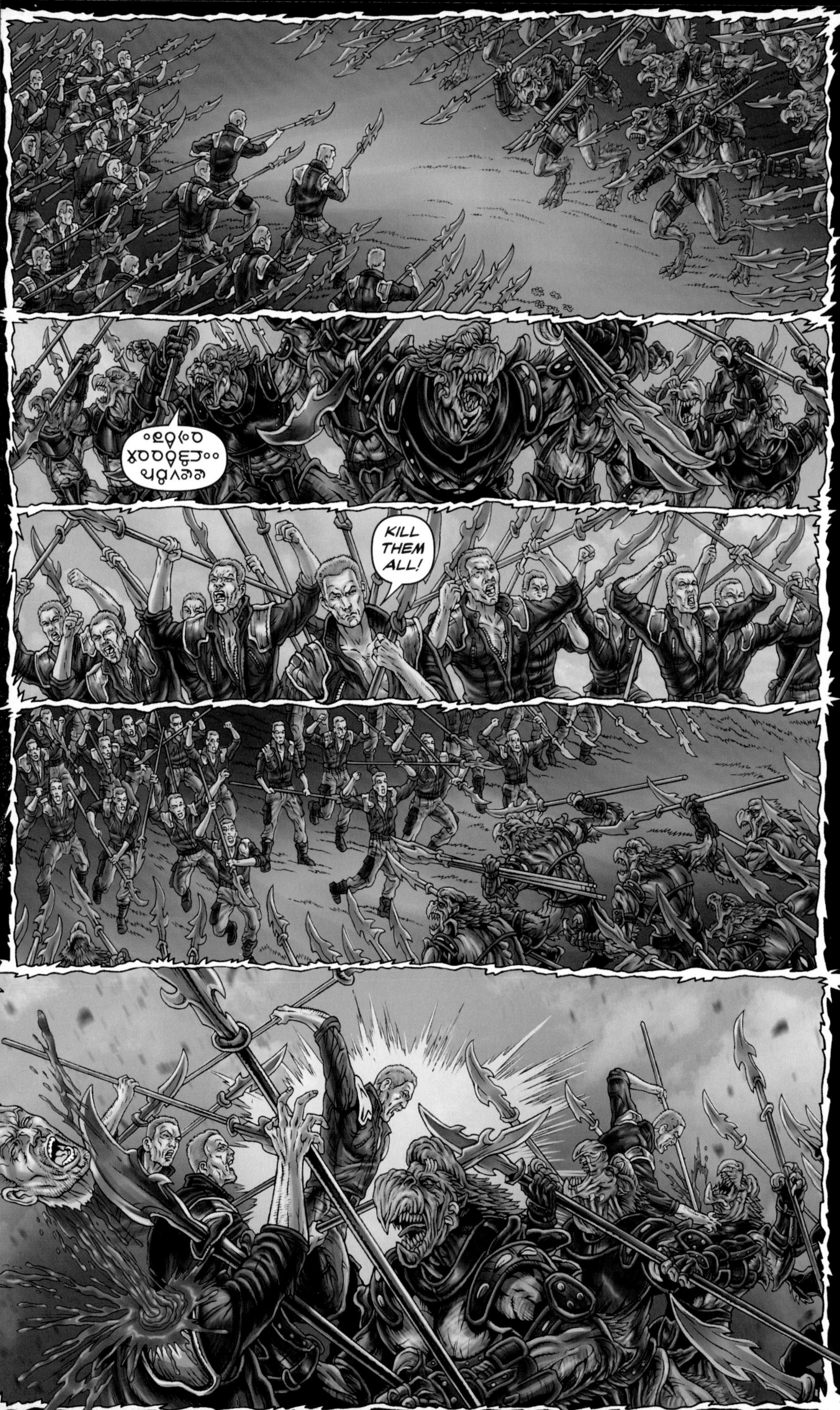
KILL THEM ALL!

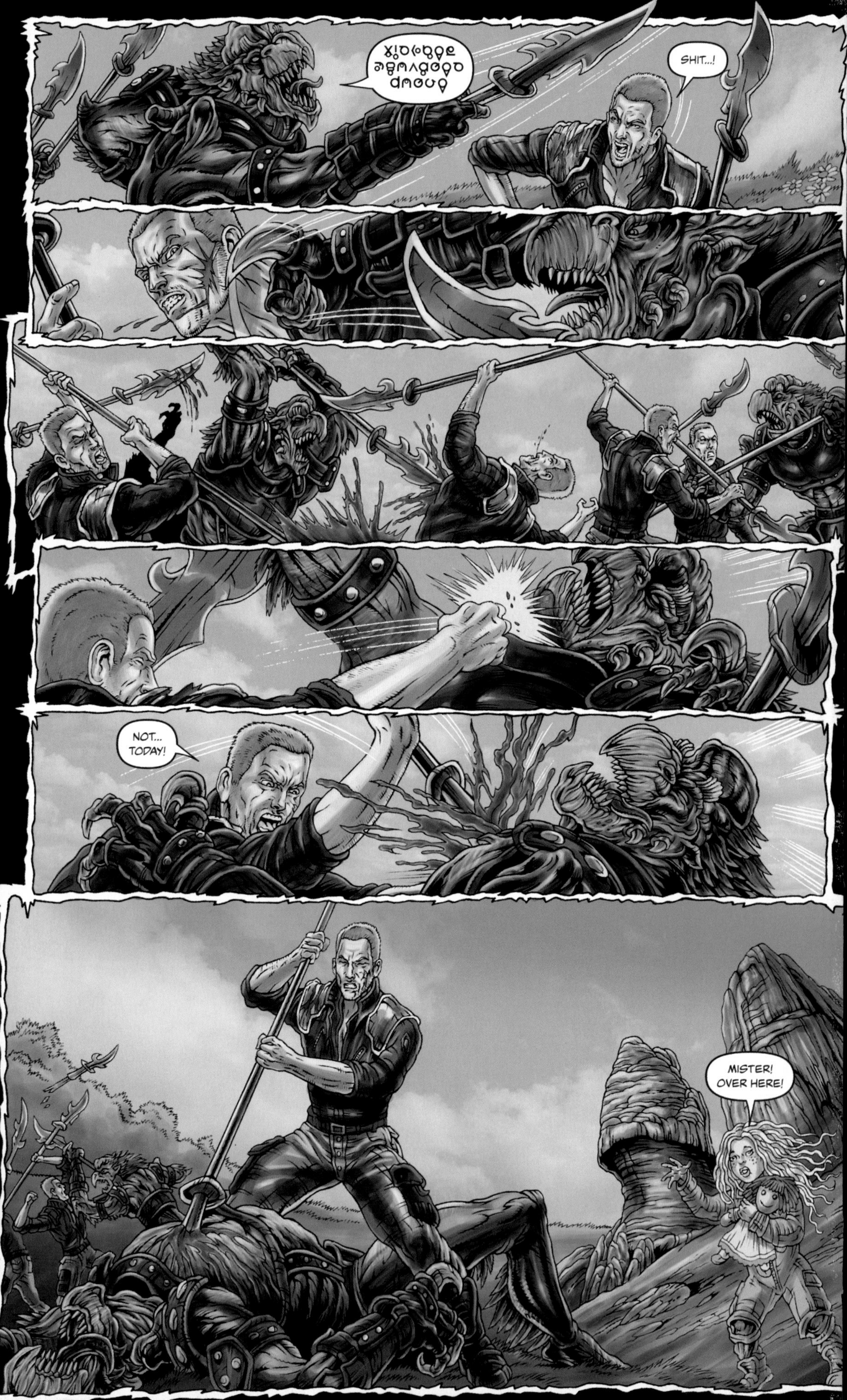
SHIT...!
NOT... TODAY!
MISTER! OVER HERE!

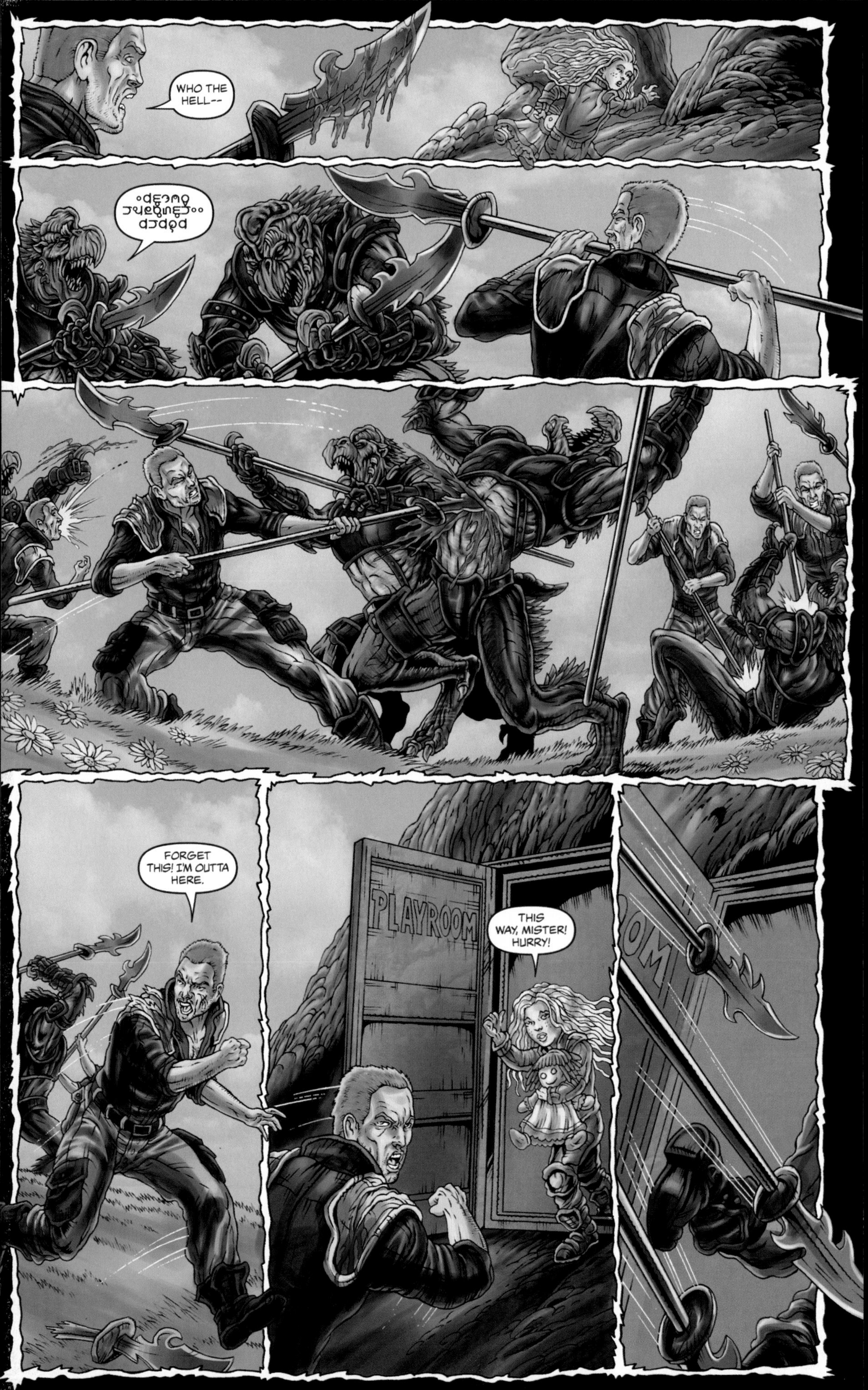
WHO THE HELL--
FORGET THIS! I'M OUTTA HERE.
PLAYROOM
THIS WAY, MISTER! HURRY!

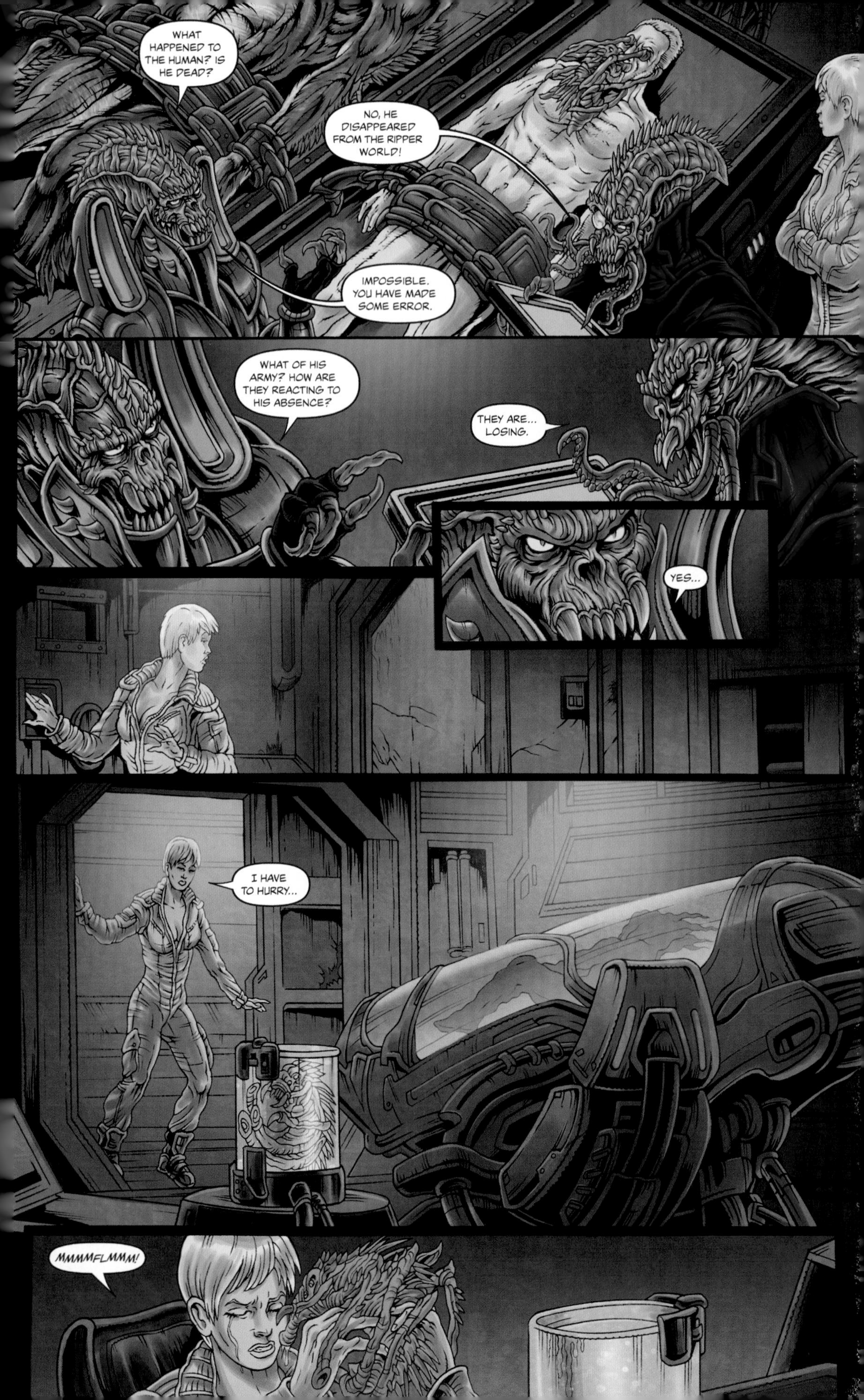

WHAT HAPPENED TO THE HUMAN? IS HE DEAD?
NO, HE DISAPPEARED FROM THE RIPPER WORLD!
IMPOSSIBLE. YOU HAVE MADE SOME ERROR.
WHAT OF HIS ARMY? HOW ARE THEY REACTING TO HIS ABSENCE?
THEY ARE... LOSING.
YES...
I HAVE TO HURRY...
MMMMFLMMM!

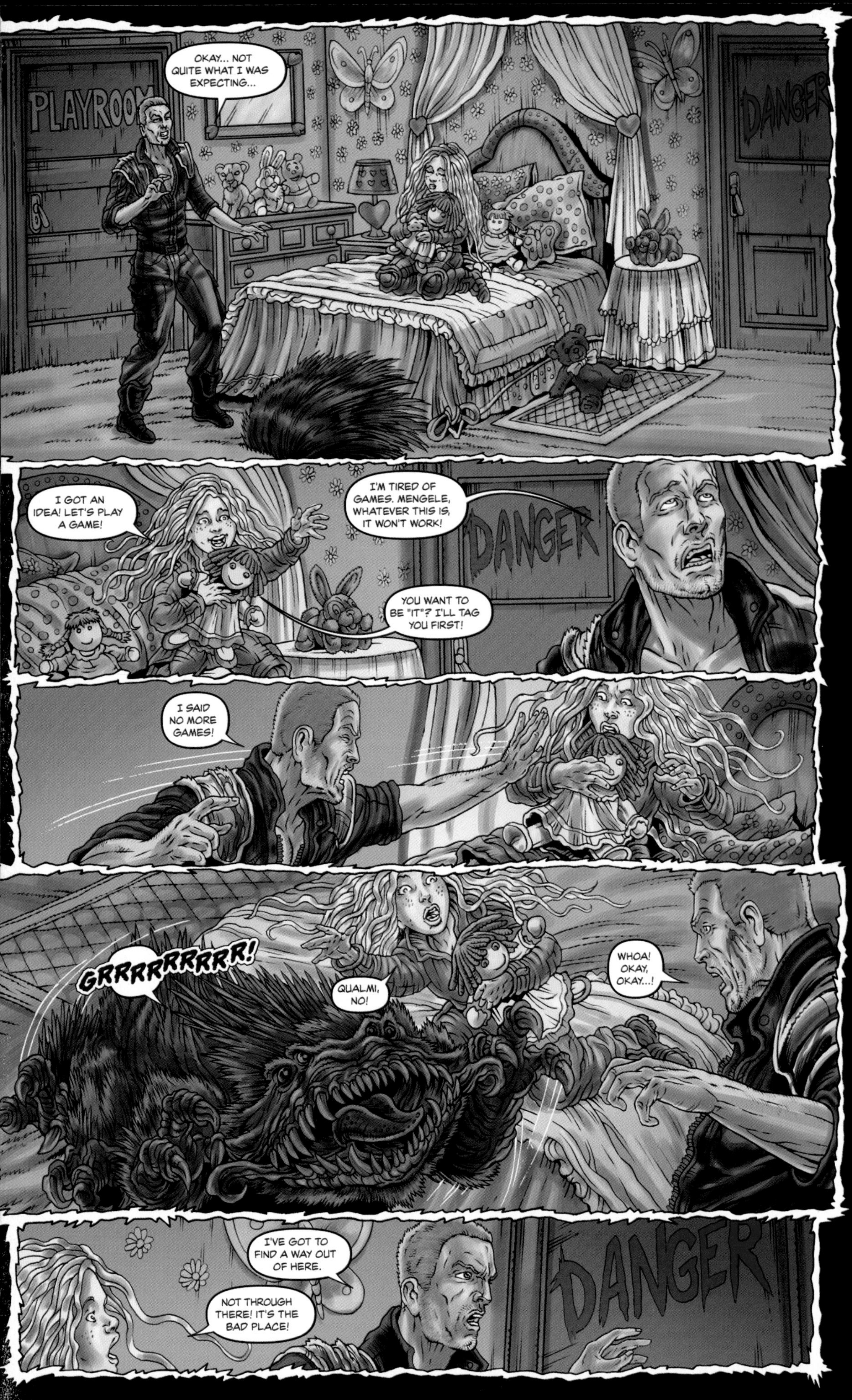
PLAYROOM
OKAY... NOT QUITE WHAT I WAS EXPECTING...
DANGER
I GOT AN IDEA! LET'S PLAY A GAME!
I'M TIRED OF GAMES. MENGELE, WHATEVER THIS IS, IT WON'T WORK!
DANGER
YOU WANT TO BE "IT"? I'LL TAG YOU FIRST!
I SAID NO MORE GAMES!
GRRRRRRRRR!
QUALMI, NO!
WHOA! OKAY, OKAY...!
I'VE GOT TO FIND A WAY OUT OF HERE.
NOT THROUGH THERE! IT'S THE BAD PLACE!
DANGER

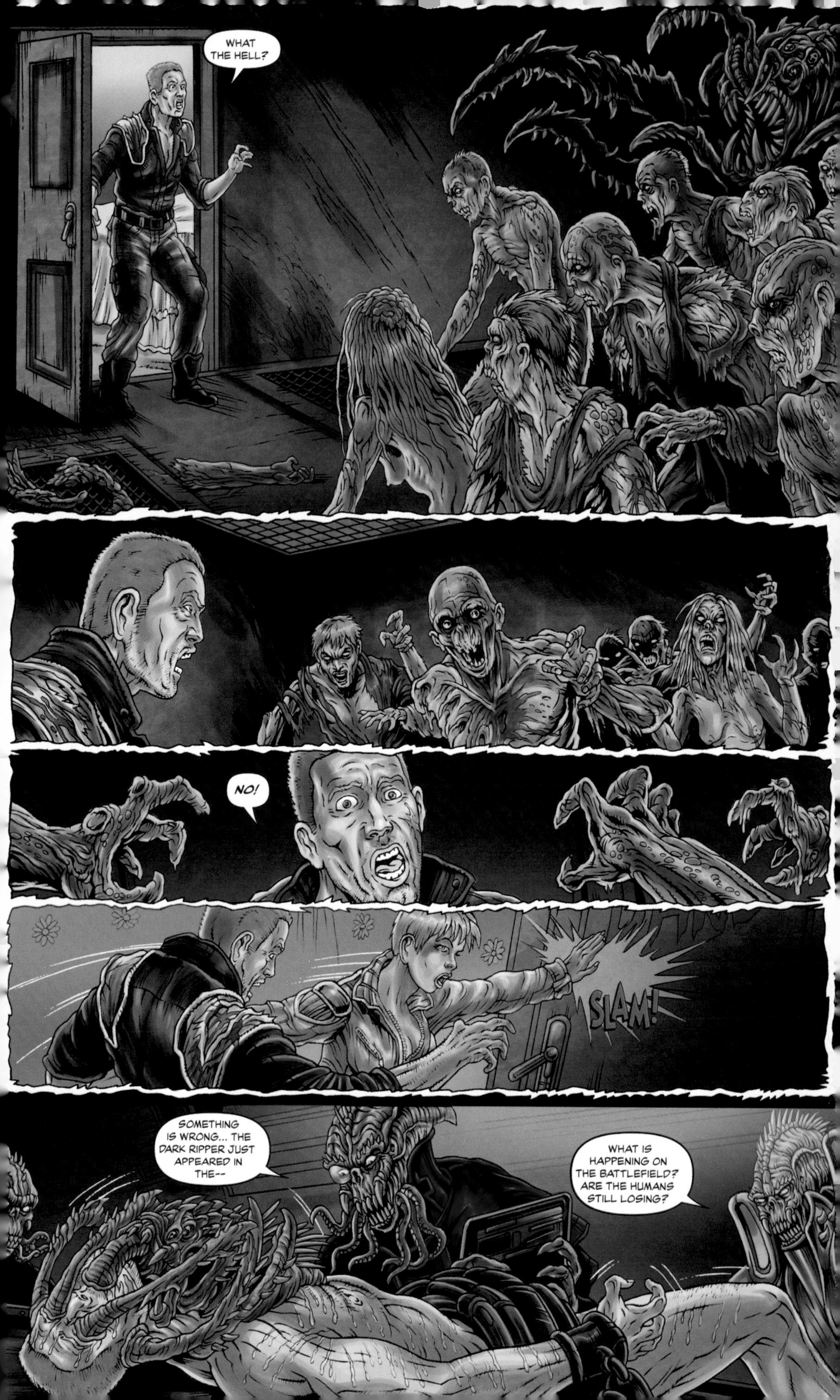
WHAT THE HELL?
NO!
SLAM!
SOMETHING IS WRONG... THE DARK RIPPER JUST APPEARED IN THE--
WHAT IS HAPPENING ON THE BATTLEFIELD? ARE THE HUMANS STILL LOSING?

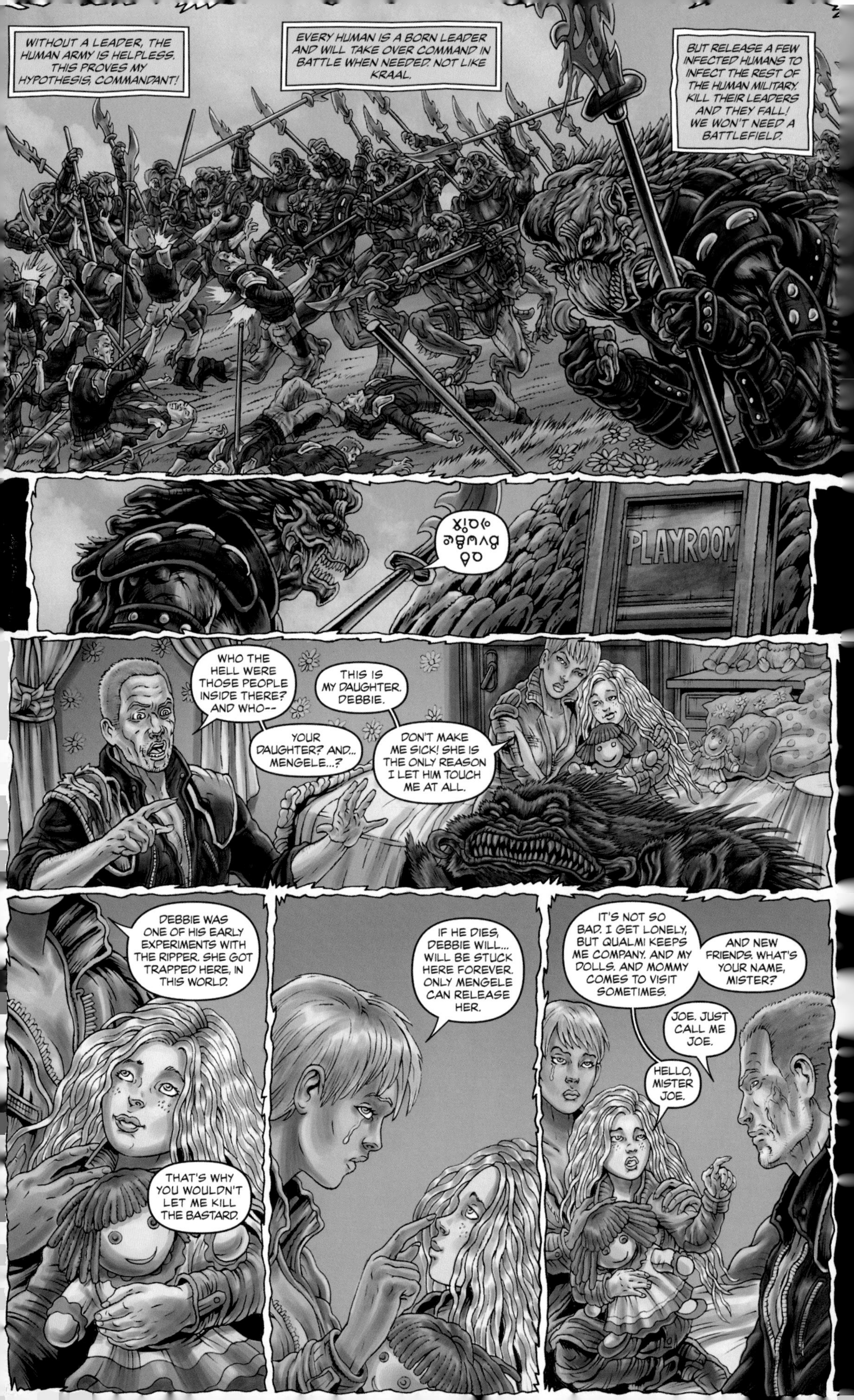
WITHOUT A LEADER, THE HUMAN ARMY IS HELPLESS. THIS PROVES MY HYPOTHESIS, COMMANDANT!
EVERY HUMAN IS A BORN LEADER AND WILL TAKE OVER COMMAND IN BATTLE WHEN NEEDED. NOT LIKE KRAAL.
BUT RELEASE A FEW INFECTED HUMANS TO INFECT THE REST OF THE HUMAN MILITARY. KILL THEIR LEADERS AND THEY FALL! WE WON'T NEED A BATTLEFIELD.
PLAYROOM
WHO THE HELL WERE THOSE PEOPLE INSIDE THERE? AND WHO--
THIS IS MY DAUGHTER. DEBBIE.
YOUR DAUGHTER? AND... MENGELE...?
DON'T MAKE ME SICK! SHE IS THE ONLY REASON I LET HIM TOUCH ME AT ALL.
DEBBIE WAS ONE OF HIS EARLY EXPERIMENTS WITH THE RIPPER. SHE GOT TRAPPED HERE, IN THIS WORLD.
THAT'S WHY YOU WOULDN'T LET ME KILL THE BASTARD.
IF HE DIES, DEBBIE WILL... WILL BE STUCK HERE FOREVER. ONLY MENGELE CAN RELEASE HER.
IT'S NOT SO BAD. I GET LONELY, BUT QUALMI KEEPS ME COMPANY. AND MY DOLLS. AND MOMMY COMES TO VISIT SOMETIMES.
AND NEW FRIENDS. WHAT'S YOUR NAME, MISTER?
JOE. JUST CALL ME JOE.
HELLO, MISTER JOE.

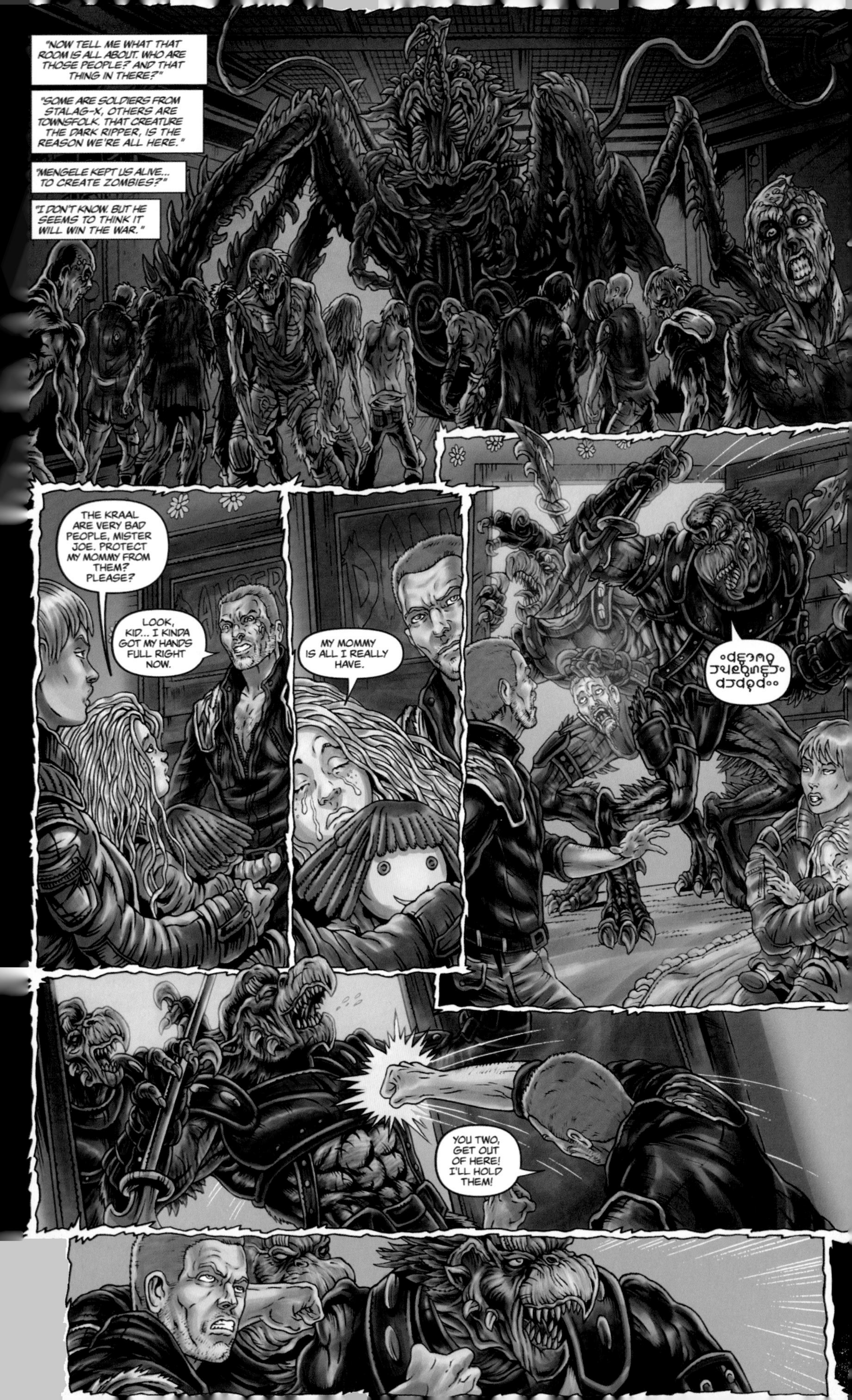
"NOW TELL ME WHAT THAT ROOM IS ALL ABOUT. WHO ARE THOSE PEOPLE? AND THAT THING IN THERE?"
"SOME ARE SOLDIERS FROM STALAG-X, OTHERS ARE TOWNSFOLK. THAT CREATURE THE DARK RIPPER, IS THE REASON WE'RE ALL HERE."
"MENGELE KEPT US ALIVE... TO CREATE ZOMBIES?"
"I DON'T KNOW. BUT HE SEEMS TO THINK IT WILL WIN THE WAR."
THE KRAAL ARE VERY BAD PEOPLE, MISTER JOE. PROTECT MY MOMMY FROM THEM? PLEASE?
LOOK, KID... I KINDA GOT MY HANDS FULL RIGHT NOW.
MY MOMMY IS ALL I REALLY HAVE.
YOU TWO, GET OUT OF HERE! I'LL HOLD THEM!

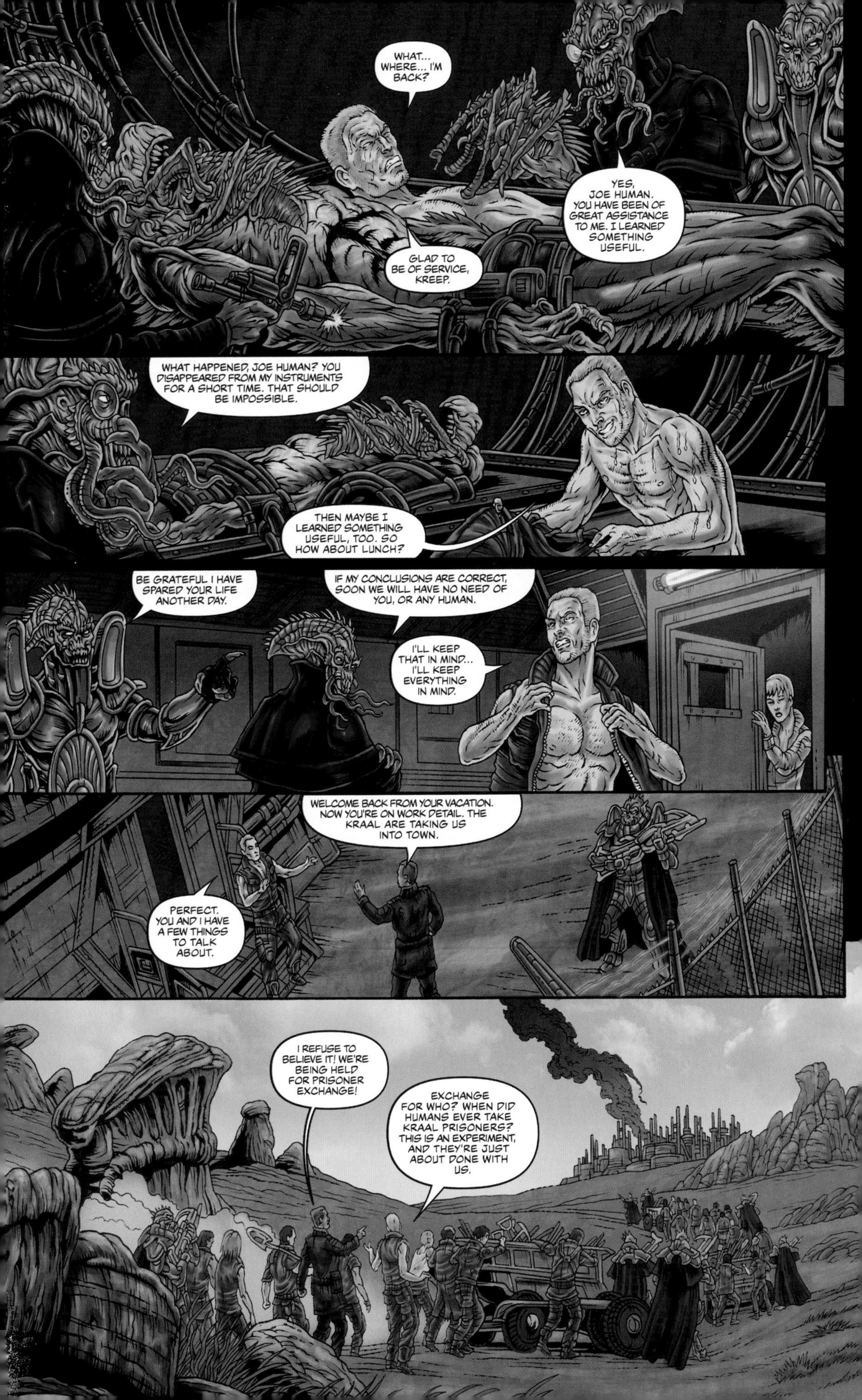
WHAT... WHERE... I'M BACK?
YES, JOE HUMAN. YOU HAVE BEEN OF GREAT ASSISTANCE TO ME. I LEARNED SOMETHING USEFUL.
GLAD TO BE OF SERVICE, KREEP.
WHAT HAPPENED, JOE HUMAN? YOU DISAPPEARED FROM MY INSTRUMENTS FOR A SHORT TIME. THAT SHOULD BE IMPOSSIBLE.
THEN MAYBE I LEARNED SOMETHING USEFUL, TOO. SO HOW ABOUT LUNCH?
BE GRATEFUL I HAVE SPARED YOUR LIFE ANOTHER DAY.
IF MY CONCLUSIONS ARE CORRECT, SOON WE WILL HAVE NO NEED OF YOU, OR ANY HUMAN.
I'LL KEEP THAT IN MIND... I'LL KEEP EVERYTHING IN MIND.
WELCOME BACK FROM YOUR VACATION. NOW YOU'RE ON WORK DETAIL. THE KRAAL ARE TAKING US INTO TOWN.
PERFECT. YOU AND I HAVE A FEW THINGS TO TALK ABOUT.
I REFUSE TO BELIEVE IT! WE'RE BEING HELD FOR PRISONER EXCHANGE!
EXCHANGE FOR WHO? WHEN DID HUMANS EVER TAKE KRAAL PRISONERS? THIS IS AN EXPERIMENT, AND THEY'RE JUST ABOUT DONE WITH US.

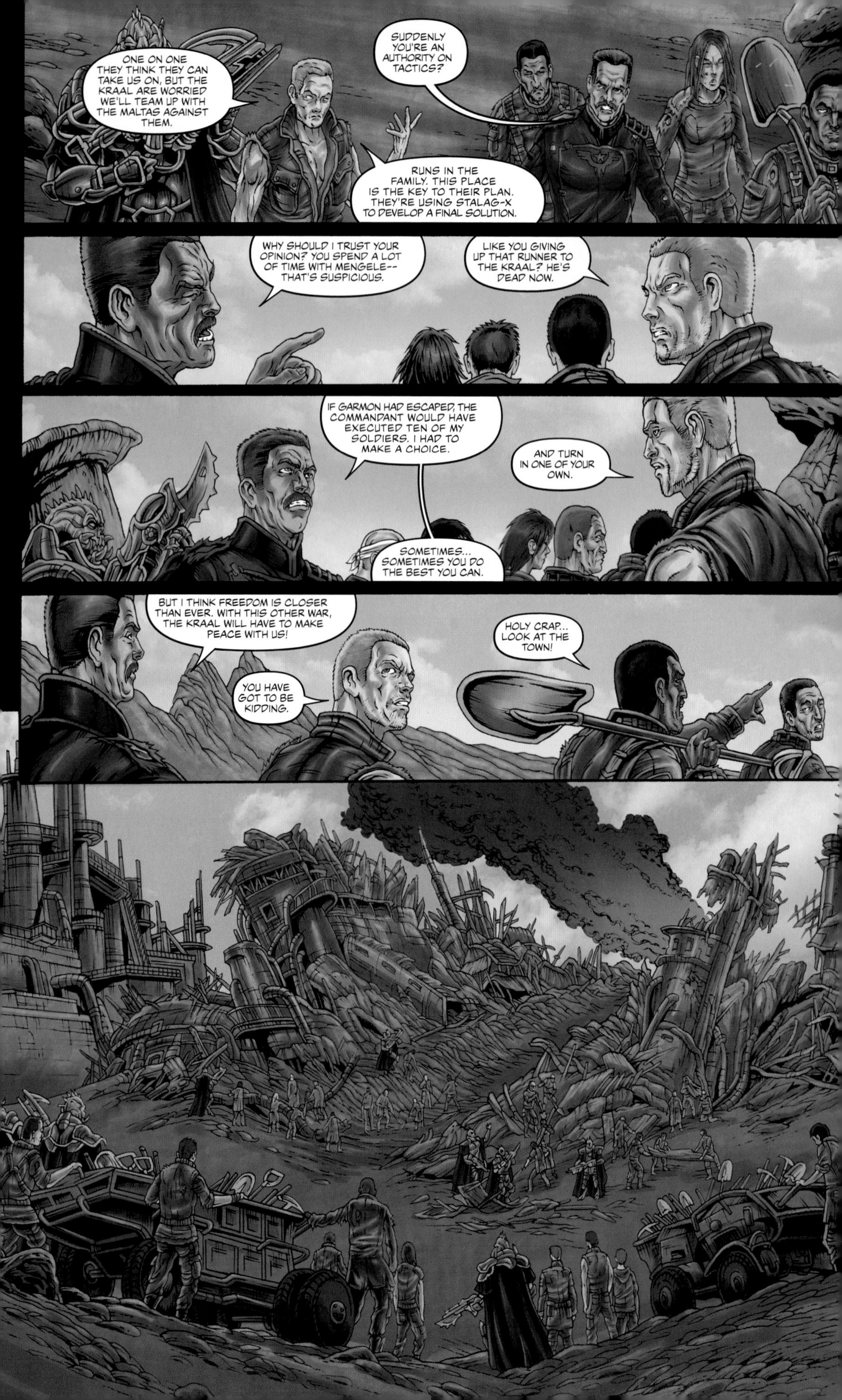
ONE ON ONE THEY THINK THEY CAN TAKE US ON, BUT THE KRAAL ARE WORRIED WE'LL TEAM UP WITH THE MALTAS AGAINST THEM.
SUDDENLY YOU'RE AN AUTHORITY ON TACTICS?
RUNS IN THE FAMILY. THIS PLACE IS THE KEY TO THEIR PLAN. THEY'RE USING STALAG-X TO DEVELOP A FINAL SOLUTION.
WHY SHOULD I TRUST YOUR OPINION? YOU SPEND A LOT OF TIME WITH MENGELE-- THAT'S SUSPICIOUS.
LIKE YOU GIVING UP THAT RUNNER TO THE KRAAL? HE'S DEAD NOW.
IF GARMON HAD ESCAPED, THE COMMANDANT WOULD HAVE EXECUTED TEN OF MY SOLDIERS. I HAD TO MAKE A CHOICE.
AND TURN IN ONE OF YOUR OWN.
SOMETIMES... SOMETIMES YOU DO THE BEST YOU CAN.
BUT I THINK FREEDOM IS CLOSER THAN EVER. WITH THIS OTHER WAR, THE KRAAL WILL HAVE TO MAKE PEACE WITH US!
YOU HAVE GOT TO BE KIDDING.
HOLY CRAP... LOOK AT THE TOWN!

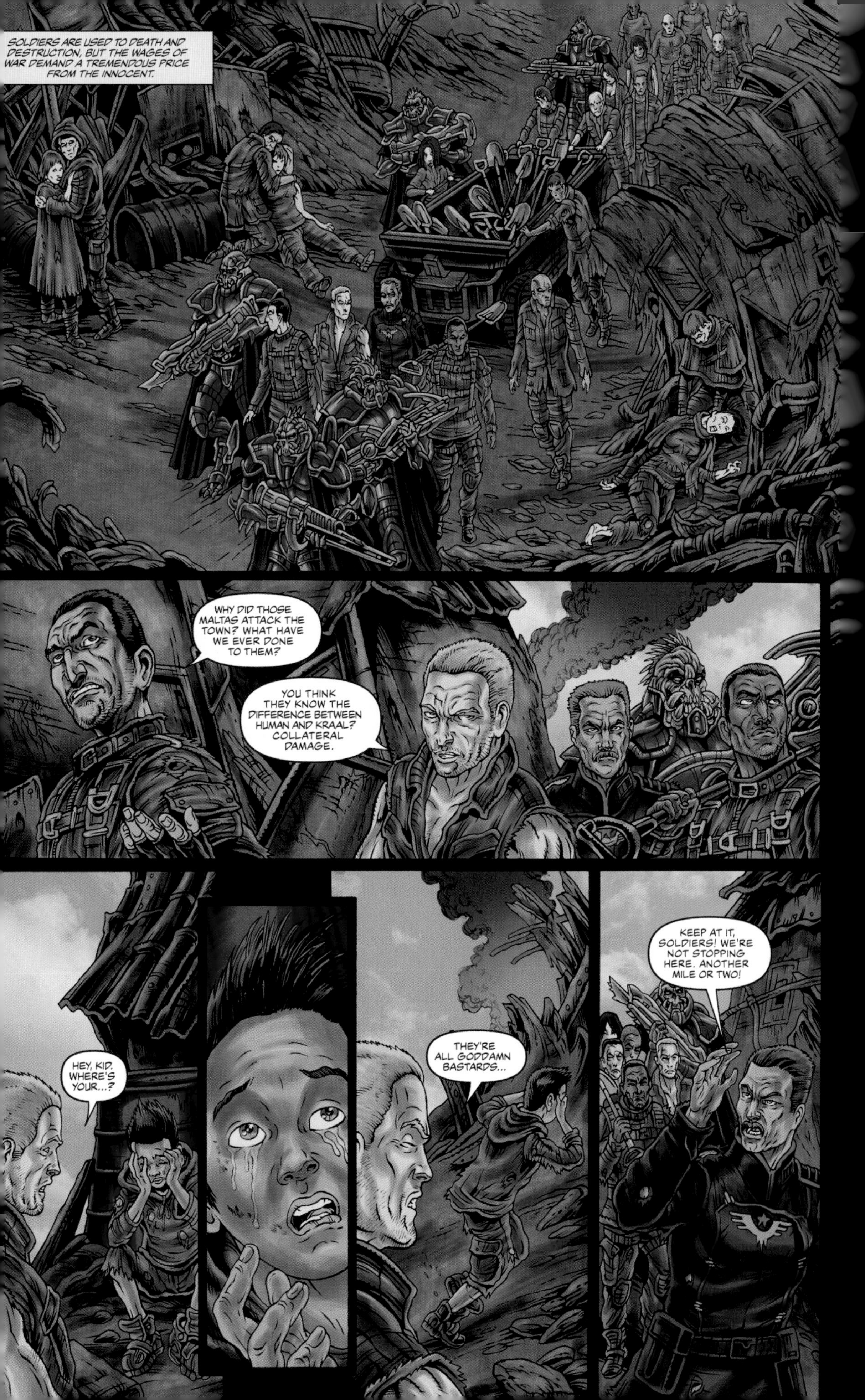
SOLDIERS ARE USED TO DEATH AND DESTRUCTION, BUT THE WAGES OF WAR DEMAND A TREMENDOUS PRICE FROM THE INNOCENT.
WHY DID THOSE MALTAS ATTACK THE TOWN? WHAT HAVE WE EVER DONE TO THEM?
YOU THINK THEY KNOW THE DIFFERENCE BETWEEN HUMAN AND KRAAL? COLLATERAL DAMAGE.
HEY, KID. WHERE'S YOUR...?
THEY'RE ALL GODDAMN BASTARDS...
KEEP AT IT, SOLDIERS! WE'RE NOT STOPPING HERE. ANOTHER MILE OR TWO!

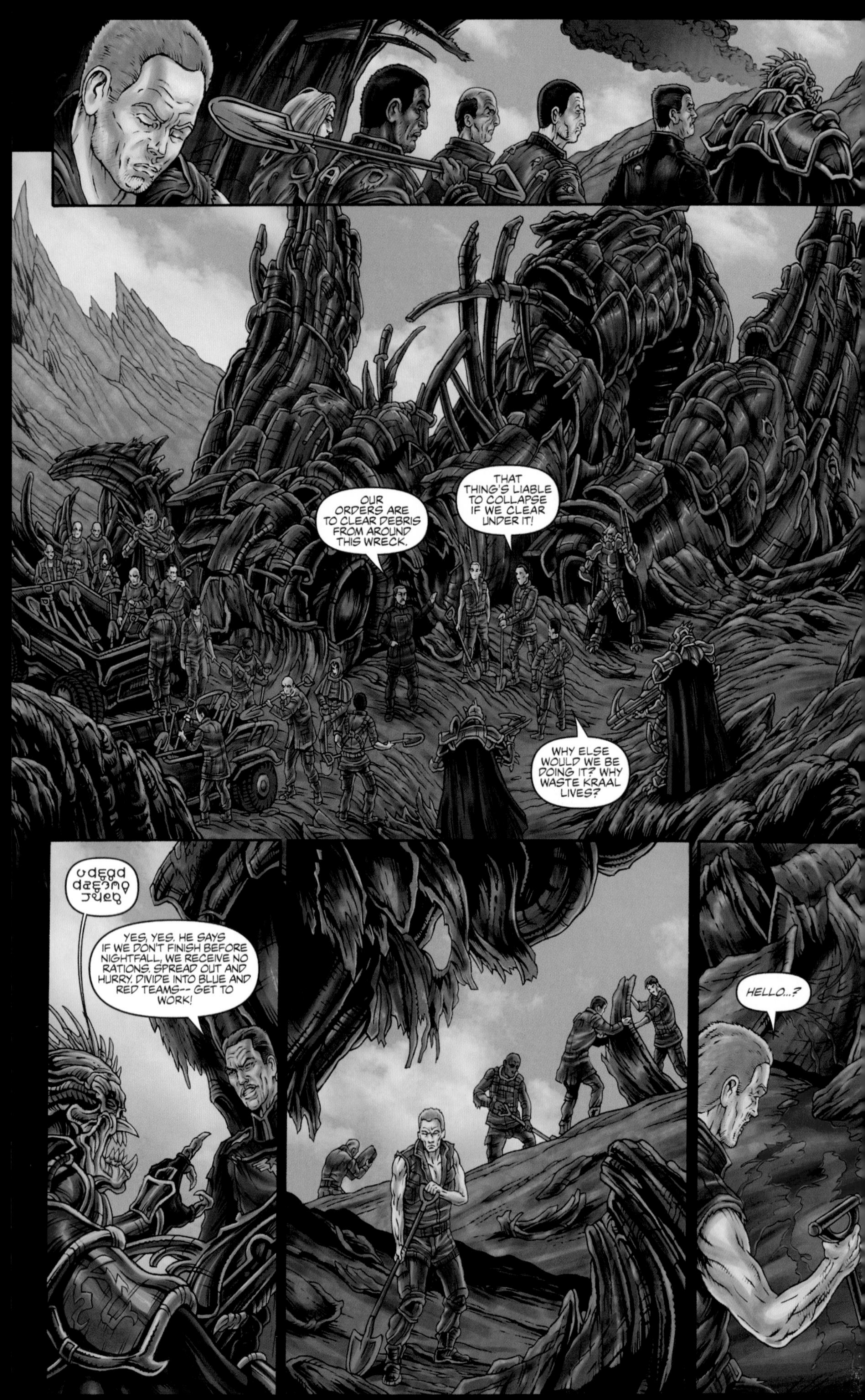
OUR ORDERS ARE TO CLEAR DEBRIS FROM AROUND THIS WRECK.
THAT THING'S LIABLE TO COLLAPSE IF WE CLEAR UNDER IT!
WHY ELSE WOULD WE BE DOING IT? WHY WASTE KRAAL LIVES?
YES, YES. HE SAYS IF WE DON'T FINISH BEFORE NIGHTFALL, WE RECEIVE NO RATIONS. SPREAD OUT AND HURRY. DIVIDE INTO BLUE AND RED TEAMS-- GET TO WORK!
HELLO...?

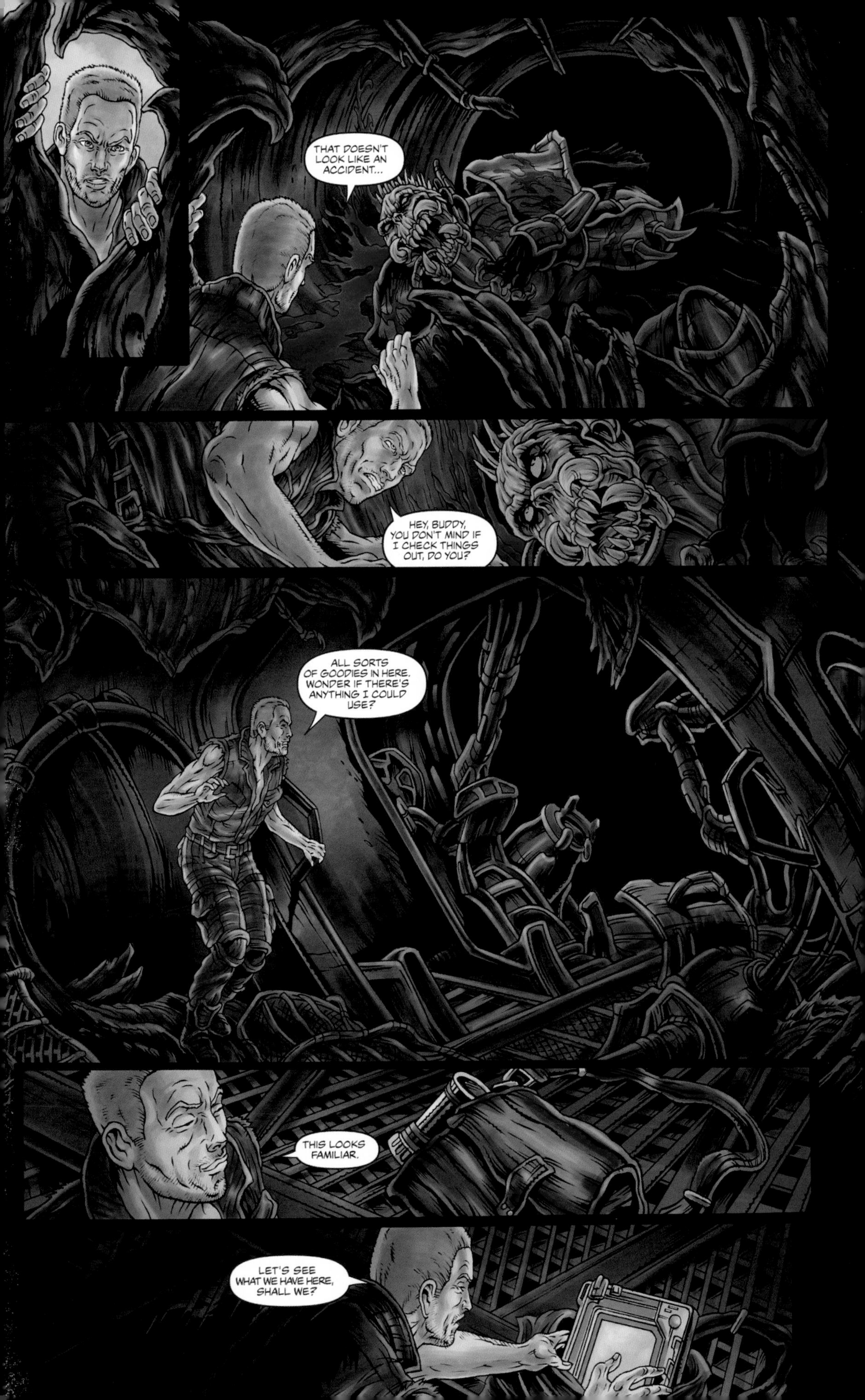
THAT DOESN'T LOOK LIKE AN ACCIDENT...
HEY, BUDDY, YOU DON'T MIND IF I CHECK THINGS OUT, DO YOU?
ALL SORTS OF GOODIES IN HERE. WONDER IF THERE'S ANYTHING I COULD USE?
THIS LOOKS FAMILIAR.
LET'S SEE WHAT WE HAVE HERE, SHALL WE?

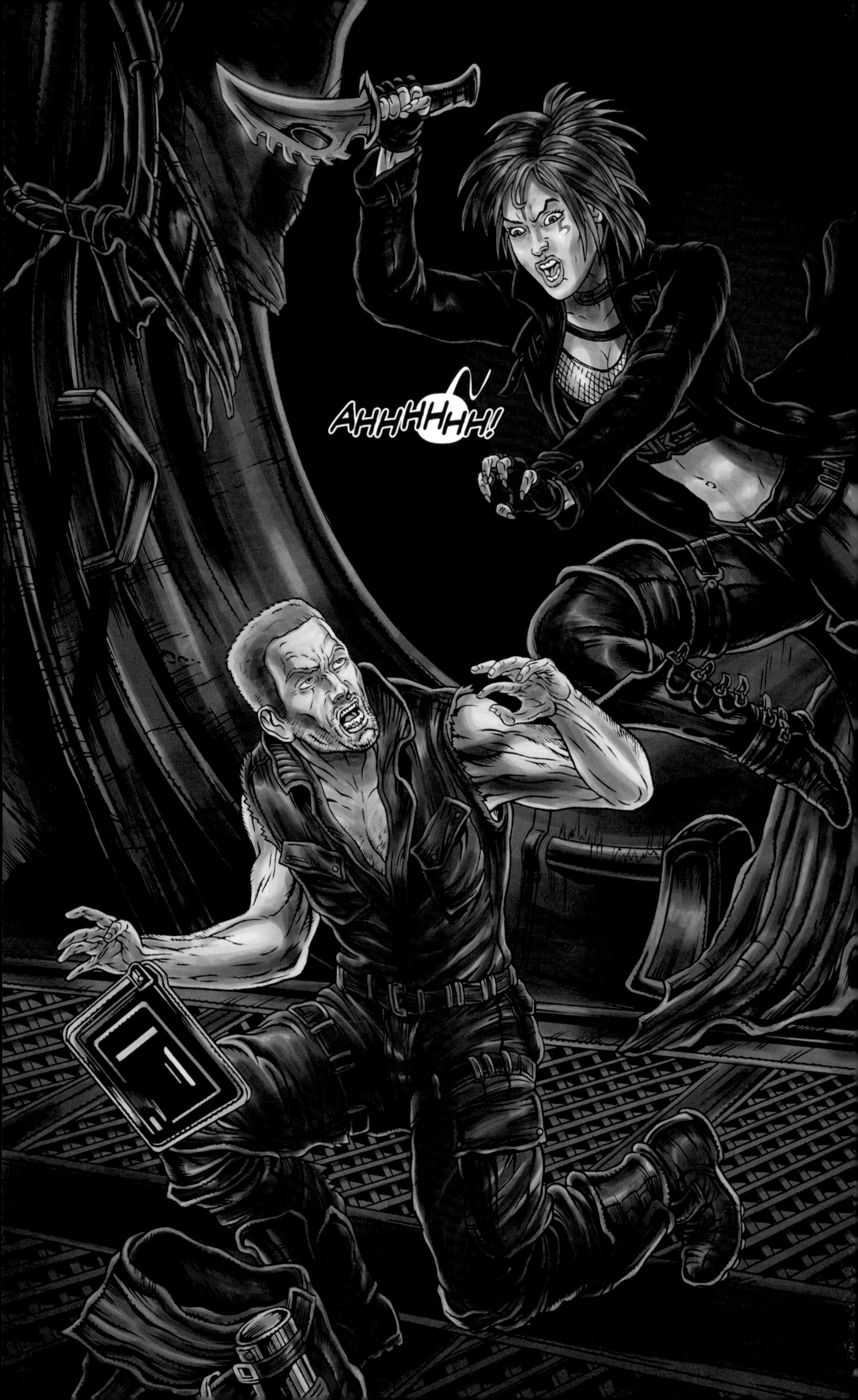
AHHHHHH!

CHAPTER

V

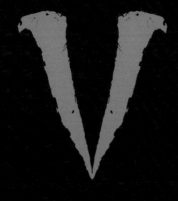

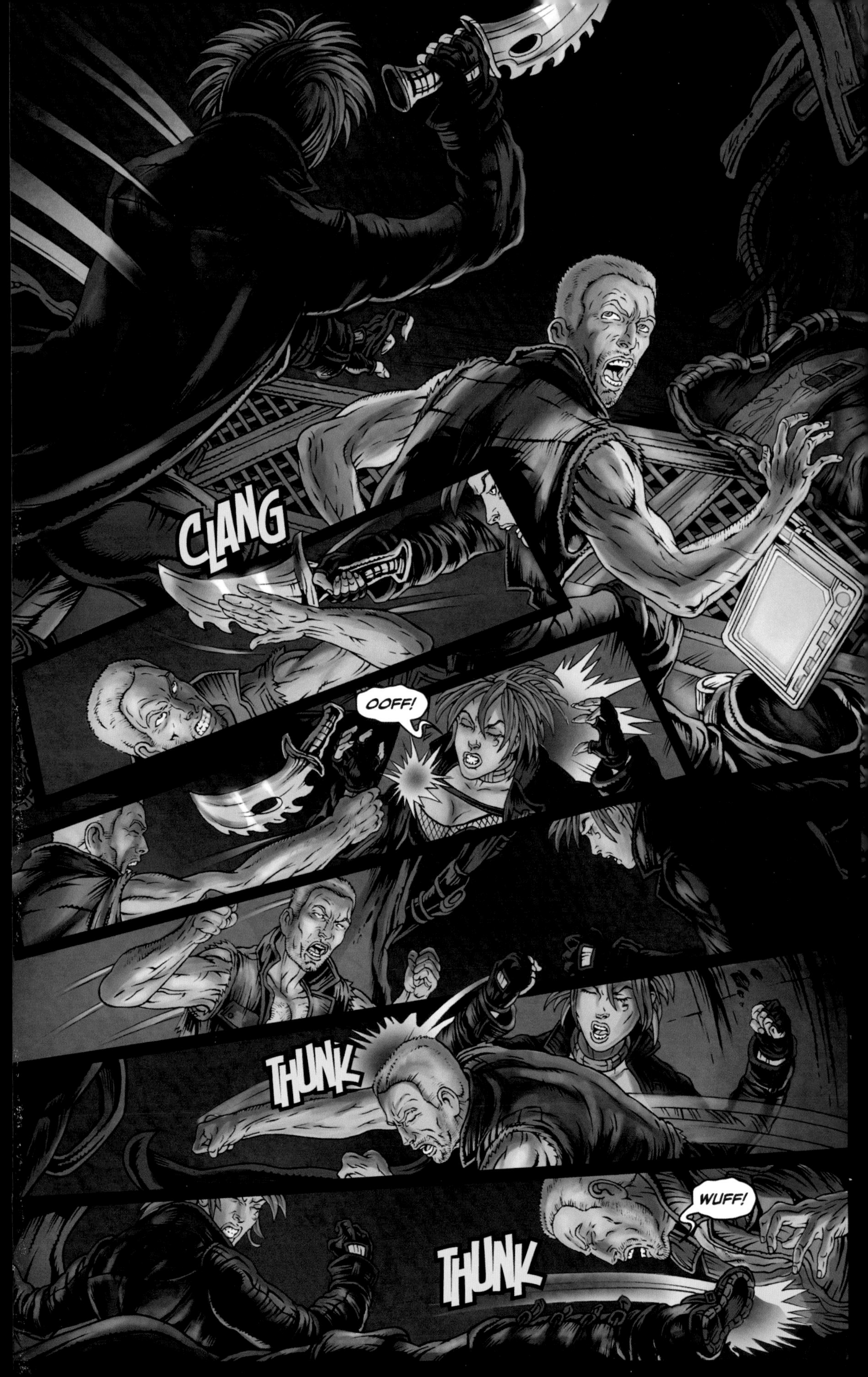
CLANG
OOFF!
THUNK
WUFF!
THUNK

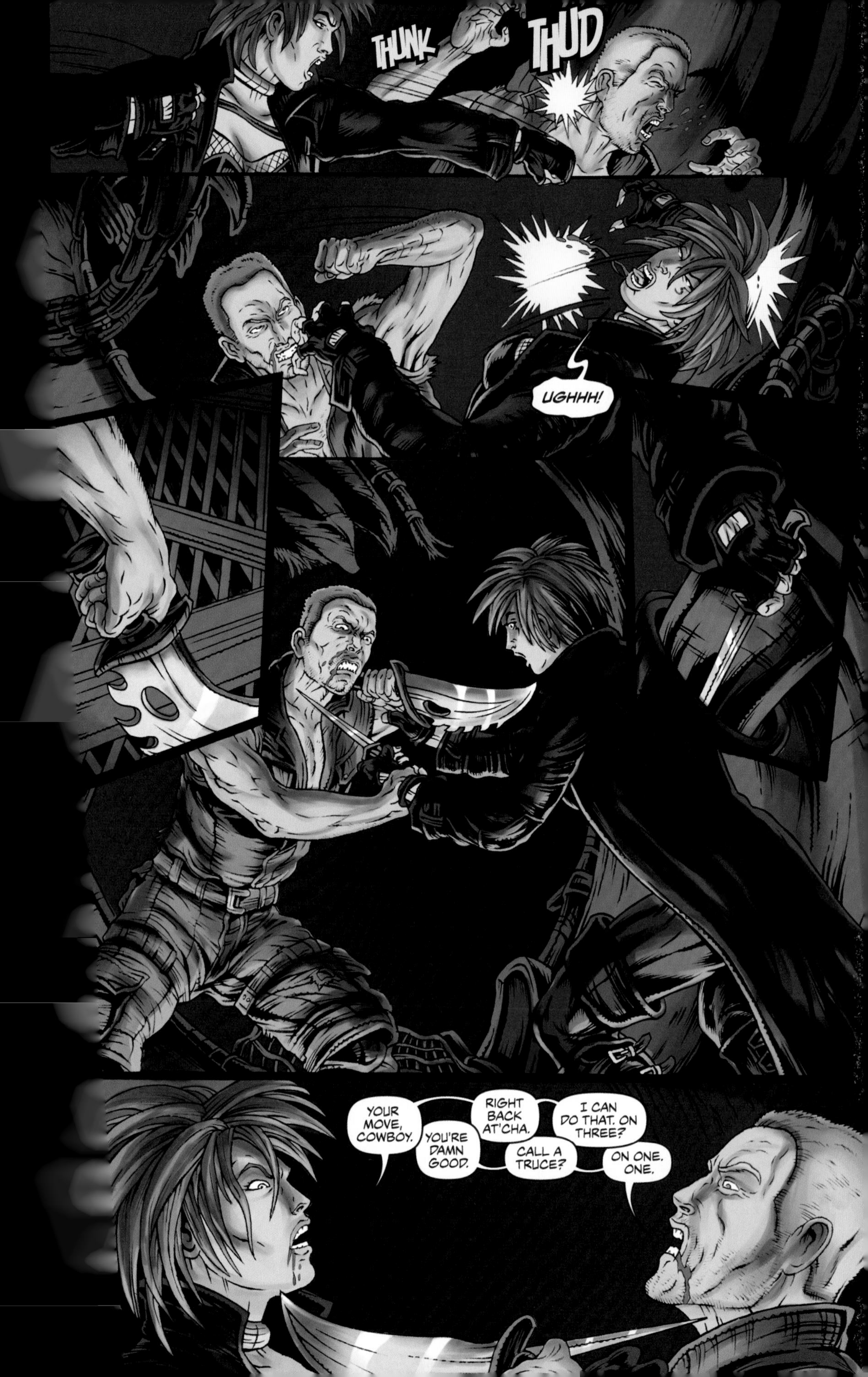
THUNK
THUD
UGHHH!
YOUR MOVE, COWBOY.
YOU'RE DAMN GOOD.
RIGHT BACK AT'CHA.
CALL A TRUCE?
I CAN DO THAT. ON THREE?
ON ONE. ONE.

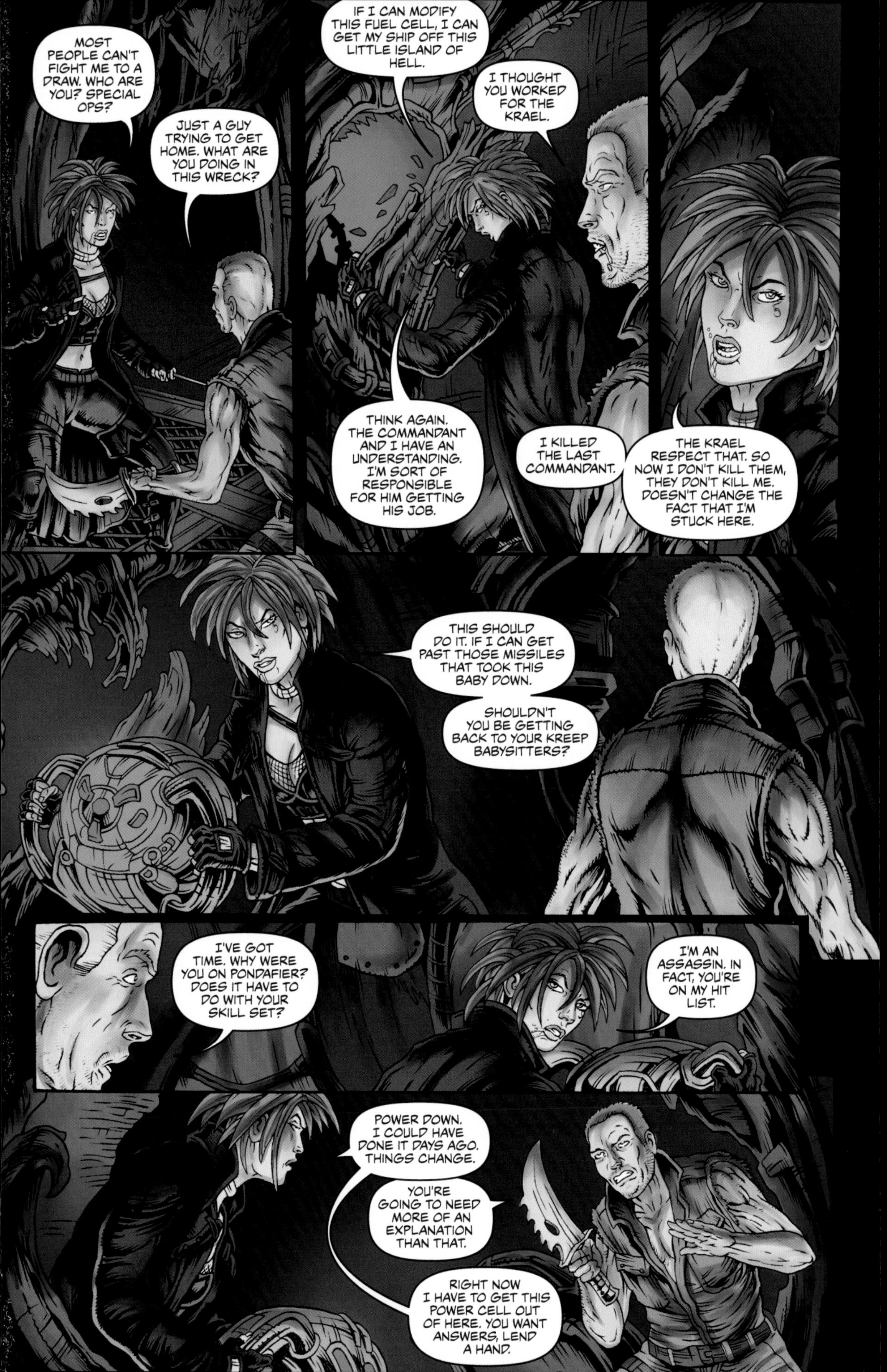
MOST PEOPLE CAN'T FIGHT ME TO A DRAW. WHO ARE YOU? SPECIAL OPS?
JUST A GUY TRYING TO GET HOME. WHAT ARE YOU DOING IN THIS WRECK?
IF I CAN MODIFY THIS FUEL CELL, I CAN GET MY SHIP OFF THIS LITTLE ISLAND OF HELL.
I THOUGHT YOU WORKED FOR THE KRAEL.
THINK AGAIN. THE COMMANDANT AND I HAVE AN UNDERSTANDING. I'M SORT OF RESPONSIBLE FOR HIM GETTING HIS JOB.
I KILLED THE LAST COMMANDANT.
THE KRAEL RESPECT THAT. SO NOW I DON'T KILL THEM, THEY DON'T KILL ME. DOESN'T CHANGE THE FACT THAT I'M STUCK HERE.
THIS SHOULD DO IT. IF I CAN GET PAST THOSE MISSILES THAT TOOK THIS BABY DOWN.
SHOULDN'T YOU BE GETTING BACK TO YOUR KREEP BABYSITTERS?
I'VE GOT TIME. WHY WERE YOU ON PONDAFIER? DOES IT HAVE TO DO WITH YOUR SKILL SET?
I'M AN ASSASSIN. IN FACT, YOU'RE ON MY HIT LIST.
POWER DOWN. I COULD HAVE DONE IT DAYS AGO. THINGS CHANGE.
YOU'RE GOING TO NEED MORE OF AN EXPLANATION THAN THAT.
RIGHT NOW I HAVE TO GET THIS POWER CELL OUT OF HERE. YOU WANT ANSWERS, LEND A HAND.

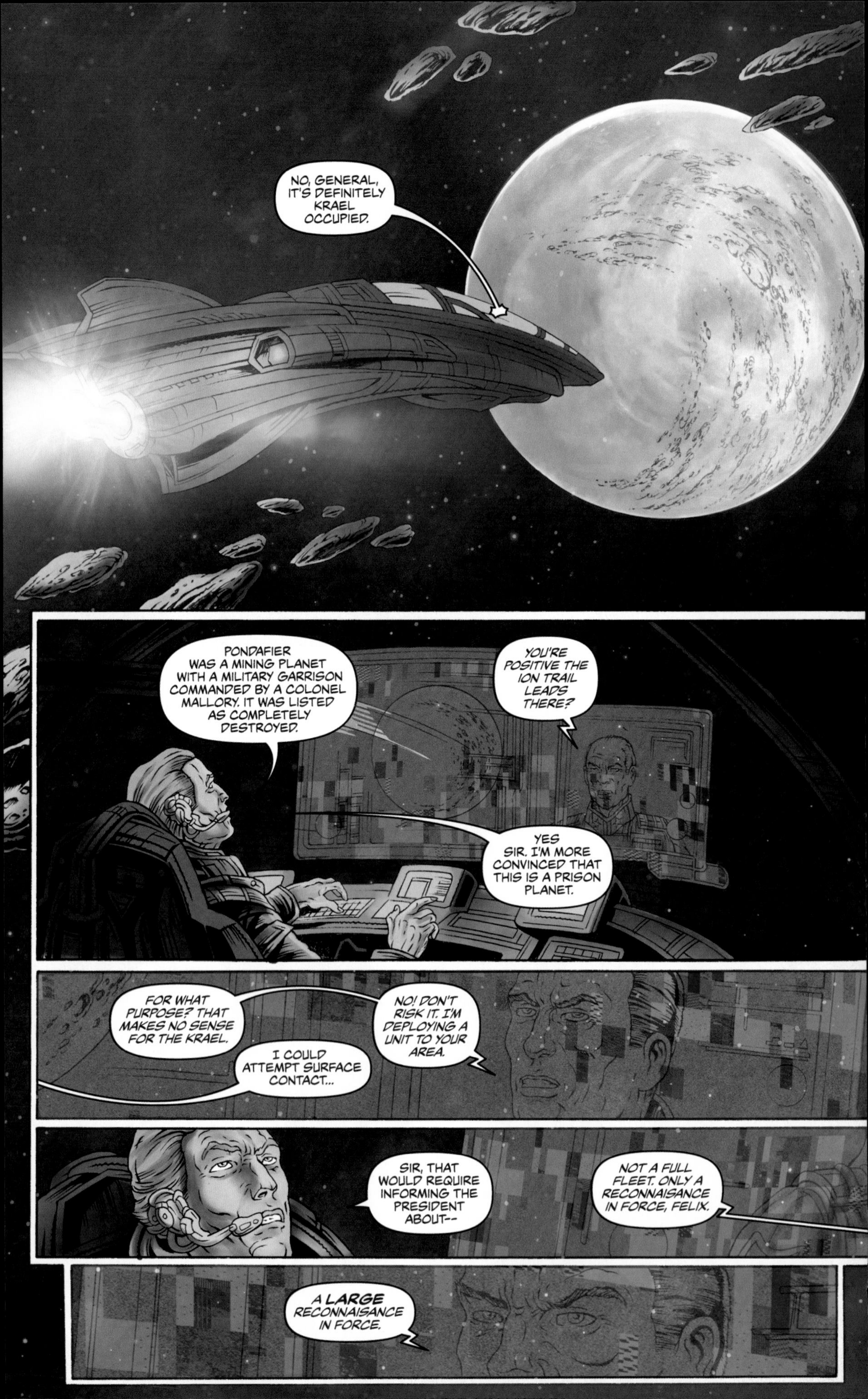

NO, GENERAL, IT'S DEFINITELY KRAEL OCCUPIED.
PONDAFIER WAS A MINING PLANET WITH A MILITARY GARRISON COMMANDED BY A COLONEL MALLORY. IT WAS LISTED AS COMPLETELY DESTROYED.
YOU'RE POSITIVE THE ION TRAIL LEADS THERE?
YES SIR. I'M MORE CONVINCED THAT THIS IS A PRISON PLANET.
FOR WHAT PURPOSE? THAT MAKES NO SENSE FOR THE KRAEL.
I COULD ATTEMPT SURFACE CONTACT...
NO! DON'T RISK IT. I'M DEPLOYING A UNIT TO YOUR AREA.
SIR, THAT WOULD REQUIRE INFORMING THE PRESIDENT ABOUT--
NOT A FULL FLEET. ONLY A RECONNAISANCE IN FORCE, FELIX.
A LARGE RECONNAISANCE IN FORCE.

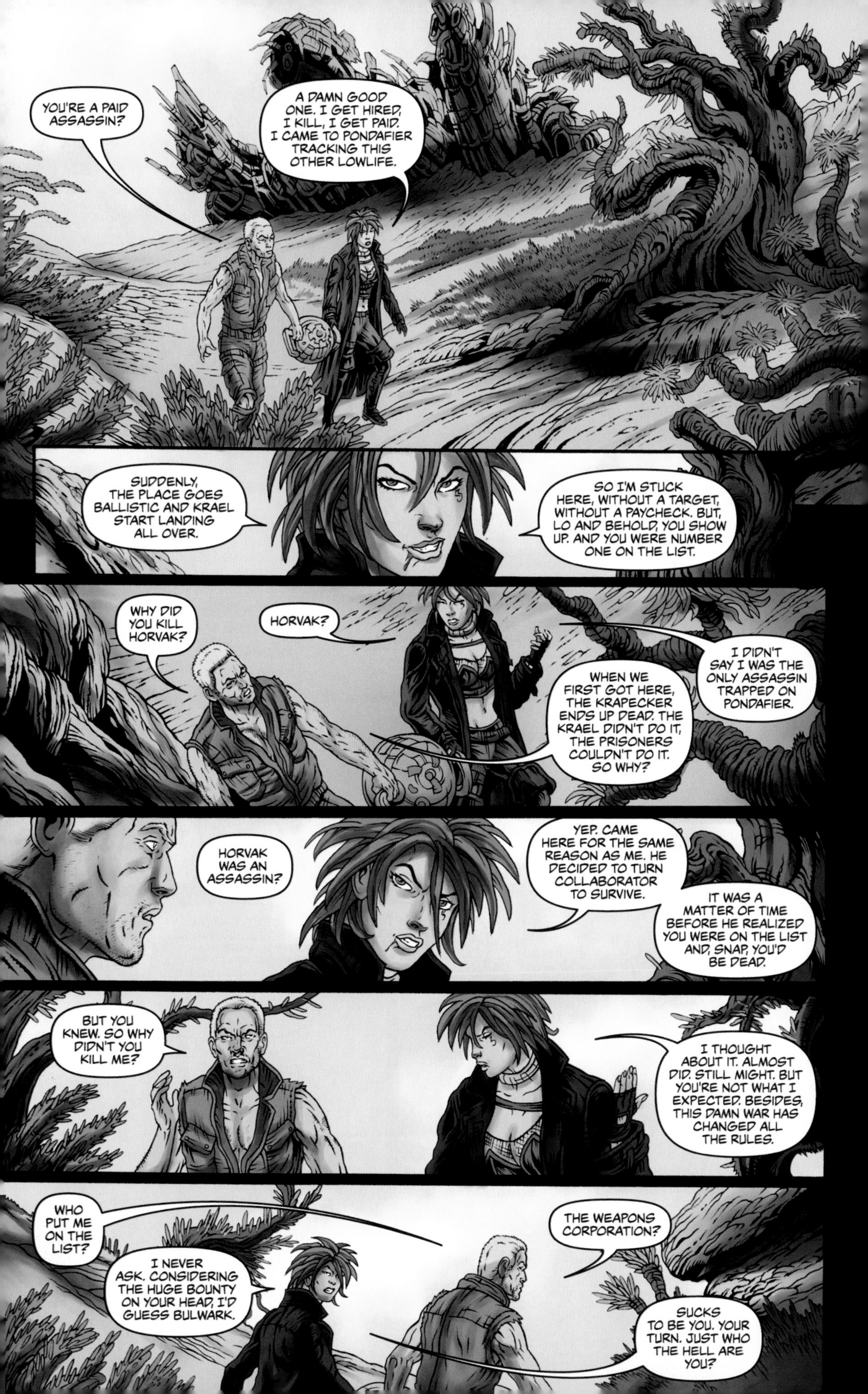
YOU'RE A PAID ASSASSIN?
A DAMN GOOD ONE. I GET HIRED, I KILL, I GET PAID. I CAME TO PONDAFIER TRACKING THIS OTHER LOWLIFE.
SUDDENLY, THE PLACE GOES BALLISTIC AND KRAEL START LANDING ALL OVER.
SO I'M STUCK HERE, WITHOUT A TARGET, WITHOUT A PAYCHECK. BUT, LO AND BEHOLD, YOU SHOW UP. AND YOU WERE NUMBER ONE ON THE LIST.
WHY DID YOU KILL HORVAK?
HORVAK?
WHEN WE FIRST GOT HERE, THE KRAPECKER ENDS UP DEAD. THE KRAEL DIDN'T DO IT, THE PRISONERS COULDN'T DO IT. SO WHY?
I DIDN'T SAY I WAS THE ONLY ASSASSIN TRAPPED ON PONDAFIER.
HORVAK WAS AN ASSASSIN?
YEP. CAME HERE FOR THE SAME REASON AS ME. HE DECIDED TO TURN COLLABORATOR TO SURVIVE.
IT WAS A MATTER OF TIME BEFORE HE REALIZED YOU WERE ON THE LIST AND, SNAP, YOU'D BE DEAD.
BUT YOU KNEW. SO WHY DIDN'T YOU KILL ME?
I THOUGHT ABOUT IT. ALMOST DID. STILL MIGHT. BUT YOU'RE NOT WHAT I EXPECTED. BESIDES, THIS DAMN WAR HAS CHANGED ALL THE RULES.
WHO PUT ME ON THE LIST?
I NEVER ASK. CONSIDERING THE HUGE BOUNTY ON YOUR HEAD, I'D GUESS BULWARK.
THE WEAPONS CORPORATION?
SUCKS TO BE YOU. YOUR TURN. JUST WHO THE HELL ARE YOU?

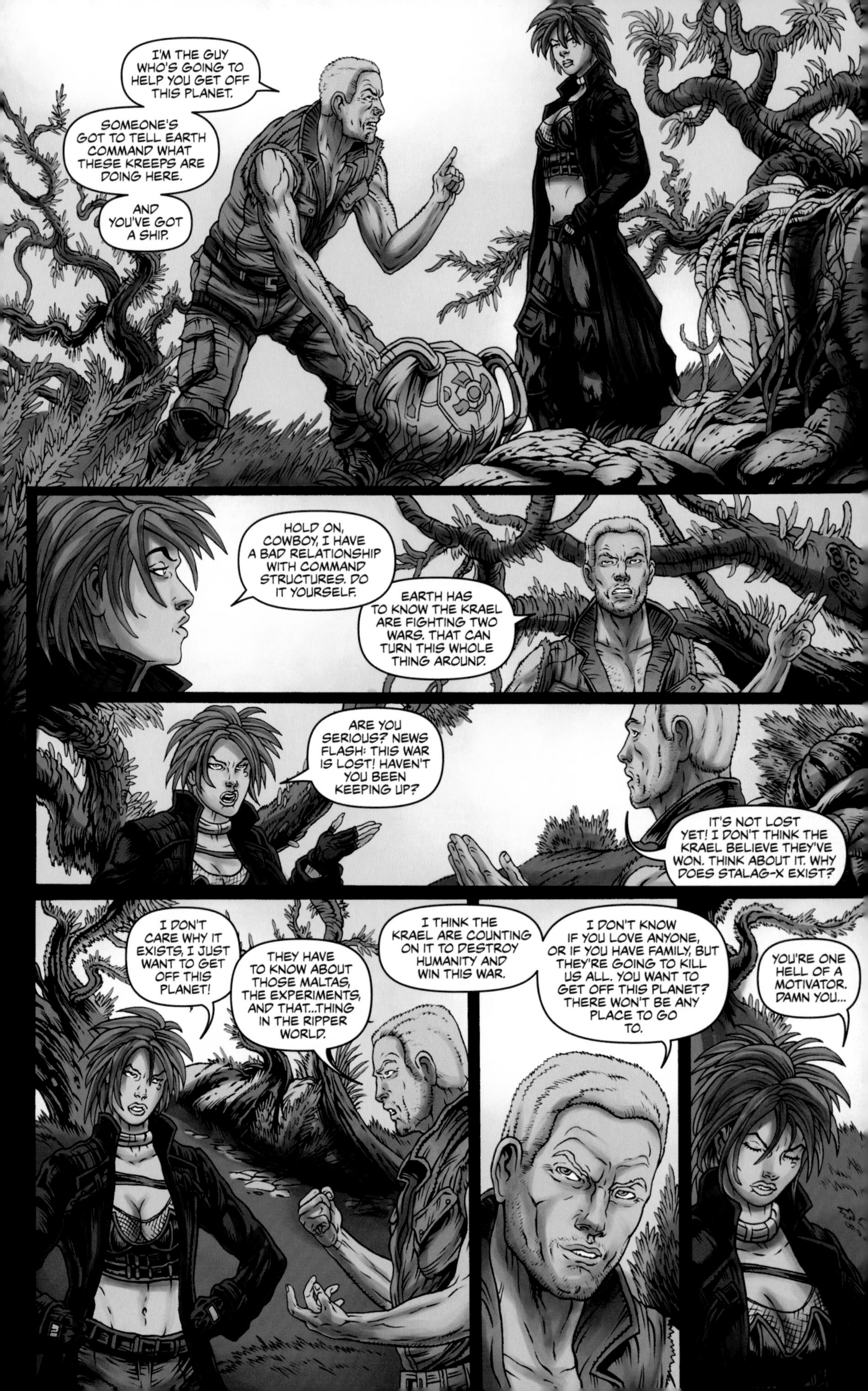
I'M THE GUY WHO'S GOING TO HELP YOU GET OFF THIS PLANET.
SOMEONE'S GOT TO TELL EARTH COMMAND WHAT THESE KREEPS ARE DOING HERE.
AND YOU'VE GOT A SHIP.
HOLD ON, COWBOY, I HAVE A BAD RELATIONSHIP WITH COMMAND STRUCTURES. DO IT YOURSELF.
EARTH HAS TO KNOW THE KRAEL ARE FIGHTING TWO WARS. THAT CAN TURN THIS WHOLE THING AROUND.
ARE YOU SERIOUS? NEWS FLASH: THIS WAR IS LOST! HAVEN'T YOU BEEN KEEPING UP?
IT'S NOT LOST YET! I DON'T THINK THE KRAEL BELIEVE THEY'VE WON. THINK ABOUT IT. WHY DOES STALAG-X EXIST?
I DON'T CARE WHY IT EXISTS, I JUST WANT TO GET OFF THIS PLANET!
THEY HAVE TO KNOW ABOUT THOSE MALTAS, THE EXPERIMENTS, AND THAT...THING IN THE RIPPER WORLD.
I THINK THE KRAEL ARE COUNTING ON IT TO DESTROY HUMANITY AND WIN THIS WAR.
I DON'T KNOW IF YOU LOVE ANYONE, OR IF YOU HAVE FAMILY, BUT THEY'RE GOING TO KILL US ALL. YOU WANT TO GET OFF THIS PLANET? THERE WON'T BE ANY PLACE TO GO TO.
YOU'RE ONE HELL OF A MOTIVATOR. DAMN YOU...

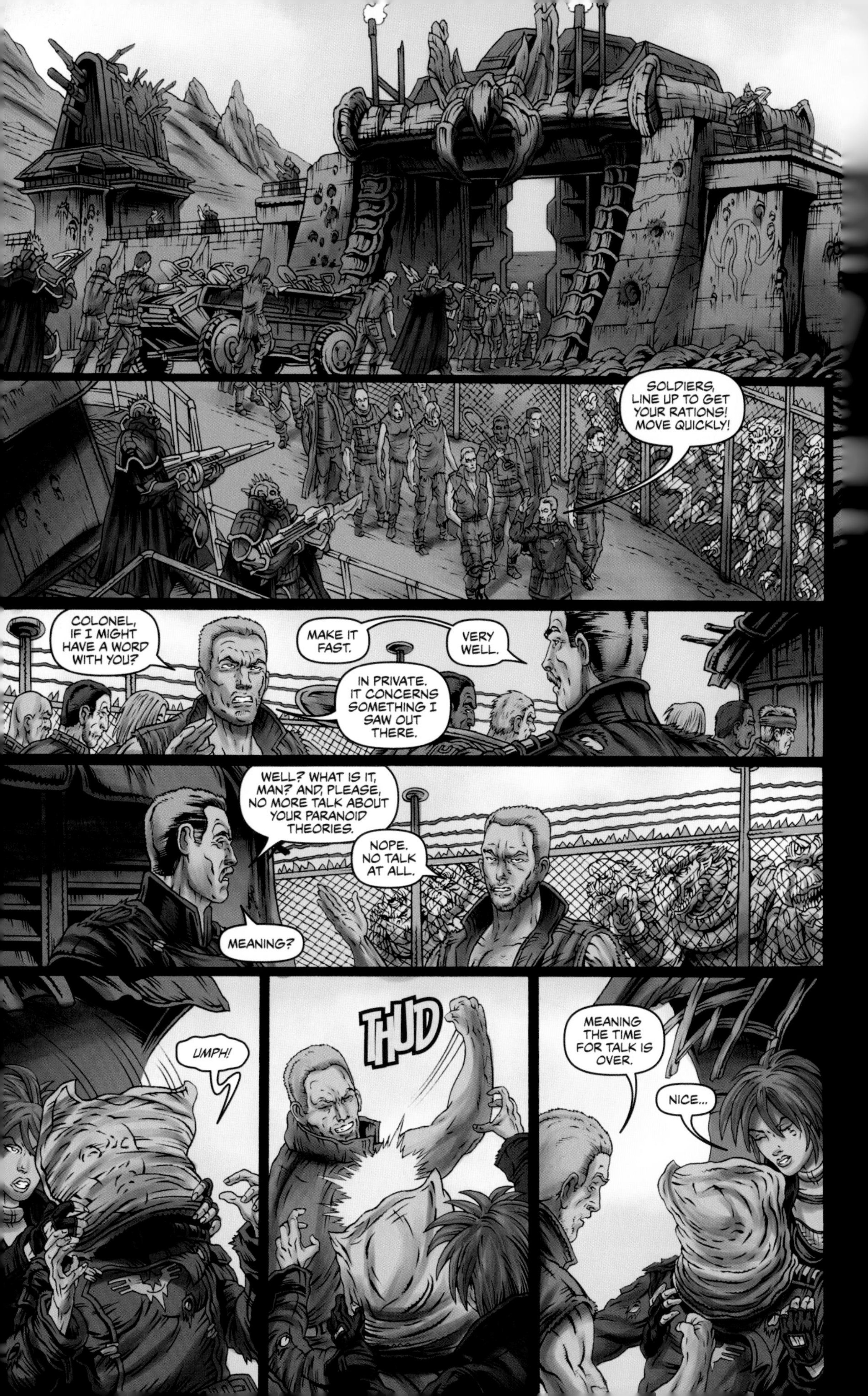
SOLDIERS, LINE UP TO GET YOUR RATIONS! MOVE QUICKLY!
COLONEL, IF I MIGHT HAVE A WORD WITH YOU?
MAKE IT FAST.
VERY WELL.
IN PRIVATE. IT CONCERNS SOMETHING I SAW OUT THERE.
WELL? WHAT IS IT, MAN? AND, PLEASE, NO MORE TALK ABOUT YOUR PARANOID THEORIES.
NOPE. NO TALK AT ALL.
MEANING?
UMPH!
THUD
MEANING THE TIME FOR TALK IS OVER.
NICE...

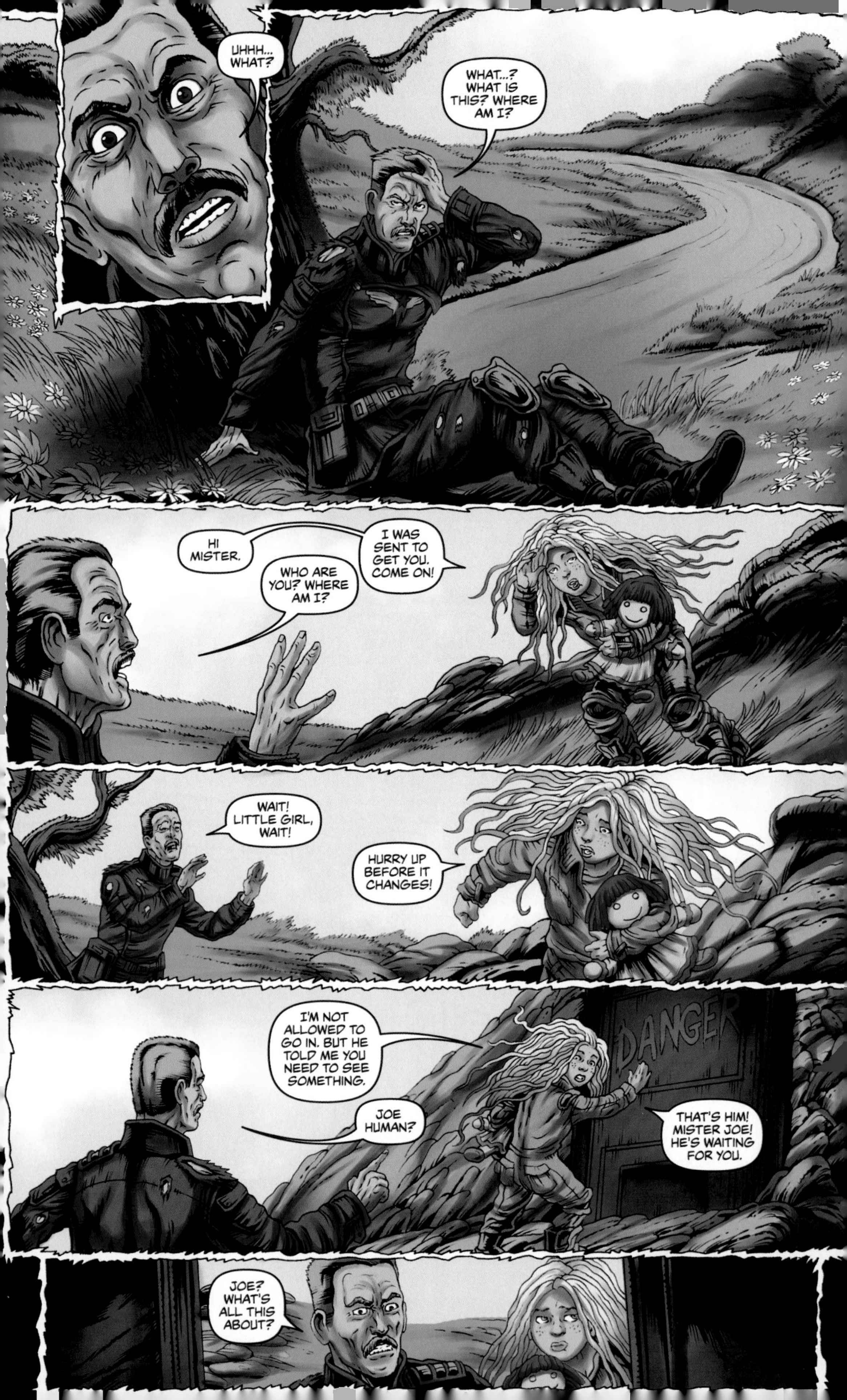
UHHH... WHAT?
WHAT...? WHAT IS THIS? WHERE AM I?
HI MISTER.
I WAS SENT TO GET YOU. COME ON!
WHO ARE YOU? WHERE AM I?
WAIT! LITTLE GIRL, WAIT!
HURRY UP BEFORE IT CHANGES!
I'M NOT ALLOWED TO GO IN. BUT HE TOLD ME YOU NEED TO SEE SOMETHING.
JOE HUMAN?
THAT'S HIM! MISTER JOE! HE'S WAITING FOR YOU.
DANGER
JOE? WHAT'S ALL THIS ABOUT?

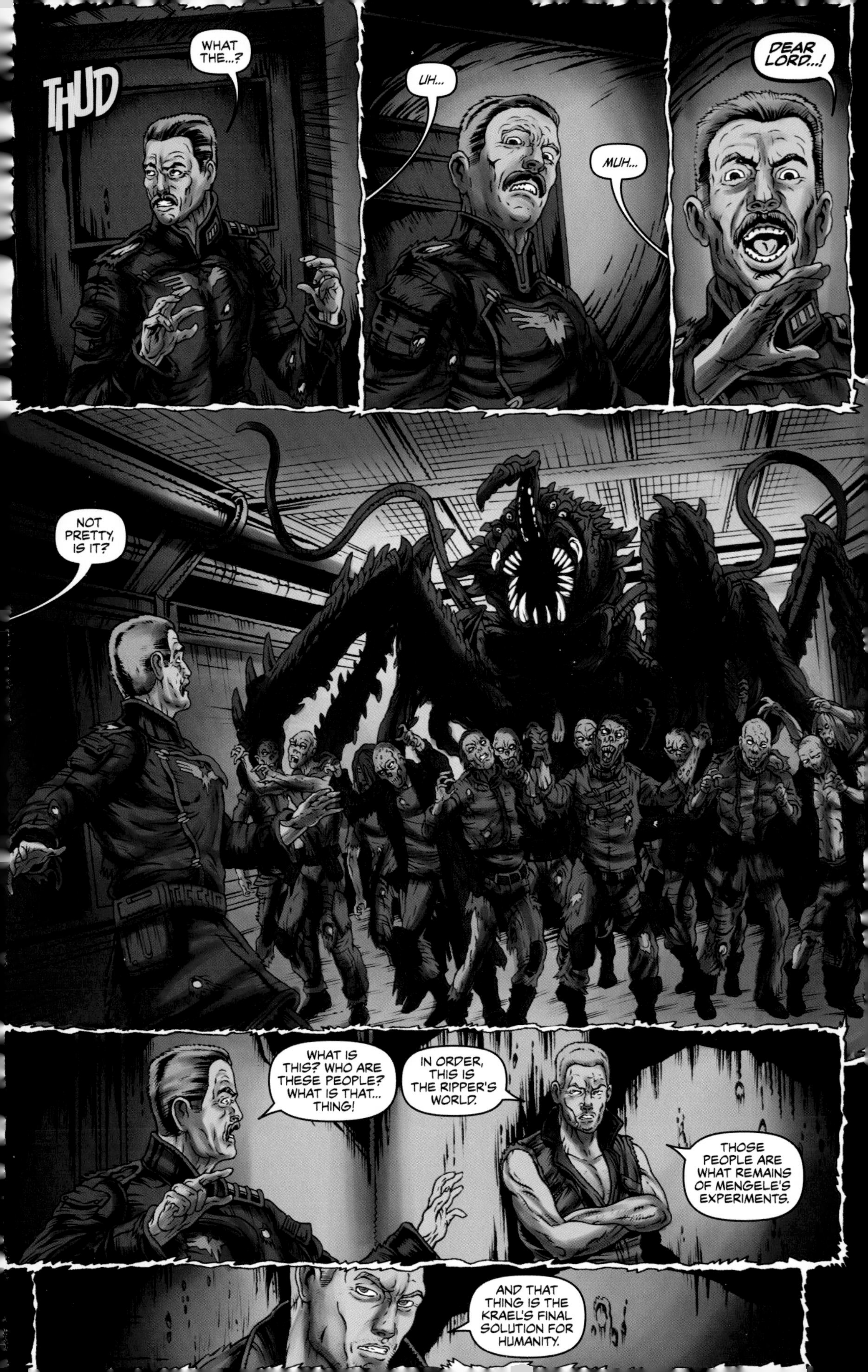
THUD
WHAT THE...?
UH...
MUH...
DEAR LORD...!
NOT PRETTY, IS IT?
WHAT IS THIS? WHO ARE THESE PEOPLE? WHAT IS THAT... THING!
IN ORDER, THIS IS THE RIPPER'S WORLD.
THOSE PEOPLE ARE WHAT REMAINS OF MENGELE'S EXPERIMENTS.
AND THAT THING IS THE KRAEL'S FINAL SOLUTION FOR HUMANITY.

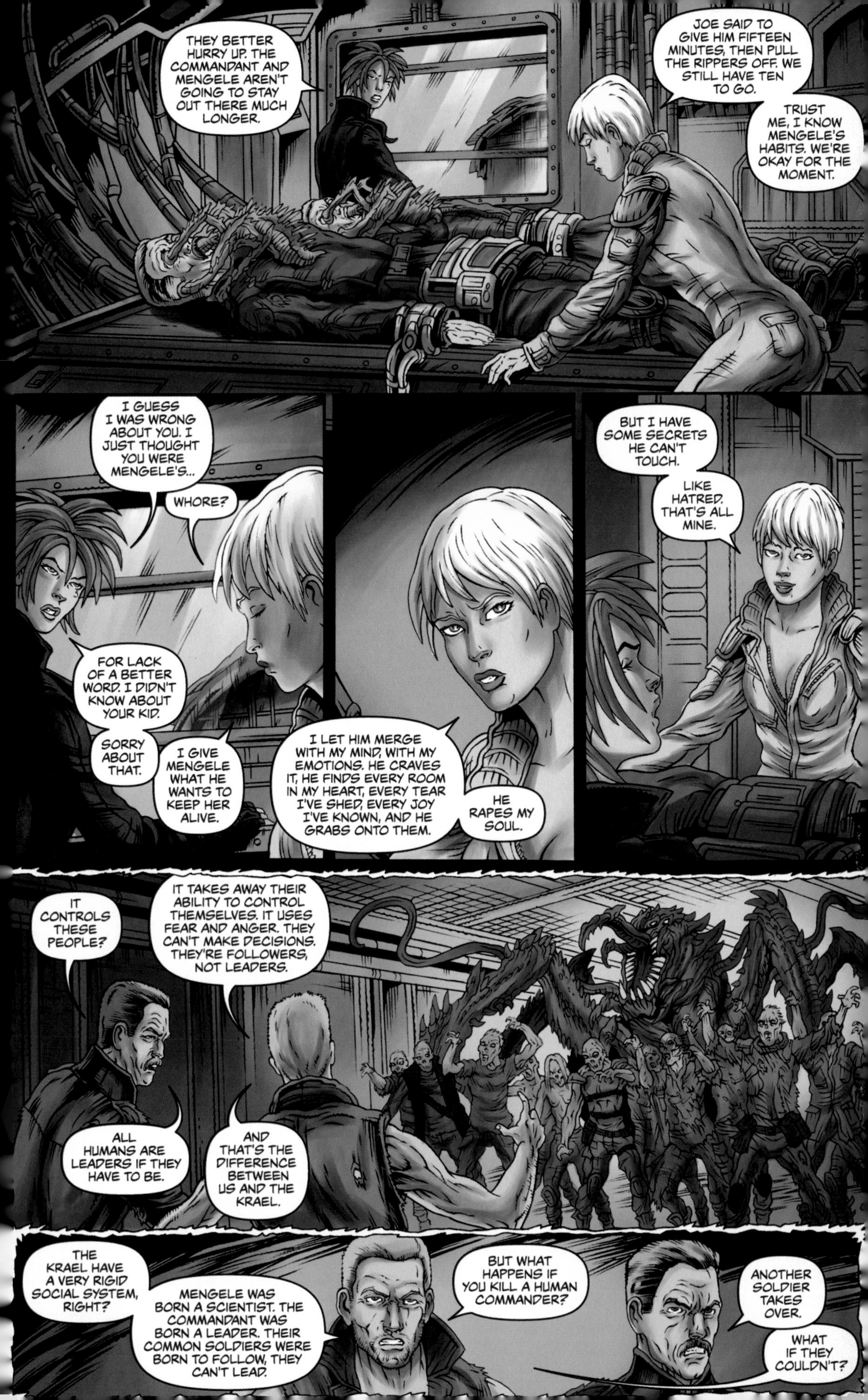
THEY BETTER HURRY UP. THE COMMANDANT AND MENGELE AREN'T GOING TO STAY OUT THERE MUCH LONGER.
JOE SAID TO GIVE HIM FIFTEEN MINUTES, THEN PULL THE RIPPERS OFF. WE STILL HAVE TEN TO GO.
TRUST ME, I KNOW MENGELE'S HABITS. WE'RE OKAY FOR THE MOMENT.
I GUESS I WAS WRONG ABOUT YOU. I JUST THOUGHT YOU WERE MENGELE'S...
WHORE?
FOR LACK OF A BETTER WORD. I DIDN'T KNOW ABOUT YOUR KID.
SORRY ABOUT THAT.
I GIVE MENGELE WHAT HE WANTS TO KEEP HER ALIVE.
I LET HIM MERGE WITH MY MIND, WITH MY EMOTIONS. HE CRAVES IT, HE FINDS EVERY ROOM IN MY HEART, EVERY TEAR I'VE SHED, EVERY JOY I'VE KNOWN, AND HE GRABS ONTO THEM.
HE RAPES MY SOUL.
BUT I HAVE SOME SECRETS HE CAN'T TOUCH.
LIKE HATRED. THAT'S ALL MINE.
IT CONTROLS THESE PEOPLE?
IT TAKES AWAY THEIR ABILITY TO CONTROL THEMSELVES. IT USES FEAR AND ANGER. THEY CAN'T MAKE DECISIONS. THEY'RE FOLLOWERS, NOT LEADERS.
ALL HUMANS ARE LEADERS IF THEY HAVE TO BE.
AND THAT'S THE DIFFERENCE BETWEEN US AND THE KRAEL.
THE KRAEL HAVE A VERY RIGID SOCIAL SYSTEM, RIGHT?
MENGELE WAS BORN A SCIENTIST. THE COMMANDANT WAS BORN A LEADER. THEIR COMMON SOLDIERS WERE BORN TO FOLLOW, THEY CAN'T LEAD.
BUT WHAT HAPPENS IF YOU KILL A HUMAN COMMANDER?
ANOTHER SOLDIER TAKES OVER.
WHAT IF THEY COULDN'T?

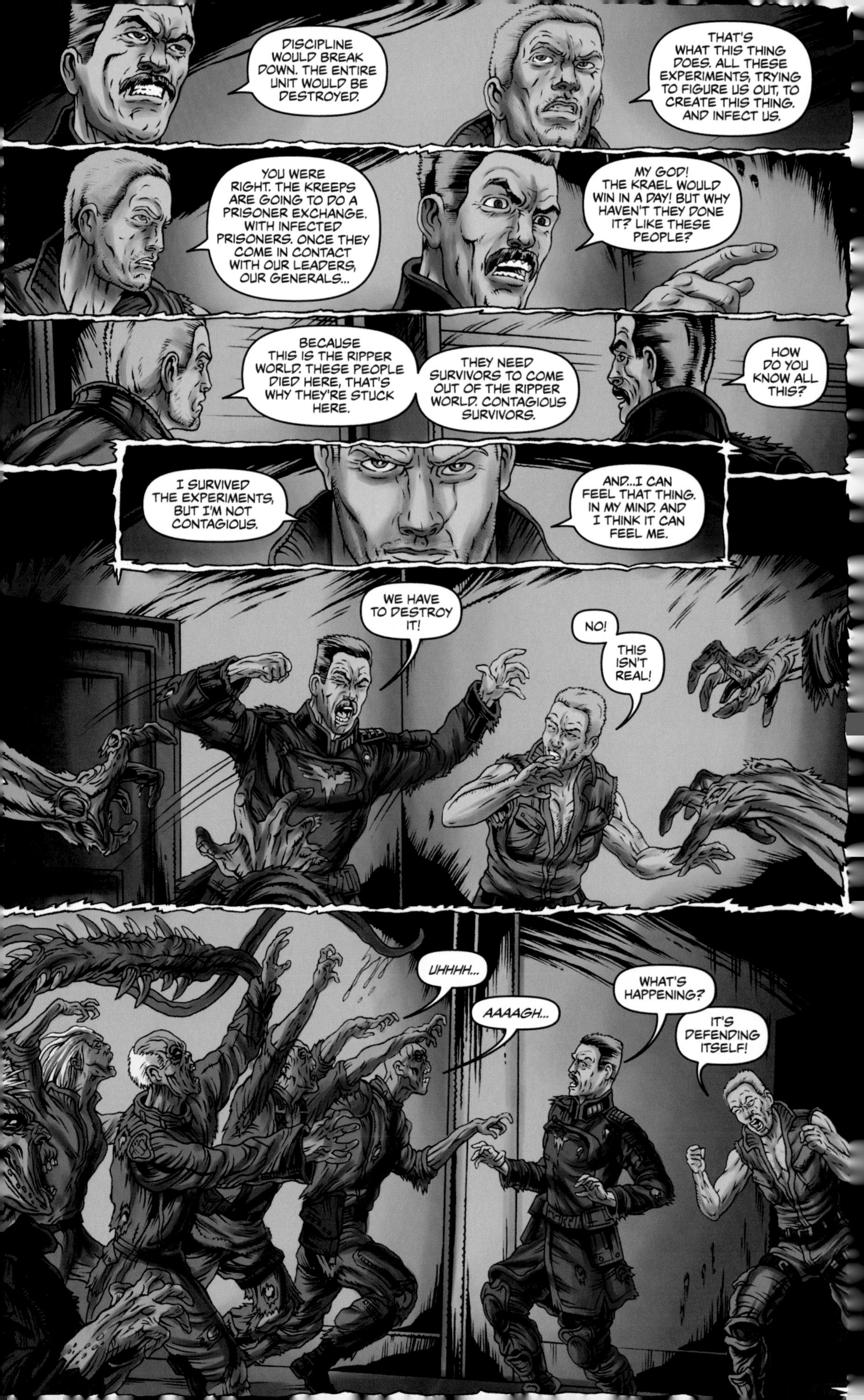
DISCIPLINE WOULD BREAK DOWN. THE ENTIRE UNIT WOULD BE DESTROYED.
THAT'S WHAT THIS THING DOES. ALL THESE EXPERIMENTS, TRYING TO FIGURE US OUT, TO CREATE THIS THING. AND INFECT US.
YOU WERE RIGHT. THE KREEPS ARE GOING TO DO A PRISONER EXCHANGE. WITH INFECTED PRISONERS. ONCE THEY COME IN CONTACT WITH OUR LEADERS, OUR GENERALS...
MY GOD! THE KRAEL WOULD WIN IN A DAY! BUT WHY HAVEN'T THEY DONE IT? LIKE THESE PEOPLE?
BECAUSE THIS IS THE RIPPER WORLD. THESE PEOPLE DIED HERE, THAT'S WHY THEY'RE STUCK HERE.
THEY NEED SURVIVORS TO COME OUT OF THE RIPPER WORLD. CONTAGIOUS SURVIVORS.
HOW DO YOU KNOW ALL THIS?
I SURVIVED THE EXPERIMENTS, BUT I'M NOT CONTAGIOUS.
AND...I CAN FEEL THAT THING. IN MY MIND. AND I THINK IT CAN FEEL ME.
WE HAVE TO DESTROY IT!
NO!
THIS ISN'T REAL!
UHHHH...
AAAAGH...
WHAT'S HAPPENING?
IT'S DEFENDING ITSELF!

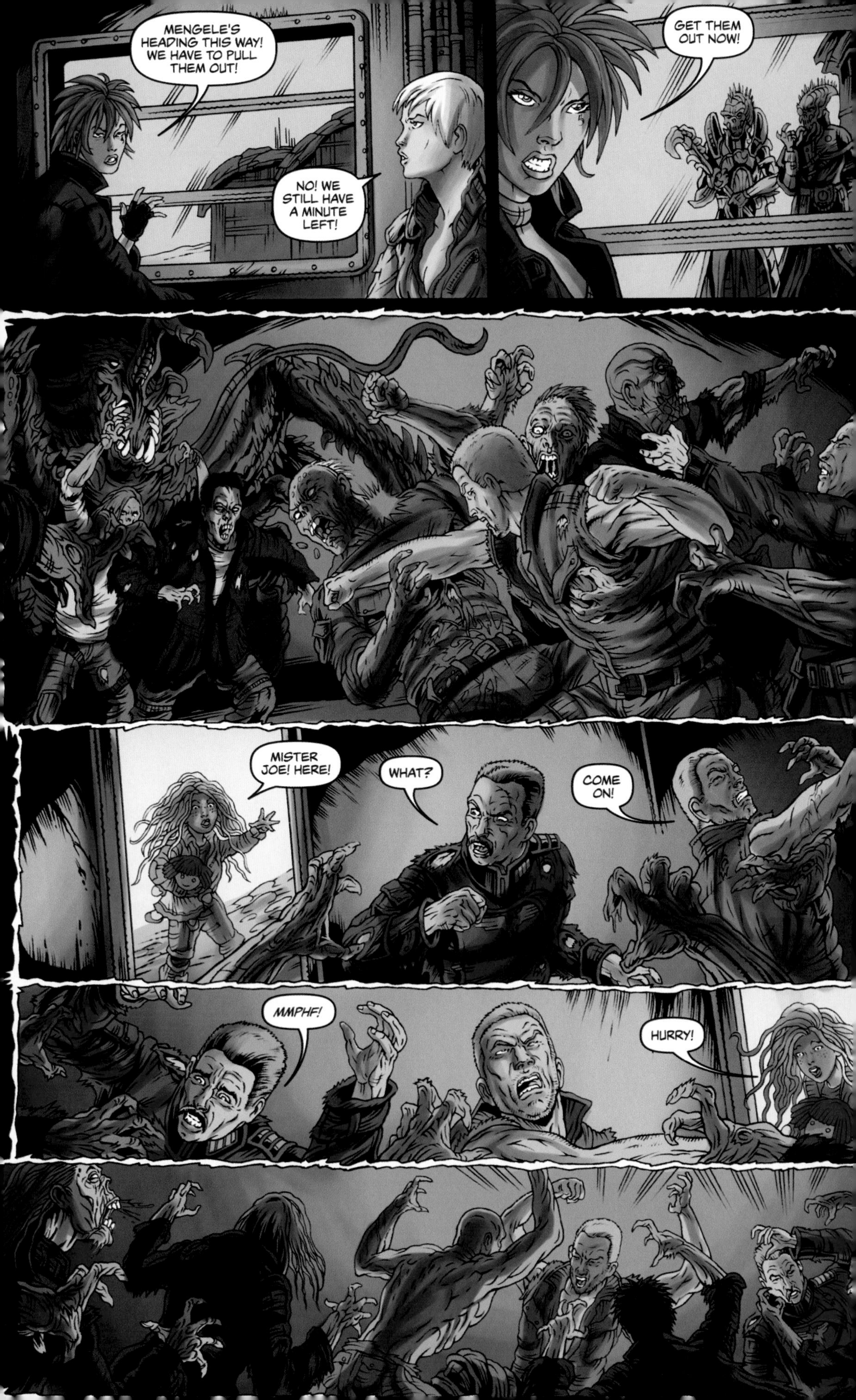
MENGELE'S HEADING THIS WAY! WE HAVE TO PULL THEM OUT!
NO! WE STILL HAVE A MINUTE LEFT!
GET THEM OUT NOW!
MISTER JOE! HERE!
WHAT?
COME ON!
MMPHF!
HURRY!

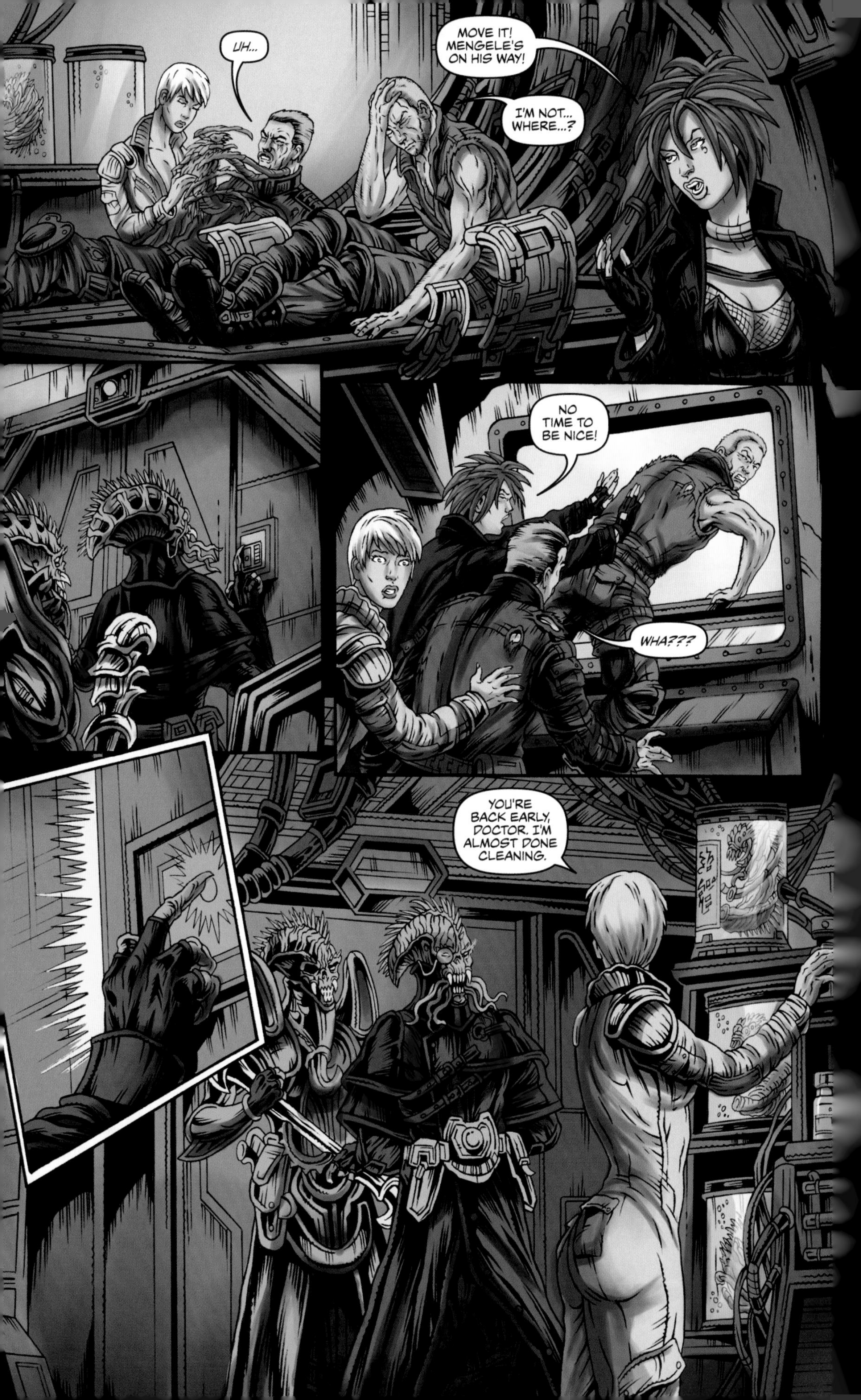
UH...
MOVE IT! MENGELE'S ON HIS WAY!
I'M NOT... WHERE...?
NO TIME TO BE NICE!
WHA???
YOU'RE BACK EARLY, DOCTOR. I'M ALMOST DONE CLEANING.

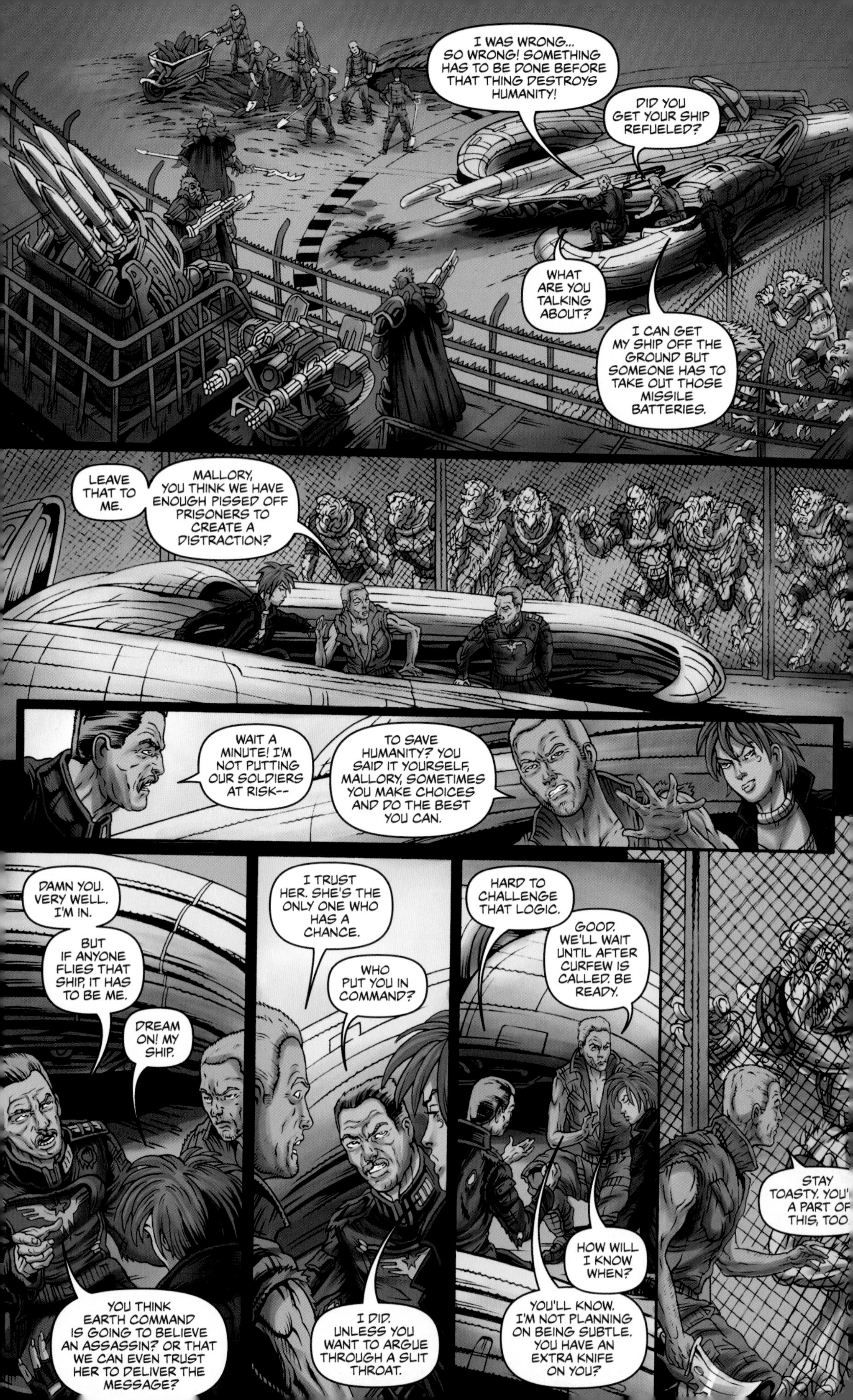
I WAS WRONG... SO WRONG! SOMETHING HAS TO BE DONE BEFORE THAT THING DESTROYS HUMANITY!
DID YOU GET YOUR SHIP REFUELED?
WHAT ARE YOU TALKING ABOUT?
I CAN GET MY SHIP OFF THE GROUND BUT SOMEONE HAS TO TAKE OUT THOSE MISSILE BATTERIES.
LEAVE THAT TO ME.
MALLORY, YOU THINK WE HAVE ENOUGH PISSED OFF PRISONERS TO CREATE A DISTRACTION?
WAIT A MINUTE! I'M NOT PUTTING OUR SOLDIERS AT RISK--
TO SAVE HUMANITY? YOU SAID IT YOURSELF, MALLORY, SOMETIMES YOU MAKE CHOICES AND DO THE BEST YOU CAN.
DAMN YOU. VERY WELL. I'M IN.
BUT IF ANYONE FLIES THAT SHIP, IT HAS TO BE ME.
DREAM ON! MY SHIP.
YOU THINK EARTH COMMAND IS GOING TO BELIEVE AN ASSASSIN? OR THAT WE CAN EVEN TRUST HER TO DELIVER THE MESSAGE?
I TRUST HER. SHE'S THE ONLY ONE WHO HAS A CHANCE.
WHO PUT YOU IN COMMAND?
I DID. UNLESS YOU WANT TO ARGUE THROUGH A SLIT THROAT.
HARD TO CHALLENGE THAT LOGIC.
GOOD. WE'LL WAIT UNTIL AFTER CURFEW IS CALLED. BE READY.
HOW WILL I KNOW WHEN?
YOU'LL KNOW. I'M NOT PLANNING ON BEING SUBTLE. YOU HAVE AN EXTRA KNIFE ON YOU?
STAY TOASTY. YOU' A PART OF THIS, TOO

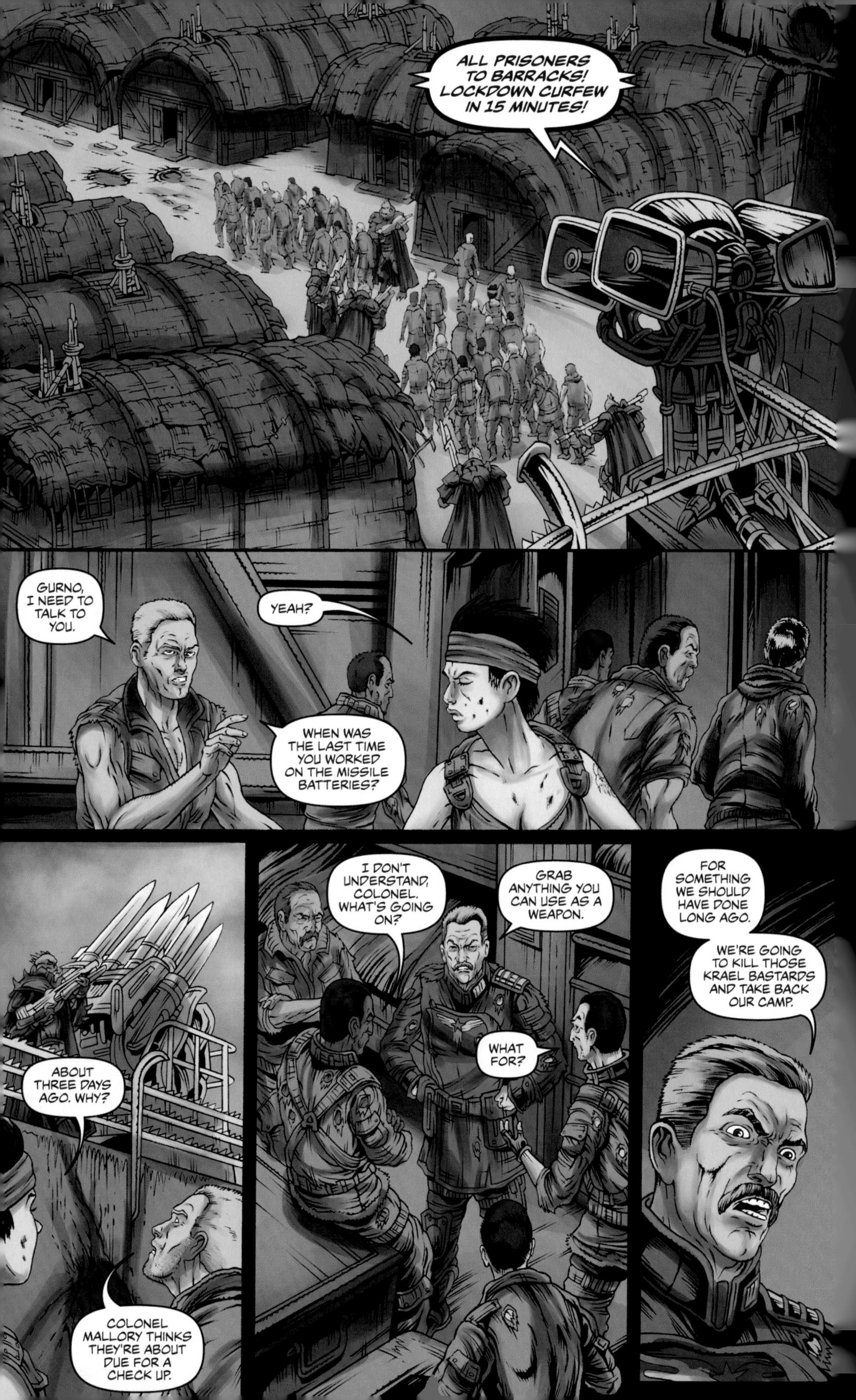
ALL PRISONERS TO BARRACKS! LOCKDOWN CURFEW IN 15 MINUTES!
GURNO, I NEED TO TALK TO YOU.
YEAH?
WHEN WAS THE LAST TIME YOU WORKED ON THE MISSILE BATTERIES?
ABOUT THREE DAYS AGO. WHY?
COLONEL MALLORY THINKS THEY'RE ABOUT DUE FOR A CHECK UP.
I DON'T UNDERSTAND, COLONEL. WHAT'S GOING ON?
GRAB ANYTHING YOU CAN USE AS A WEAPON.
WHAT FOR?
FOR SOMETHING WE SHOULD HAVE DONE LONG AGO.
WE'RE GOING TO KILL THOSE KRAEL BASTARDS AND TAKE BACK OUR CAMP.

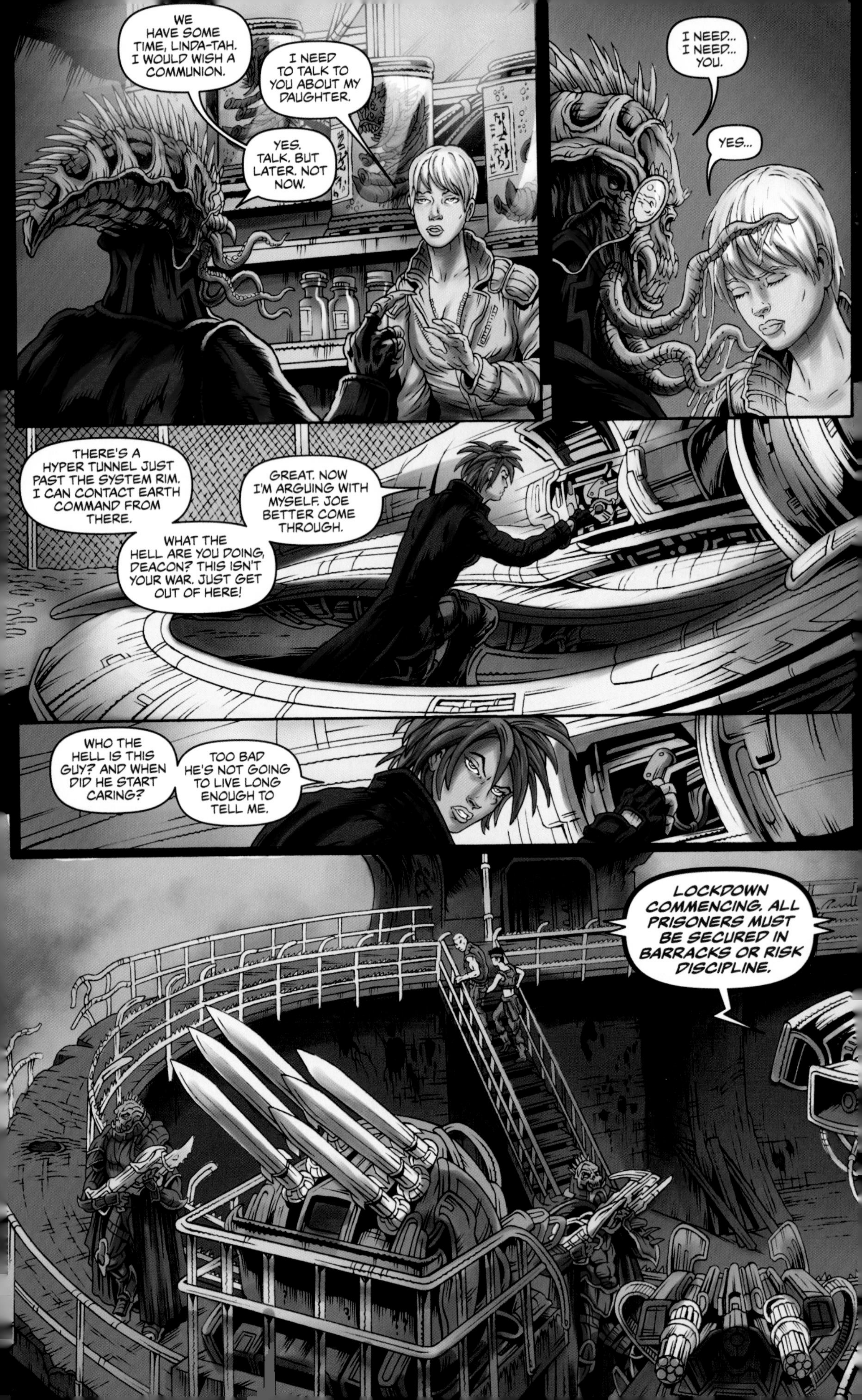
WE HAVE SOME TIME, LINDA-TAH. I WOULD WISH A COMMUNION.
I NEED TO TALK TO YOU ABOUT MY DAUGHTER.
YES. TALK. BUT LATER. NOT NOW.
I NEED... I NEED... YOU.
YES...
THERE'S A HYPER TUNNEL JUST PAST THE SYSTEM RIM. I CAN CONTACT EARTH COMMAND FROM THERE.
WHAT THE HELL ARE YOU DOING, DEACON? THIS ISN'T YOUR WAR. JUST GET OUT OF HERE!
GREAT. NOW I'M ARGUING WITH MYSELF. JOE BETTER COME THROUGH.
WHO THE HELL IS THIS GUY? AND WHEN DID HE START CARING?
TOO BAD HE'S NOT GOING TO LIVE LONG ENOUGH TO TELL ME.
LOCKDOWN COMMENCING. ALL PRISONERS MUST BE SECURED IN BARRACKS OR RISK DISCIPLINE.

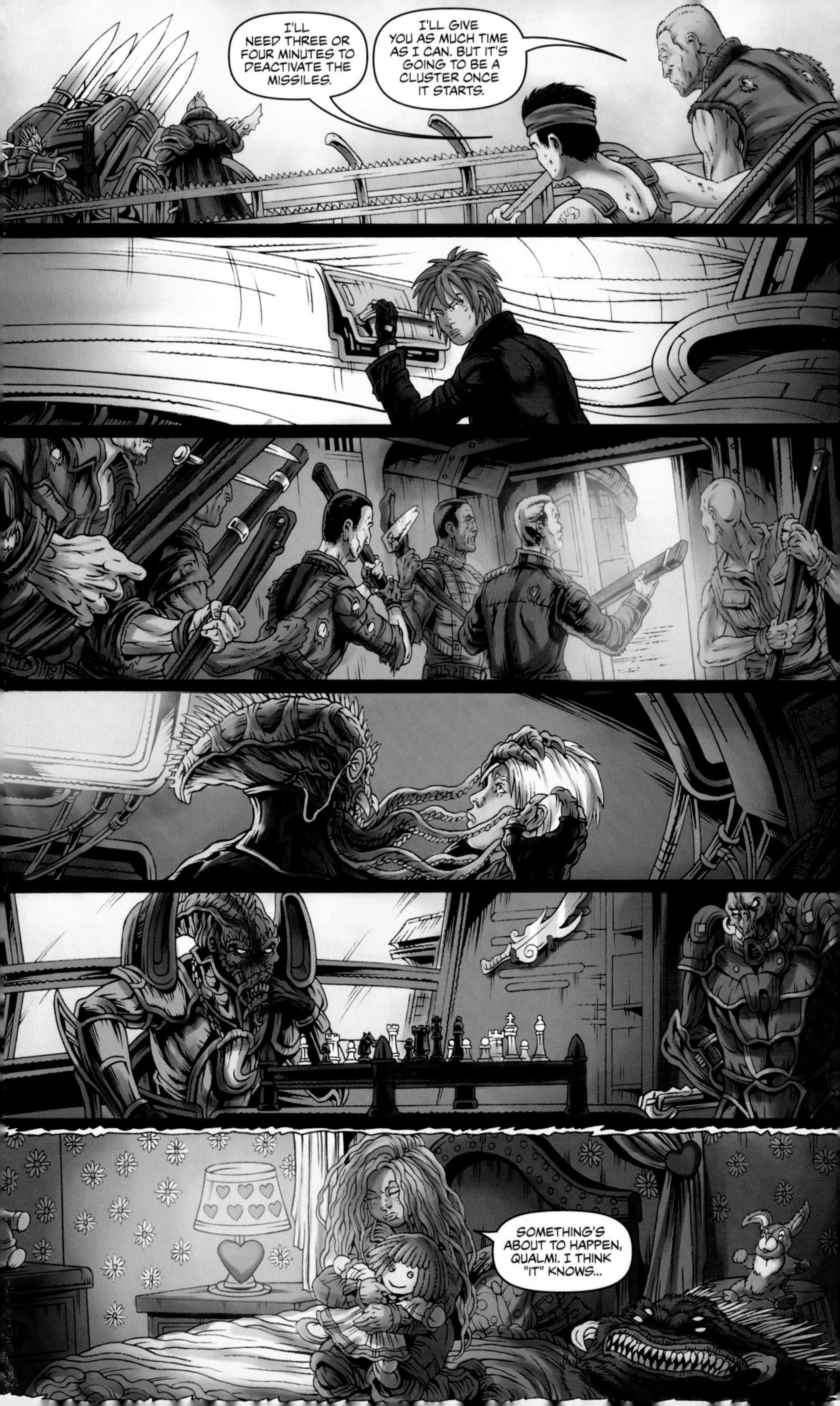
I'LL NEED THREE OR FOUR MINUTES TO DEACTIVATE THE MISSILES.
I'LL GIVE YOU AS MUCH TIME AS I CAN. BUT IT'S GOING TO BE A CLUSTER ONCE IT STARTS.
SOMETHING'S ABOUT TO HAPPEN, QUALMI. I THINK "IT" KNOWS...

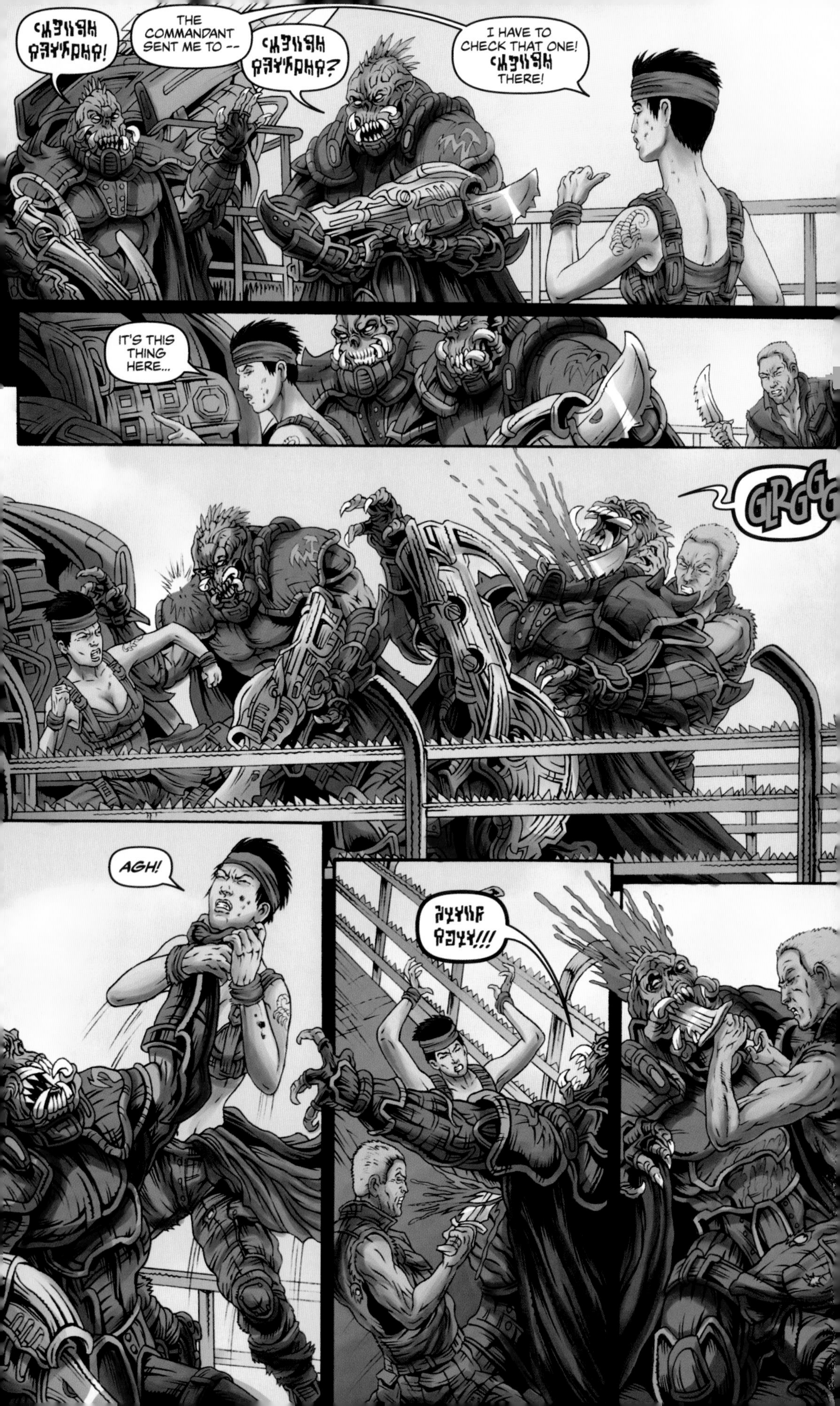
THE COMMANDANT SENT ME TO --
I HAVE TO CHECK THAT ONE! … THERE!
IT'S THIS THING HERE...
GLRGG
AGH!

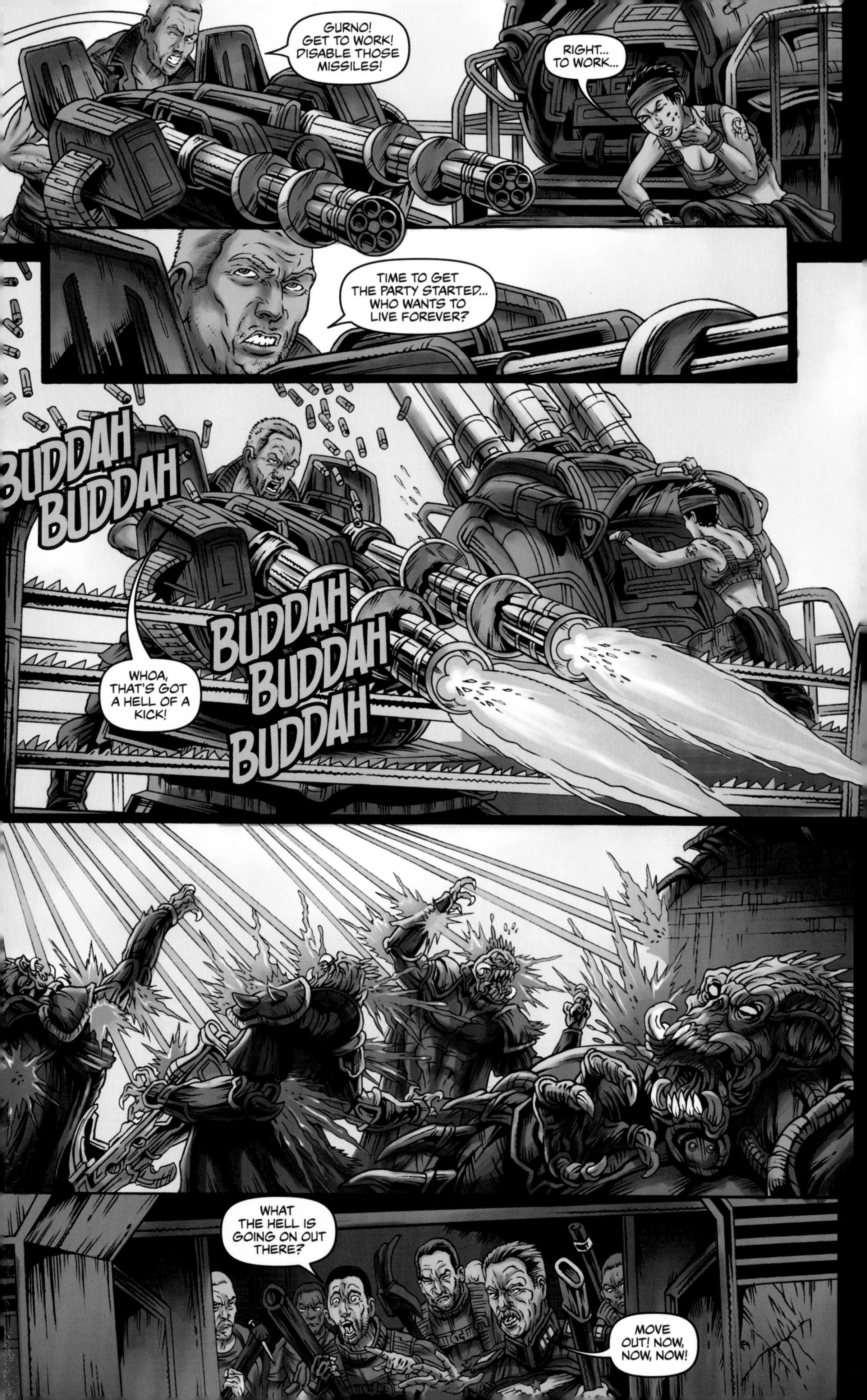
GURNO! GET TO WORK! DISABLE THOSE MISSILES!
RIGHT... TO WORK...
TIME TO GET THE PARTY STARTED... WHO WANTS TO LIVE FOREVER?
BUDDAH BUDDAH
WHOA, THAT'S GOT A HELL OF A KICK!
BUDDAH BUDDAH BUDDAH
WHAT THE HELL IS GOING ON OUT THERE?
MOVE OUT! NOW, NOW, NOW!

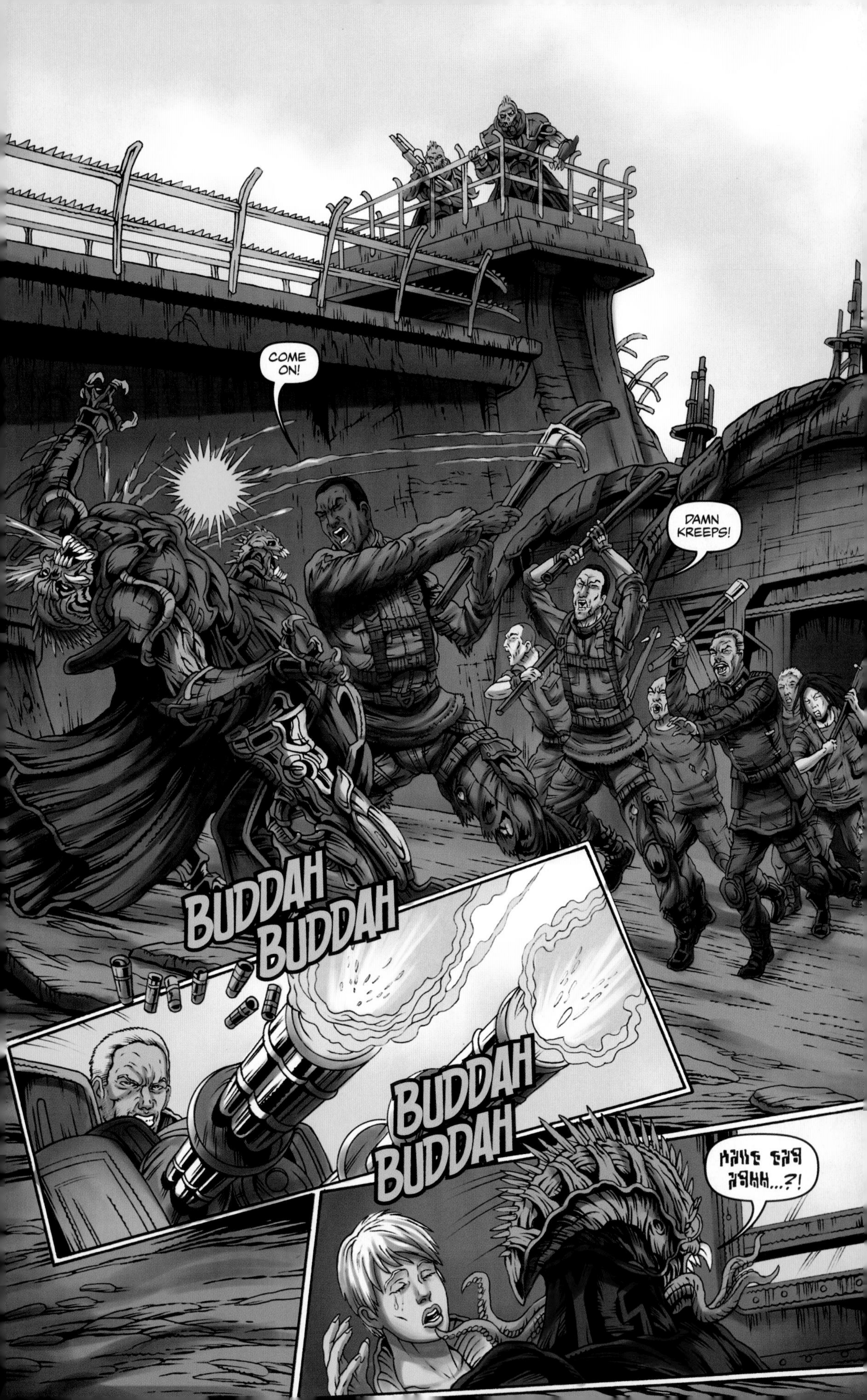
COME ON!
DAMN KREEPS!
BUDDAH BUDDAH
BUDDAH BUDDAH

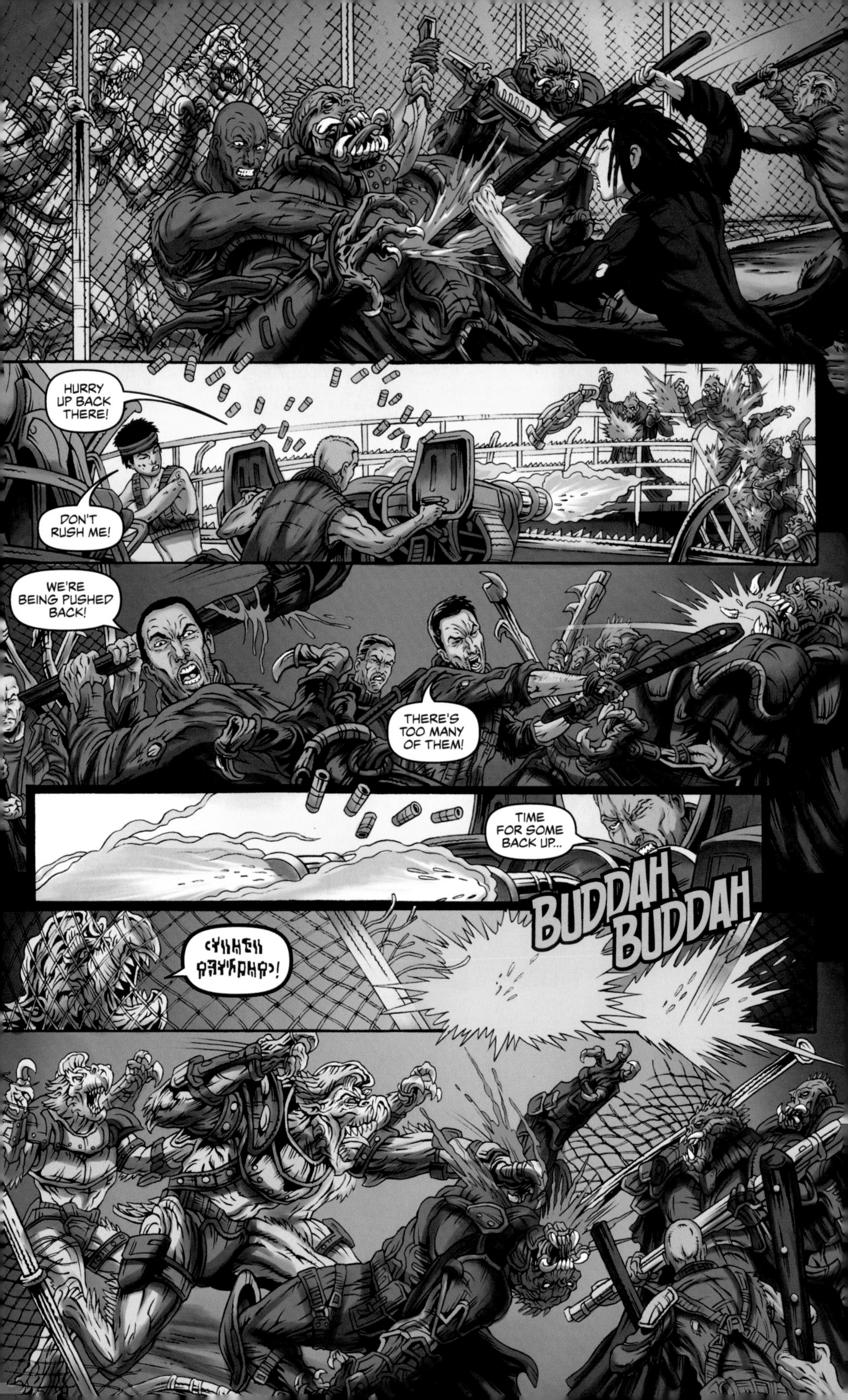
HURRY UP BACK THERE!
DON'T RUSH ME!
WE'RE BEING PUSHED BACK!
THERE'S TOO MANY OF THEM!
TIME FOR SOME BACK UP...
BUDDAH BUDDAH

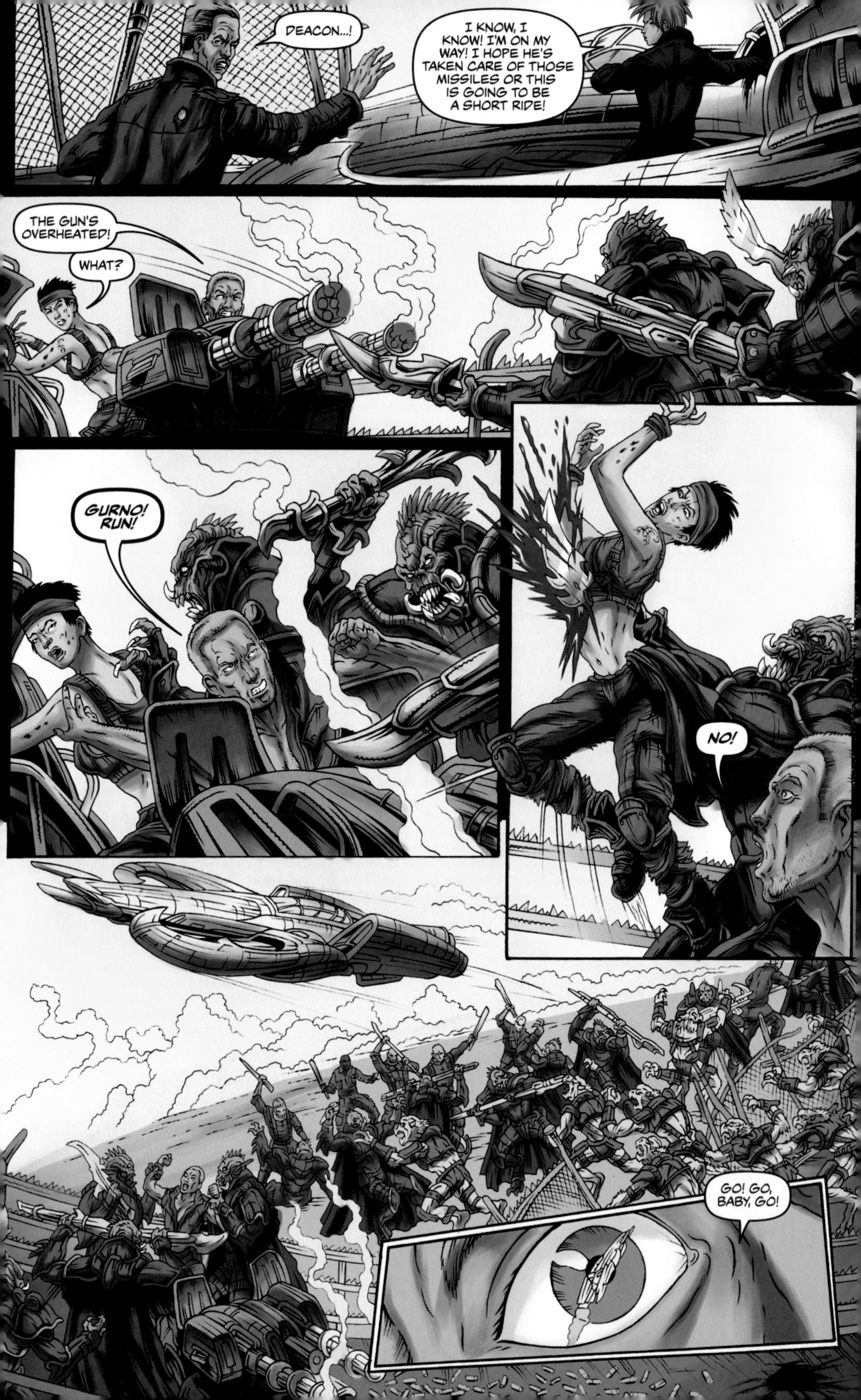
DEACON...!
I KNOW, I KNOW! I'M ON MY WAY! I HOPE HE'S TAKEN CARE OF THOSE MISSILES OR THIS IS GOING TO BE A SHORT RIDE!
THE GUN'S OVERHEATED!
WHAT?
GURNO! RUN!
NO!
GO! GO, BABY, GO!

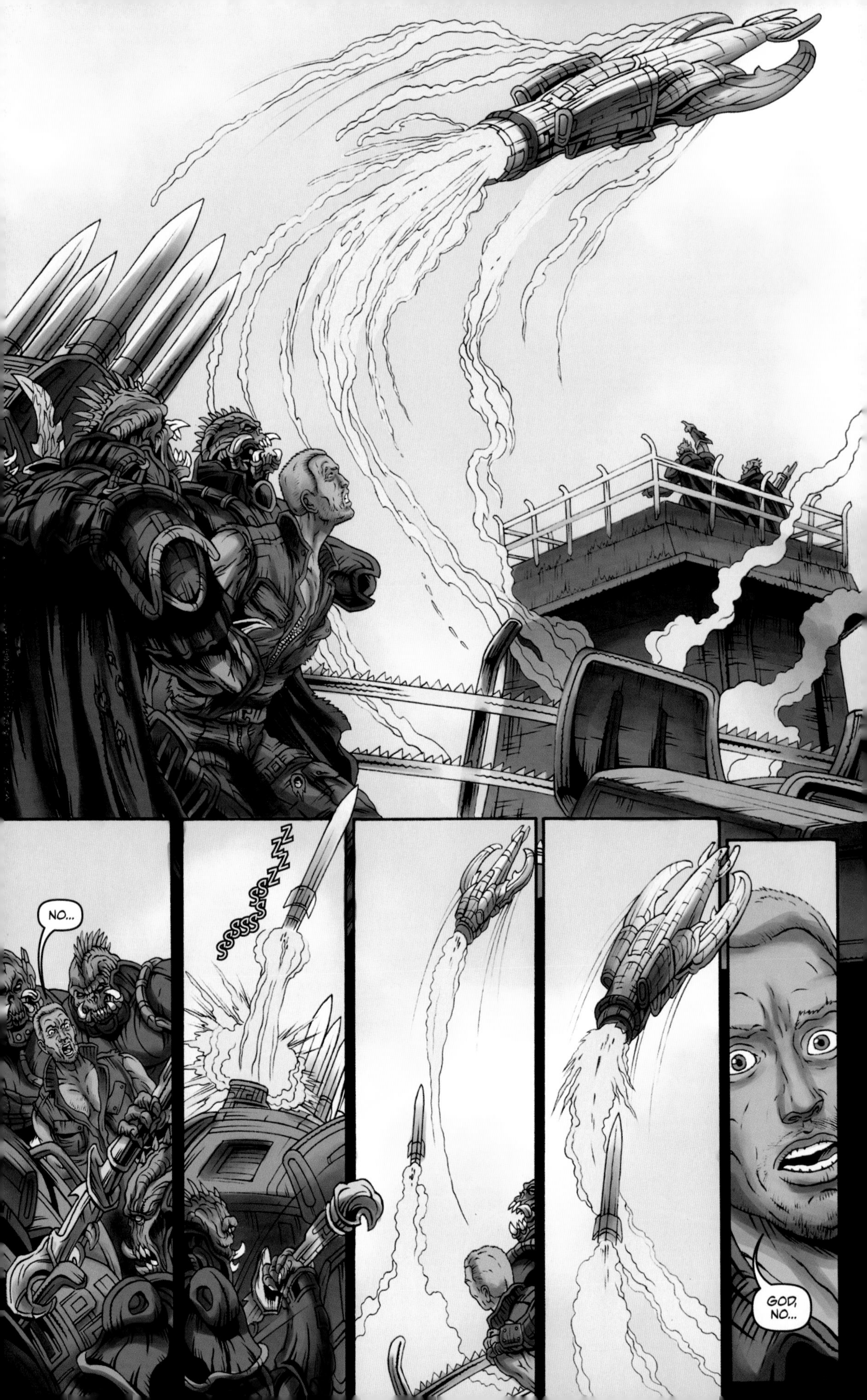
NO...
SSSSSSSZZZZ
GOD, NO...

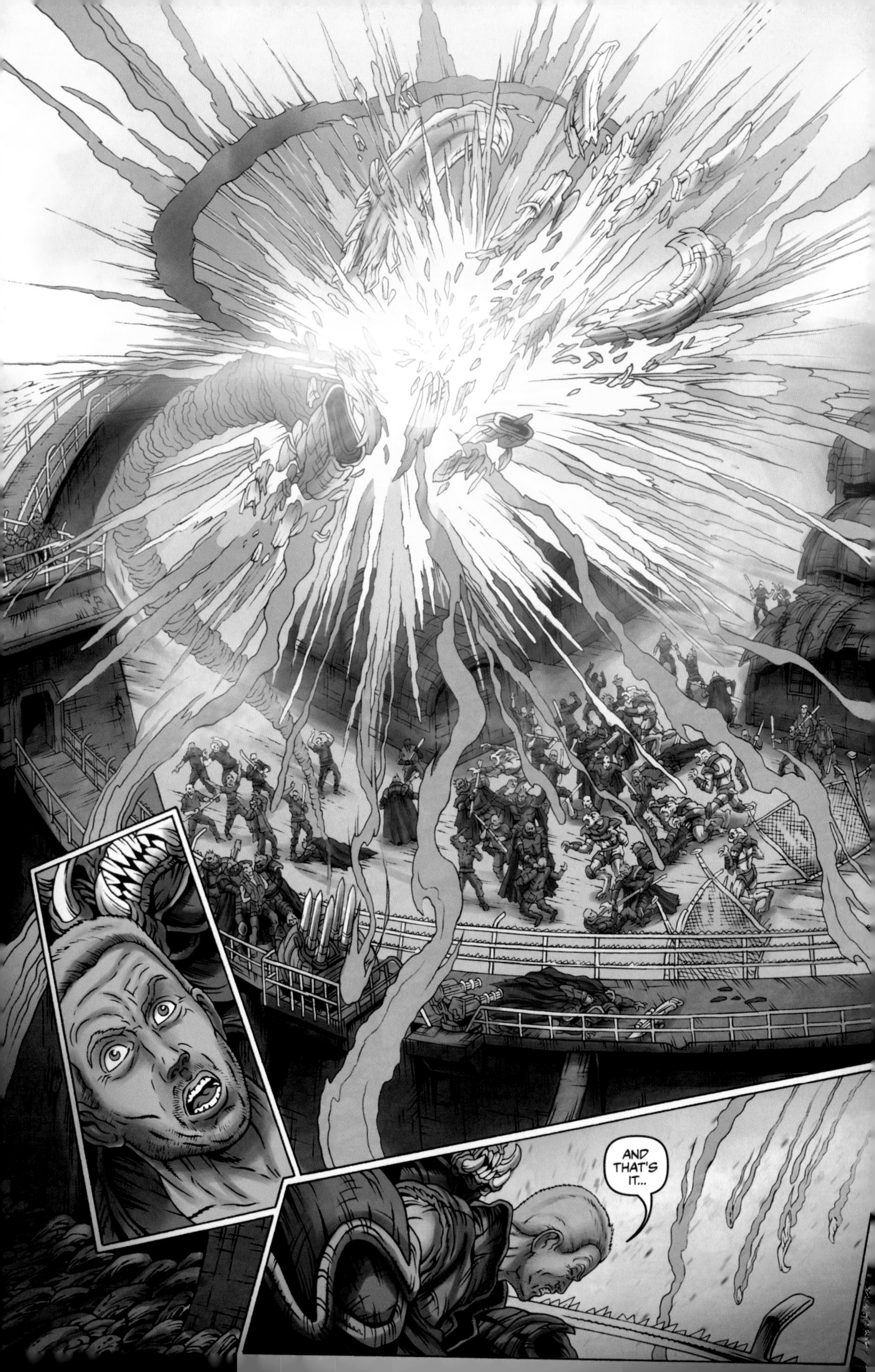
AND THAT'S IT...

CHAPTER VI

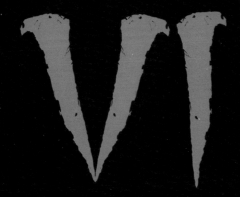

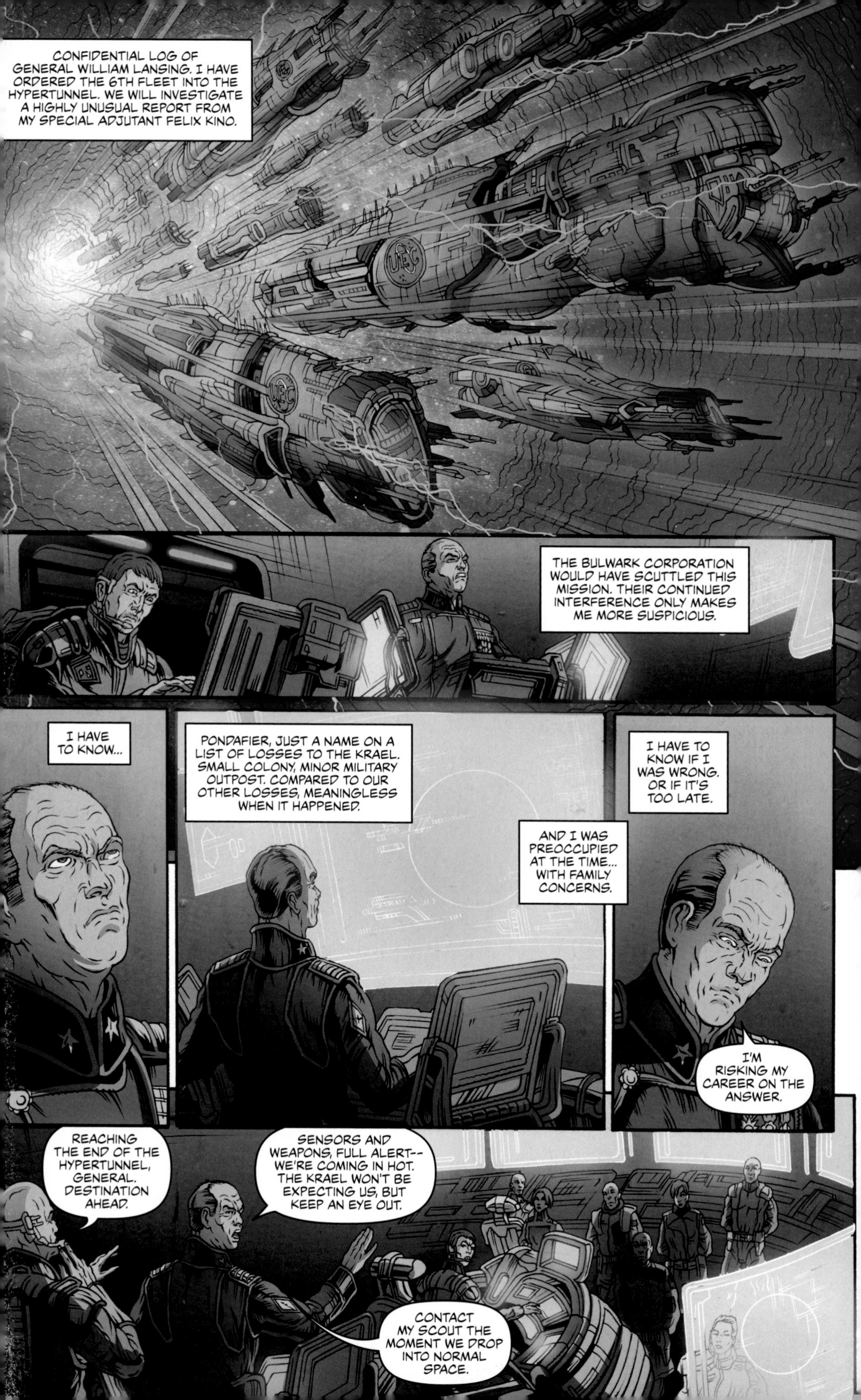
CONFIDENTIAL LOG OF GENERAL WILLIAM LANSING. I HAVE ORDERED THE 6TH FLEET INTO THE HYPERTUNNEL. WE WILL INVESTIGATE A HIGHLY UNUSUAL REPORT FROM MY SPECIAL ADJUTANT FELIX KINO.
THE BULWARK CORPORATION WOULD HAVE SCUTTLED THIS MISSION. THEIR CONTINUED INTERFERENCE ONLY MAKES ME MORE SUSPICIOUS.
I HAVE TO KNOW...
PONDAFIER, JUST A NAME ON A LIST OF LOSSES TO THE KRAEL. SMALL COLONY, MINOR MILITARY OUTPOST. COMPARED TO OUR OTHER LOSSES, MEANINGLESS WHEN IT HAPPENED.
AND I WAS PREOCCUPIED AT THE TIME... WITH FAMILY CONCERNS.
I HAVE TO KNOW IF I WAS WRONG. OR IF IT'S TOO LATE.
I'M RISKING MY CAREER ON THE ANSWER.
REACHING THE END OF THE HYPERTUNNEL, GENERAL. DESTINATION AHEAD.
SENSORS AND WEAPONS, FULL ALERT-- WE'RE COMING IN HOT. THE KRAEL WON'T BE EXPECTING US, BUT KEEP AN EYE OUT.
CONTACT MY SCOUT THE MOMENT WE DROP INTO NORMAL SPACE.

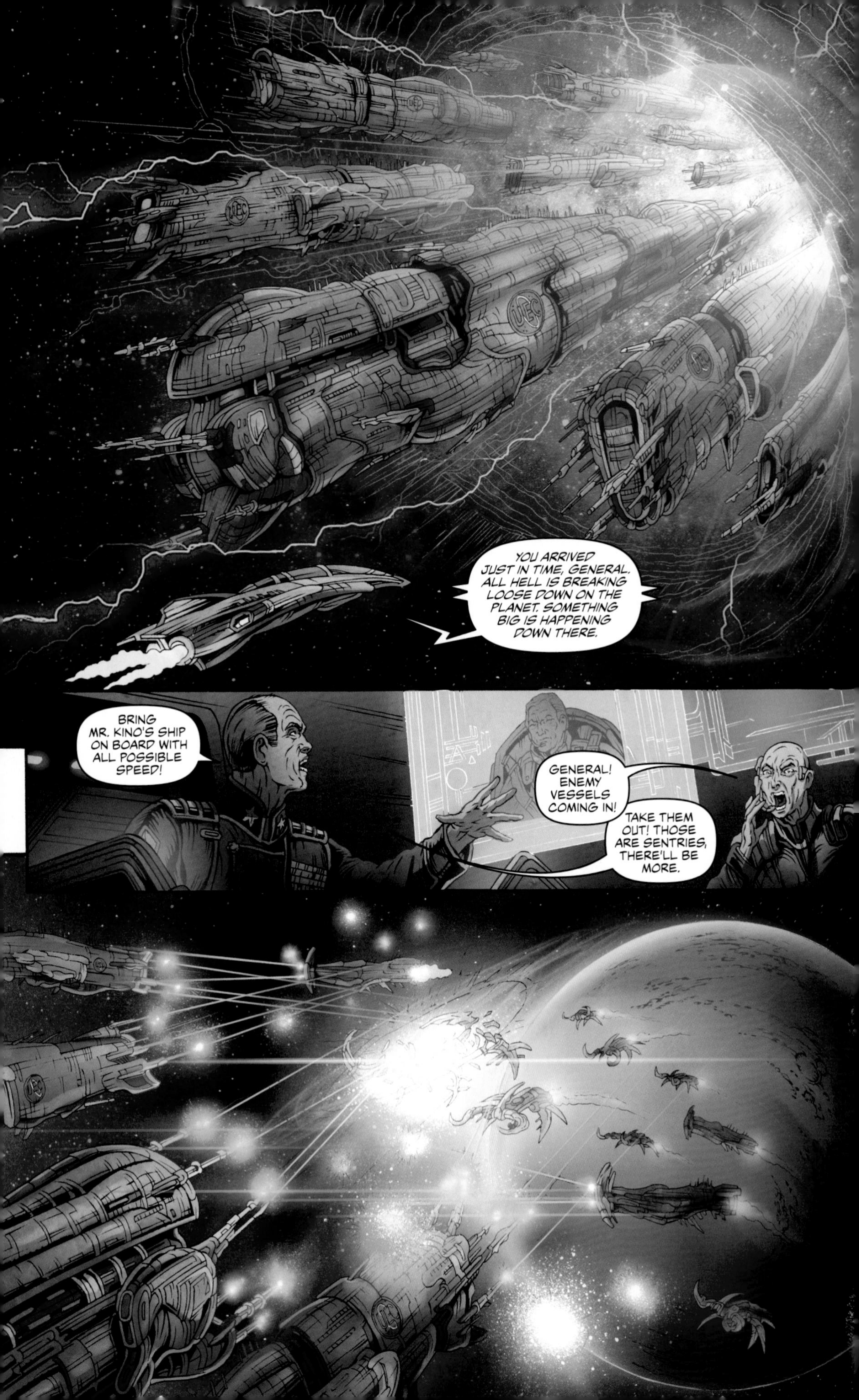
YOU ARRIVED JUST IN TIME, GENERAL. ALL HELL IS BREAKING LOOSE DOWN ON THE PLANET. SOMETHING BIG IS HAPPENING DOWN THERE.
BRING MR. KINO'S SHIP ON BOARD WITH ALL POSSIBLE SPEED!
GENERAL! ENEMY VESSELS COMING IN!
TAKE THEM OUT! THOSE ARE SENTRIES, THERE'LL BE MORE.

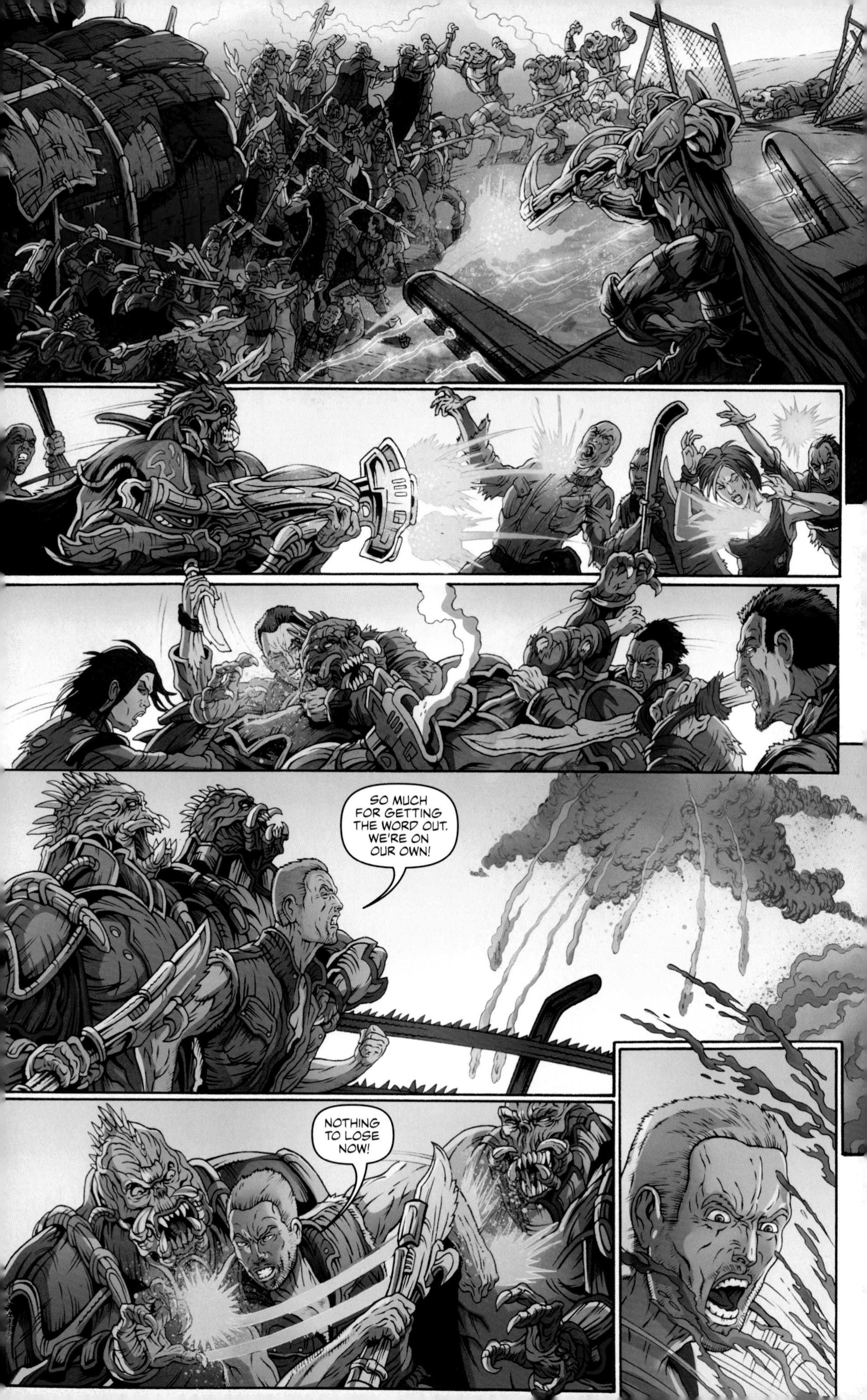
SO MUCH FOR GETTING THE WORD OUT. WE'RE ON OUR OWN!
NOTHING TO LOSE NOW!

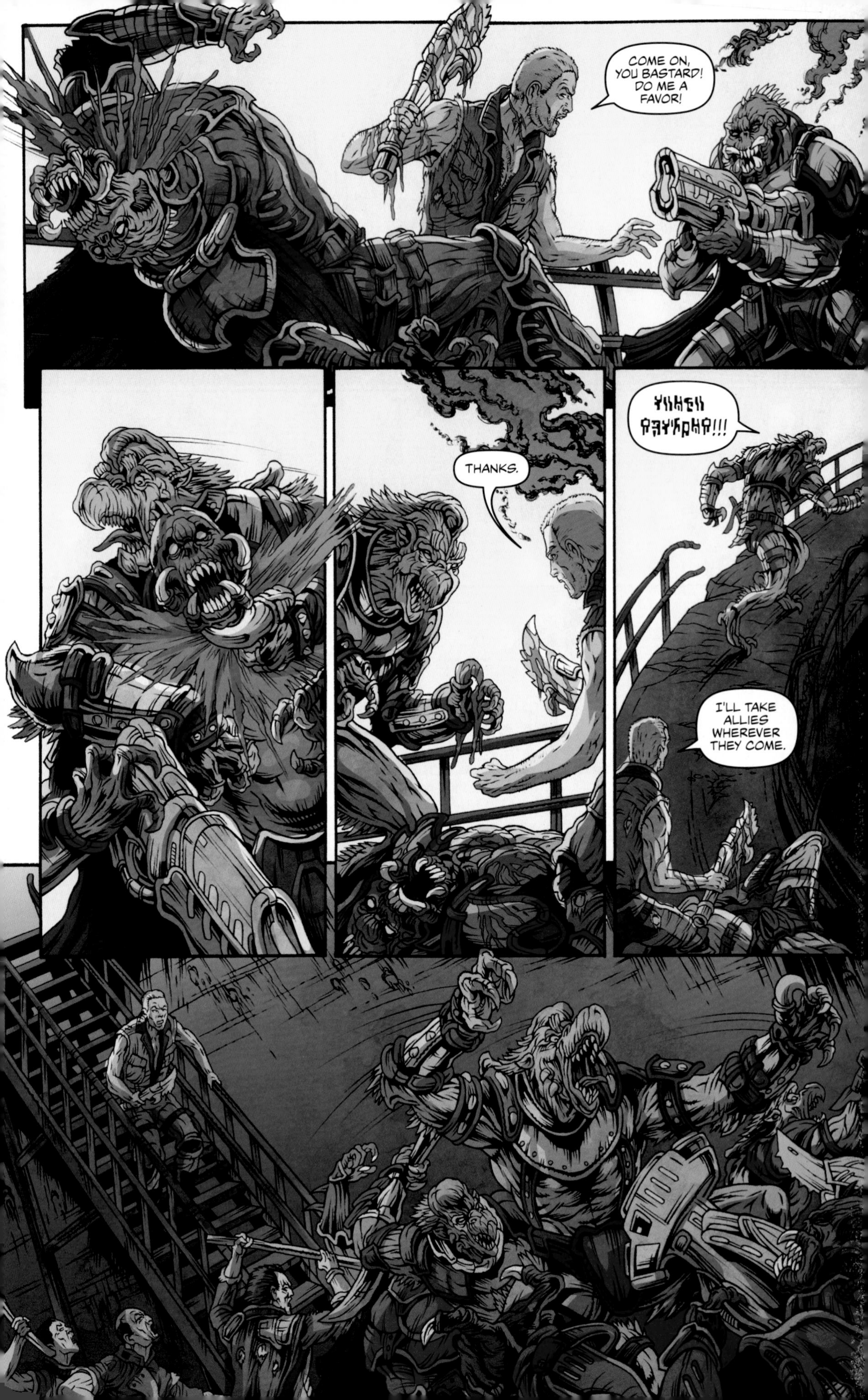
COME ON, YOU BASTARD! DO ME A FAVOR!
THANKS.
I'LL TAKE ALLIES WHEREVER THEY COME.

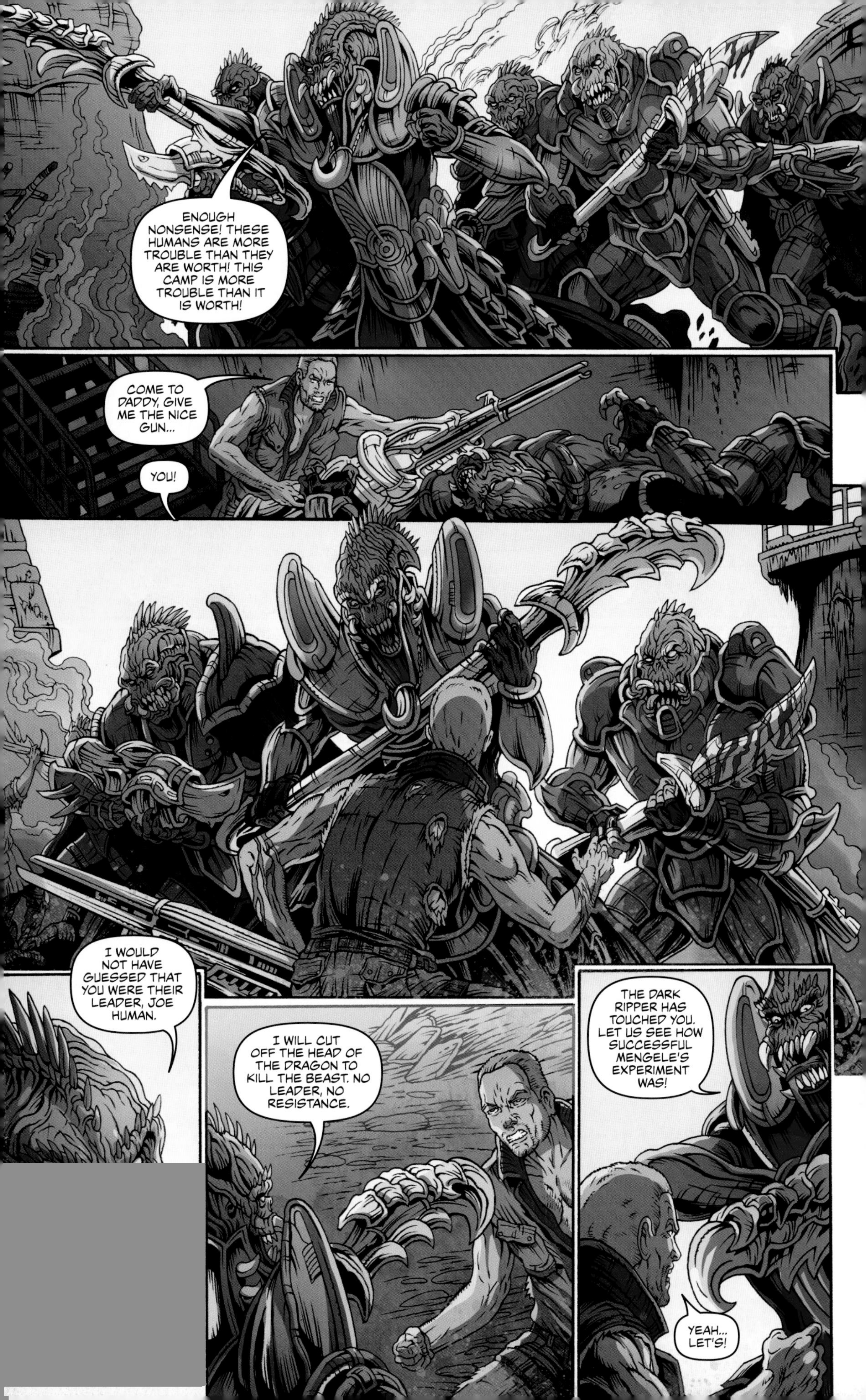
ENOUGH NONSENSE! THESE HUMANS ARE MORE TROUBLE THAN THEY ARE WORTH! THIS CAMP IS MORE TROUBLE THAN IT IS WORTH!
COME TO DADDY, GIVE ME THE NICE GUN...
YOU!
I WOULD NOT HAVE GUESSED THAT YOU WERE THEIR LEADER, JOE HUMAN.
I WILL CUT OFF THE HEAD OF THE DRAGON TO KILL THE BEAST. NO LEADER, NO RESISTANCE.
THE DARK RIPPER HAS TOUCHED YOU. LET US SEE HOW SUCCESSFUL MENGELE'S EXPERIMENT WAS!
YEAH... LET'S!

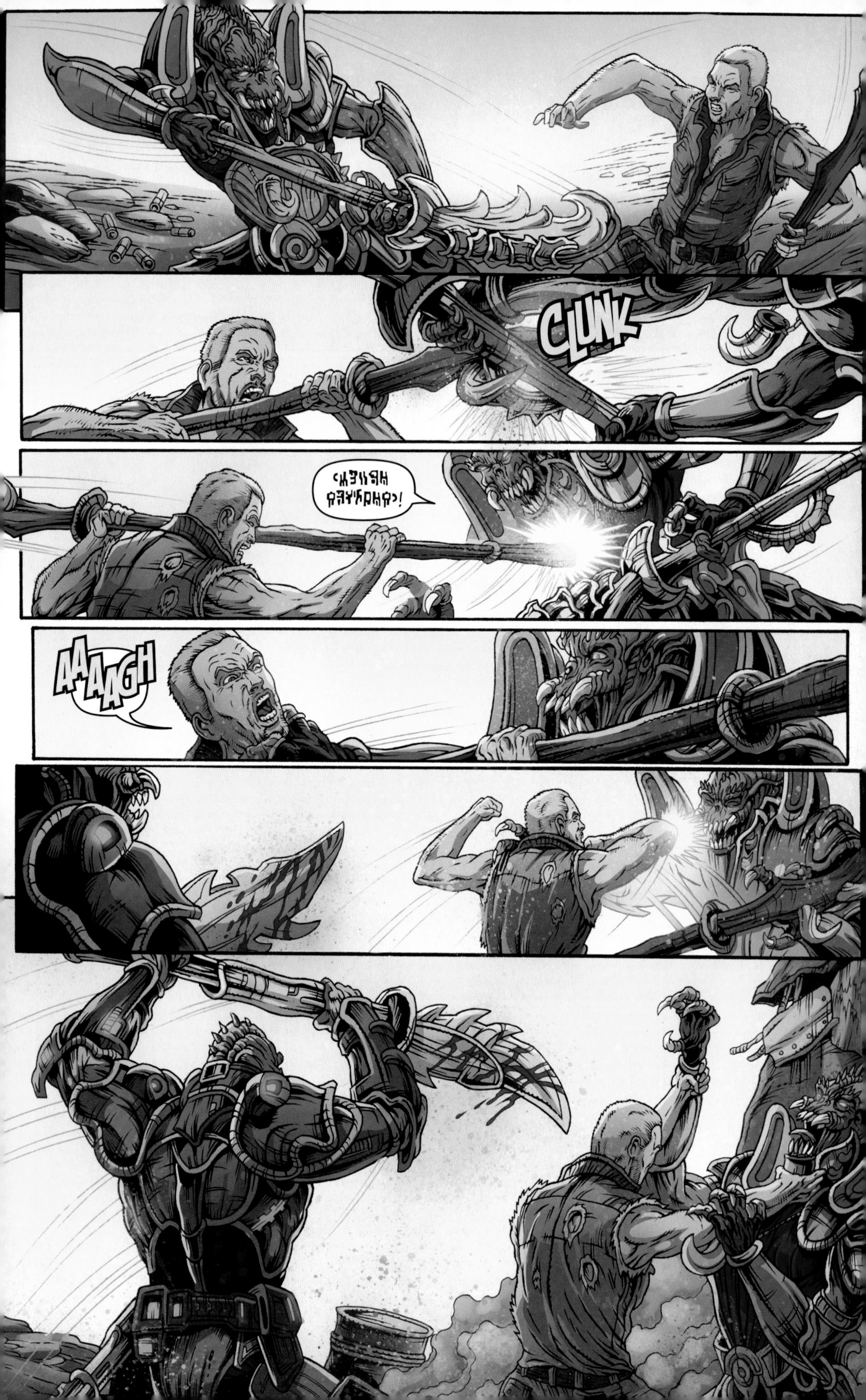
CLUNK
AAAAGH

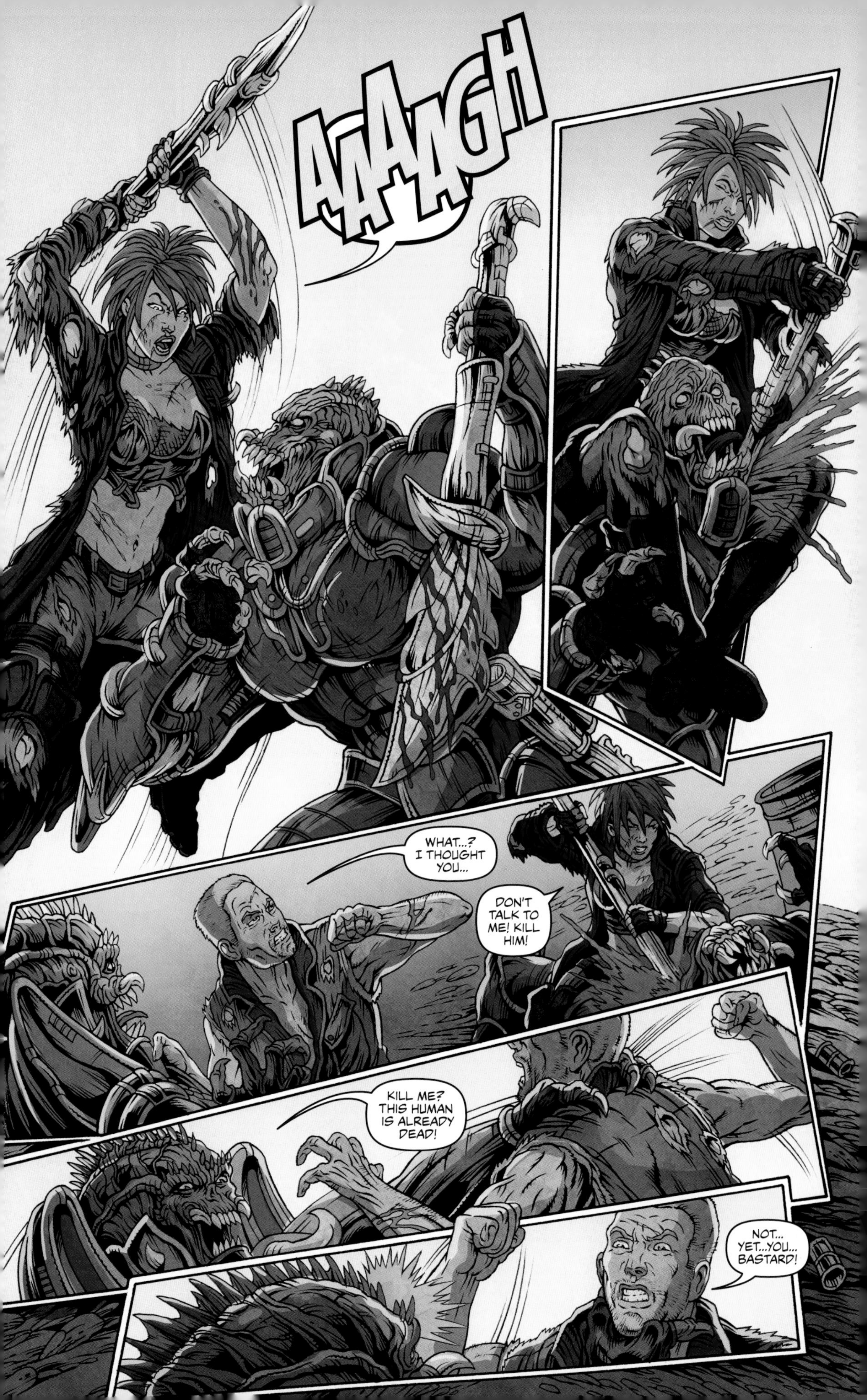
AAAAGH
WHAT...? I THOUGHT YOU...
DON'T TALK TO ME! KILL HIM!
KILL ME? THIS HUMAN IS ALREADY DEAD!
NOT... YET...YOU... BASTARD!

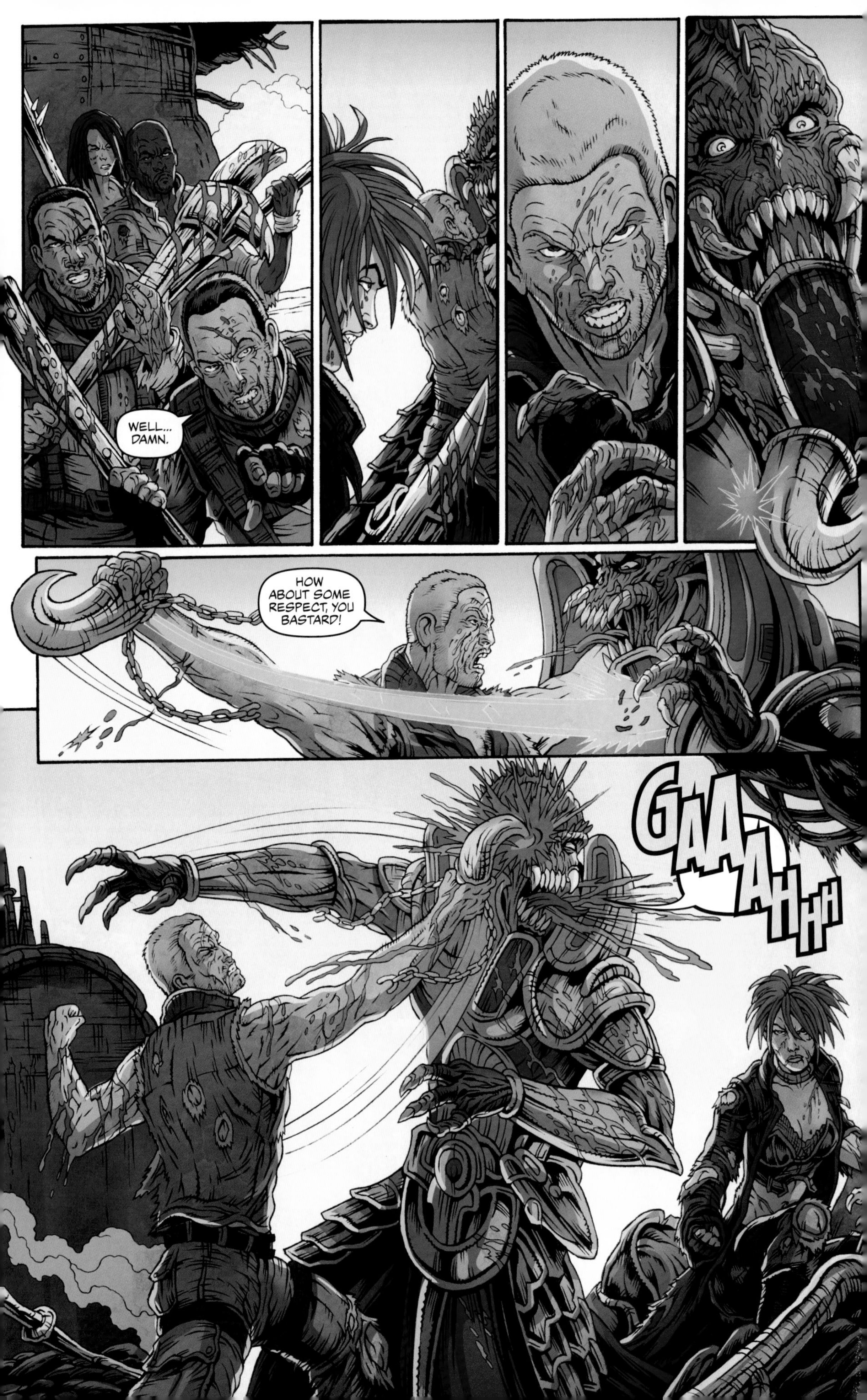
WELL... DAMN.
HOW ABOUT SOME RESPECT, YOU BASTARD!
GAAAAHHH

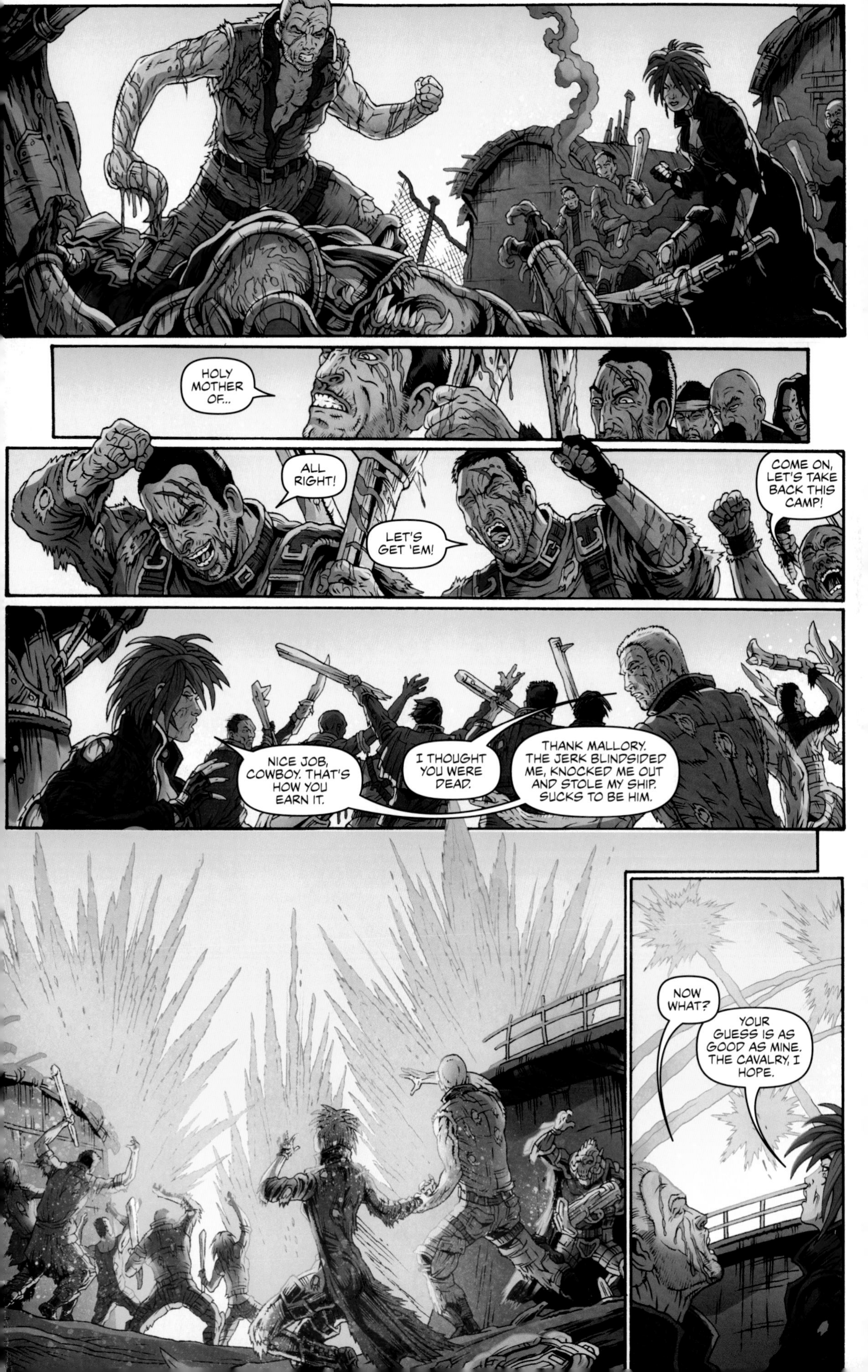
HOLY MOTHER OF...
ALL RIGHT!
LET'S GET 'EM!
COME ON, LET'S TAKE BACK THIS CAMP!
NICE JOB, COWBOY. THAT'S HOW YOU EARN IT.
I THOUGHT YOU WERE DEAD.
THANK MALLORY. THE JERK BLINDSIDED ME, KNOCKED ME OUT AND STOLE MY SHIP. SUCKS TO BE HIM.
NOW WHAT?
YOUR GUESS IS AS GOOD AS MINE. THE CAVALRY, I HOPE.

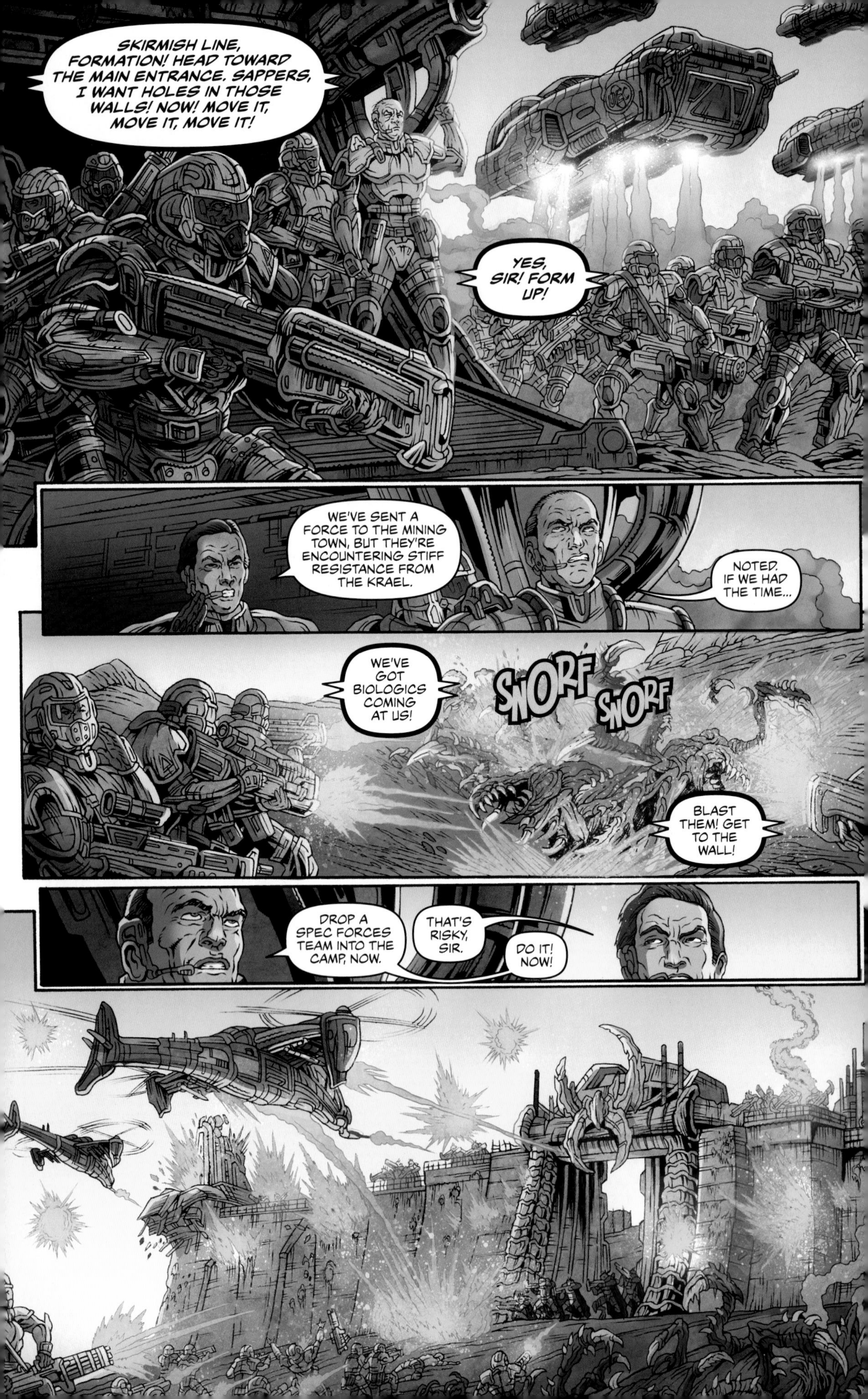
SKIRMISH LINE, FORMATION! HEAD TOWARD THE MAIN ENTRANCE. SAPPERS, I WANT HOLES IN THOSE WALLS! NOW! MOVE IT, MOVE IT, MOVE IT!
YES, SIR! FORM UP!
WE'VE SENT A FORCE TO THE MINING TOWN, BUT THEY'RE ENCOUNTERING STIFF RESISTANCE FROM THE KRAEL.
NOTED. IF WE HAD THE TIME...
WE'VE GOT BIOLOGICS COMING AT US!
SNORF
SNORF
BLAST THEM! GET TO THE WALL!
DROP A SPEC FORCES TEAM INTO THE CAMP, NOW.
THAT'S RISKY, SIR.
DO IT! NOW!

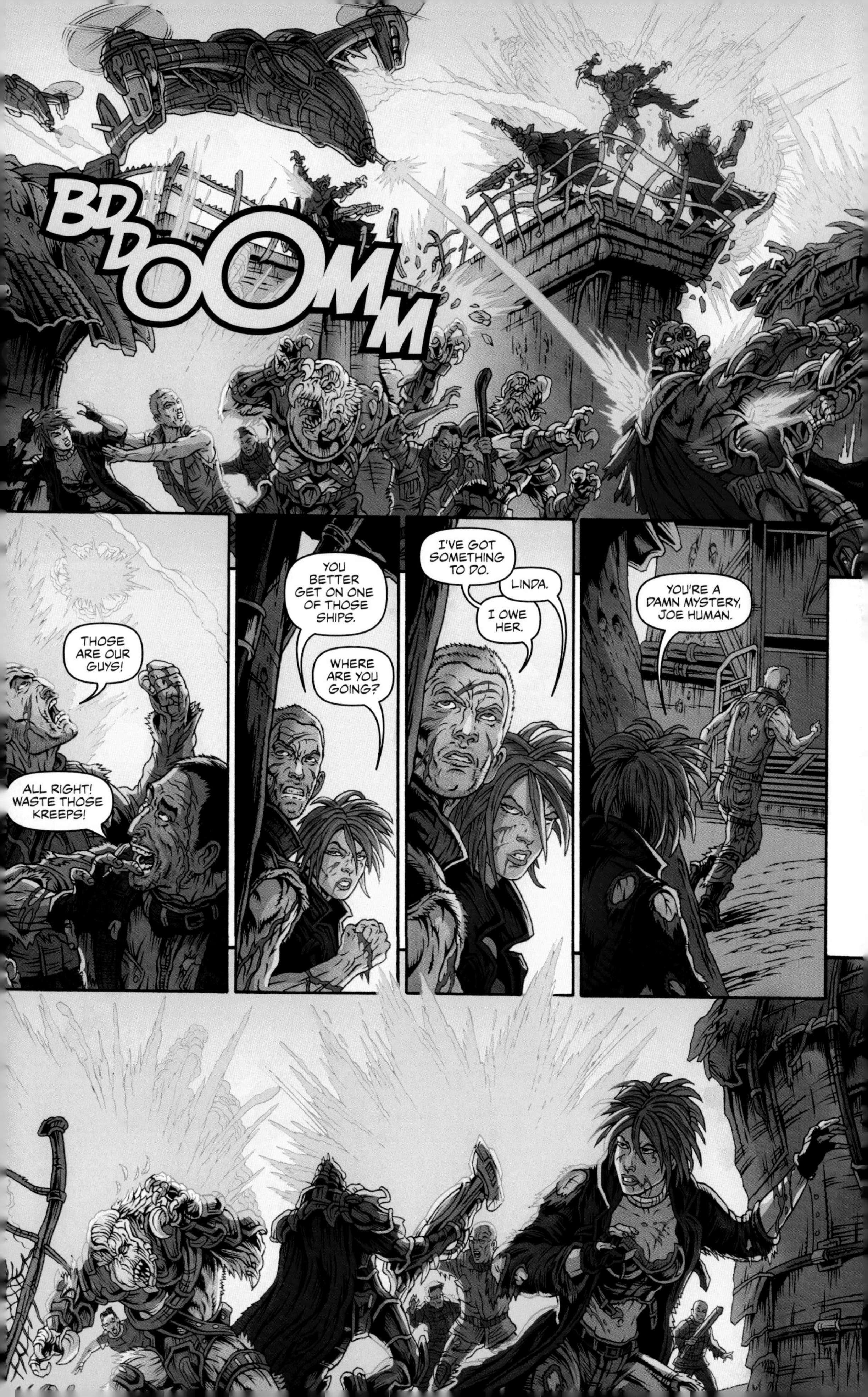
BDDOOMMM
THOSE ARE OUR GUYS!
ALL RIGHT! WASTE THOSE KREEPS!
YOU BETTER GET ON ONE OF THOSE SHIPS.
WHERE ARE YOU GOING?
I'VE GOT SOMETHING TO DO.
LINDA.
I OWE HER.
YOU'RE A DAMN MYSTERY, JOE HUMAN.

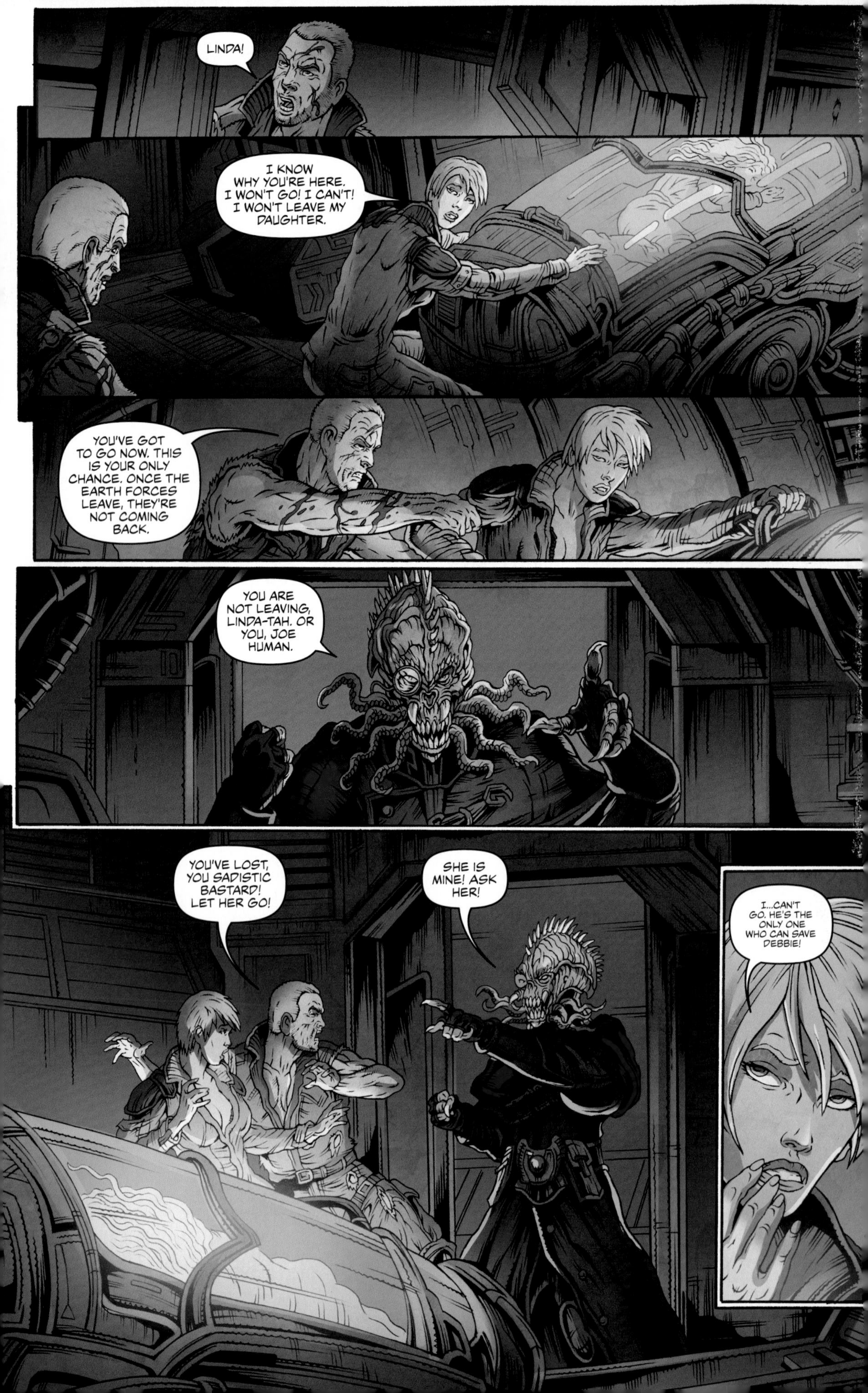
LINDA!
I KNOW WHY YOU'RE HERE. I WON'T GO! I CAN'T! I WON'T LEAVE MY DAUGHTER.
YOU'VE GOT TO GO NOW. THIS IS YOUR ONLY CHANCE. ONCE THE EARTH FORCES LEAVE, THEY'RE NOT COMING BACK.
YOU ARE NOT LEAVING, LINDA-TAH. OR YOU, JOE HUMAN.
YOU'VE LOST, YOU SADISTIC BASTARD! LET HER GO!
SHE IS MINE! ASK HER!
I...CAN'T GO. HE'S THE ONLY ONE WHO CAN SAVE DEBBIE!

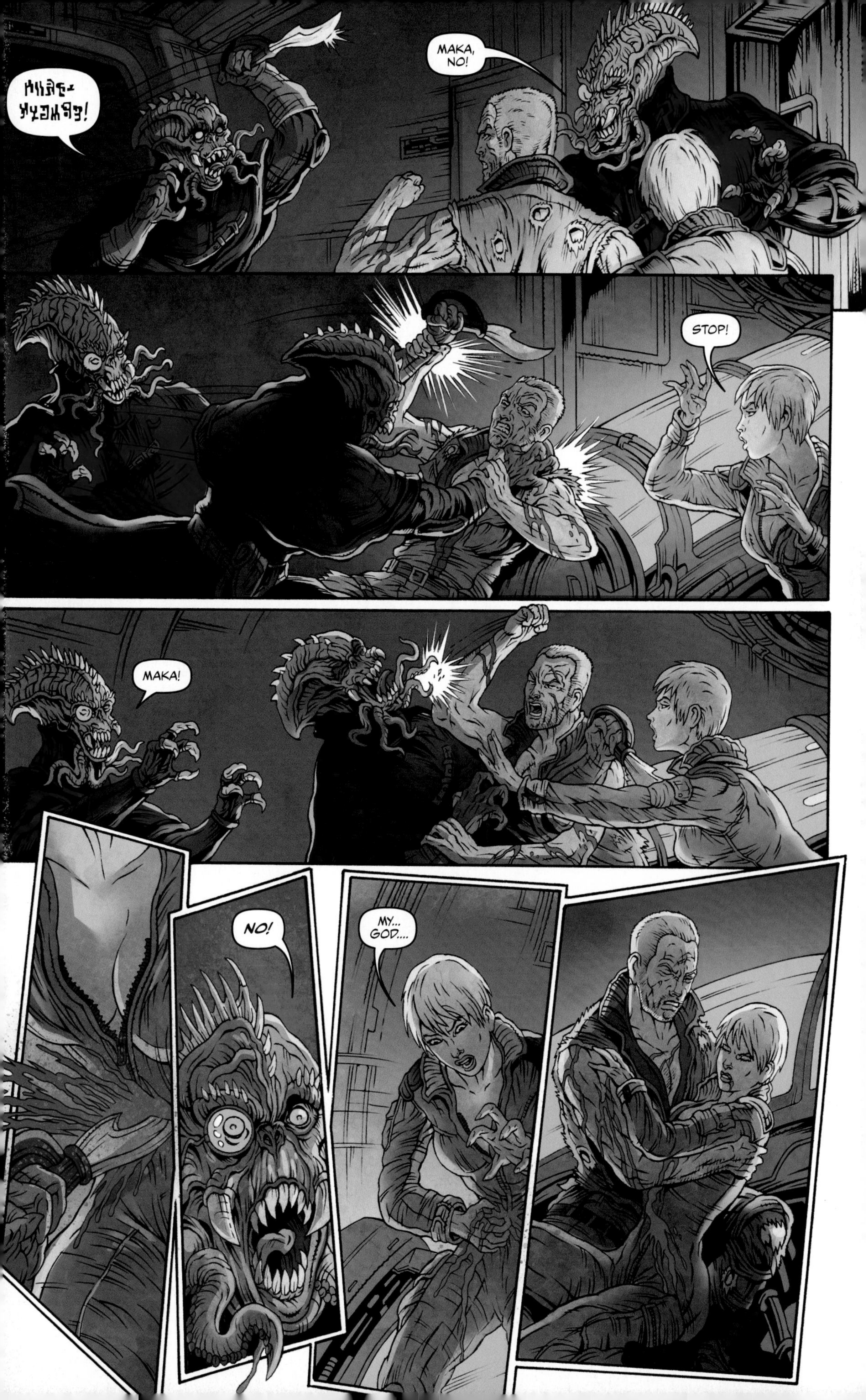
MAKA, NO!
STOP!
MAKA!
NO!
MY... GOD....

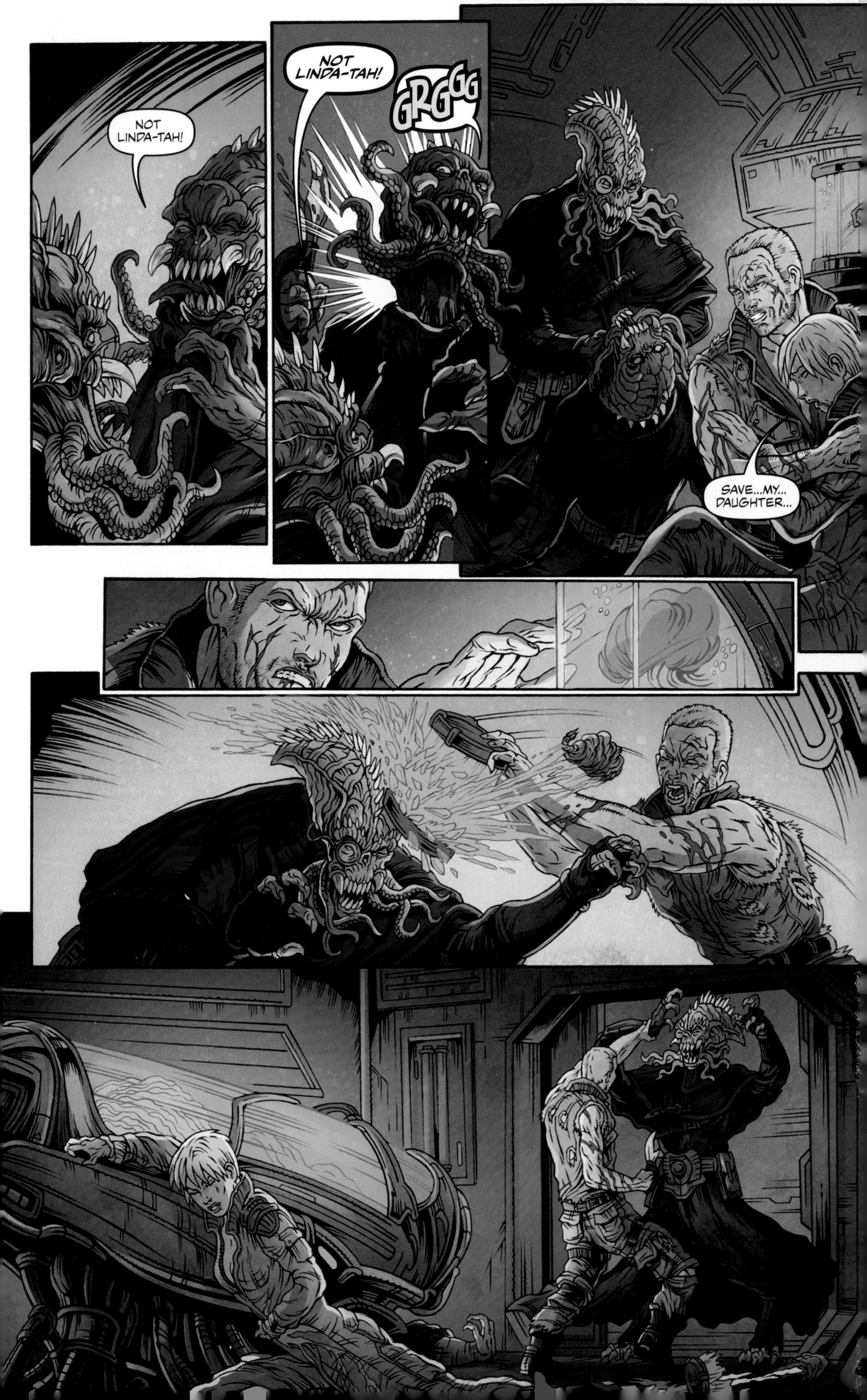
NOT LINDA-TAH!
NOT LINDA-TAH!
GRGGG
SAVE...MY... DAUGHTER...

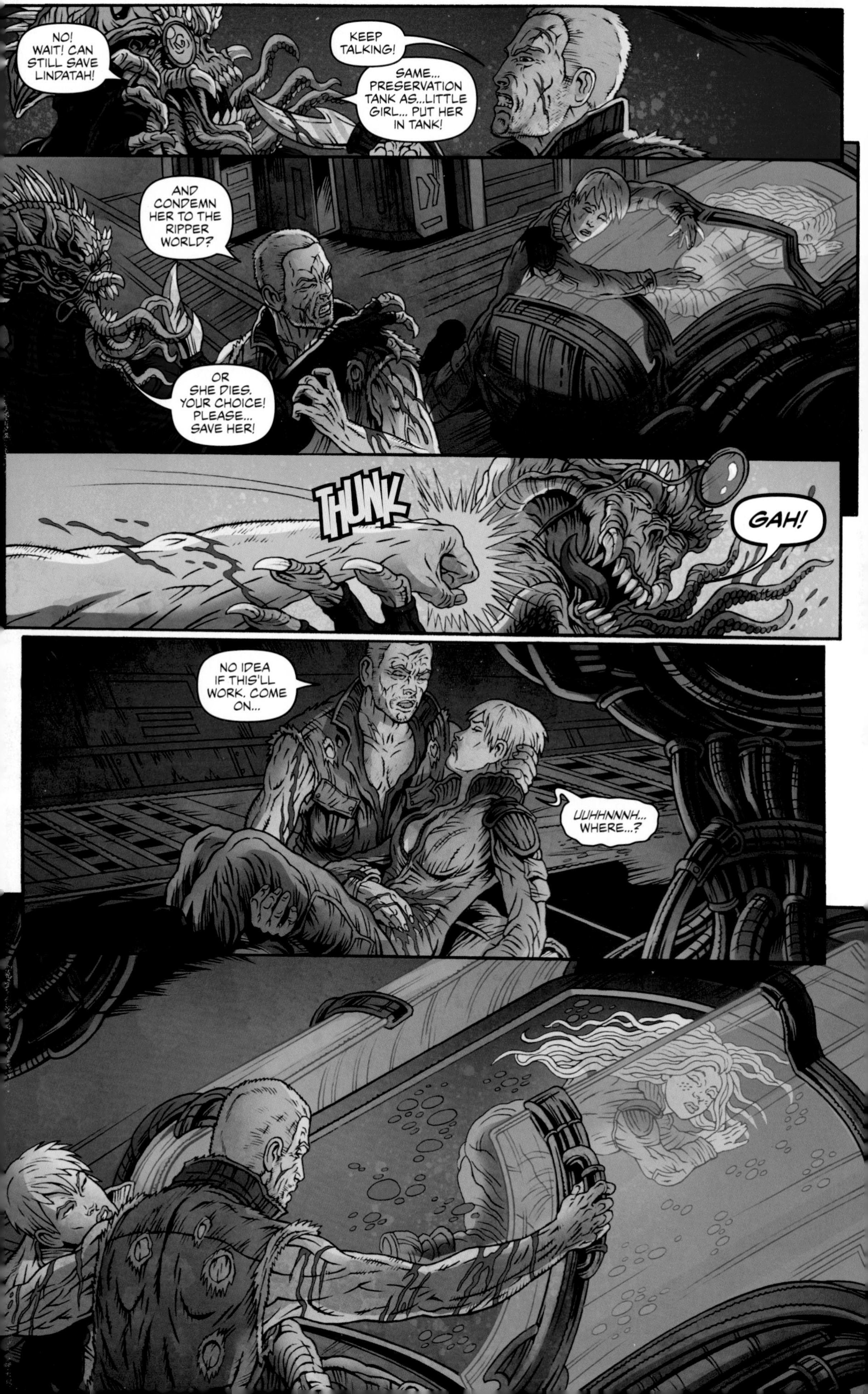
NO! WAIT! CAN STILL SAVE LINDATAH!
KEEP TALKING!
SAME... PRESERVATION TANK AS...LITTLE GIRL... PUT HER IN TANK!
AND CONDEMN HER TO THE RIPPER WORLD?
OR SHE DIES. YOUR CHOICE! PLEASE... SAVE HER!
THUNK
GAH!
NO IDEA IF THIS'LL WORK. COME ON...
UUHHNNNH... WHERE...?

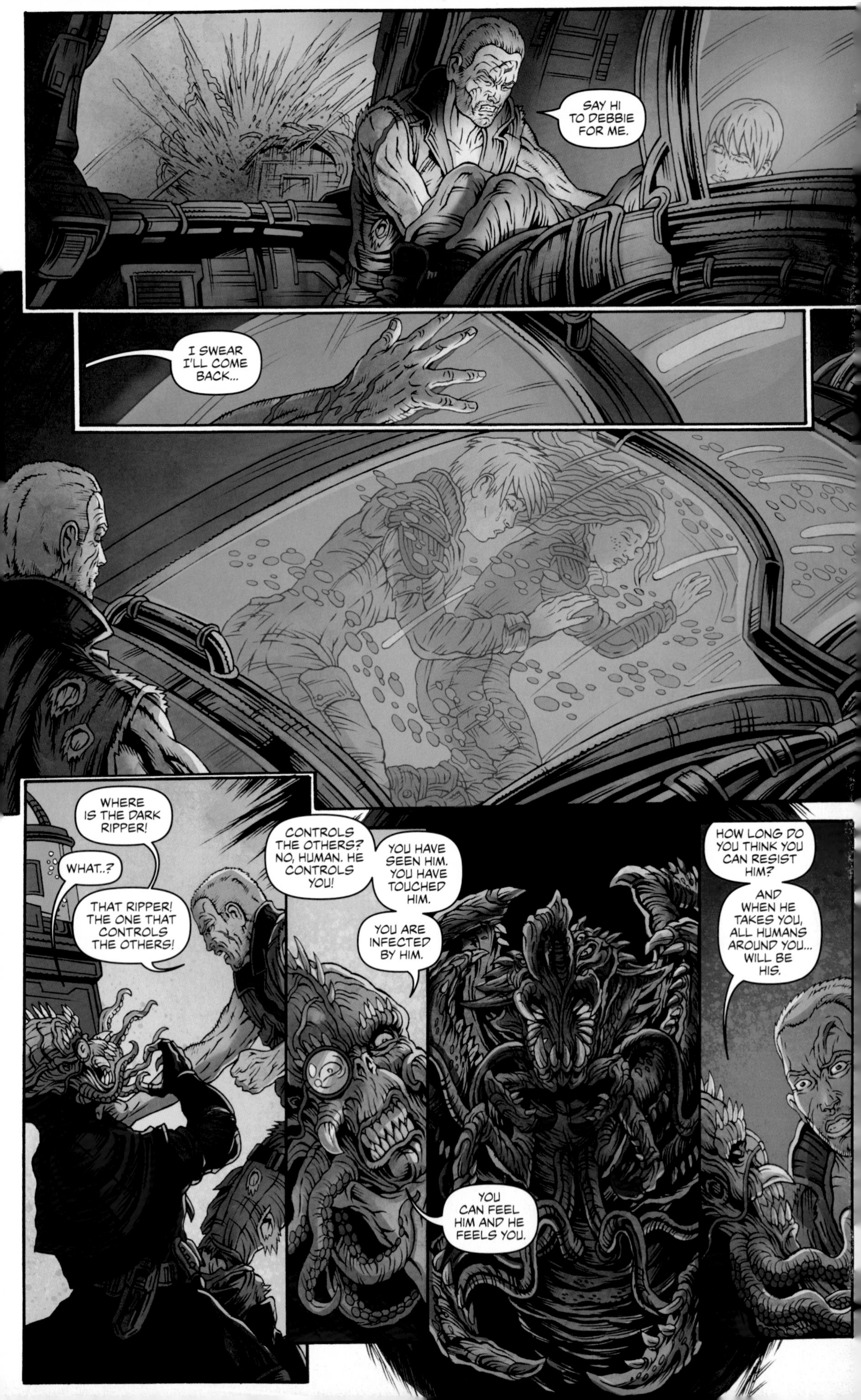
SAY HI TO DEBBIE FOR ME.
I SWEAR I'LL COME BACK...
WHERE IS THE DARK RIPPER!
WHAT..?
THAT RIPPER! THE ONE THAT CONTROLS THE OTHERS!
CONTROLS THE OTHERS? NO, HUMAN. HE CONTROLS YOU!
YOU HAVE SEEN HIM. YOU HAVE TOUCHED HIM.
YOU ARE INFECTED BY HIM.
YOU CAN FEEL HIM AND HE FEELS YOU.
HOW LONG DO YOU THINK YOU CAN RESIST HIM?
AND WHEN HE TAKES YOU, ALL HUMANS AROUND YOU... WILL BE HIS.

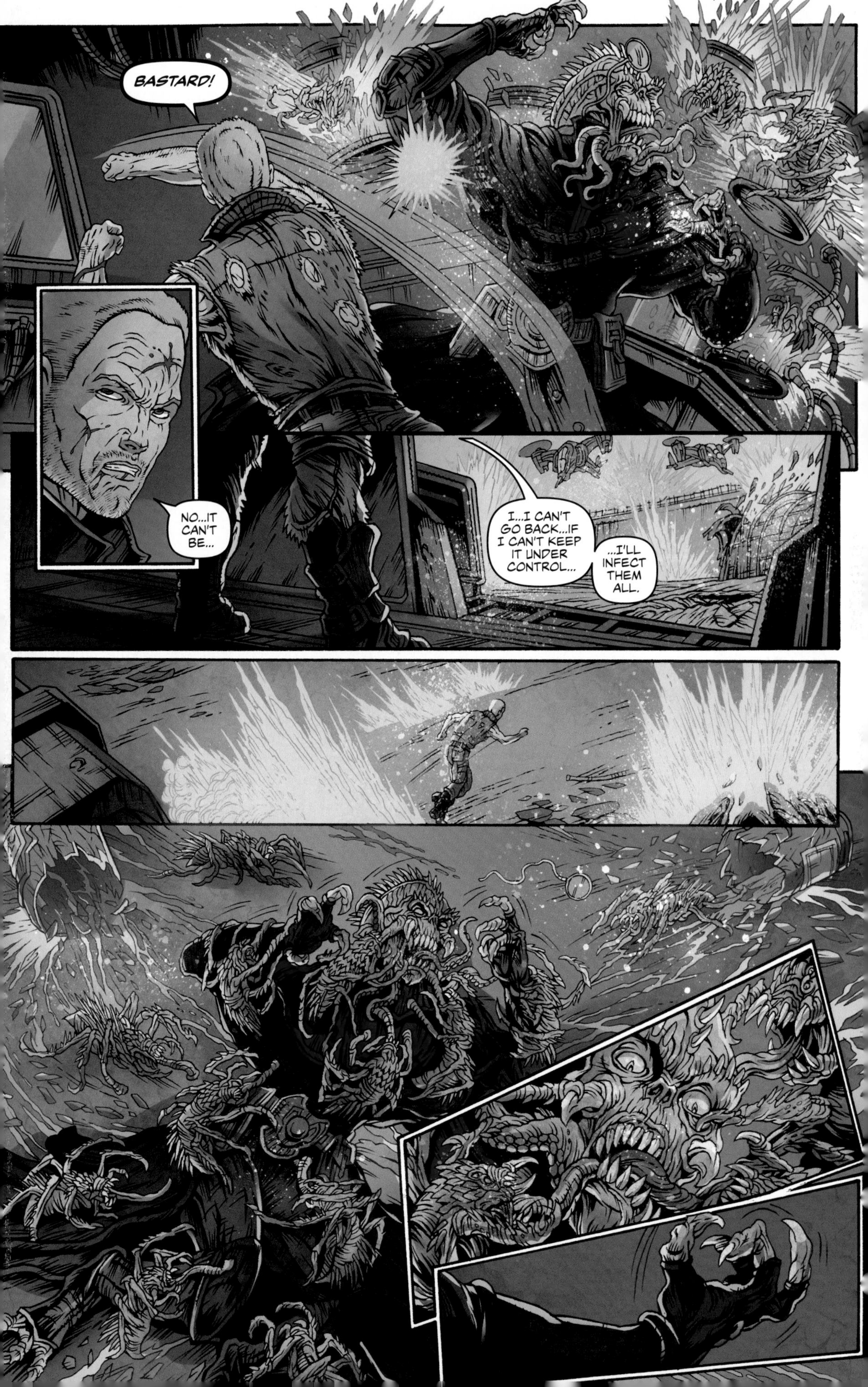
BASTARD!
NO...IT CAN'T BE...
I...I CAN'T GO BACK...IF I CAN'T KEEP IT UNDER CONTROL...
...I'LL INFECT THEM ALL.

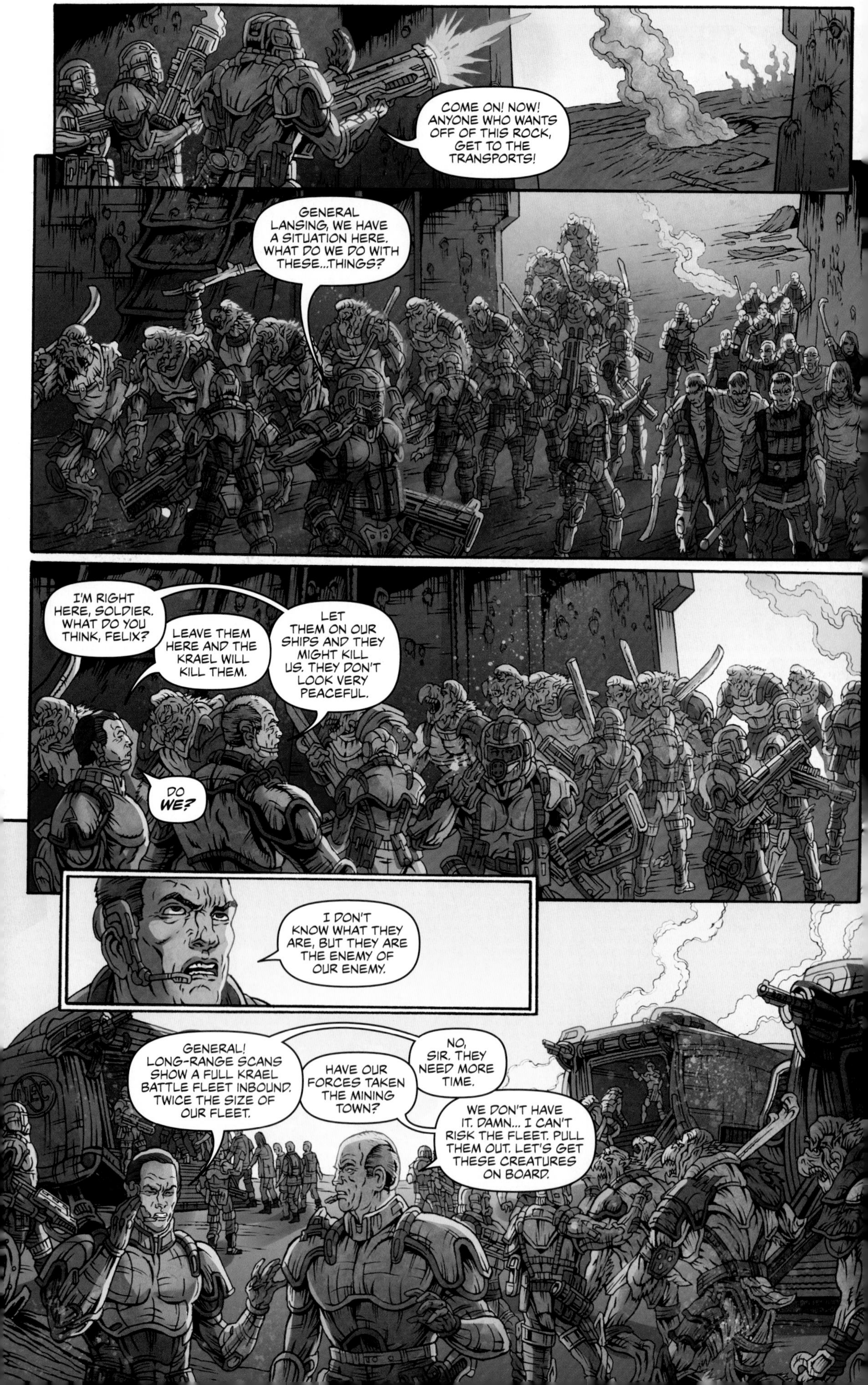
COME ON! NOW! ANYONE WHO WANTS OFF OF THIS ROCK, GET TO THE TRANSPORTS!
GENERAL LANSING, WE HAVE A SITUATION HERE. WHAT DO WE DO WITH THESE...THINGS?
I'M RIGHT HERE, SOLDIER. WHAT DO YOU THINK, FELIX?
LEAVE THEM HERE AND THE KRAEL WILL KILL THEM.
LET THEM ON OUR SHIPS AND THEY MIGHT KILL US. THEY DON'T LOOK VERY PEACEFUL.
DO *WE?*
I DON'T KNOW WHAT THEY ARE, BUT THEY ARE THE ENEMY OF OUR ENEMY.
GENERAL! LONG-RANGE SCANS SHOW A FULL KRAEL BATTLE FLEET INBOUND. TWICE THE SIZE OF OUR FLEET.
HAVE OUR FORCES TAKEN THE MINING TOWN?
NO, SIR. THEY NEED MORE TIME.
WE DON'T HAVE IT. DAMN... I CAN'T RISK THE FLEET. PULL THEM OUT. LET'S GET THESE CREATURES ON BOARD.

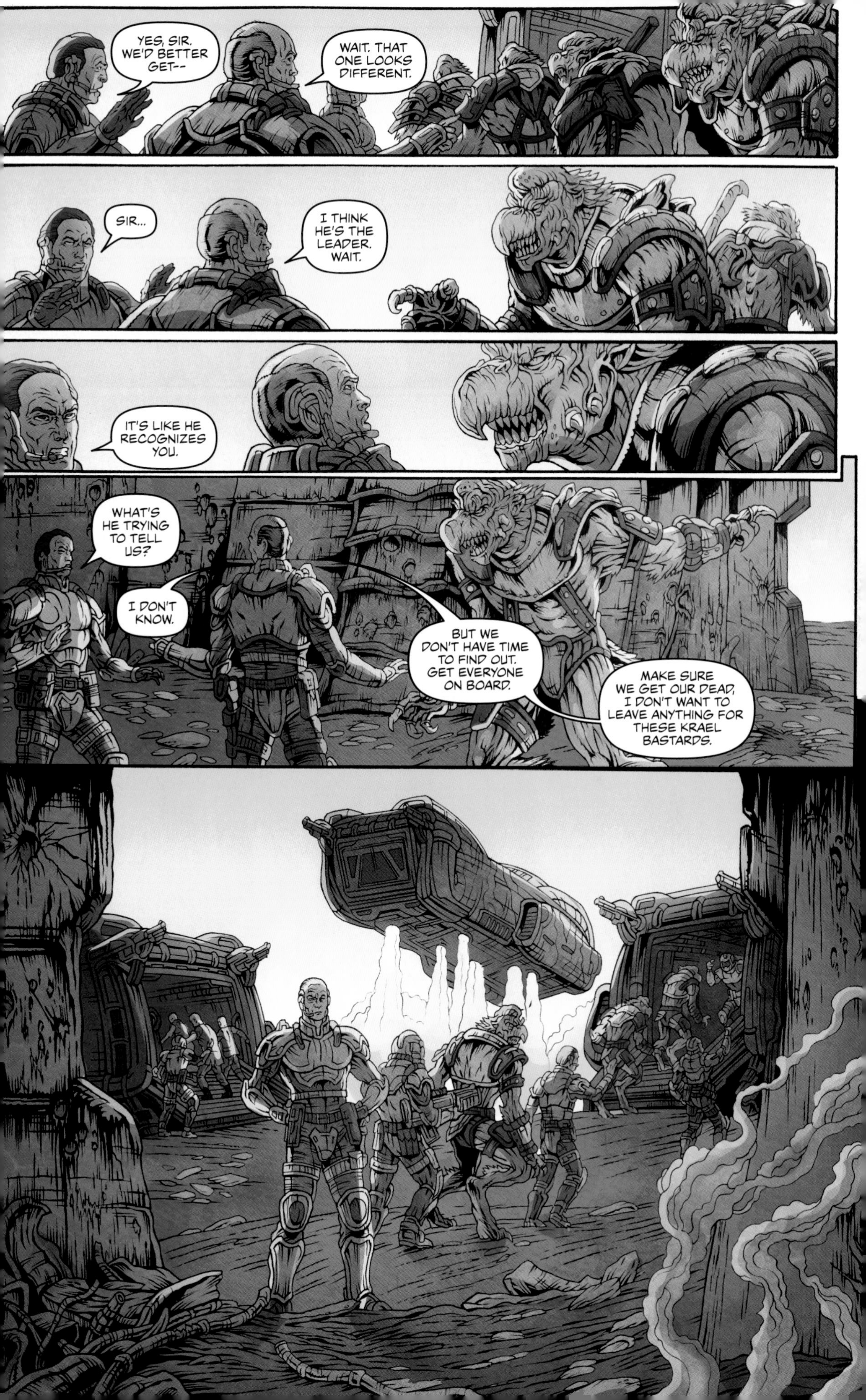
YES, SIR. WE'D BETTER GET--
WAIT. THAT ONE LOOKS DIFFERENT.
SIR...
I THINK HE'S THE LEADER. WAIT.
IT'S LIKE HE RECOGNIZES YOU.
WHAT'S HE TRYING TO TELL US?
I DON'T KNOW.
BUT WE DON'T HAVE TIME TO FIND OUT. GET EVERYONE ON BOARD.
MAKE SURE WE GET OUR DEAD, I DON'T WANT TO LEAVE ANYTHING FOR THESE KRAEL BASTARDS.

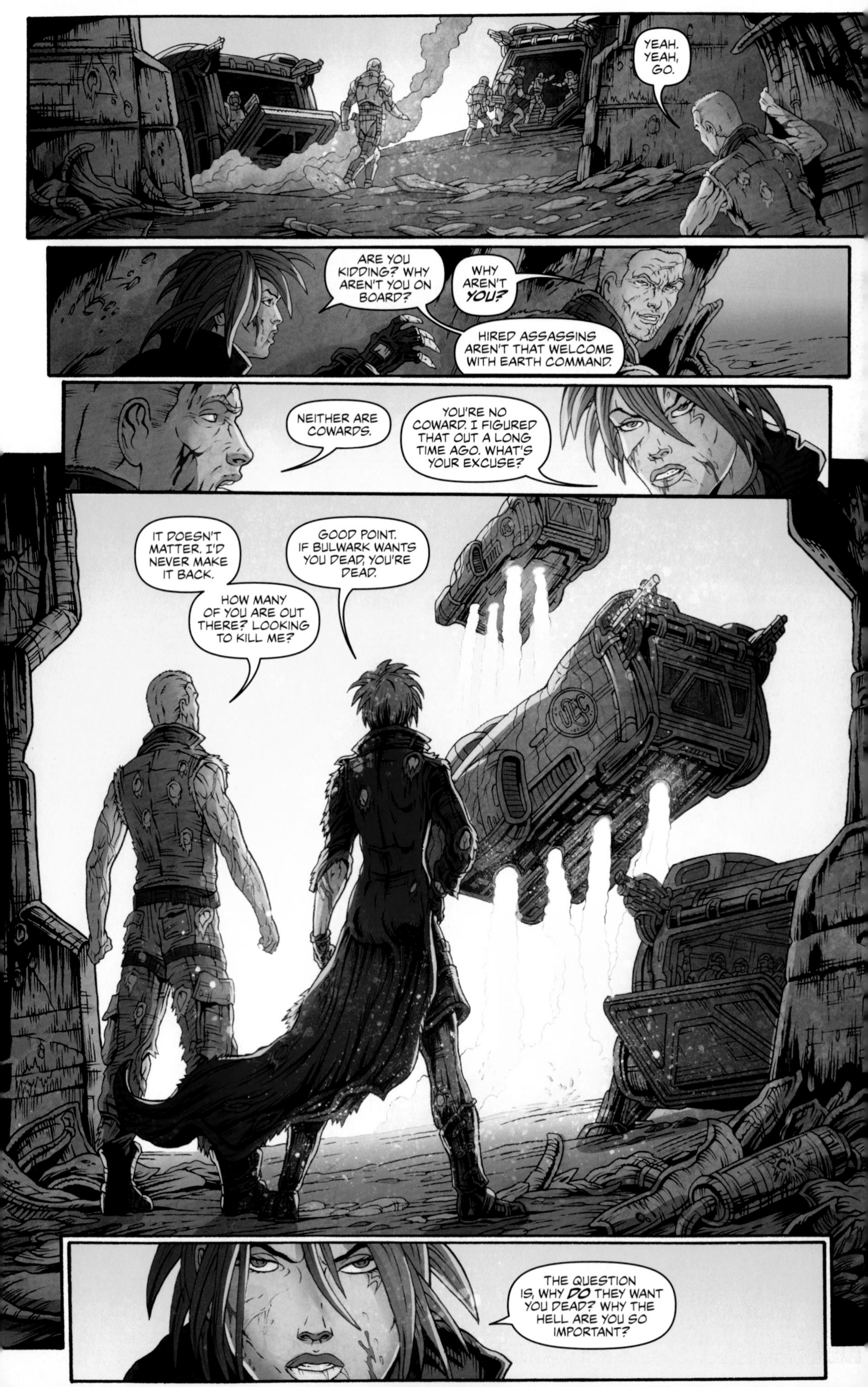
YEAH. YEAH, GO.
ARE YOU KIDDING? WHY AREN'T YOU ON BOARD?
WHY AREN'T ***YOU?***
HIRED ASSASSINS AREN'T THAT WELCOME WITH EARTH COMMAND.
NEITHER ARE COWARDS.
YOU'RE NO COWARD. I FIGURED THAT OUT A LONG TIME AGO. WHAT'S YOUR EXCUSE?
IT DOESN'T MATTER. I'D NEVER MAKE IT BACK.
HOW MANY OF YOU ARE OUT THERE? LOOKING TO KILL ME?
GOOD POINT. IF BULWARK WANTS YOU DEAD, YOU'RE DEAD.
THE QUESTION IS, WHY ***DO*** THEY WANT YOU DEAD? WHY THE HELL ARE YOU SO IMPORTANT?

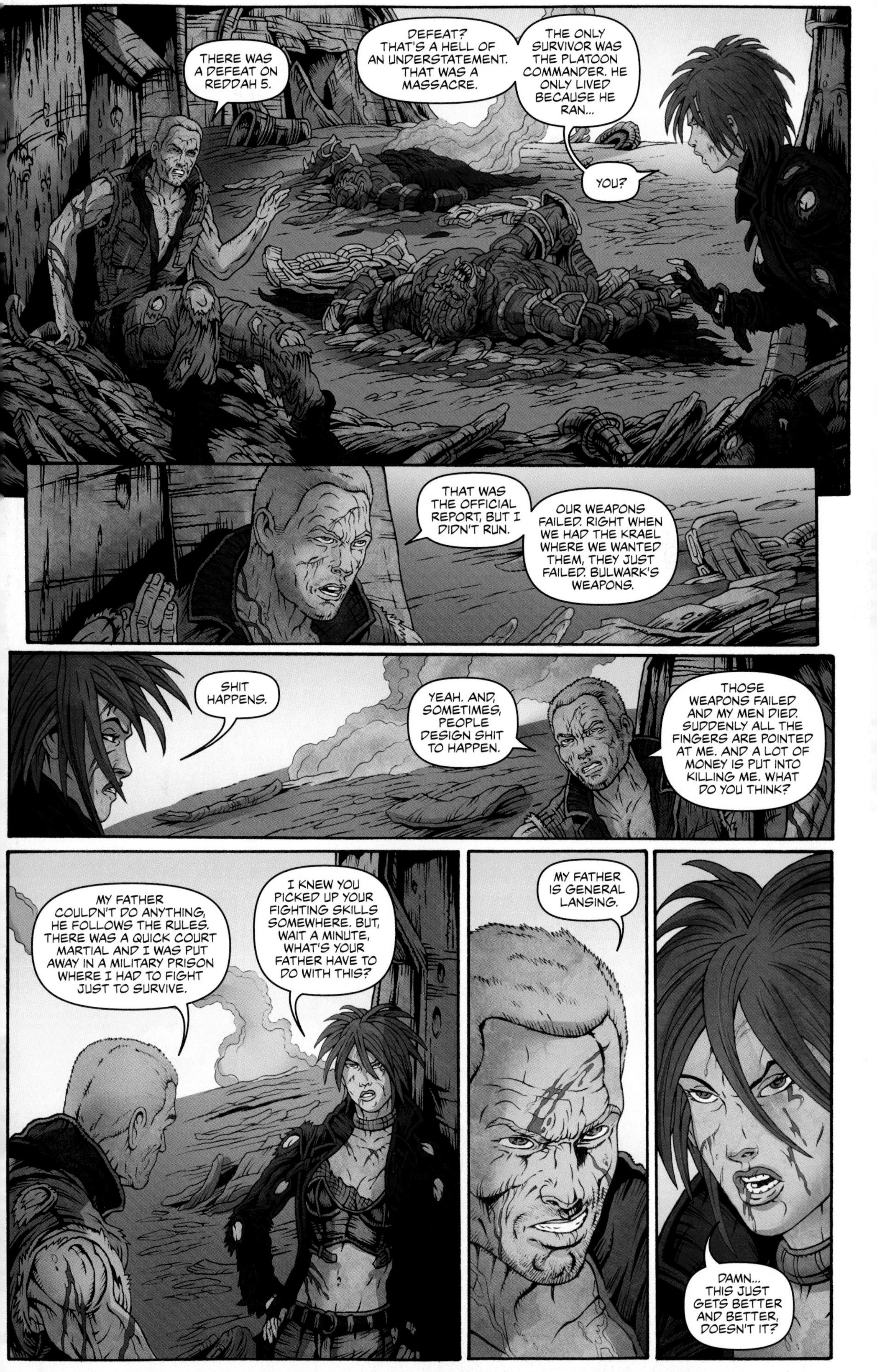
THERE WAS A DEFEAT ON REDDAH 5.
DEFEAT? THAT'S A HELL OF AN UNDERSTATEMENT. THAT WAS A MASSACRE.
THE ONLY SURVIVOR WAS THE PLATOON COMMANDER. HE ONLY LIVED BECAUSE HE RAN...
YOU?
THAT WAS THE OFFICIAL REPORT, BUT I DIDN'T RUN.
OUR WEAPONS FAILED. RIGHT WHEN WE HAD THE KRAEL WHERE WE WANTED THEM, THEY JUST FAILED. BULWARK'S WEAPONS.
SHIT HAPPENS.
YEAH. AND, SOMETIMES, PEOPLE DESIGN SHIT TO HAPPEN.
THOSE WEAPONS FAILED AND MY MEN DIED. SUDDENLY ALL THE FINGERS ARE POINTED AT ME. AND A LOT OF MONEY IS PUT INTO KILLING ME. WHAT DO YOU THINK?
MY FATHER COULDN'T DO ANYTHING, HE FOLLOWS THE RULES. THERE WAS A QUICK COURT MARTIAL AND I WAS PUT AWAY IN A MILITARY PRISON WHERE I HAD TO FIGHT JUST TO SURVIVE.
I KNEW YOU PICKED UP YOUR FIGHTING SKILLS SOMEWHERE. BUT, WAIT A MINUTE, WHAT'S YOUR FATHER HAVE TO DO WITH THIS?
MY FATHER IS GENERAL LANSING.
DAMN... THIS JUST GETS BETTER AND BETTER, DOESN'T IT?

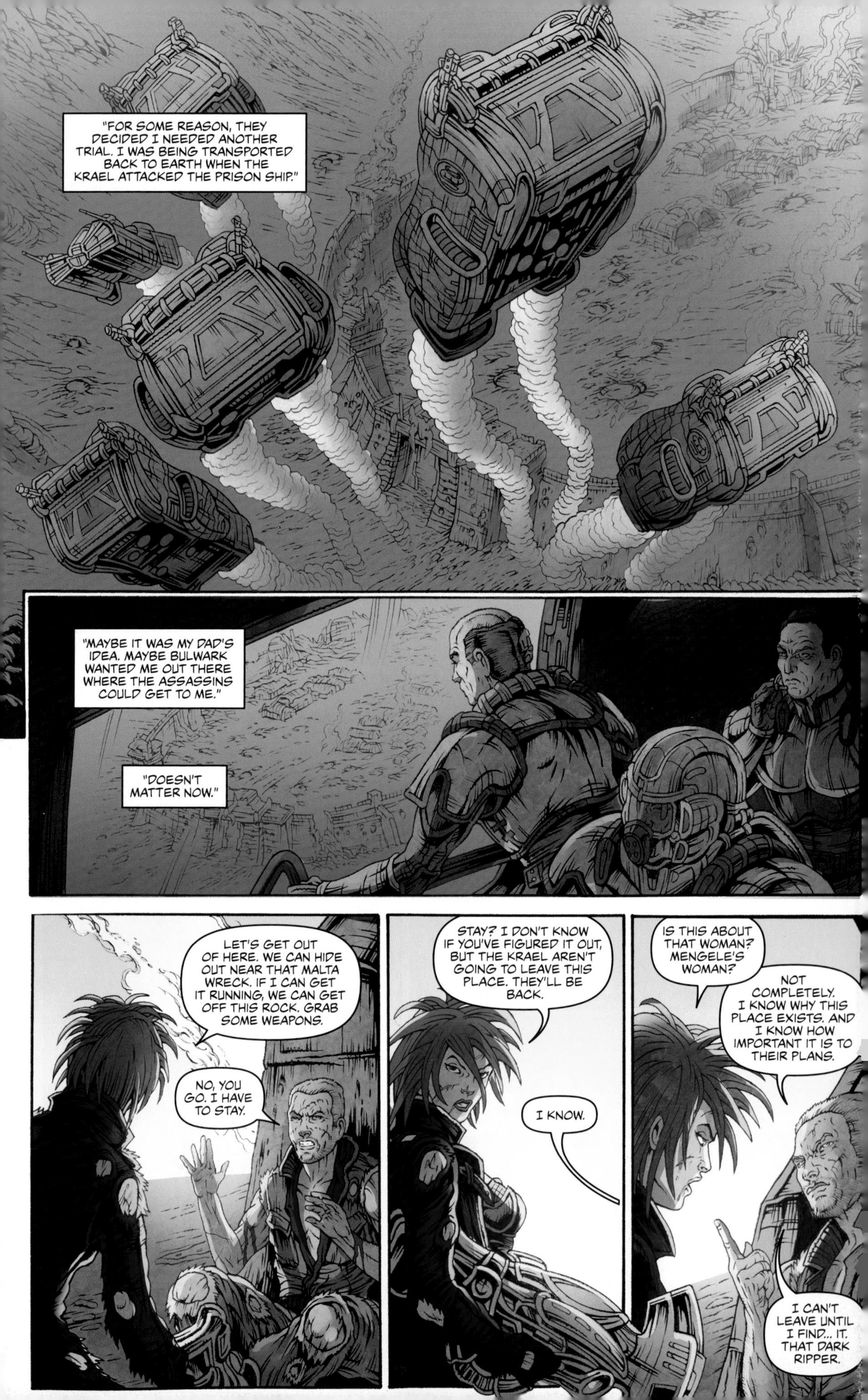
"FOR SOME REASON, THEY DECIDED I NEEDED ANOTHER TRIAL. I WAS BEING TRANSPORTED BACK TO EARTH WHEN THE KRAEL ATTACKED THE PRISON SHIP."
"MAYBE IT WAS MY DAD'S IDEA. MAYBE BULWARK WANTED ME OUT THERE WHERE THE ASSASSINS COULD GET TO ME."
"DOESN'T MATTER NOW."
LET'S GET OUT OF HERE. WE CAN HIDE OUT NEAR THAT MALTA WRECK. IF I CAN GET IT RUNNING, WE CAN GET OFF THIS ROCK. GRAB SOME WEAPONS.
NO, YOU GO. I HAVE TO STAY.
STAY? I DON'T KNOW IF YOU'VE FIGURED IT OUT, BUT THE KRAEL AREN'T GOING TO LEAVE THIS PLACE. THEY'LL BE BACK.
I KNOW.
IS THIS ABOUT THAT WOMAN? MENGELE'S WOMAN?
NOT COMPLETELY. I KNOW WHY THIS PLACE EXISTS. AND I KNOW HOW IMPORTANT IT IS TO THEIR PLANS.
I CAN'T LEAVE UNTIL I FIND... IT. THAT DARK RIPPER.

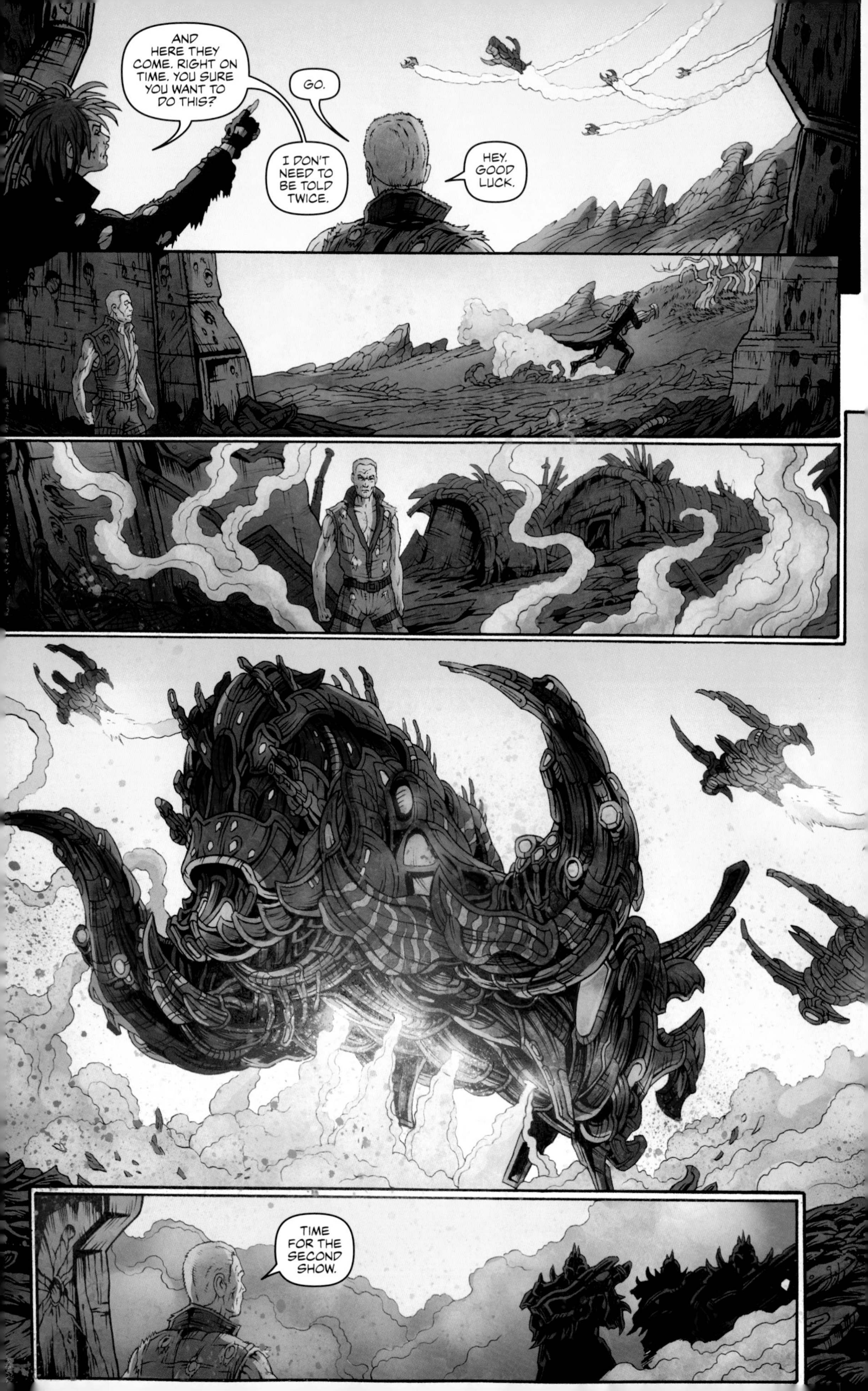
AND HERE THEY COME. RIGHT ON TIME. YOU SURE YOU WANT TO DO THIS?
GO.
I DON'T NEED TO BE TOLD TWICE.
HEY. GOOD LUCK.
TIME FOR THE SECOND SHOW.

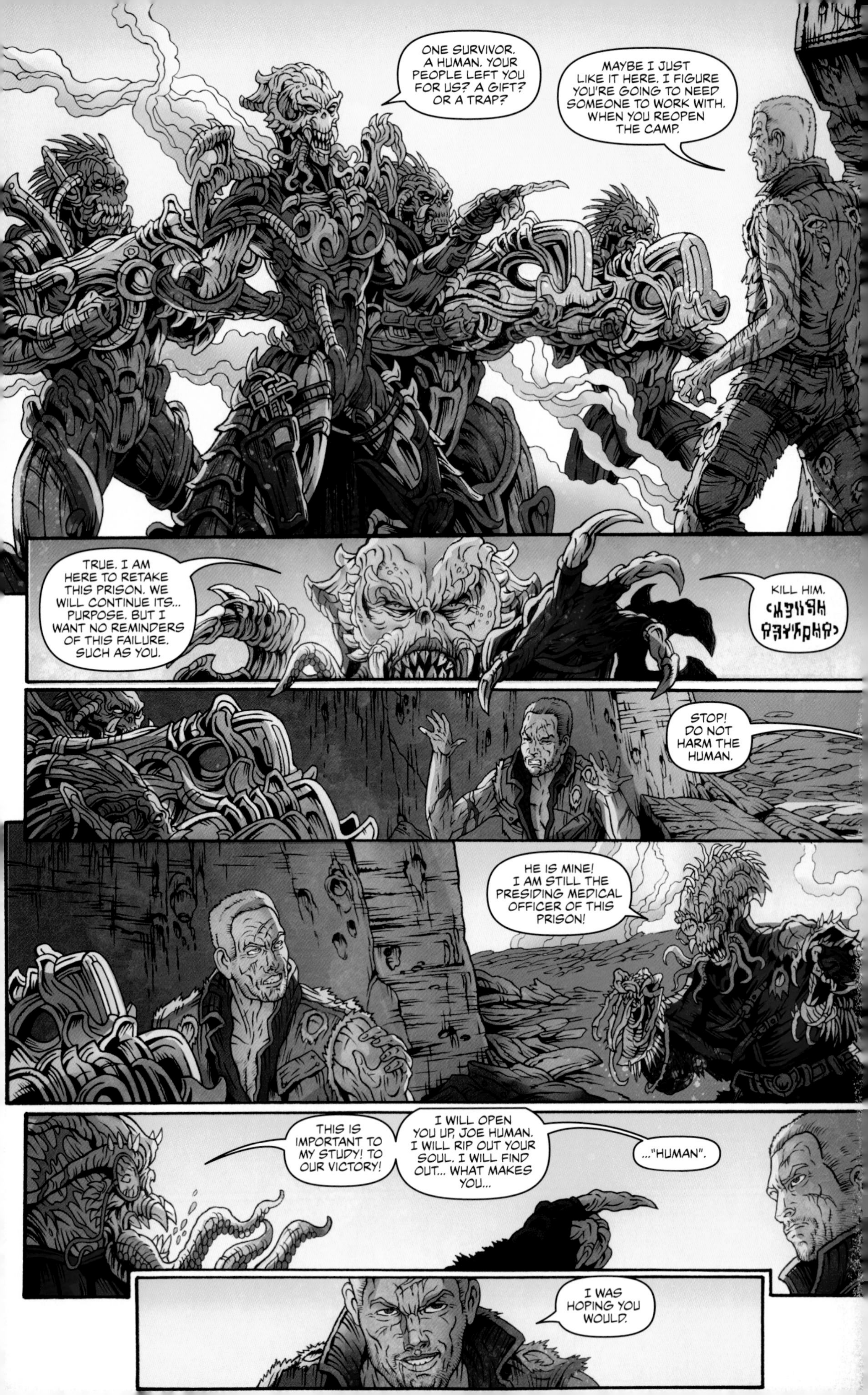
ONE SURVIVOR. A HUMAN. YOUR PEOPLE LEFT YOU FOR US? A GIFT? OR A TRAP?
MAYBE I JUST LIKE IT HERE. I FIGURE YOU'RE GOING TO NEED SOMEONE TO WORK WITH. WHEN YOU REOPEN THE CAMP.
TRUE. I AM HERE TO RETAKE THIS PRISON. WE WILL CONTINUE ITS... PURPOSE. BUT I WANT NO REMINDERS OF THIS FAILURE. SUCH AS YOU.
KILL HIM.
STOP! DO NOT HARM THE HUMAN.
HE IS MINE! I AM STILL THE PRESIDING MEDICAL OFFICER OF THIS PRISON!
THIS IS IMPORTANT TO MY STUDY! TO OUR VICTORY!
I WILL OPEN YOU UP, JOE HUMAN. I WILL RIP OUT YOUR SOUL. I WILL FIND OUT... WHAT MAKES YOU...
..."HUMAN".
I WAS HOPING YOU WOULD.

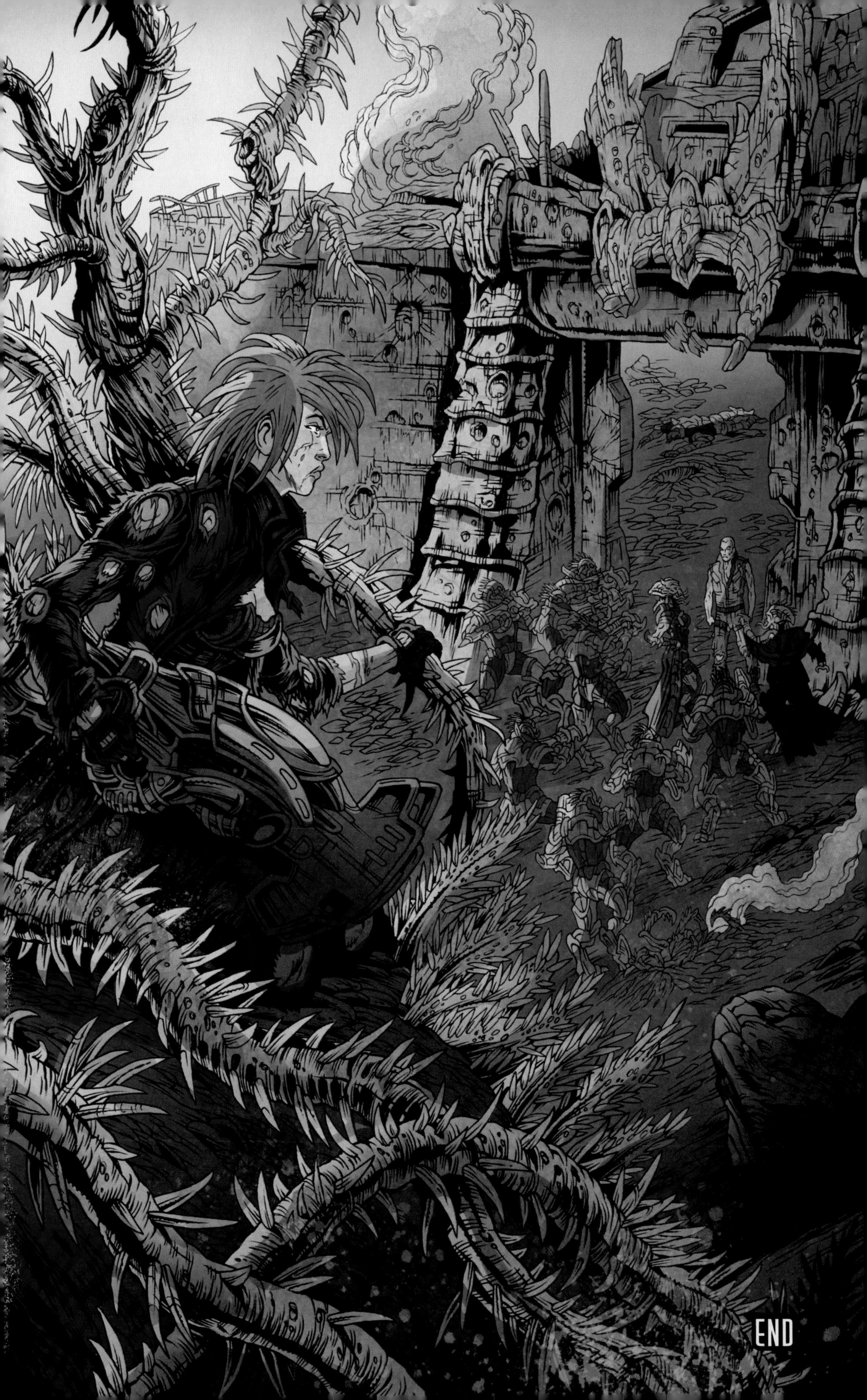
END

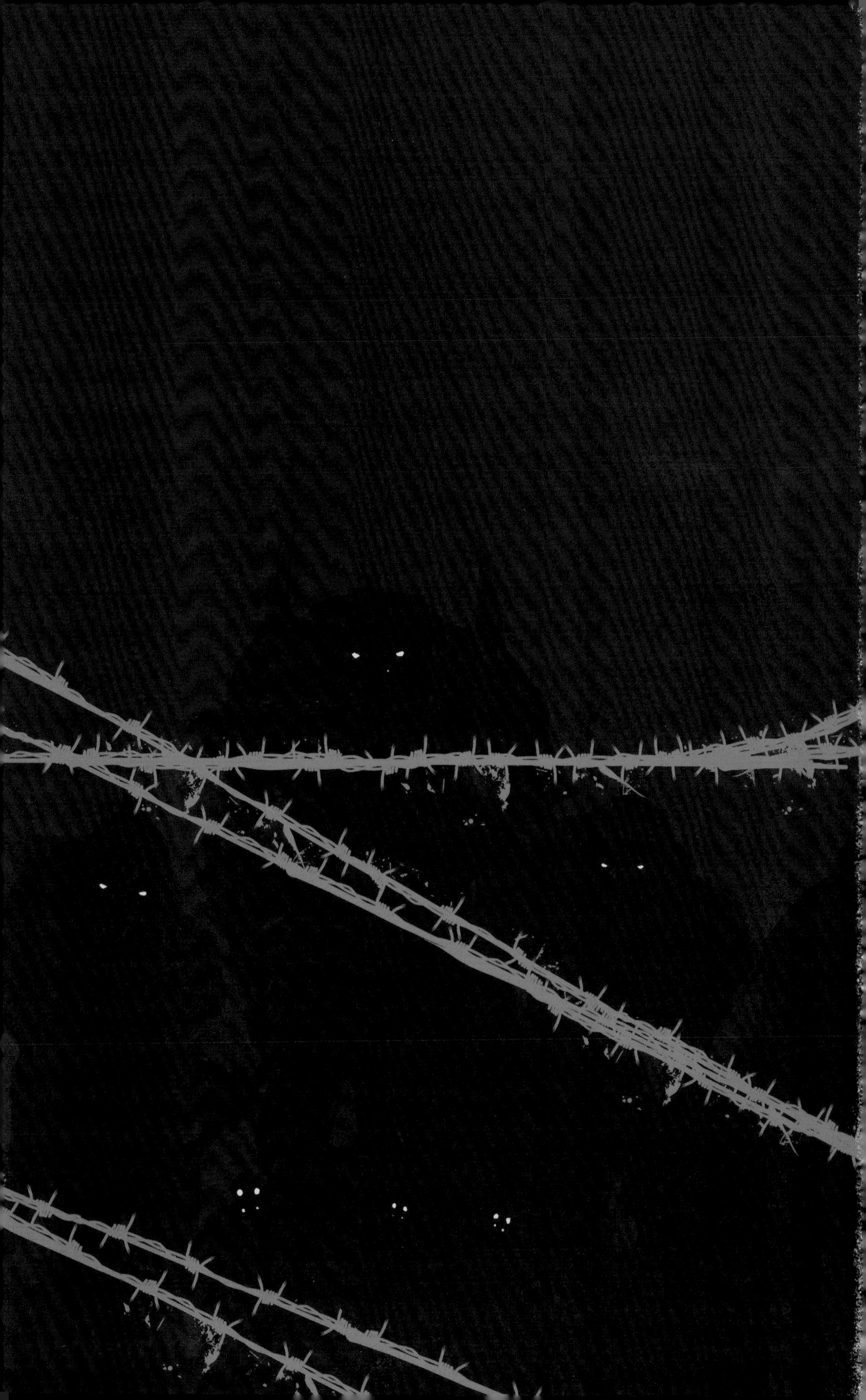

DEACON'S STORY

NOT A PRISONER

WRITTEN BY

KEVIN J. ANDERSON STEVEN L. SEARS

ILLUSTRATED BY

NATHAN GOODEN

She spent her days wondering whether the Krael commandant would scream when she killed him. **She didn't worry about how she would kill him. Deacon had no doubt of that, otherwise she'd be stuck here on this backwater planet. But the devil was in the details.

Deacon formed part of a plan as she hid among the rocks outside the harsh prisoner-of-war camp the alien invaders had built here on Pondafier. Originally a military base, one of the few Commonwealth outposts left over from the Outer Planet rebellion, it had fallen easily to the Krael. The monstrous aliens had killed the few defenders, strengthened its defenses, and built specialized facilities within the old outpost boundaries.

The camp's walls were high and imposing, capped with crackling pulse barriers making the air stink like ozone. Krael guard patrol walked around the tops of the wall. Inside the camp, the hideous creatures cracked down on their numerous prisoners, human soldiers they had seized from Commonwealth warships or dragged away as wounded from battlefields on unlucky planets.

The Krael never took prisoners, everyone knew that

Deacon didn't know what went on inside that place, much less why it even existed. The Krael never took prisoners, everyone knew that, so this place, which had become known by the local colonists as Stalag-X, was a true anomaly. She had watched as they herded human prisoners within the walls, sometimes allowing well-guarded groups to emerge for the "fresh air" of hard labor around the camp.

Although Deacon was on the outside and solo, she was just as trapped as the others since the Krael invasion had clamped down like a strangler smothering a victim. Some might have called her lucky. The human POWs were treated as animals, only slightly worse than the downtrodden settlers who lived in the overthrown settlement of Colony. Starved into submission, the colonists were no more than domesticated cattle. She didn't understand why the vicious Krael had

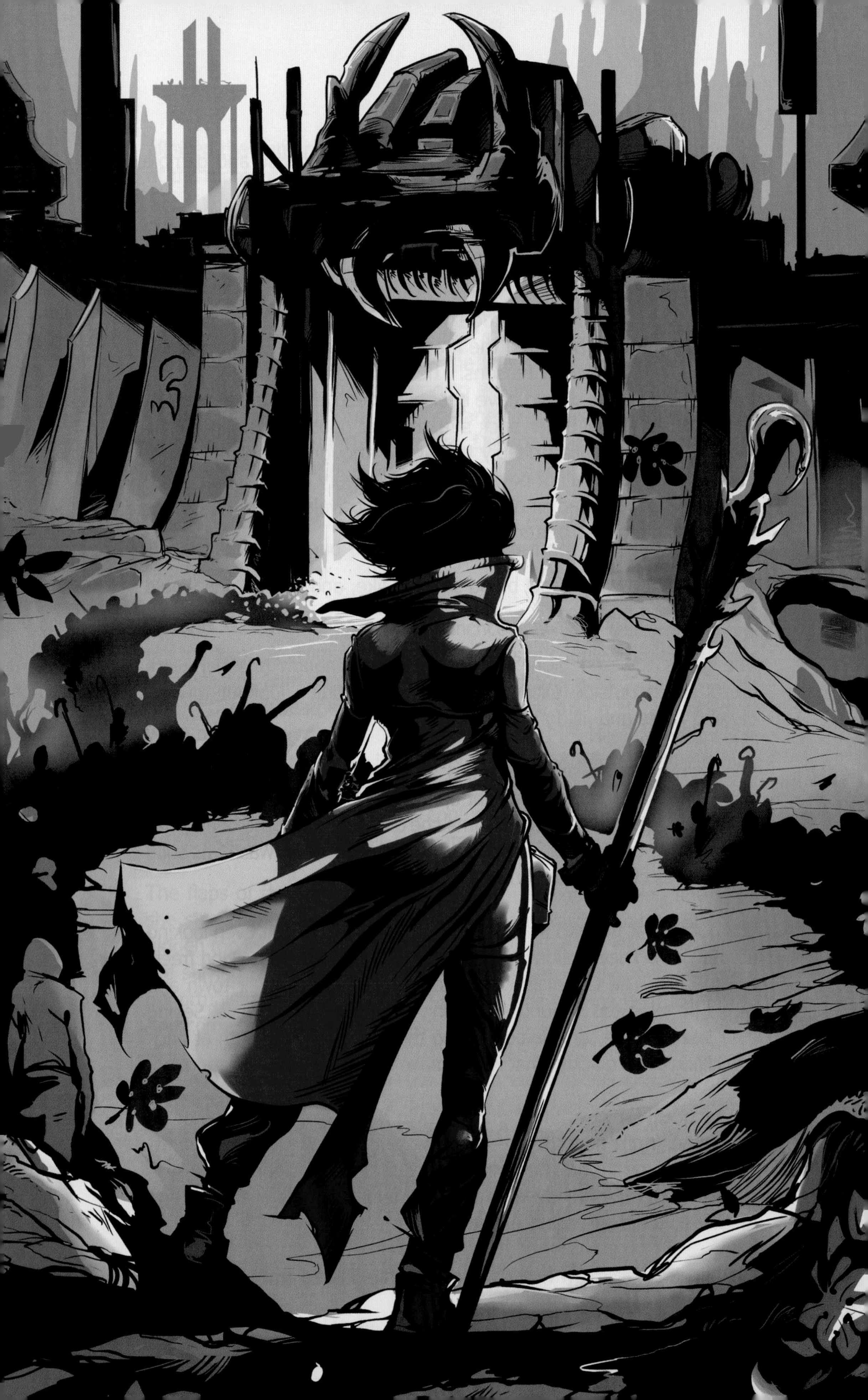

ers as they silently nudged each other or nodded toward her. Their bruised and dirty faces grew slack with wary curiosity.

Deacon ignored them, caring only about the two Krael guards. They wore armor with bulbous plates and spiny shoulder guards, thick collars and scale overlapping ridges across their chests and legs. The creatures had leathery faces, blazing yellow eyes, and curved tusks that framed their mouths. They were ugly with faces only a mother could love, if their mother were a tarantula who'd had an illicit affair with a pug dog. They carried prodding staffs with thick handles, metal knobs, and a hooked blade that could either gut or decapitate a victim. An imposing, intimidating weapon, Deacon thought. Brute force, ugly, intimidating, but not necessarily practical at a distance. She wasn't thinking distance, her mission was to get close and personal.

In any event, she thought, this should be quick.

The Krael on the towers were a different matter. With their big mounted guns they could rake the area with high-intensity pulses or projectiles. She hoped they would let the guards handle the situation. In any event, she thought, this should be quick.

One way or another.

A shout from the walls told her the Krael had seen her, but they didn't fire immediately as the two guards turned their attention toward her. As much as anyone could read the Krael, she thought she could read confusion, indecision, disbelief. So far, so good.

The enormous gates opened as she approached and two more guards stepped from the interior of the camp and took positions near the back of the POW work crews. Deacon had no doubt that if the humans decided to make a break for it, take a chance on freedom right now, they'd be slaughtered. She could only hope they would be smart enough not to interfere, not because she had any particular feelings for the prisoners—they'd chosen their lot the moment they put on military gear—but because it would be a useless attempt and she'd most likely get killed in the process. The prisoners didn't move, just watched.

The foremost two alien guards stepped forward, shifting their prodding staffs into attack position, clenching the handles with clawed hands. Inside the stalag she glimpsed rows of low hastily constructed barracks, numerous human prisoners standing to be counted in ranks, many of them still wearing tattered United Commonwealth uniforms.

She decided that was also a good sign. It meant the Commandant would likely be in the open courtyard. Deacon walked forward without flinching as if the monstrous guards were no more than panhandlers to be ignored.

She heard the dull creak of the guns on the tower being focused on her as if a lone woman carrying a stick might be an invading army. She tried not to smile at that, though she doubted the Krael would recognize the nuances of human emotions. She walked forward with square shoulders, not sure how much time the surprise would grant her. She had observed that Krael acted quickly when responding to their basic emotions, but they tended to be confused when forced to consider their actions. It was a part of their caste system; each level of responsibility was delegated to the one above them. The fact that they hadn't cut her down the moment she appeared meant they were waiting for orders.

One of the ugly creatures grunted something in a guttural language that sounded halfway between a belch and a chainsaw. Deacon kept walking. In the pocket of her trench coat she carried her burst tablet, the miniaturized receiver that downloaded all background information and dossier packets the Service relayed whenever a subspace buoy emerged and transmitted new data. One part of that vital database was a first-order approximation of translation software so she could, to a certain extent, communicate with the ugly creatures. The tablet spoke in an uninflected, bland, human voice that bore little relation to the growling anger the guard had spoken.

"Halt. Maintain your distance. Do not retreat."

She calculated two more steps. The Krael repeated his command, louder. She risked another step, then came to a stop and glared at him. It was a test of wills, but Deacon was in her element, the poker table of professional assassins. Killing was only ten percent of what she actually did. The rest of it was strategy. That required knowing your opponent, which is why she had spent the last eight months studying the Krael on Pondafier before deciding to act.

In her peripheral vision, she could see the human POWs stir nervously, sure that the Krael were about to rip this foolish young woman apart. Deacon ignored them; the humans were irrelevant to her equation.

She was focused on the alien's body language. She waited. The Krael leaned forward, and she saw his feet dig in, preparing for his charge.

"I've come for your Commandant," she said abruptly, and the device translated for her. She watched the two guards recoil and stiffen holding up their spiked staffs. The translation was apparently reasonably accurate, and her calculations were correct. She had confused them again.

"You are a prisoner," said the other guard. The translator had difficulty with the last word which, Deacon knew, meant that the inflection had changed. It was more a question of uncertainty.

She responded in a sharp bark, "I'm no prisoner. I'm not from Colony Town and I'm not a soldier." She gestured deprecatingly into the camp, then repeated, "I've come for the Commandant."

She mused on the fact that, aside from the POWs, she was probably the greatest free human expert in Krael behavior just by benefit of being here, watching them first-hand from hiding. The propaganda about how well the war was going for Earth was just that: propaganda. She had seen the space wrecks and floating bodies. She had lost count of how many mass graves she had come upon in her travels.

It was well known the Krael never took prisoners, never, yet here she was facing an entire POW camp.

Clearly Earth Command would love to have this information, but that wasn't part of her mission, nor were these POWs part of her mission. She was stuck here on Pondafier, and the only way she could go home and collect payment for her assignment was to get off this damn planet. Quite simply, she had completed her mission, and the Krael were in her way.

The second guard spoke and the translation conveyed his obvious question. "Why do you wish to see the Commandant?"

"I intend to kill him," she said. For effect, she examined her nails on her free hand, bit at a loose hangnail and spit it to the side, then returned her glare to the Krael. The human prisoners nearby gasped a few seconds before the guards reacted to the subsequent translation. The Krael flinched, startled at the response. Deacon knew the time had come. She took one more step forward. "Or do I kill you to get to him?" she stated flatly. The translation echoed against the walls of the camp.

Though the Krael were not human, they still reacted predictably to provocation. The first huge guard lurched toward her, spreading his four curved mouth tusks, flashing his fangs. He lifted his weapon, and Deacon stood her ground, waiting, letting his inertia commit him. When he leaned forward to deliver his fatal blow, Deacon shifted her weight and spun her ironwood stick, whipping it like a scorpion's stinger. She drew back her arm, jammed her open palm into the out-side of his elbow, turning as she plunged the sharp crystal thorn tip deep into the yellow jelly of his eye. She pushed deep and yanked it back out faster than even the liquid could spurt out.

The guard jerked and snapped his head back as his knees buckled. Deacon jammed the crystal-tipped spear again, this time deep into his mouth, pushing it to the back of his throat. She forced the sharp point up into his palate, ramming it through the bone and into his brain. She yanked the spear out again and danced back two steps. Everything happened in only a fraction of a second.

The Krael began to fall, ooze coming out of his punctured eye, a gur-gling sound emerging from his throat as his breath mixed with the blood and brain matter gushing into his mouth. Deacon stood upright and, almost casually, stabbed a third time hard into his throat. Krael blood spilled out onto the dust of the road. She noted that it smelled like copper and vinegar.

The second guard roared, and Deacon had to calculate this carefully. If he reached her, he was going to kill her. If he didn't, the guns on the wall would rain down hell around her. If she killed him, the result would be the same. She had three obvious options, and all of them left her dead.

The Krael swung his weapon up toward her staff. This was a feint, she saw immediately, and went with it. As their weapons collided, he shoved his body toward her, expecting her motion to be defensive and off balance. Deacon ignored his shift, though. She released the staff, slammed her elbow into his jaw, and linked her arm around the Krael's head, lifting herself up and around to the back of his body. She allowed the momentum to spin them completely around until they were both facing the walls of the stalag, and the guns now aimed on

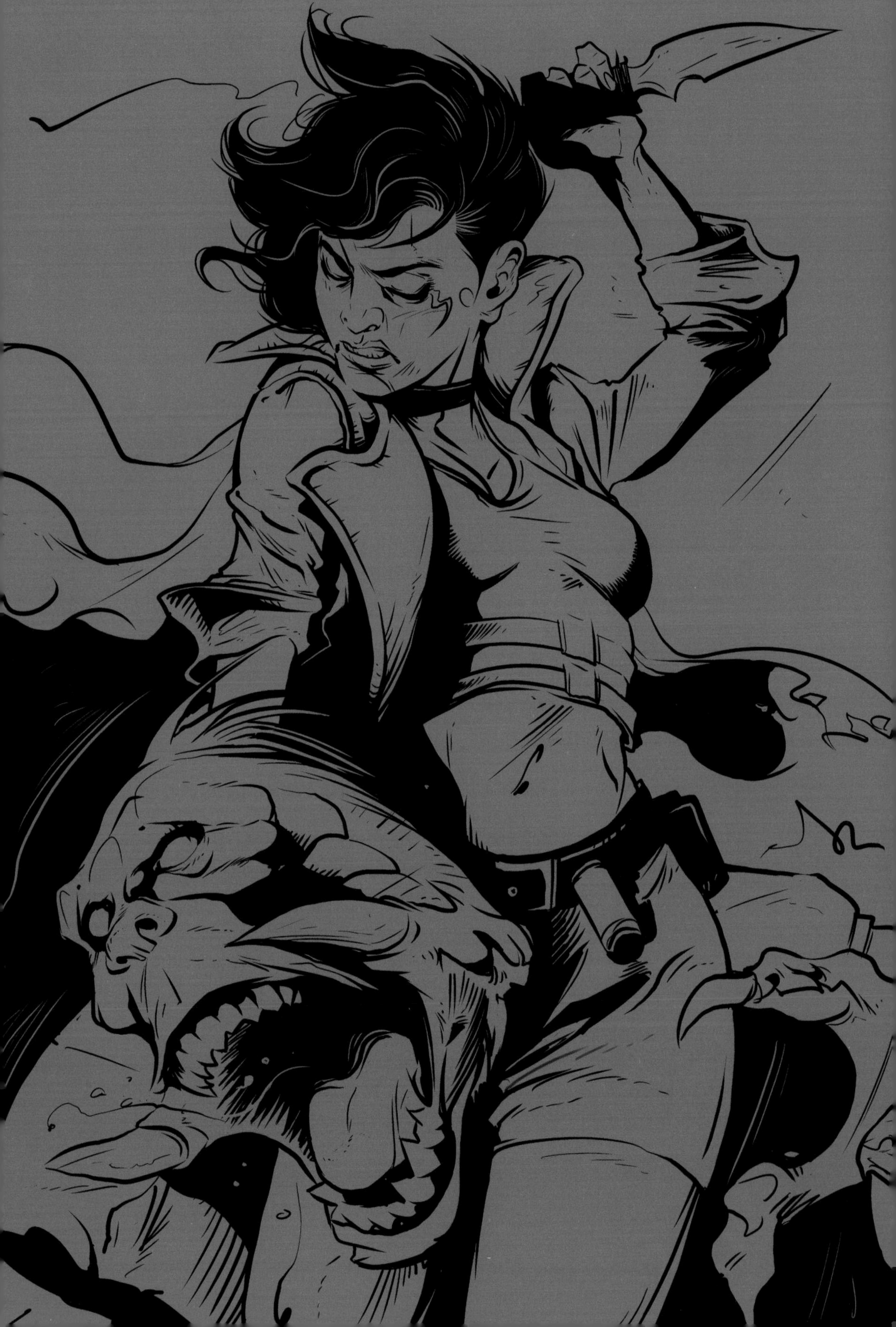

her. She pulled her knife, put it to the neck of the Krael, tightening her grip around his throat.

She had three options. Deacon picked the fourth. She dropped her knife and released the Krael, letting him fall to the ground, heaving, and raised her empty hands into the air.

The few seconds passed in geologic terms, seemingly an eternity. She heard the wind whistling past her ear. She could sense the tension of the human POWs watching. She expected to feel the expanding air of a heat blast, the smell of the ozone in her nostrils. She lowered her hands slowly, stared at the open gate and waited.

The Krael guard at her feet was still wheezing. Apparently she had broken his jaw. On the ground next to him was a large tooth. One of his curved and fearsome looking tusks from around his mouth. She slowly bent down to snatch it up.

"My trophy," she said. The Krael stumbled to his feet, seemingly confused. "Now take me to your Commandant." He stumbled back toward the gate and disappeared inside. The remaining Krael kept their weapons aimed on her. The human prisoners stared, awed and impressed. Several were grinning, and a few even silently applauded. They seemed to think she was a rescuer, some savior who would bring them freedom. She wished them well, but Deacon was getting out of here on her own.

Movement at the gate caught her attention. Four Krael had returned, marching through the prisoners in the yard to the front gate and standing in a square position, their bladed weapons at their sides. Their intent was unmistakable. She walked forward, into the center of the square. They turned as one, the rear two bringing their blades up toward her back.

As they started to walk, she heard a familiar "snorfing" sound behind her. The strange sand creatures the Krael had hibernating under the ground around Stalag-X as watchdogs had been activated. She didn't have to look back to know they were feasting on the forgotten Krael she had killed. A gruesome, but efficient way to dispose of those who had lost honor by being defeated.

The first part of her plan was a success. DEACON WAS NOW A PRISONER OF THE KRAEL.

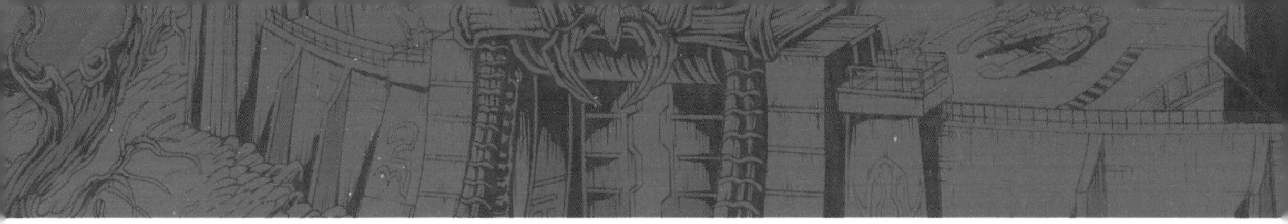

She sat cross-legged on the sand in the middle of the open camp yard, while the human POWs were on the other side of electric-phase fencing. The Krael guards kept their distance, wary. They had relieved her of the deadly staff, but let her keep her knife, as if they didn't consider it much of a threat. She could make do.

Her eyes were closed as if resting, but she focused all her senses and sensibilities on her predicament and the task ahead.

She'd done her threat assessment the moment she entered the stalag. It was a natural thing for her, intuitively examining every new environment for any advantages and disadvantages, far more of the latter than the former. Though she'd been observing Stalag-X for several months, she could not have known exactly what the Krael had done to the interior of the former human military base. She was quite familiar with the standard layout of Commonwealth bases, but the Krael had modified this one to their own use.

The local Colony Town had also been taken and repurposed, and the settlers didn't have a chance. Pondafier was never going to be an exotic getaway for the Space Cruise companies, but it wasn't a bad planet when she'd first arrived on a routine assassination mission. The Krael invasion had screwed everything up.

Deacon's target had shown up on her burst tablet with the new data received from the Service, a clandestine subnet listing board for those who did commerce in illegal affairs. It was a safe way for an employer to stay anonymous while guaranteeing payment to professionals like herself. The money was transferred into an escrow account until receipt of proof of completion. It was an open system, with the money paid to whomever actually accomplished the task. First come, first served. That had resulted in a lot of clusterfucks with more than one assassin getting in the way of others, all after the same target. But those free-for-alls were for lower-level killers.

DEACON WASN'T A LOW-LEVEL KILLER. Her record entitled her to a Premium listing, giving her access to the high-value targets where the real money was. Less competition, though much more risk. Deacon had been contracted as Premium for years, picking up targets, reading the mission data, warnings and weaknesses, useful details for an assassin. The galaxy had enough scattered planets of diverse people, beliefs and enmities that she never lacked for work.

The initial outbreak of the Krael war, when the aliens attacked and wiped out human colonies and military ships on the rim systems, didn't really affect Deacon's business at first. She'd been inconvenienced, but she hadn't paid much attention to politics. She would study the listings from the Service and choose a target that sounded interesting. She'd been out on the far rim when she saw the urgent high-level target appear, last known location on Pondafier.

And a price tag that made the job very worthwhile.

A missing part in the dossier, as always, was why the target was so important. Deacon never bothered to ask. The job was a job, and she didn't care whether the victim was a genocidal dictator, a religious cult leader, or simply a cheating ex-husband targeted by a jilted lover. Everyone bleeds the same.

Since Pondafier was nearby, she had altered her course to take the job. There was always a small chance that some other assassin might hurry to the backwater planet and beat her to the victim, but she doubted it. This was just too far out on the rim, and the well-armed Earth Command military base south of town made Pondafier a less-than-desirable place for assassins to ply their trade. Perhaps the target thought the sheer isolation offered him some protection. And maybe it did, from others. Not from her.

She had studied the public information available on the target as she brought in her ship to land in a clearing not far from Colony Town. The target's name was Anson Garbo, a wealthy executive who had pulled up roots and decided to become a hardscrabble colonist.

NOT LIKELY.

He had worked in various technologies with all the major companies, Bulwark being the most notable. It was the largest pan-galactic corporation, everyone of note worked for Bulwark at one time or another. Since the beginning of the Krael war, Bulwark's size had tripled along with the number of Earth government contracts it received.

Bulwark paid its employees well, so if this Anson Garbo had chucked that paycheck, he must have some really nasty people after him. She suspected that Garbo was probably embezzling or involved in industrial espionage. Someone wanted him dead, even though he'd gone to ground in the far armpit of the rim, where he was not likely to sell any stolen information or live large off of his illicit earning. He was a scared rabbit. That was plain enough.

Someone was willing to pay a hell of a lot of money for this scared rabbit.

She had landed her ship in a clearing surrounded by slowly waving thorn vines. Out of habit, she removed a cache of weapons and supplies, hiding them in case of emergency. Making those preparations seemed silly because Pondafier was such an obscure planet with a nonthreatening town. But Deacon had learned that worst-case scenarios occurred more often than anyone would expect. Early in her career, she had spent six months in a revitalization pod because she'd underestimated the abilities of a group of farmers defending a friend. Not again.

She had a long rifle if she wanted to kill the target at a distance, but she would still have to come forward and use her cranial drill to acquire the proof of death sample. She had her long knife in case she wanted to be personal, and she could kill with her bare hands, barring anything else. Deacon liked to improvise. If the plans were too specific, too cut and dried, then her job would become just that—a job.

For her, killing people was never personal. She wasn't a sick psychopath like that asshole Margrev. Deacon was a professional and learned early to bury any emotion. The last time she'd let passion drive her was her first assignment, the head of an interstellar cartel dealing in clone slavery and organ trade. The target was surrounded by security, untouchable by his enemies. Deacon had killed him quickly and silently, along with his bodyguards.

SHE WAS TWELVE AT THE TIME.

The only training she'd previously had was watching her parents and sister being slaughtered by that particular cartel, and that was enough to start her career. But she left that anger and hatred behind in the bloody loading bay of their slave ship. Anger and personal vendettas had no place now; they could get her killed.

Perhaps it was her own version of therapy, an attempt to blot out the memory of her family's slaughter. Perhaps it was guilt for being helpless when she'd been young. Sometimes she thought of it as justifiable revenge on a hateful God. It didn't matter. Deacon didn't care about causes or reasons. War or not, she was a gun for hire, and someone wanted this Anson Garbo dead.

The population of Colony Town was less than eight hundred. The buildings mainly prefab structures, though the people had added some personal touches. The settlers worked hard to be self-sufficient, if not profitable. The local biologic-mineral plant called ironwood was their main export. When cured and treated, ironwood was among the strongest materials in the galaxy. But aside from their exotic wood exports, Pondafier was an invisible world. These people considered it home, and who was she to judge?

Since he was a relative newcomer to this planet, Garbo shouldn't be hard to find.

No matter how much she wanted to keep a low profile, Deacon called attention to herself, just by being there. They didn't get a lot of tourists. The long rifle slung over her back, her knife at her side, her trench coat loose around her, all drew attention she strolled down the wide streets made of baked, hardened dirt and crushed gravel beaten down by large tires of Colony wood-processing trucks. She saw storefronts, tradesmen, mechanics, merchants and clothiers, which implied to Deacon that Colony Town was thriving enough that people could dabble in businesses beyond mere day-to-day survival. Large reptilian beasts with stubby horns and big eyes plodded down the street chased by laughing children who seemed to treat them as pets instead of meat sources or beasts of burden.

Shopkeepers emerged to look at Deacon. An old man sat on a low metal cargo crate using a whirring diamond blade to carve a mis-shapen hunk of ironwood into some design. She locked eyes with him and he nodded curtly at her, but continued his work without showing undue alarm. She kept walking as if she knew where she was going.

She chose not to go to the seediest-looking establishment, where one might expect to find information for any price. She didn't think Garbo was that sort of target. Rather she went to a small cafe that served meals with families at tables outside.

One of the servers approached her, a short man with sandy hair and a toothy grin. "Haven't seen you around. Table for one, or....?" He peered around, as if looking for a companion. Deacon shot him a friendly smile, another skill she had cultivated.

"I'm looking for a man, Anson Garbo. He's an old friend who moved here recently."

The sandy-haired man turned his eyes upward, accessing his memory cells. He frowned and shook his head.

"Garbo's outside of town," said another server as he set down a plate of sliced meats and boiled green tubers in front of a rough-looking man. He stood up and wiped his hands on his apron. "He hardly ever comes into town. He bought the Gallagher homestead in a canyon just south of here. About ten klicks from the military base. He keeps to himself."

"That's Anson!" Deacon said. "It'll be good to see him."

The customer picked at the green tubers in front of him then peered up at her. "Kinda strange. Garbo's never gotten a visitor before."

Deacon's demeanor went from warm to ice in a nanosecond as she turned her hard eyes to him.

"Have you gotten any offworld visitors either?"

The man flushed and turned away. "No. Sorry." He went back to his meal, his curiosity quelled by the warning bells in his head.

Deacon left, knowing they would all remember her. Once she killed Garbo, everyone in town would realize who had murdered him. Even if it became an entrenched fight, she doubted any misguided local justice would be a problem. She would soon be long gone from Pondafier, flying off in her ship, ready for the next mission. The long list of names the Service sent to her burst tablet would never run out. Job security.

The western sky turned bronze as the sun settled toward the horizon. She'd have to take the long route to avoid the military base, but she didn't want to explain herself to Earth Command soldiers on patrol. She kept to the long canyons, weaving through the old riverbeds. The target wasn't actually that hard to find.

Deacon saw the secondhand prefab hut that Anson Garbo had apparently bought from the estate of an old miner who had died the year before. Canyon shadows cast gray blankets over the ground, creeping along as the sun set. Lights glowed in the prefab hut.

Deacon approached cautiously, aware that Garbo might have set up motion sensors and traps. But all she found was a spiny lizard on top of a boulder. It flicked out a forked tongue and burbled a warning as it displayed needle-like fangs. She tossed a pebble and the lizard scuttled away.

She heard casual movement inside the prefab house, saw lights, a shadow – a single figure. He had prepared no defenses, this was just a normal day for him. His last day.

A polite person would knock, but assassins didn't need to be polite.

She pulled a small flash-bang from her coat and using the hard heel of her boot, she kicked open the flimsy door. It slammed against the inner wall as she tossed in the flash-bang, which went off with a blinding light and sudden concussive sound. Deacon rolled in to the opposite wall as the man inside let out a high shrill scream.

Garbo stumbled backward from the small single-burner stove where he had been cooking and accidentally pulled the pot of boiling soup off the burner, spilling thick brown gravy down his leg, which changed his cry to an entirely different squeal of pain. Still blinded by the flash-bang, he swung the soup ladle in front of him like a weapon.

Deacon took three strides, grabbed him by the front of his shirt and threw him into a wooden chair. She snatched the ladle from his hand and swatted him across the face with it. He stared up at her in fear.

"Just to verify," Deacon said in a casual tone, looming above him. "You're Anson Garbo, right?"

"What do you want?" he wailed, pawing at the hot spilled soup on his pants. "Leave me alone. My leg... "

She wasn't in a hurry to kill him. He was still insensible from the effects of the flash-bang and it went against her sense of ethics to kill a target in his condition. Thunder rolled in the distance. She stood up, tossing the deadly ladle aside and evaluated the target.

Garbo's shirt was rugged, but more stylish than serviceable. His skin sagged as if he had lost a great deal of weight in recent months. His brown eyes looked haunted. His hair was unkempt, the leftovers of what had once been a fine haircut now grown out in all directions.

"You...you've come to take me back?" he asked as he looked up at her, his sight beginning to return.

"Not in my job description. I've got a contract for your life."

His breath caught in his throat. "No, I should have been safe here," he said with a broken voice. "They know I've got insurance! I placed copies of the information elsewhere. If I'm—"

She grabbed his throat, squeezed hard. "I don't care."

He pawed at her arm in an attempt to finally fight back, but Deacon pulled his free wrist and stepped backward, pushing his locked arm down and driving him to the floor. She twisted his arm behind him, placing her boot on his back.

"You don't understand what's going on!" Garbo screamed. "The Krael war, the human colonies that've fallen --"

"I know about the colonies and the battles," she said. "Lots of widows and orphans."

The thunder rolled louder in the distance, accenting her words. "It's not that. It's them! Some of those colonies didn't have to --"

She twisted his arm harder. "Not interested."

"Please. Just take me back! With this information, you could change everything!"

Deacon knelt with her face next to his. She could smell the soup mixed with the sour smell of urine from his pants. "Did you miss the 'I don't care' part?"

"But it's Bulwark!"

That confirmed what she suspected. Garbo had worked for Bulwark, stole something, and then fled. Bulwark was one of the few companies that could afford a priority assassination. She knew he would keep babbling, pleading for his life, finally offering to bribe her. There was a series of stages the condemned went through, the last bargaining for life. She had heard it all.

"I'll match whatever they're paying you!" he screamed.

Deacon shook her head, surprised that he'd gone right for the final bargaining chip. "Do you want to hire me? Fill out the forms and transfer the money to the Service. I'll be happy to work for you." She took out her knife. "But I'm still going to finish this contract."

With a swift vicious blow she crashed the thick hilt of her dagger against the side of Garbo's temple, breaking the skull precisely on the sweet spot. It was a mercy move, because she knew it rendered him instantly unconscious. He slumped forward with a low moan. She turned the dagger around, placed the tip carefully at the base of his skull.

"IT'S NOTHING PERSONAL," she whispered and shoved down, severing his spine and killing him.

She closed her eyes, letting her subconscious bury whatever guilt she might have, then went to work with her cranial drill. It was a simple to operate, inserting the extraction tube into the victim's ear in order to remove tissue from the medulla. The DNA would prove his identity and guarantee the target was deceased. She also took high-res images, just to make it a complete package. Before long the Service would be notified, Anson Garbo's name would be removed from the list, and the payment would be transferred to her account.

The sound of thunder increased in intensity, so she would have to wait out the storm in this quiet hut before making her way back to the ship so she could leave. As far as assignments went, there had been no complications. Easy.

Little did she know that the "thunder" was a Krael special force overrunning the military base. The alien invasion was already in the process of occupying Colony Town. Her space cruiser was just hours away from being discovered, since she hadn't bothered to hide it with any sophisticated or long-term camouflage. Krael patrols would soon roam the landscape, and the sound of their scout craft would send her scurrying for cover.

For the first time in her life, Deacon had known what it felt like to be the prey.

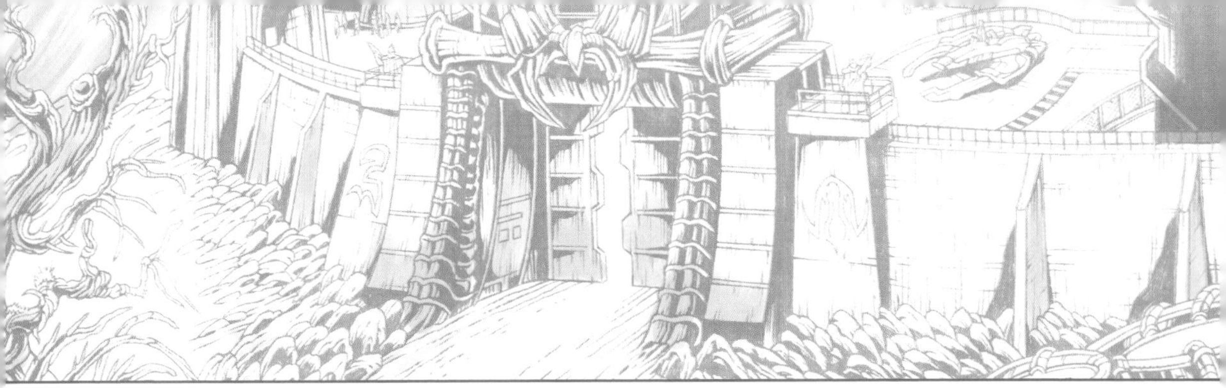

NOW, IN THE CAMP YARD, SHE INHALED DEEPLY AS SHE OPENED HER EYES AND GLANCED AROUND THE INTERIOR OF STALAG-X.

The human POWs looked defeated, some of them wounded, others gaunt and skeletal. She saw defiance in the eyes of some, despair in others. The Krael guards were bloated with their own confidence. Their fangs and claws, their armor and sharp weapons were enhanced for effect, but little more than costumes to her.

She had waited long enough. "The Commandant! What is taking him so long? Is he afraid?" Her tablet translated her words, and she hoped it also conveyed the defiance in her voice. "I have places to go. I need my ship back, and I want to be off this damned planet."

Some of the human prisoners shook their heads, as if concluding she was mad or suicidal. But she didn't have any intention of negotiating for her freedom. She wanted to kill the Commandant, simple as that.

Deacon had downloaded all the known knowledge of the Krael on her burst tablet—which, admittedly, wasn't much. Her direct observations, combined with Earth Command intel reports, confirmed what she suspected about their military-social structure. The Krael were a segregated species, each one born into a specific caste, Warrior caste, Science caste, Command caste, maybe more, each with differentiated skills and duties. The Warrior caste was subservient to the Command caste; the Science caste was more ambiguous as to its place in the hierarchy. She knew the leader of the Science caste here on Pondafier was the equal of the Commandant. She hoped that wouldn't be a problem, but she could be flexible.

As if on cue, the very representative of the Science caste emerged from a small building next to the POW barracks. Taller, with a smoother skull and higher cranium, he looked less threatening than a typical Krael. But the fear the human POWs suddenly showed at his appearance put Deacon on notice. This creature was no one to play around with.

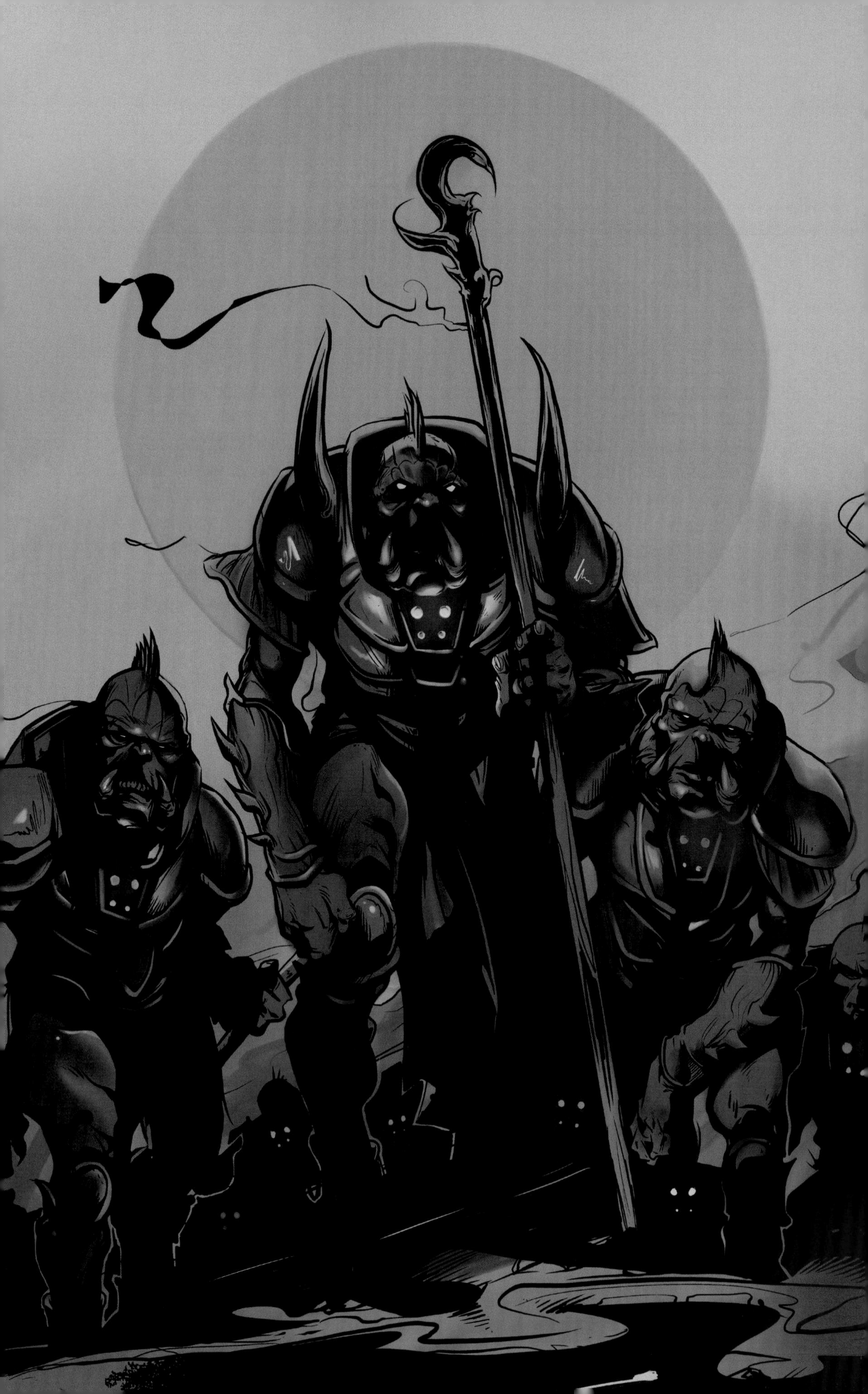

His claws tapped on a small energy weapon on his belt. "You are an interesting human. Very interesting. I should like to study you."

Deacon covered her shock. He had spoken in Standard English! She'd never seen any data that even hinted the Krael were capable of human speech.

Momentary doubt swept over her. Deacon's target had been, from the beginning, the Commandant. She was betting on the Krael ascension of power, that killing an opponent considered higher than your caste would bestow a certain amount of respect from the others. So far, she'd been proven correct, since she was still alive after killing the Krael guard. But something about this new scientist Krael made her rethink her plan. What if he was the absolute power here? If he knew Standard English, that meant he had studied humans. And, perhaps he would figure out what she was up to.

Before the scientist Krael could step closer, she heard a loud command and the ranks of alien guards suddenly stiffened. The Commandant of Stalag X strode out from the large headquarters building near the gate.

He was powerful, well-built, and obviously a veteran of many battles. He glided forward with confidence, his yellow eyes fixed on her. The Krael scientist bowed as the Commandant passed, and the deference was a welcome sight to Deacon.

She stood from the sand as he approached, facing the Commandant directly. She held her hands open to her side, demonstrating her own confidence.

The Commandant studied her, then pointed his finger to the ground with emphasis. His guttural voice issued a command in his native tongue. The Scientist spoke to Deacon directly, rather than waiting for her tablet to translate. "Commandant K'Grau, most high of the Clan of—"

The Commandant interrupted, also in Standard English. "I don't need your translation. You taught me their language for a reason, so I could command the prisoners."

"I'm not a prisoner," Deacon interrupted him. "I'm not from this planet. I'm not your enemy, and I'm sure as hell not going to kneel. Give me my ship back, and I'll leave."

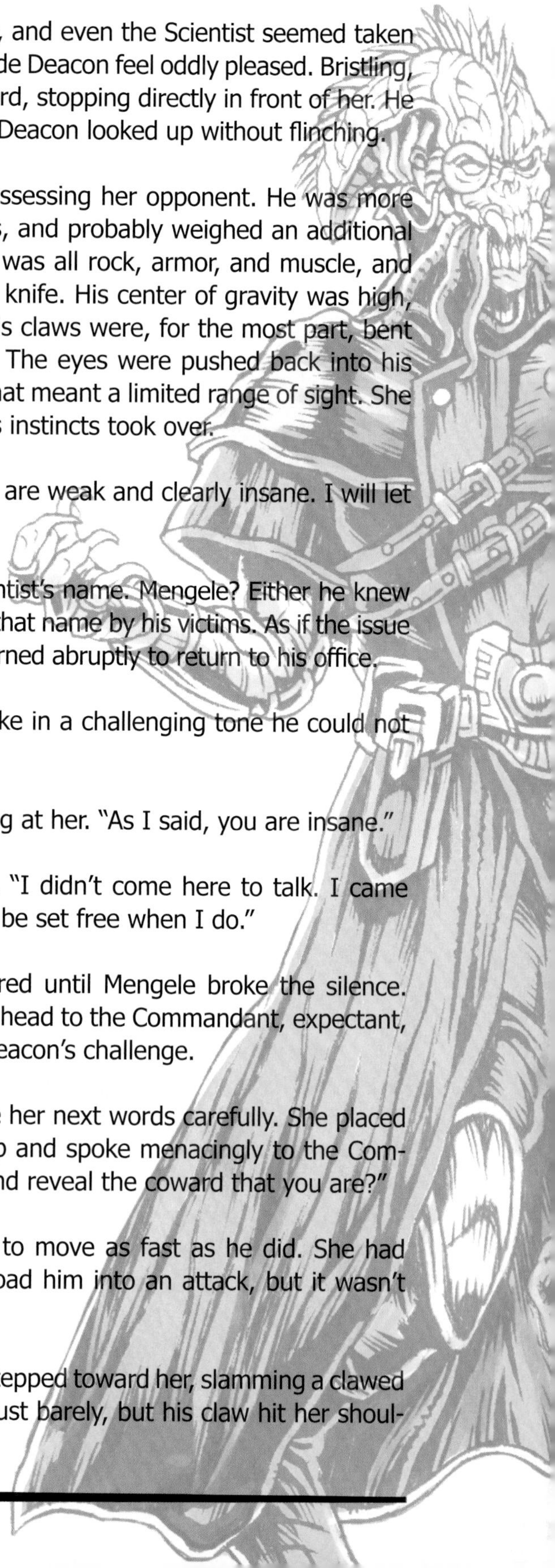

The Krael guards shifted angrily, and even the Scientist seemed taken back by her response, which made Deacon feel oddly pleased. Bristling, the Commandant trudged forward, stopping directly in front of her. He glared down into her eyes, and Deacon looked up without flinching.

In her mind, she was already assessing her opponent. He was more than a head taller than she was, and probably weighed an additional two hundred pounds. His body was all rock, armor, and muscle, and all they had left her with was a knife. His center of gravity was high, too high. She could use that. His claws were, for the most part, bent inwards. That, too, was useful. The eyes were pushed back into his skull. Good for protection, but that meant a limited range of sight. She processed it all as her assassin's instincts took over.

The Commandant snarled, "You are weak and clearly insane. I will let Mengele dissect you."

She almost chuckled at the Scientist's name. Mengele? Either he knew Earth history or he'd been given that name by his victims. As if the issue was settled, the Commandant turned abruptly to return to his office.

"You are afraid of me!" She spoke in a challenging tone he could not ignore.

He paused and turned, glowering at her. "As I said, you are insane."

"Maybe," Deacon replied loudly. "I didn't come here to talk. I came here to kill you. And I expect to be set free when I do."

The world fell still. No one stirred until Mengele broke the silence. "Very interesting." He turned his head to the Commandant, expectant, underlining the importance of Deacon's challenge.

Deacon knew she had to choose her next words carefully. She placed a hand on the dagger at her hip and spoke menacingly to the Commandant. "Or do you submit? And reveal the coward that you are?"

She honestly didn't expect him to move as fast as he did. She had prepared two more taunts to goad him into an attack, but it wasn't necessary.

The Commandant roared as he stepped toward her, slamming a clawed hand at her face. She dodged, just barely, but his claw hit her shoulder, spinning her backward. The movement took her by surprise, but Deacon regained her balance, pirouetted and then landed, her knees bent. She crouched forward, arms back, knife already in her hand. The Commandant drew the ceremonial curved blade at his waist and then the second one from his other hip.

His muscular arm swept the long knife toward her as she danced out of the way, spun and kicked him in the knee. His armor protected his leg, but she made him stumble. Deacon slammed her elbow into his neck and the Commandant lurched back. The four curved tusks around his mouth spread out then clamped together. His yellow eyes blazed with anger as he lunged forward.

She ducked under his arm but he moved with surprising speed, kicking up at her, catching her in the ribs and flipping her over. Deacon rolled sideways seeing stars behind her vision, feeling the breath knocked out of her. The Krael guards began stomping in rhythm, a low chanting grunt from their throats as they watched their leader deliver another kick to the side of Deacon's head.

She flipped completely into the air, blood spinning off the new gash in her scalp. The Commandant didn't even wait for her to land, but pressed his attack, lunging forward to finish her off. Deacon sucked in oxygen to recharge her energy. Pain shot through her ribs as she sprang back to her feet and launched herself sideways to avoid the sweep of the Commandant's knife.

"All right, time to stop playing around," she said with a labored gasp. She mentally chided herself for being too cocky. This was going to take every bit of skill and strategy she could muster.

Her mind scanned every memory she had of the dossier on Krael physiology, all the information that had been extracted from autopsies of mangled bodies from Krael battle fields. One thing that had caught Deacon's eye was a large cluster of nerve endings covered by a swollen sac under each arm. Human scientists disagreed about its purpose, but Deacon had noticed the Krael armor seemed to be reinforced in that particular location. Whatever that nerve sack was for, they made the effort to protect it. It must be very sensitive—and, thus, a target. The problem was she had only one shot at it.

In order to have the best chance, Deacon had to change her strategy. She had to lose.

The guards were stomping harder, chanting louder, their bloodlust rising with Deacon's impending death. Mengele watched with interest, the talons of his hand settling lightly on his side arm.

The Commandant struck at her again. Deacon dodged, but more slowly this time. Her muscles screamed as she tried to stay just one step ahead of the Krael's blows. She tried a desperate dive for his midsection, grabbing him in a wrestler's hold, vainly attempting to knock him off balance. The Commandant's boots dug into the ground as he braced himself. He brought both elbows down in the middle of her back. She collapsed, still desperately trying to hold onto him.

The Commandant knew he had her. His knee caught her directly under her chin, the impact loosening her grip and knocking her onto the ground. Deacon lay on her back, dazed and vulnerable. The Commandant lifted his arms high overhead, spinning the blades into a strike position, ready to plunge them into her heart.

Deacon smiled through her bloody lips. She was inside his defense and underneath his arms. Perfect.

With a scream, she jabbed up with the butt of her hand at the nerve sack. She struck him precisely at the right point, directly under the armor, hammering hard.

From the roar that came out of his fanged mouth, Deacon knew her strategy had been vindicated. With a groan like a falling herd beast, the Commandant lurched backward. She rolled to her feet, still staggering from the beating she had been given, but with a rush of adrenaline.

The Commandant tried to turn away, to protect his vulnerable side. In doing so, he exposed the nerve sack under his other arm. Deacon slammed her foot into it, staggering him to his knees, forcing him to drop his knives. She grabbed one as he desperately threw a punch at her. She dove over his shoulder, grabbing his neck with her free hand, using her momentum to spin across his body and under his arm again.

She stabbed the knife into the vulnerable nerve sack. The Commandant shrieked. The Krael guards backed away in shock, looking to each other as if lost. Mengele leaned forward, his eyes squinting as the scientist in him studied her.

Deacon yanked the knife free as the Commandant raised his other arm to grasp at her. She couldn't turn down such an obvious opportunity and slashed along his arm, separating the ligaments in his elbow and rendering his arm useless.

She knew she could kill him now, she could kill him immediately. But that wouldn't be good enough. She needed to make a statement, and every one of the Krael watching her needed to understand loud and clear, especially Mengele. And, more, the human part of her wanted revenge.

In three quick plunges, the blade sank deep into the Commandant's back, his thigh, and the back of his neck. Each strike brought a howl of pain and a shocked reaction from the Krael guards. Fear?

The Commandant reached up with his uninjured arm, but she grabbed the wrist, stepped over it, and bent it backwards against her leg, making a loud snap as the bone fractured.

The Commandant fell backward, and Deacon pressed upon him, jamming her knee on his neck, pinning him to the ground. His arms and legs flailed uselessly.

Her breath was hard and labored as she looked down at him. "It's nothing personal" she whispered as she plunged the knife into his eye with both hands, pressing with her body and twisting it as it dug through his skull and brain.

If Garbo's death was painless, she made sure this one was anything but.

The Commandant's body stiffened and jerked as his nerves flared with pain then went dead.

Silence settled on the stalag as Deacon rested on the hilt of the knife for a moment, then slid off to the side. She tried to walk away, but her body deserted her. She fell to her knees, gasping. The blood from her wounds dripped to the sand and seeped in.

Out of the corner of her eye, she saw a shadow approaching. Mengele strode forward. He paused momentarily by the body of the Commandant, briefly settling his hand under the body's ear, then nodded. Deacon watched warily as the Scientist drew his sidearm and approached her. He knelt next to her, placed the barrel of his gun against her head, and peered into her face.

Deacon laughed dryly; all her strategy, all her plans, worthless.

"Humans intrigue me" he said to her. "I would like to study you. I would like to dissect you. I would like to connect you to the Ripper."

"Get it over with," she sneered at him.

Mengele stood and reholstered his weapon. "Go." He nodded toward the open stalag gate. "You killed our Commandant and gained your freedom."

"I want my ship back..." she demanded, a part of her still not believing what had just happened.

Mengele shook his head. "You have earned our respect, but not our assistance. Leave. You are not a prisoner."

Mengele turned and walked toward his building, not looking back. Deacon's breath caught in her throat. She had won!

The Krael guards separated as she stumbled out the gate and into the wilderness of Pondafier.

She was going to survive, but she would have to find a way off this planet.

She needed to get her ship back.

And collect her reward for a mission well done.

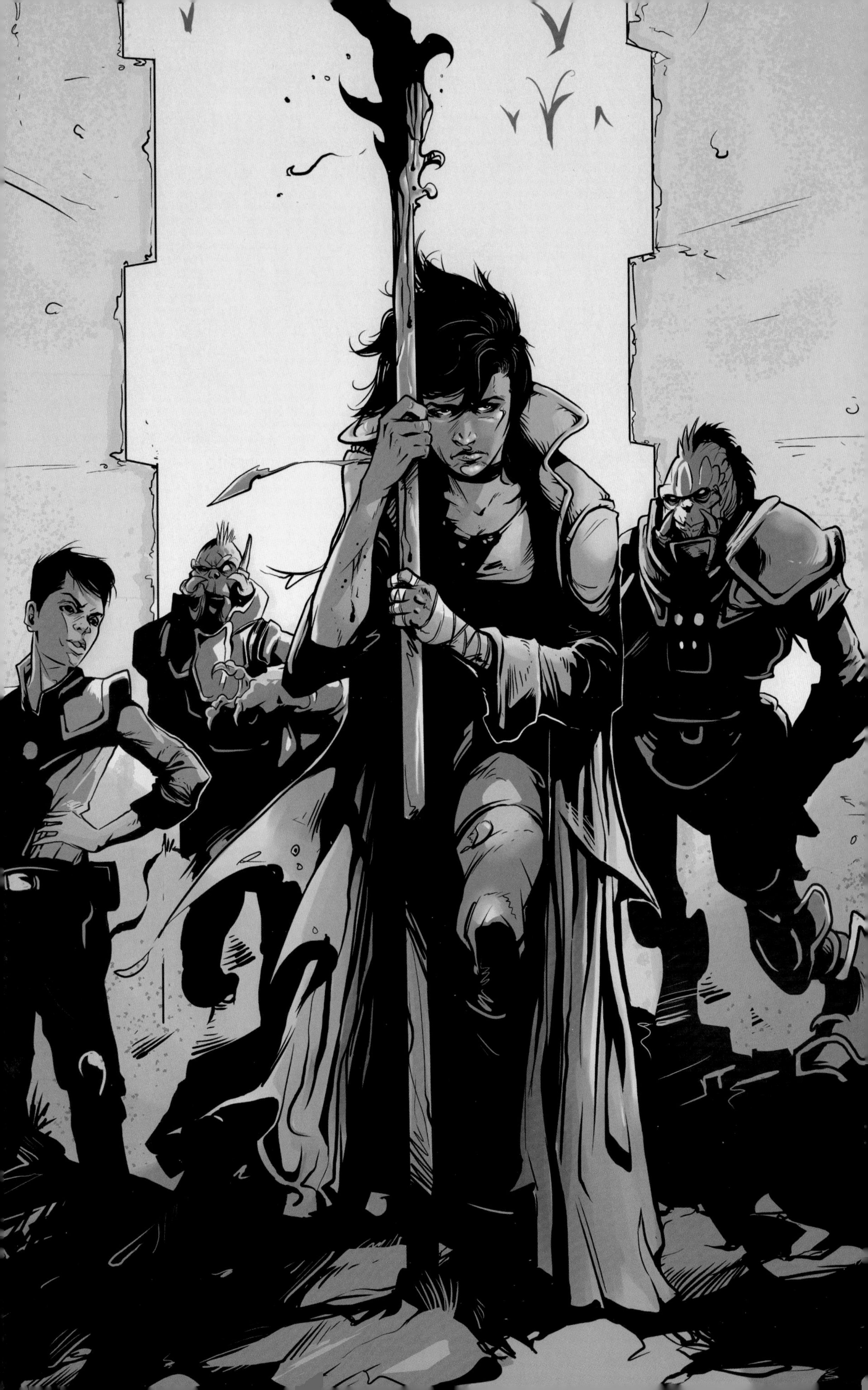

GALLERY X

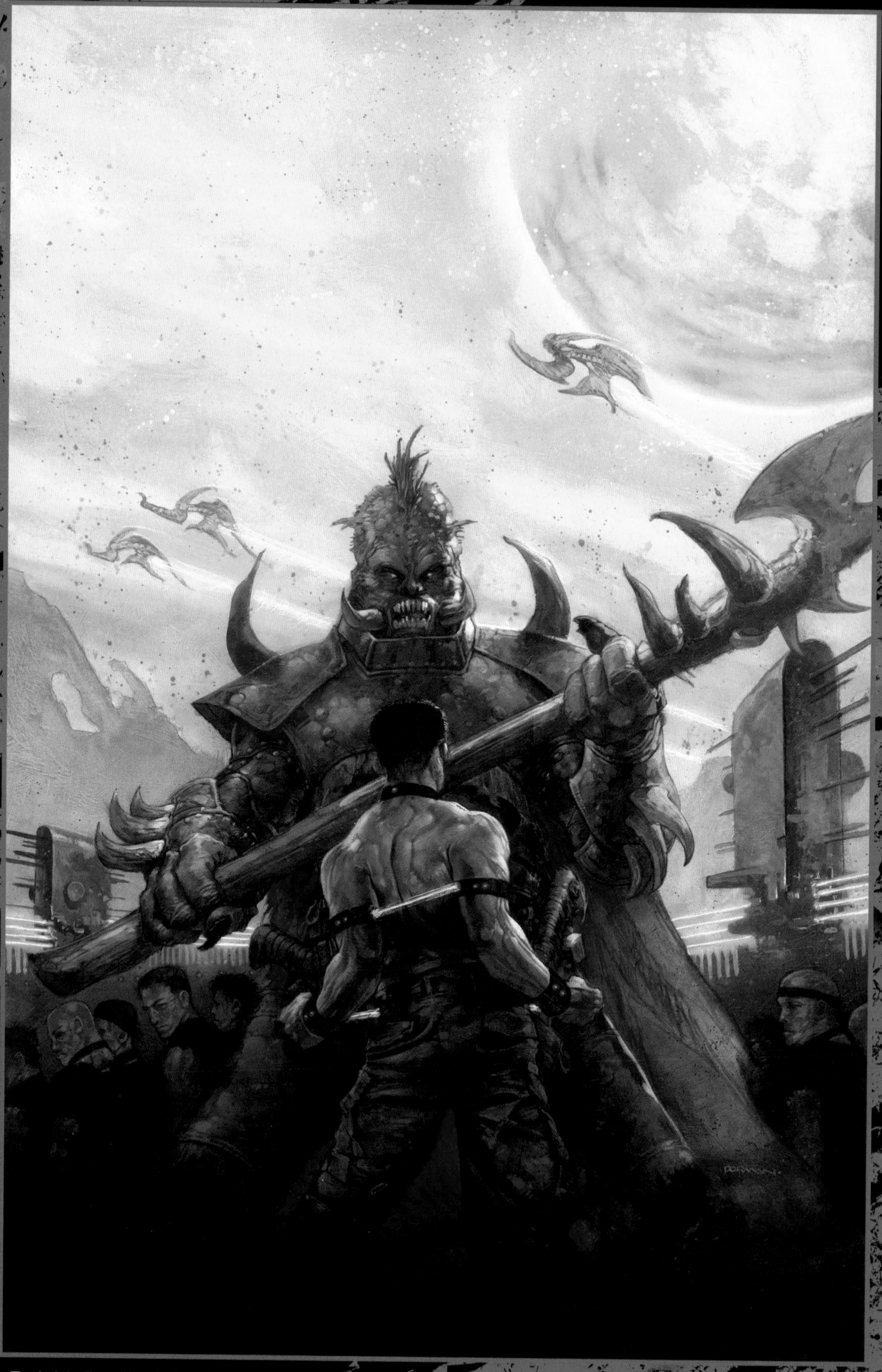

DAVE DORMAN

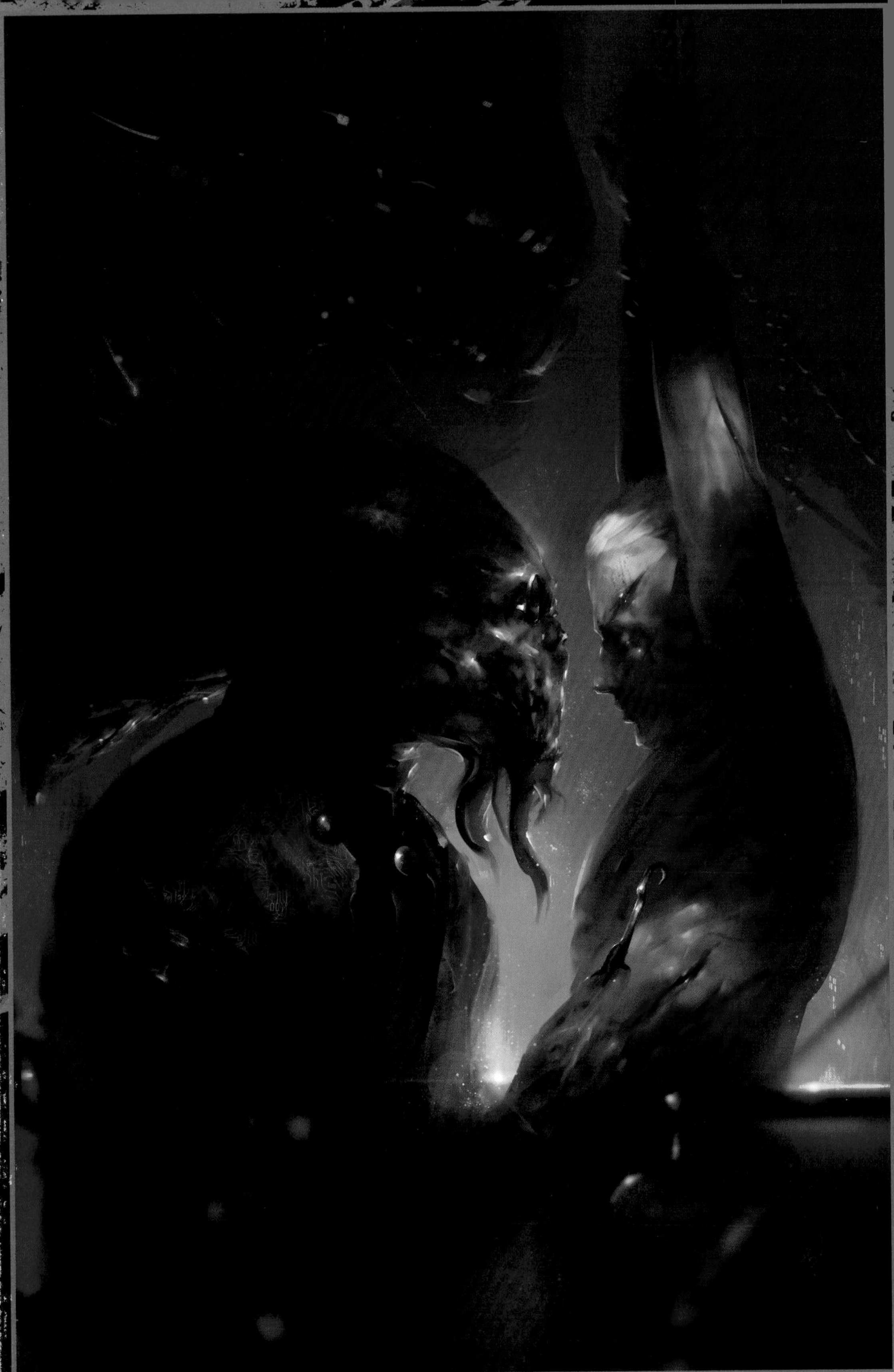

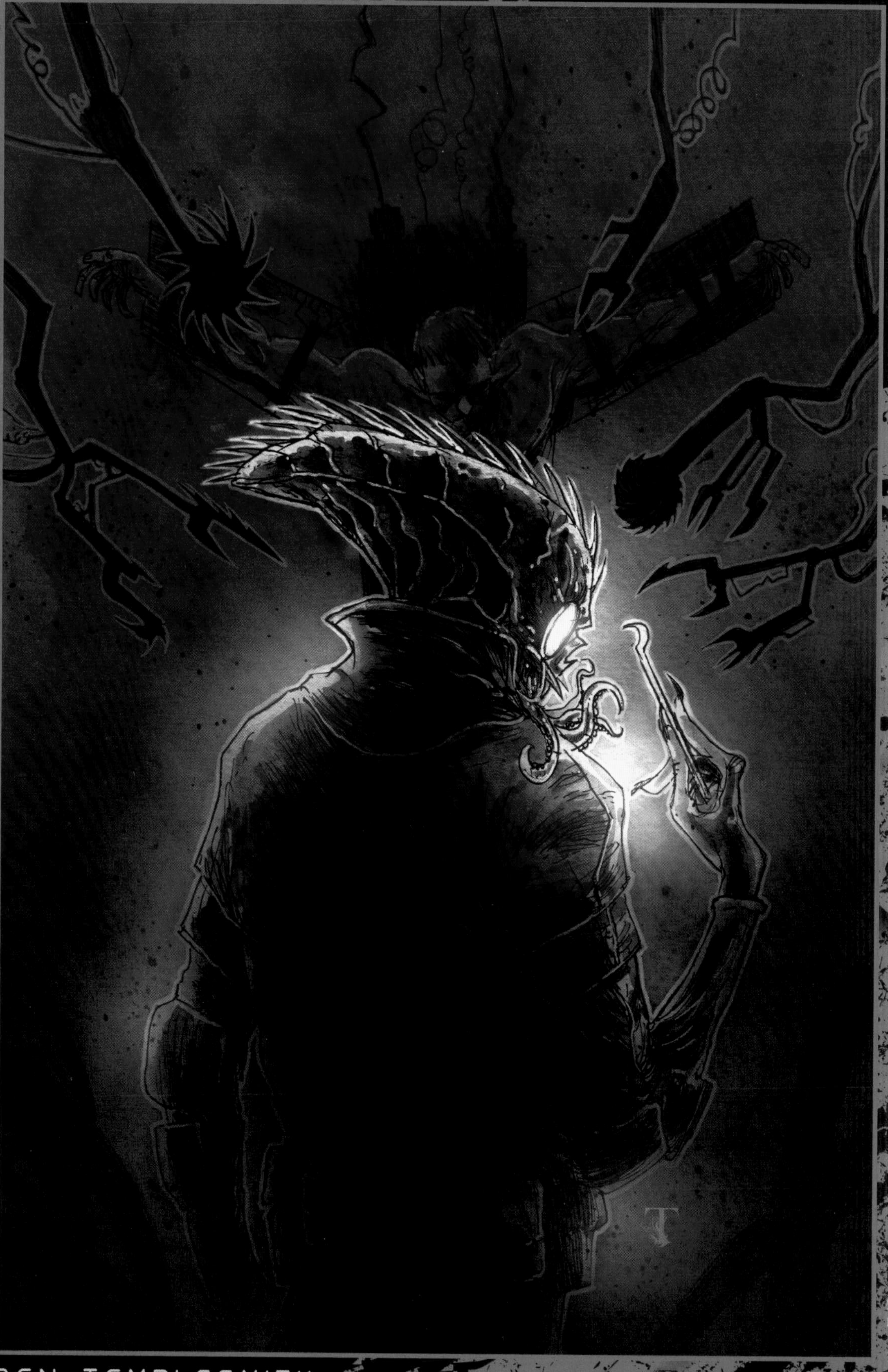

BEN TEMPLESMITH

YA ANDE /GN
Anderson, Kevin J.,
Stalag X /

DEC 0 8 2018